The Emerald Comb

KATHLEEN MCGURL

HQ

ONE PLACE. MANY STORIES

HQ
An imprint of HarperCollins*Publishers* Ltd
1 London Bridge Street
London SE1 9GF

First published in Great Britain by
HQ, an imprint of HarperCollins Ltd 2020

A catalogue record for this book is
available from the British Library.

ISBN: 9780008389215

MIX
Paper from
responsible sources
FSC
www.fsc.org
FSC™ C007454

This book is produced from independently certified FSC™ paper
to ensure responsible forest management.

For more information visit: www.harpercollins.co.uk/green

Printed by CPI Group (UK) Ltd, Croydon CR0 4YY

St Clair Family Tree – as researched by Katie

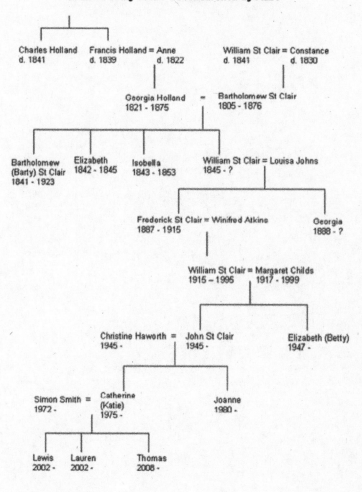

Charles Holland
d. 1841

Francis Holland = Anne
d. 1839   d. 1822

William St Clair = Constance
d. 1841   d. 1830

Georgia Holland   =   Bartholomew St Clair
1821 - 1875   1805 - 1876

Bartholomew
(Barty) St Clair
1841 - 1923

Elizabeth
1842 - 1845

Isobella
1843 - 1853

William St Clair = Louisa Johns
1845 - ?

Frederick St Clair = Winifred Atkins
1887 - 1915

Georgia
1888 - ?

William St Clair = Margaret Childs
1915 – 1995   1917 - 1999

Christine Haworth = John St Clair
1945 -   1945 -

Elizabeth (Betty)
1947 -

Simon Smith = Catherine
1972 -   (Katie)
              1975 -

Joanne
1980 -

Lewis
2002 -

Lauren
2002 -

Thomas
2006 -

Prologue

Kingsley House
North Kingsley
Hants
November 1876
To my dearest son, Barty St Clair

This is my confession. I am the only soul still living who knows the truth. It will pain me to write this story, but write it I must, before I depart this life. I have not long to live, and I fear death – heaven will not be my final resting place. Dear Barty, when you have read this in its entirety you will understand why I know I am destined for that other, fiery place, to burn with guilt and shame for all eternity.

You must read this alone, sitting in the worn, red armchair by the fireside in the drawing room of Kingsley House. Or perhaps you will sit in my study, at my old walnut desk. Where ever you choose, have a glass of whiskey to hand to fortify yourself. You will need it.

Read this only after I am dead, after I am buried. Read this and understand why you must <u>never sell Kingsley House</u>.

1

You must live in it until the end of your days, guarding its secrets, as I have.

Tell no one the contents of this confession. Not even your brother, William. Especially not your brother, William. It would grieve him, he who worshipped his mother and believed she could do no wrong, even more than it will grieve you. You will understand this when you have reached the end of my story.

Destroy this document when you have read it. You must carry the shameful secret within you, as I have done, but at least you will not also carry guilt.

There, I have written an introduction, but I must rest before I begin my story. Bear with me, my dearest son, while I recoup the strength I need to write this sorry tale.

Your ever loving, repentant father,
Bartholomew St Clair

2

Chapter One

Hampshire, November 2012

The weather matched my mood. A dark, low sky with a constant drizzle falling meant I needed both headlights and wipers on as I drove up the M3. Whenever I'd pictured myself making this trip I'd imagined myself singing along to the car radio beneath blue skies and sunshine. The reality, thanks to a row with my husband, Simon, couldn't have been more different. All I'd asked of him was to look after our kids for a single Saturday afternoon, while I went to take some photos of Kingsley House, where my ancestors had once lived. Not much to ask, was it? I'd planned it for weeks but of course he hadn't listened, and had made his own plans to go to rugby training. Then when it was time for me to leave, he'd made such a fuss. I'd ended up grabbing my bag and storming out, leaving him no choice but to stay and be a parent for once, while the kids watched, wide-eyed. Perhaps that's unfair of me. He's a wonderful parent, and we have a strong marriage. Most of the time.

It was a half-hour drive from our home in Southampton to North Kingsley, a tiny village north of Winchester. Just enough time to calm myself down. Funny thing was, if I'd wanted to do something girly like go shopping or get my nails done, Simon would have happily minded the kids. But because I was indulging my hobby, my passion for genealogy, he made things difficult. I loved researching the past, finding out where my family came from. Simon's adopted. He's never even bothered to trace his biological parents. God, if I was adopted, I'd have done that long ago. I can't understand why you wouldn't want to know your ancestry. It's what makes you who you are.

The rain had eased off; I'd calmed down and was buzzing with excitement when I finally drove up the narrow lane from the village and got my first glimpse of Kingsley House. Wet leaves lay clumped together on its mossy gravel driveway. Paint peeled from the windowsills, and the brickwork was in need of repointing. An overgrown creeper grew up one wall almost obscuring a window, and broken iron guttering hung crookedly, spoiling the house's Georgian symmetry.

Kingsley House was definitely in need of some serious renovation. I fell instantly and overwhelmingly in love with it. It felt like home.

Gathering my courage, I approached the front door. It was dark green and panelled, with a leaded fanlight set into the brickwork above. There was no bell-push or knocker, so I rapped with my knuckles, wondering if it would be heard inside. Was there even anyone at home to hear it? There were no cars outside, and no lights shone from any window despite the deepening afternoon gloom. Maybe the house was uninhabited, left to rot until some developer got his hands on it. Or perhaps the owners were away. I'd checked the house out on Google Street View before coming, and had the idea it was occupied.

I knocked again, and waited a couple of minutes. Still no response. But now that I was here, I thought I might as well get a good look at the place. After all, my ancestors had lived here for a hundred years. That gave me some sort of claim to the house, didn't it? The windows either side of the front door had curtains drawn across. No chance of a peek inside from the front, then.

To the left of the house there was a gate in the fence. One hinge was broken so that the gate hung lopsided and partially open. I only needed to push it a tiny bit more to squeeze through. Beyond, a paved path led past a rotting wooden shed to a patio area at the back of the house. I tiptoed round. A huge beech tree dominated the garden, its auburn autumn leaves adding a splash of colour to the dull grey day.

French windows overlooked the patio, and the room beyond was in darkness. Cupping my hands around my eyes I pressed my nose to the glass. It was a formal dining room, with ornately moulded cornices and a fine-looking marble fireplace. Had my great-great-great-grandfather Bartholomew and his wife dined in this very room, back in the early Victorian era? It sent shivers down my spine as I imagined their history playing out right here, in this faded old house.

'You there! What do you think you're up to?'

I jumped away from the window and turned to see a gaunt old man in a floppy cardigan approaching from the other side of the building, waving his walking stick at me. Behind him was a neatly dressed elderly lady. She was holding tightly onto his arm, more to steady him than for her own benefit. The owners were not on holiday, then. I silently cursed myself. Today was really not going according to plan. First the row with Simon and now being caught trespassing.

The man waved his stick again. 'I said, what do you think you're up to, snooping around the back of our house?'

'I'm…er…I was just…' I stuttered.

'Just wondering if the place was empty and had anything worth stealing, I'll bet,' said the lady.

'No, not at all, I was only…'

'Vera, call the police,' said the old man. His voice was cracked with age. His wife hesitated, as if unsure about letting go of his arm to go to the phone.

5

I held out my hands. 'No, please don't do that, let me explain.'

'Yes, I think you had better explain yourself, young lady,' said Vera. 'Harold dear, sit yourself down before you topple over.' She pulled a shabby metal garden chair across the patio and gently pushed him into it.

He held his stick in front of him like a shotgun. 'Don't you come any closer.'

God, the embarrassment. I felt myself redden from the chest up. They looked genuinely scared of me.

'I'm sorry. I did knock at the door but I guess you didn't hear.'

'There's a perfectly serviceable bell, if you'd only pulled on the bell-rope,' said Vera.

Bell-rope? Presumably part of an original bell system. I shrugged. 'I'm sorry, I didn't notice the rope.'

Vera shook her immaculate grey perm and folded her arms. 'In any case, you had no answer, so why did you come around to the back?'

I gaped like a goldfish for a moment as I searched for the right words. I'd imagined meeting the current inhabitants of my ancestors' house so many times, but I had never once thought it would happen like this. We really had got off on the wrong footing. I could see my chances of getting a look inside vanishing like smoke on the wind.

'The thing is, I was interested in the house because' – I broke off for a moment as they both glared at me, then the words all came out in a rush – 'my ancestors used to live here. I've researched my family tree, you see, and found my four-greats grandfather William St Clair built this house, then his son Bartholomew inherited it and lived here after he got married, then *his* son, another Bartholomew but known as Barty lived here right up until—'

'1923!' To my utter astonishment both the old people chorused the date.

'You're a St Clair then, are you?' said Vera, looking less fierce but still a little suspicious.

'I was Catherine St Clair before I got married. Plain old Katie Smith now.'

I put out my hand and thankfully she took a tentative step forward and shook it. The atmosphere instantly felt less frosty.

'Vera Delamere. And this is my husband, Harold.'

I shook his gnarled and liver-spotted hand too, while he stayed sitting in his chair. 'I'm so sorry to have frightened you. I shouldn't have come around the back. I was just so desperate for a glimpse inside. And I wasn't even sure if the house was occupied at all…' Oops, was I implying it looked derelict? I felt myself blushing again. I thought quickly, and changed the subject. 'You know about the St Clairs?'

'Not all of them, but we've heard of Barty St Clair,' said Harold. 'When we moved here in 1959 a lot of people hereabouts remembered him still. He was quite a character, by all accounts.'

'Really? What do you know about him? He was my great-great-great-uncle, I think.' I counted off the 'greats' on my fingers.

Vera sat down beside Harold and gestured to me to take a seat as well. 'I remember old Mrs Hodgkins from the Post Office telling me about him. Apparently he wouldn't ever let anyone in the house or garden. He wasn't a recluse – he'd go out and about in the village every day and was a regular in the pub every night. But he had this great big house and let not a soul over the threshold – no cook or cleaner, no gardener, no tradesmen. Mrs Hodgkins thought he must have had something to hide.'

'Ooh, intriguing!' I said. 'Perhaps he had a mad wife in the attic or something like that.'

Vera laughed. I smiled. Thank goodness we'd broken the ice now. 'Well, by the time we moved in there was no evidence of any secrets. Mind you, that was many years after Barty St Clair's day. It was a probate sale when we bought it. It had been empty for a few years and was in dire need of modernising.' She sighed, and gazed at the peeling paint on the patio doors. 'And now it's in dire need of modernising again, but we don't have the energy to do it.'

She stood up, suddenly. 'Why are we sitting out here in the damp? Come on. Let's go inside. I'll make us all a cup of tea, and then give you a tour, Katie.'

Harold chuckled. 'Then you'll see for certain we have nothing worth stealing, young lady.'

I grinned as I watched Vera help him to his feet, then followed them around to the kitchen door on the side of the house. I felt a tingle of excitement. Whatever secrets the house still held, I longed to discover them.

Chapter Two

Hampshire, November 1876

Kingsley House, November 1876

My dear Barty

    I have rested for a day or so, filled my ink-well, replenished my paper store and summoned the courage I need to begin my confession. And begin it I must, for the date of my death grows ever nearer.

    Barty, I shall write this confession as though it were a story, about some other man. I will write 'he did this', and 'he said that', rather than 'I did', and 'I said'. At times I will even write as if in the heads of other characters, as though I know their thoughts and am privy to their memories of those times. It is from conversations since then, and from my own conjectures, that I am able to do this, and I believe it is the best way to tell what will undoubtedly become a long and complex tale. It is only by distancing myself in this way, and telling the tale as though it were a novel, that I will be able to tell the full truth. And you deserve the full truth, my true, best-loved son.

We shall begin on a cold, snowy evening nearly forty years ago, when I first set eyes upon the woman who was to become my wife.

Brighton, January 1838

Bartholomew St Clair leaned against a classical pillar in the ballroom of the Assembly Rooms, watching the dancers whirl around. There was a good turnout for this New Year's ball. He ran his fingers around the inside of his collar. The room was warm, despite the freezing temperatures outside. He could feel his face flushing red with the heat, or maybe that was due to the volume of whiskey and port he'd consumed since dinner.

He scanned the room – the dancing couples twirling past him, the groups of young ladies with their chaperones at the sides of the room, the parties of men more interested in the drink than the dancing. He was looking for one person in particular. If his sources were correct, the young Holland heiress would be at this ball – her first since she came out of mourning. It could be worth his while obtaining an introduction to her. Rumour had it she was very pretty, but more than that, rich enough to get him out of debt. A couple of bad investments had left him in a precarious position, which only a swift injection of capital would resolve.

He watched as a pretty young girl in a black silk gown spun past him, on the arm of a portly man in military uniform. Her white-blonde hair was in striking contrast to her dress, piled high on top, with soft ringlets framing her face. She was smiling, but something about the way she held herself, as distant from her dancing partner as she could, told Bartholomew she was not enjoying herself very much. He recalled that the Holland girl was currently residing with her uncle, an army captain. This could be her.

The dance ended, and now the band struck up a Viennese

waltz. Bartholomew kept his eyes fixed on the girl as she curtsied to her partner, shook her head slightly and made her way across the room towards the entrance hall. He straightened his collar, smoothed his stubbornly curly hair and pushed through the crowds, to intercept her near the door.

'You look hot,' he said. 'May I get you some refreshments?'

She blushed slightly, and smiled. 'I confess I am a little warm. Perhaps some wine would revive me.'

He took a glass from a tray held by a passing waiter, and gave it to her with a small bow. 'I am sorry, I have not even introduced myself. Bartholomew St Clair, at your service.'

She held out her hand. 'Georgia Holland. I am pleased to meet you.'

So it was her. She was even prettier viewed close-up, in a girlish, unformed kind of way, than she was at a distance. He raised her hand to his lips and kissed it. Her skin was soft and smooth. 'Would you like to sit down to rest? Your dancing appears to have exhausted you.'

'It has, rather,' she replied, as he led her towards some empty chairs at the side of the room. 'I am unused to dancing so much. This is my first ball since…' She bit her lip.

'Since…a bereavement?' he asked, gently. Sadness somehow suited her.

'My father,' Georgia whispered. She looked even prettier with tears threatening to fall. 'He died a year ago. I have only just begun to rejoin Society.'

'My condolences, Miss Holland. Are you all right? Would you like me to fetch someone for you?'

She shook her head. 'I am quite well, thank you. You are very kind.' She took a sip of her wine, then placed it on a small table beside her chair. She stood, and held out her hand. 'It has been a pleasure meeting you, Mr St Clair. But I think I must take my leave now. My uncle is here somewhere. Perhaps he will call a cab to take me home.'

Bartholomew jumped to his feet. 'I shall find your uncle for you. Though I could fetch you a cab myself.' And accompany you home in it, he hoped, though it would not be the normal course of behaviour.

'My uncle is my guardian,' she said. 'I live with him. So I must at least inform him that I wish to leave.' She scanned the room. 'Ah, there he is.' She indicated the portly man in a captain's uniform with whom he'd first seen her dancing.

So that was the person he needed to impress. From the way she'd held herself when dancing with him, it seemed there was no love lost between them, on her side at least. Interesting. Bartholomew took her arm, and led her through the crowds towards the captain, who was talking with a group of people in a corner of the room. She seemed tiny at his side – her slightness contrasting with his fine, strongly built figure.

'Uncle, this is Mr St Clair. He has very kindly been looking after me, when I felt a little unwell after our last dance.'

Bartholomew bowed, and shook the captain's plump, sweaty hand. 'Pleased to meet you, sir.'

'Charles Holland. Obliged to you for taking care of the girl.'

'Excuse me, sir,' said Bartholomew. He took a step forward and spoke quietly. 'Your niece wishes to return home. With your permission, I shall call a cab for her.'

Holland turned to regard him carefully. 'Very well,' he said. 'You wish to continue taking care of my niece. You may do so. She has money, as you are no doubt already aware.'

'Sir, I assure you, your niece's fortune is not of interest…'

Holland waved his hand dismissively. 'Of course it is, man. It's time she married and became someone else's responsibility. You look as likely a suitor as anyone else, and perhaps a better match than some of the young pups who've been sniffing around. You may take her home.' He nodded curtly and turned back to his companions.

Bartholomew opened his mouth to say something more, but thought better of it. What rudeness! But if Charles Holland didn't much care who courted his niece or how, at least it made things easier. He glanced at her. She was standing, hands clasped and eyes down, a few feet away. Probably too far to have heard the exchange between himself and her uncle. He took her arm and led her towards the cloakroom and the exit.

Outside, a thin covering of an inch or two of snow lay on everything, muting sound and reflecting the hazy moonlight so that the world appeared shimmering and silver. Georgia shivered and pulled her cloak more tightly around her.

'Come, there should be a cab stand along Ship Street,' Bartholomew said, steadying her as she descended the steps to the street. He grimaced as he noticed her shoes – fine silk dancing slippers, no use at all for walking in the snow.

'It's a beautiful night,' she said. 'I should like to see the beach, covered in snow. It always seems so wrong, somehow, to have the sea lapping at snow. Can we walk a little, just as far as the promenade, perhaps?'

'But your shoes! You will get a chill in your feet, I fear.'

'Nonsense. They will get a little cold but the snow is not deep. And the night air has quite revived me. I feel alive, Mr St Clair! Out of that stuffy ballroom, I feel I want to run and skip and – oh!'

He clutched her arm as she slipped in the snow. 'Be careful! Hold on to me, or you will do yourself more damage than cold feet.'

She tucked her arm through his and held on. Bartholomew enjoyed the warmth of her hand on his arm, the closeness of her hip to his. Her breath made delicate patterns in the cold night air, and he imagined the feel of it against his face, his lips... Yes, she would do nicely. He smiled, and led her across King's Road onto the promenade. It was deserted, and the snow lay pristine – white and untouched, apart from a single line of dog paw prints. On the beach, the partially covered pebbles looked like piles of frosted almonds.

Georgia sighed. 'So pretty.'

'Indeed,' said Bartholomew, watching her as she made neat footprints in the snow, then lifted her foot to see the effect. She had tiny, narrow feet, and the slippers had a small triangular-shaped heel.

'See my footprints? We could walk a little way, and then you could pick me up and carry me, so when others come this way it will look as though I had simply vanished.' She giggled, and pushed back the hood of her cloak to gaze up at him.

Her eyes glinted mischievously, and even in the subdued moonlight he could see they were a rich green. He was seized by the urge to take her in his arms and kiss her.

'Let's do it!' he said, taking her hand to walk a dozen more steps along the prom. Then he scooped her up, his pulse racing at the feel of her arms about his neck, her slight figure resting easily in his arms. Her hood fell back and tendrils of her golden hair fell across his shoulder. For a moment he stood there, holding her, gazing into her eyes and wondering whether she would respond to a kiss.

'Well, come on then, Mr St Clair – you must walk now, and make your footprints look no different to before. You must not stagger under my weight, or it will be obvious what has happened. Gee up, Mr St Clair!' She gently kicked her legs, as though she was riding him side-saddle.

'Yes, ma'am!' he laughed, and walked on along the prom. After a little way she twisted to try to see the footprints he'd left, and he, feeling he was losing his grip on her, put her down. She instantly walked on a few more steps and turned back to see the effect.

'Look, I appeared from nowhere!'

'Like an angel from heaven,' he said. 'Come, I must escort you home. It is late, and the snow is beginning to fall again.'

Georgia tilted her head back and let a few large flakes land on her face. 'It's so refreshing. Thank you, Mr St Clair. Since meeting you I have had a lovely evening. We can walk to my uncle's house, if you like – he lives in Brunswick Terrace.'

Bartholomew noted she had not said 'we live' – clearly she did not feel as though her uncle's house was her home.

'On a fine evening, Miss Holland, I could think of nothing better than to take your arm and stroll along the promenade as far as Brunswick. But I shall have to postpone that pleasure for another day. Your feet will freeze, even more than they already have. Look, we are in luck, here is an empty cab.'

He waved at the cabman who brought his horse to a skidding stop beside them. They climbed aboard and Georgia gave the address. She shivered and pressed her arm tightly against his. Minutes later the cab halted outside the grand terrace, its white-washed walls gleaming in the wintry moonlight.

Bartholomew paid the cabman and asked him to wait. He helped Georgia down from the cab and led her up the entrance steps of her uncle's house. The door opened as they approached, and a maid ushered them inside, into a grand hallway where the remains of a fire smouldered in the grate.

'Oh, Miss Georgia, I am so glad you are back. Mr Holland were back a half-hour ago and he said you had left the ball before him. I were fretting about you.' She bustled around, taking Georgia's cloak and exclaiming over the state of her shoes.

'Agnes, I am perfectly all right. Kind Mr St Clair has been looking after me. We decided to walk part of the way home.'

The maid glanced accusingly at Bartholomew. She was a striking-looking woman, blonde like her mistress but with more mature features, as though she had grown into her looks. She was an inch or two taller, and looked, he thought, as Georgia might in a few years' time, when she'd outgrown her childish playfulness. Beautiful, rather than pretty.

'Sir, forgive me for speaking out of turn but my mistress were not wearing the right sort of shoe for a walk in the snow. See, the silk is ruined and her poor feet are froze. Sit you down here,

15

Miss Georgia, and I will fetch a bowl of warm water to wash them.' With another stern look at Bartholomew, she hurried along the hallway towards the kitchen stairs.

'Agnes has been with me since I was fourteen. She does fuss, rather.' Georgia sat on an uncomfortable-looking carved-back chair and rubbed at her feet. 'But a warm foot-bath sounds just what I need. Perhaps, Mr St Clair, you would help me rub some life back into my toes?' She looked up at him, a half-smile flirting with the corners of her mouth.

But Bartholomew was still gazing in the direction the maid had taken. For all Miss Holland's coquettish ways, she was young and immature. Bartholomew was no stranger to women – he'd been near to proposing once to a merchant's daughter in Bath, but she had accepted a better offer from a baronet's son. He'd had a brief affair with the bored wife of a naval captain, until she tired also of him. And of course, there had been plenty of women of the night, who waited outside the Assembly Rooms to accompany lone men to their lodgings.

None of these women, however, had ever had quite the effect on him that the maid, Agnes, had. A thrill had run through him the moment his eyes met hers, leaving him hot with desire, his palms tingling, his heart racing. She was returning now, with the basin of water. She glared again at Bartholomew.

'Sir, you are still here? You may think me bold to suggest it, but I think you ought to leave, afore the snow becomes too deep for cabs. I can ask the footman to fetch you a brandy if you need fortification before venturing out.'

He felt his blood thrill again at the forthrightness of the woman. A lady's maid, who thought nothing of speaking to guests in her employer's house, as though they were her wayward sons.

'A brandy would be excellent, yes.' He nodded at her, and she pulled on the bell-cord. A moment later a footman arrived, and Agnes sent him for the brandy. He was back a minute later, closely followed by Charles Holland, who had exchanged his captain's jacket for a woollen dressing gown.

'Is that my niece back home at last? What do you think you are doing, keeping my staff up and waiting for you on such a night?' He stopped in his tracks when he noticed Bartholomew. 'Ah, I see. Sir, I thank you for bringing her home. Please, call on her again tomorrow morning. You will be most welcome.' He nodded curtly and left.

Georgia smiled up at him. 'You will come back tomorrow, won't you? As my uncle said, you will be made most welcome.'

Bartholomew started. He'd almost forgotten about Georgia. The maid, Agnes, had filled his mind completely. But maids don't have money, he reminded himself. And it was money he needed most. He dragged his gaze away from Agnes and returned Georgia's smile.

'Miss Georgia, you are forgetting yourself,' scolded Agnes. 'Come, dry your feet. I will help you upstairs. Sir, please ring the bell should you require anything more.'

Bartholomew gulped back the brandy brought by the footman, relishing the fiery warmth it brought to his belly. He watched as the two women crossed the black-and-white tiled hallway and made their way up the stairs. Each of them gave him one backwards glance – Miss Holland's smile was cheeky and inviting; the maid's glare was challenging, but with a half-smile and a raised eyebrow as though she had guessed the effect she'd had on him.

Without a doubt he would return tomorrow. And the day after, and the day after that. He left his empty glass on a side table and let himself out of the house. Thankfully the cab was still there, though the cabman grumbled about how long he'd had to wait in the dreadful weather. Bartholomew gave the address of his lodgings in Kemptown and sat back, huddled in his cloak, planning his ideal future which involved both of the women he'd met that night.

Chapter Three

Hampshire, November 2012

I followed Vera Delamere through a tired 1970s kitchen into a large wood-panelled hallway, and then through to a cosy sitting room. She flicked on the lights, and crouched at the fireplace which was already laid with a mixture of logs and coal. As she struck a match, Harold shuffled in and sat down beside the fire, leaning his stick against the side of the mantelpiece.

'Good-oh, we could do with a bit of warmth in here,' he said, and she turned to smile fondly at him. They'd obviously been together for a very long time. I hoped Simon and I would be like them, one day. If we managed to resolve our differences and stay together long enough.

I looked around the room. A large built-in shelving unit occupied one wall. It was made of dark wood, and was clearly very old. It was beautiful.

'That was here when we moved in,' Mrs Delamere said, nodding at the shelves. 'Riddled with woodworm, unfortunately, though we have had it treated.'

'It's gorgeous. I wonder if it was here when my ancestors lived here?'

'I'll go and make the tea,' said Vera. 'Sit down, Katie, do. By the fire, there. It'll get going in a moment.'

I sat opposite Harold in a well-worn fireside chair. 'This is a lovely cosy room.'

Harold nodded. 'We think this was originally a study. There's a much bigger sitting room across the hall, but it's too hard to heat it. When there's only Vera and me, this room's just right for us. So, you're a St Clair, are you? I thought old Barty hadn't had any children. Certainly no one to leave the house to.'

'You're right, he didn't. I'm descended from his younger brother, William.'

'Ah, that would explain it,' said Harold, nodding with satisfaction.

Vera bustled in with the tea tray. She gave it to Harold to balance on his lap for a moment as she tugged at a shelf in the old unit. It folded out, creating a desk, and she put the tea tray on it.

We chatted comfortably about the history of the house and my research while we drank the tea, then Vera offered me a tour of the house.

Harold had fallen asleep in his chair, his head nodding forward onto his chest. Vera gently took his tea cup out of his hand and put it on a side table. I followed her back into the huge hallway. 'Are you sure you don't mind showing me around? I must admit I'm dying to see the house.'

'Oh, it's quite all right. Lovely to have a visitor, if truth be told. Well, here's the living room. Drawing room, I suppose I should call it.'

She ushered me into a large, cold room, with a window to the front of the house. It had a grand fireplace which looked original, brown floral seventies carpet and cream woodchip wallpaper. Family photographs showing a younger Vera and Harold with two cheeky-looking boys jostled for position on the mantelpiece, and heavy crushed-velvet curtains hung at the window.

'We don't come in here much, except in the summer when it's the coolest room in the house,' Vera said.

She led the way back through the hallway and into the dining room I'd peered into from outside. I crossed to the window and looked out. The garden was surprisingly small for such a large old house, and I commented on this.

'It would have had much more land originally,' Vera explained. 'Most of it was sold off before we moved in. There would have been stables and other outbuildings – we think those stood where Stables Close is now. But what's left is a lovely garden. It catches the evening sun. And we're very fond of that tree.' She pointed to a huge beech which stood against a crumbling garden wall.

'I bet your children enjoyed climbing that,' I said.

'Oh, they did, they did! Tim would be sitting up there where the main trunk forks, and Mike would push past him and go up higher. I couldn't watch, but Harold always thought it was better for boys to climb trees than artificial climbing frames in sterile playgrounds.'

I laughed. 'My dad always says the same thing. My sister and I were both tomboys and spent half our childhoods up trees.'

'Good for you! I think it's essential for children to play outside. Shall we continue with the tour?'

She took me down a dark corridor to the kitchen with its walk-in pantry and a rather damp utility room which might once have been called a scullery. Then upstairs, where four large bedrooms and a bathroom occupied the first floor, and another two smaller attic bedrooms filled the second floor. I loved every inch of it. I suspected none of it had seen a lick of paint or a roll of new wallpaper since the sixties or seventies but the house oozed charm and character. I tried to imagine my ancestors here: Barty and his brother William, my great-great-grandfather, running up and down the stairs as boys; their father Bartholomew writing letters in the study downstairs; their mother serenely embroidering a sampler by the fireside in the drawing room. There would have been servants here too, living in those attic bedrooms.

We finished the tour and went back downstairs. Harold was still dozing beside the fire in the old study. 'Thank you so much, Mrs Delamere,' I said. 'I have really enjoyed imagining my ancestors living here. It's a wonderful house.'

'It is, yes.' She shook her head. 'Sadly it's too much for Harold and me nowadays. We shall soon have to think about moving out and into somewhere smaller. But I hate the thought of developers carving it up into flats, and I'm certain that's what would happen. We've been approached by a couple of developers already.'

'Mmm, yes, I can see you'd want it to stay as it is.'

'Oh, I wouldn't mind the idea of it being done up inside. Lord knows it needs it – tastes have changed and I know it's very dated. But I'd want to think of it remaining as a single family home. Ah, well.' She caught hold of my hands and leaned in to kiss my cheek. 'Katie, it's been so lovely to meet you. I hope you'll come again – I'd love to hear more about how you researched your ancestors, and how you knew they lived here.'

'Well, it was all via the census records,' I said, as I slipped on my coat. 'They're available on the Internet now, which makes it all pretty easy.'

Vera smiled. 'I'm afraid we don't even own a computer.'

As I left the house I sensed someone's eyes on me, and turned to look back. Vera was standing at the study window, watching me go with a wistful expression on her thin face. I waved, and she smiled and waved back. I crossed the street and took a few photos of the house for my records, then headed back home to Southampton. As I drove back down the motorway I wondered what kind of mood Simon would be in. Hopefully he'd have got over himself by now. I was buzzing with excitement about having seen inside my ancestors' home and wanted to be able to share it with him.

***

Simon was in the kitchen, stirring a pot of bolognese sauce for the kids' tea. I put my arms around him from behind, stretched up and kissed the back of his neck.

'Mind out! You nearly made me knock the pan over.' He shrugged himself out of my hug.

'Sorry. I'll take over if you like.' I gave the pot a stir then waltzed off around the kitchen. Our four-year old, Thomas, came in pushing a small yellow digger along the floor and making engine noises. He giggled when he saw me dancing. I scooped him up and danced with him.

'Hey, not while I'm cooking!' said Simon, brandishing his wooden spoon. 'There's no space in here for mucking about. I take it from your happy dance that you found what you were looking for?'

'Yes, I found the house!'

'What house was this?'

'Oh, Simon, I told you this morning!' I put Thomas down. He retrieved his digger and resumed excavations in the hallway. 'It was the house where the St Clairs lived, for over a hundred years. My great-great-grandfather William St Clair would have been born there, and his father Bartholomew before him.'

'Ah, yes. You've been rummaging around in the pointless past again while I look after the future, a.k.a. our children. So you got a photo of this house?'

'More than that – I went inside! The owners are a lovely elderly couple called Harold and Vera Delamere and they remember how the older folk in the village told them stories of Barty St Clair when they moved it. Apparently he was a bit strange. Very sociable but wouldn't let anyone in the house. Maybe he was hiding something – ooh, maybe there're some skeletons in my ancestors' closets!'

'Good stuff. I don't get this obsession with your ancestors, but whatever floats your boat, I suppose.' He grinned, and patted my shoulder. His way of apologising for the morning's row. I smiled back, accepting the apology.

'Kids! Dinner's ready!' Simon called. He plonked three plates of spag bol on the table, then left the kitchen. Looked like supervising the kids' dinner time was going to be my job, then. Fair enough. I'd had my time off. I helped Thomas climb up onto a chair, and ruffled Lewis and Lauren's hair as they sat at the table.

'Hey, mind the gel!' Lewis ducked away from my hand. Only ten but already spending hours in front of the mirror before school each day.

'What do you want to put gel in your hair for, you're not a girl.' His twin sister Lauren flicked his ear. 'With those spikes you'll puncture the ball when you next play rugby with Dad.'

'You don't head the ball in rugby, *derrr*,' retorted Lewis. 'Don't you know *anything*?'

'More than you, stupid.' Lauren swished her blonde mane over her shoulder and stuck out a bolognese-encrusted tongue in his direction.

'That's enough, you two,' I said. 'Eat up and if you can't speak nicely to each other don't speak at all.'

They glared across the table at each other but otherwise got on with it. Little Thomas, as usual, was keeping his head down and out of trouble. He caught my eye and flashed me a winning smile. Apart from the strand of spaghetti that was slithering down his chin it was one of those expressions you just wish you'd caught on camera.

I made myself a cup of tea while the children finished their dinners. Once they were finished and the kitchen was clean, I sat down at the table sipping my cup of tea, and drifted off into a pleasant fantasy in which the Delameres sold up and somehow Simon and I could afford to buy the house, move in and discover all its secrets.

Chapter Four

Hampshire, December 2012

'I know,' I said, decisively, 'let's take Mum and Dad out for Sunday lunch at the pub this weekend, rather than cook it here. It's always a squash when they come for dinner, and it'd be lovely to have someone else do all the work.' It was a few weeks after my visit to Kingsley House. Simon and I had managed not to row again, mainly because I'd not said a single word more about my ancestry research, and he'd foregone another rugby practice to take the whole family out to see *The Polar Express* at the cinema.

Simon put down the book he was reading and peered over his glasses at me. 'OK, and maybe your dad will want to pay…'

I threw a cushion at him. 'No, we'll pay, you tight git. It's supposed to be Dad's birthday dinner, after all. Anyway, we can easily afford to since your promotion and pay rise.'

He hugged the cushion and threw his feet up onto the sofa. It was a cold, dark evening – one of those where you wish you had an open fireplace instead of a gas fire, when you just want to cuddle up with a blanket and a good book. And maybe a glass of wine.

'Fancy a glass of wine?' I said.

'Yeah, go on then.' Simon swung his legs off the sofa and stood up to fetch a bottle. 'Arrgh, what did I tread on?' He hopped around then sat back down to investigate the damage to his foot.

'Lego, I expect. Lewis had some in here earlier.'

'When's he going to grow out of Lego?' grumbled Simon, kicking the offending piece under the Christmas tree.

'About the same time as Thomas grows into it,' I replied. 'I'll get the wine, seeing as you're incapacitated.'

'Thanks. What we really need is a bigger house. One with a playroom, so we can keep the lounge clear of toys and the kids can injure themselves on their own Lego without involving us.'

I went to fetch a couple of glasses and a bottle of Pinot Noir from the kitchen. Simon was right – we had outgrown this house. The two boys had to share a room, which didn't work very well because of the difference in their ages. The kitchen was a reasonable size but had to double as a dining room. Just about OK for the five of us but hopeless if we had visitors. And the garage was stuffed to bursting with bikes, gardening tools and DIY debris.

'Do you mean it?' I asked, as I returned with the wine.

'Mean what?'

'What you said about wanting a bigger house.'

He frowned, stared at the ceiling as though looking for an answer written on it, then sat upright. 'Yeah, I think I do. How do you feel about moving?'

'Well, I love this house, but we do need more space.'

'Right then, let's start house-hunting.' He grabbed my laptop from the side table which doubled as a desk, and started tapping the keys.

'Really? Right now?' Was he serious or just fooling? Sometimes it was hard to tell with Simon.

'No time like the present, eh? And no harm in looking.' He grinned and patted the seat beside him. I sat down, and a moment later we were browsing a list of houses in Southampton which matched our criteria: four bedrooms, garden, two reception rooms. It was nice to do something together, as well.

I pointed to a Victorian three-storey semi. 'That one looks good.'

'Bit pricey.'

'What can we afford?'

'Dunno, I'd have to do the figures. Say four hundred thousand maximum – that'll give us an idea of what's available. Good job I got that promotion.'

They all looked nearer the half-million mark. I began to get despondent as Simon scrolled through. There was no point compromising on size – might as well stay where we are. We wanted to stay in Hampshire near our parents. Mine helped out with childcare occasionally and Simon's mum – adoptive mum – was suffering from dementia and needed support. And there needed to be good schools nearby.

'Winchester would be good. That'd cut fifteen minutes off my commute to London,' said Simon.

'Yes, I like Winchester too.' I reached over and selected Winchester from a dropdown list of areas, and we began browsing a new set of houses.

'Period or modern?' Simon asked.

'Period, definitely. Something with character. More wine?'

'Why not? Period for me, too. Cor, look at this one!' He clicked on a thumbnail image to expand it. I gasped – I'd seen that house before. Kingsley House, up for sale! Simon would click onto the next house instantly if he knew, so I quickly covered my gasp with an exclamation.

'Wow, gorgeous! What's the asking price?'

'Hmm, four-four-five. Bit out of our price range. Looks a bit run down. Could be worth a look, though.'

'Really? You want to go and see it?' My heart beat a little faster at the idea of having another look at that house. I wondered whether anything had happened to Vera and Harold Delamere to make them put it up for sale. They'd mentioned feeling they ought to move somewhere smaller but had seemed reluctant to put the house on the market. I hoped they were OK. I'd thought of them and the house many times since my visit.

Simon frowned at me. 'Well, that's how house-hunting works, isn't it? You find something you like the look of, then go to see it.'

'It's just all a bit sudden. Have we actually decided we want to move?'

'Do *you* want to?'

'Well, it makes sense, so I guess I do...'

'Great! So do I.' He clinked glasses with me. 'So if we've made the decision to move, we might as well start looking at properties sooner rather than later. Don't you think?'

And so it was that on Saturday I found myself standing outside Kingsley House again, grinning from ear to ear, with a slightly grizzly Thomas who'd just woken up holding my hand. Simon had dropped us off and was busy parking the car further up the lane. The older children and the estate agent were with him. I tugged on the bell-rope and heard a distant jangling inside.

Vera opened the door and broke into a wide smile when she saw me on the doorstep. 'Katie, how lovely to see you! But, I'm afraid we're expecting visitors in a moment. The house is up for sale, you see.'

'I know – it's us who've come to see it,' I said, shaking her hand.

'You? Oh, how lovely! When the estate agent said a Mr and Mrs Smith wanted to see the house I didn't think for a moment it'd be you!'

'I know, it's such a common name, not like St Clair. Listen.' I spoke hurriedly, seeing Simon, Lewis, Lauren and the estate agent walking up the lane 'My husband doesn't know I was here before. I'd be obliged if you didn't mention it. He's not...well...he doesn't get the whole ancestry thing, you know? I think it would put him off the house.'

Vera raised her eyebrows, but nodded. 'All right. Mum's the word. And who's this?' She crouched down to Thomas's level, but he became suddenly shy and buried his face against my leg. She stood up again as Simon and the others crunched across the gravel driveway. 'Come in, everyone. Would you like to take the little one into the study? I'm sure I can find something to amuse him while the rest of you look around the house.'

The estate agent, Martin, a skinny youth in a shiny suit, introduced everyone as Vera ushered us all inside. Martin set off on a tour with Simon, Lewis and Lauren, while I followed Vera into the study with Thomas.

Harold was dozing beside the fire, in much the same place I'd left him on my last visit. 'He's not been so good,' Vera whispered to me. 'That's why we're having to move. We're going into one of those little retirement flats, in a new development near our son in Bournemouth.' She sighed. 'It'll break our hearts to leave this place, but the time has come.'

She gently shook Harold's arm to wake him up. 'Harold, look who's here to view the house.'

He blinked twice at me, then smiled. 'Katie St Clair! So are you going to buy our house, then?'

I laughed. 'Well, I'll have to see what my husband, Simon, thinks. He's having a look around now, with the kids.'

'And you'd better go to join him, or it'll look odd,' said Vera. 'Now, Thomas, shall I fetch you something to play with? I've got a box of old Matchbox cars somewhere. I used to keep them for our grandchildren. But they're all grown-up now.' She opened a low cupboard in the old shelving unit and pulled out a Tupperware container. Thomas trotted over and started rummaging through it happily, pulling out diggers and police cars, tractors and racing cars. Harold pulled out one and showed him how the doors opened.

'Look, Thomas. It's an old Ford Anglia. Like the first car I ever owned!'

Thomas inspected the battered toy. 'Daddy's got a Galaxy. We came in it today. It's red.'

'Oh, I like Galaxies,' said Harold. 'Lovely big cars.'

Behind him, Vera gestured to me to follow her out to the hallway, leaving the 'boys' to discuss cars.

'It's lovely to see him playing with a child,' said Vera. 'Does him good.'

'Thomas loves cars. Your Tupperware box is the perfect thing to keep him happy.'

'You'd better go and join the tour. I believe they're upstairs now. I'll make us some tea, and squash for the children?'

'Perfect,' I said, and trotted upstairs to find Simon and the kids who'd reached the two attic bedrooms.

'Mum, I want to have *this* room,' said Lauren. 'I love the slopey ceilings. But I don't want Lewis in the other room up here. I want this floor all to myself. Can I?'

'Sweetheart, we haven't even decided whether to buy this house or not. It's a bit over our price range.' I looked at Simon as I said this. He was chewing his lip, a sign that he was deep in thought. 'What do you think, Simon?'

'Got loads of potential. And I've always quite fancied a project house. Do you like it?'

'I love it. Absolutely love it,' I said. Martin grinned, no doubt seeing pound signs spinning in front of his eyes.

'You can't have seen much of it yet,' said Simon. 'But it is the kind of place which grabs you, isn't it?'

He had no idea just how much it had grabbed me. I nodded, as we went back down the narrow stairs to the first floor.

A few minutes later, our tour was over. Lewis and Lauren went out to explore the garden, while Martin watched them nervously from the kitchen. Simon and I returned to the study where Thomas was parking cars along the edge of the hearth rug. Harold looked up as we entered.

'Mrs Smith, do please sit down.' He gestured to the chair

opposite him, beside the fire. 'We've been thinking. Are you serious about wanting to buy this house?'

I sat, and glanced at Simon standing beside me, wondering how we should reply. I loved the house and could think of nowhere I'd rather live, but it was out of our price range. How could we say we were serious about it when we knew we couldn't possibly afford it? Simon looked lost for words too. Before either of us had chance to frame an answer, Harold continued.

'Because if you are, I think we would be very happy to sell the house to you. Vera and I always hoped another family would buy the house, rather than a developer. We'd hate it to be mucked about with and turned into flats. We've had plenty of offers from developers, but have turned them all down, hoping a family would come and look at it. And we decided,' here he looked at Vera who nodded encouragingly, 'that if a family we liked came to see the house, we would reduce the price for them.'

I stared at him, and then at Simon. Was I hearing this right? They'd reduce the price if we wanted to buy? I blinked, and opened my mouth to speak, but again, Harold got in there first.

'I think four hundred thousand would be plenty for us. The retirement flat we want to buy is much less than that. No sense in us being greedy. Would you like to discuss it?'

I nodded, dumbly. Simon looked stunned.

Harold smiled and reached across to pat my hand. 'You mustn't feel you're cheating us, you know. We don't need the full asking price. You'd be doing us a favour by keeping it out of the developers' hands. Isn't that right, Vera?'

Her eyes were bright as she answered. 'Oh, yes. We'd love you to buy this house. Especially as—' She stopped herself in time, and put a hand to her mouth.

'Can we have a minute to talk about this?' said Simon. He went out to the hallway and nodded at me to follow him.

Vera called to the estate agent. 'Martin, could you come in

here a moment, please. Harold would like a word. Leave Mr and Mrs Smith to have another poke around by themselves, perhaps.'

Simon pulled me into the kitchen and stared at me. 'Four hundred? Wow! I was working out whether we could stretch to four twenty as a cheeky offer but if they'll come down that much – we'd be stupid not to go for it! We could sell it straight on and make a profit if nothing else.'

I felt my heart sink. Is that all he was thinking about – making a quick buck? 'We couldn't sell it on – they want a family to live here. Anyway I want to live here, don't you?'

'It needs a lot of work…'

'We could do it! I could project-manage it – Thomas will be starting reception class in school after Easter and I'll have time. I know I was going to go back to work part time, but I could do up the house first… Oh, Simon, I adore this house, and would absolutely love to live here and do it up! The kids seem to like it too…' Lewis and Lauren were investigating the beech tree. As we watched, Lauren gave her brother a leg up to the first branch.

Simon turned to me and put his hands on my shoulders. 'Calm down, Katie! I love the house too. And we could add value to it by doing it up. Look at this kitchen – hasn't been touched in thirty years! But we'd be living in a building site for ages bringing this place up to scratch. Have you any idea how stressful that would be?'

'We can do it bit by bit. I don't mind the mess. Anyway the house is big enough that we could live in some rooms while we do up others. There are *six* bedrooms, Simon! Oh, let's go and tell them yes, please!'

He gazed into my eyes, then pulled me into a crushing hug. 'All right, let's do it. But remember, we still have to find a buyer for our place.'

I kissed him. At some stage I supposed I would have to tell him about the history of this house, but that could wait. If he'd known about my ancestors living here, he'd never even have come to see it. I'd come clean later. When it was too late to back out.

We called to the kids to come inside. Their cheeks were flushed from the crisp winter air, and Lewis had grass stains on both knees.

'Awesome garden, Mum! I love that tree. Are we going to buy this house?' He glanced at his filthy hands and wiped them on the back of his jeans.

'When we move in, I want *both* of the rooms at the top. One for a bedroom and one for a playing room. Mum, can I?' Lauren clung onto my arm, jumping up and down.

'Steady on! There's a lot of water to go under the bridge before we move in. But, yes, I would think you can have *one* room at the top if that's what you want. And *share* the other as a playroom.'

'Yes!' Lauren punched the air, as we all crowded into the little sitting room cum study.

Harold looked at me expectantly. 'Well?'

'We love it. We *all* love it.' Thomas looked up from the hearth rug as I said this, and nodded his little blond head seriously.

'Four hundred?' asked Harold, raising his eyebrows.

'Deal,' said Simon, stepping across the room and shaking the old man's hand. Vera smiled broadly at me, her eyes shining. Whether with excitement or unshed tears I wasn't sure.

Martin coughed. 'Um, by rights the offers should go through me, and may I say it's a little on the low side...'

'It's all right,' said Harold. 'Remember we said we'd reduce for the right people? Mr and Mrs Smith, and young Thomas here and his brother and sister – they are the right people. And that's all there is to it.' He looked up at Simon. 'How soon can you move?'

***

'Two roast beef, one salmon and one roast chicken. And for the kids, two burger and chips, and one pasta bolognese. Have I got that right?' Simon ticked off the orders on his fingers as he recited them.

'Yes, that's the lot,' I said, watching him go to the bar to place the food order. Dad had already bought a round of drinks – insisting on paying, despite it being his birthday. I sipped my wine, and opened up the freebie bag of colouring pens and puzzles the barman had handed over for Thomas. Lauren and Lewis were on their Nintendos. I guessed they were on some kind of multi-player game, as every now and again one would cheer and the other look sulky.

Mum settled herself back into her chair. 'Now then. What's all this about you buying a new house? I know you could do with more space, but it seems so sudden. You didn't even tell us you were house-hunting!'

'We'd only just started,' I said. 'But when the right house comes up straight away, well, you just have to go for it. We saw it yesterday, and have already agreed to buy it.'

'Goodness, that was quick!'

'They offered it to us at an amazing price,' I said, grinning.

'Well, that's very exciting!' said Mum. 'Tell us about it, then, love. How many rooms does it have?'

'Six bedrooms, two reception rooms, three if you count the study. And a large kitchen with separate utility room and pantry.'

'Pantry!'

'Well, a walk-in food cupboard, really.'

'And what will you do with all those bedrooms?'

'Convert one to an en-suite,' said Simon, returning with a wooden spoon, painted with the number seventeen. 'There's only one bathroom and I think it definitely needs another.'

'Nan, I'm having a room on the top floor,' said Lauren, looking up from her game.

'Lovely, dear!'

'We'll be able to have a proper guest room, Mum,' I said. 'So you can come to stay without being stuck on the living room floor.'

'Christmas at yours next year, then?' asked Mum.

33

That was a nice idea. 'Why not?'

'As it's an old house, I guess there are proper fireplaces so Santa can come down the chimney instead of through the back door?' Dad winked at me over Thomas's head.

'I saw Santa,' said Thomas. 'On a bicycle.'

'That was just someone dressed up,' said Lewis. 'Not the real one.'

Thomas's lip quivered and I frowned at Lewis to shut him up. Mum put her arm around Thomas. 'I'll take you to see the real Santa,' she said. 'He's going to be at the shopping centre next week. He might give you a present, if you're good.' She looked at me. 'I can't wait to see the house. When will you move in?'

'When we've sold our place,' Simon said. 'We've not even put it on the market yet. With the way the market is at the moment it might take ages to sell.'

Trust Simon to put a dampener on things. I hadn't really given much thought to selling our current house. But of course he was right. I shouldn't get too excited about moving to North Kingsley. What if we couldn't sell our place, and meanwhile the Delameres got fed up of waiting and sold to someone else?

I must have looked worried, because Dad reached over and patted my hand. Simon picked up his pint.

'Don't fret, Katie,' he said. 'Since the Delameres have agreed such a good price for their house, we can price ours to sell quickly. They're moving into an empty retirement flat. We could be in by Easter, with a following wind. As long as the survey's OK. We'll have to think hard if it turns out to be riddled with dry rot or rising damp.'

I didn't listen to that last bit about surveys. Simon wasn't going to spoil it for me. I was too busy considering the totally gorgeous idea of moving in spring. Simon, Mum and Dad began a discussion on house prices while I allowed my mind to wander, imagining the fields around North Kingsley bright with the fresh green growth of a new season, the hedgerows laden with elderflower and hawthorn blossom, cute rabbits hopping along the verges, swallows dipping and diving overhead. The kids would be out in the woods, exploring the countryside, learning the names of wild flowers and birds. We'd get a dog – with such wonderful country walks all around it'd be a crime not to. I'd plant up the garden with hollyhocks and lupins, and Simon would make the kids a tree house in the branches of the beech. And of course, I'd be living in the very rooms where Georgia and Bartholomew once lived.

It would all be so perfect.

'Katie, how's the old family tree research coming on?' Dad's voice broke into my thoughts. He's the one person in my family who is truly interested in my genealogical research. I guess because he's a St Clair too. But now wasn't a great time to discuss it.

'Um, I haven't spent too much time on it lately…'

'Like hell you haven't,' said Simon. 'You've barely done anything else. Didn't you go taking photos of some old house to do with your ancestors a few weeks ago?'

'Oh, really?' said Dad. 'Fascinating! You must show me them. Where was the house?'

Trust Simon to remember that now. I felt myself blush. I hated keeping secrets from him but I wouldn't put it past him to pull out of the house purchase if he thought I was only interested in it because of its connection to my family. I had to wait until the deal was secure before telling him.

'Oh, er, it's not far. Twenty, thirty miles away, something like that. I'm still researching other St Clair facts, too. Like where they're all buried. I want to find their gravestones, and get some photos of those, too.'

'So have you drawn up the family tree yet? I'd love to see it,' said Dad.

'It's all on Ancestry.' For once, I was desperate to steer the conversation away from genealogy.

'Email me the link, will you? I'll have a look at it this week, see if I can find any more details for you. I wouldn't mind getting involved in all this research now I'm retired.'

I smiled and nodded. I'd have to forget to send him it. Otherwise he might follow up links and find Kingsley House, and recognise it from the estate agent details Simon had shown him. That would be awkward, to say the least.

Chapter Five

Brighton, April 1838

For the thousandth time, Bartholomew patted the pocket in which he'd stowed the trinket, to make sure it was safely tucked away. It wasn't the first gift he'd given Georgia, but it was by far the most expensive. A silver hair comb, set with emeralds along its spine. He'd had it made in London by a Bond Street jeweller, and hoped she would love it. As the stagecoach rumbled southwards along the bumpy Brighton road, Bartholomew was glad he would be able to deliver *this* gift in person, rather than send it as he'd done with the last few presents.

It had been a few weeks since he'd last been in Brighton. Trouble with his investments had called him to his Mayfair town-house, and it had taken him longer than expected to get everything back on track. His agent, Collins, should be able to take care of business from here on, freeing Bartholomew to live the idle life of a gentleman, as was his right. More than ever, he needed capital, and that could only come from marrying someone with money. Like Georgia Holland. There were rumours of a substantial inheritance, currently in trust for her but which would pass to her husband on the occasion of her marriage. She was pretty and charming, if a little immature, and could be a good choice of wife. He had not renewed the lease on his Brighton lodgings – Charles Holland had invited him to stay in the Brunswick Terrace house.

Well, he'd see the pretty little Georgia soon enough, and would ask for her hand at the earliest opportunity. If he played his cards right, he could be out of debt within a few months. And, of course, there was the added attraction of Georgia's alluring lady's maid. He felt a twinge of excitement at the thought of seeing *her* again.

The countryside passed by in a rush of bright new foliage, sweet white blossom, rich earthy scents of newly ploughed and planted fields. The spring sunshine cast a glow of hope for the future over everything. Bartholomew smiled. There was a world of possibilities ahead of him.

When he arrived at Brunswick Terrace, the door was opened by the footman, Peters. 'Welcome, sir. The master is awaiting you in the drawing room. I shall take your luggage up to your room.'

'Thank you.' As he gave his hat and travelling cloak to Peters, Bartholomew noticed the maid, Agnes, on the turn of the stairs. He caught her eye, and raised one eyebrow. In return, she gave an almost imperceptible nod of her head, sending a thrill rushing through him. What did she mean by that nod? Could it be – an invitation?

'Miss Georgia said to inform you she is indisposed,' said Peters. 'I believe her maid is attending to her now.' He held the drawing-room door open.

Bartholomew was still gazing after Agnes. That woman had the most regal bearing of any woman, high- or low-born, he'd ever seen. She was slight but carried herself tall, graceful as a swan. She looked back at him once, a half-smile on her face, as though she was as pleased to see him as he was to see her.

He entered the drawing room, where a log fire was blazing in the grate, even though the day was warm and sunny. Charles Holland was sitting in an armchair near the fire, his back to the window. He had a brandy glass in his hand, and as Bartholomew approached he gulped it back and motioned for Peters to pour another.

'Welcome, welcome, St Clair,' he said, waving at Bartholomew to sit opposite him.

Pulling the chair a little away from the fire, Bartholomew sat down, but declined the brandy offered to him by Peters. He'd have welcomed its warming glow, but one brandy often led to another, and another. It was early yet, and he wanted to keep his wits about him during this interview with Georgia's uncle.

'I thank you for your hospitality, sir,' he said. 'It is most kind of you to offer me room in your house.'

Holland snorted. 'You're here because I assume you are going to propose to my niece, sooner or later. I thought if you were here under her nose for a few weeks it might hurry things along. She's got money, you know. Plenty of it. In trust now, but goes to whichever poor blighter marries her.'

Bartholomew blinked. 'Sir, I am not after her money, please don't think that…'

'Hmph. Most of 'em are. Granted, she's a pretty enough little thing but there's too little flesh on her for some men's liking, and she can be far too spirited. You'll need to tame her, somewhat. You ready for that, man?'

'I like her spirit,' Bartholomew said, remembering the night they'd met, when she'd walked in the snow in dancing slippers, and made him carry her.

'So did a young chap she met last week,' said Holland. 'Son of a wine merchant, I believe, name of Perry. He's called here every day. She's having her portrait painted, and the poor sop waited mutely for hours while she sat for the artist. If you want my niece – and Lord knows you're welcome to her, I make no secret of the fact I want her off my hands – you'll need to act quickly. I'll give my blessing. Frankly I think an older, settled chap like yourself will be better for her than a love-struck pup like Perry.' He gulped back his brandy and reached for the decanter to pour another. 'Sure you won't join me?'

'Perhaps just a small one.'

Holland poured a generous measure into a large brandy glass and handed it to him. 'So, St Clair, as Georgia's official guardian I should ask you about your property and income and such like. Don't give a damn, myself, but it's the done thing as I understand it, and sooner or later some busybody's bound to ask about my niece's fiancé. So I'd best have the detail, man.'

Bartholomew cleared his throat. He'd been expecting this question, but not quite in this form. 'Well, sir, I am comfortably off. I have a townhouse in Mayfair which is my usual residence when in town, and two other properties near the Regent's Park, which are let out. I expect to inherit a small country estate in Hampshire from my father in time, but I may not keep that for long.' Best not to mention that all the London properties were mortgaged to the hilt, and he was barely able to keep up the repayments.

'Hampshire? Nice county. Know it well, from my youth. Where's your father's place, exactly?'

'North Kingsley, on the London road out of Winchester. The house is called Kingsley House.'

Holland snorted. 'Never heard of it.'

The captain's dismissal made Bartholomew feel defensive about his childhood home. 'It's not large, but is comfortable, and very pleasantly situated. Any woman would be happy living there.' He swallowed his brandy, and set the glass on a small table beside his chair.

Holland immediately reached for it and poured him another. 'How long till you inherit?'

Bartholomew blinked. The directness of the man! 'Sir, my father is old and frail. Only the Lord above knows how much

40

longer he will live, but I would not expect it to be more than a couple of years.'

'Until then, what's your income?'

'I have upwards of £800 a year from my investments. Your niece, should she accept me, will want for nothing.' At least, he had been generating £800 a year from his investments, up until losing thousands when an East Indiaman had sunk off the Cape. Bartholomew drank again from his brandy glass.

'Well, that's settled then. I'll ring for her to join us.' Holland heaved himself out of his chair and pulled on a bell-cord which hung beside the fireplace.

Bartholomew frowned. 'I believe your footman said she was indisposed?'

'Indisposed, my foot. She was dancing late at the Assembly Rooms last night with young Perry, and gave herself a headache. Fetch my niece,' he said to Peters, who responded with a small bow. 'Tell her she has an important visitor and I want her downstairs at once.'

Peters left the room. Holland nodded at Bartholomew's glass, and raised his eyebrow. Might as well be hanged for a sheep as a lamb, thought Bartholomew, as he held out his glass for yet another refill. It was indeed a fine brandy.

A moment later there was a tap at the door. Bartholomew stood, straightened his collar and arranged a smile on his face to greet Georgia.

But when Holland called 'Come!' and the door was pushed open, it was Agnes, the maid, who stepped quietly into the room, her attitude deferential but at the same time, her head held high and confident.

'Beg pardon, sir, but Miss Georgia is not well. She asks your forgiveness, and sends her apologies to Mr St Clair, but fears she cannot be in company for today.' She gave a pretty curtsey, then turned to Bartholomew. 'If it please you, sir, she says she would like to meet you after breakfast tomorrow, and if the weather be fine, perhaps take a stroll along the beach.'

She nodded, curtsied once more, and left the room, not waiting for an answer.

Bartholomew smiled. A fine woman, and one who, if he played his cards right, would soon be a part of his household.

'Thought you'd be upset, man,' said Holland. 'Travelling all this way to see my niece, only for her to stay abed. Well, plenty more days I suppose. You need to supplant that young Perry in her affections. Give her some jewellery – the ladies always like that kind of thing.'

'I am indeed sorry I cannot renew my acquaintance with Miss Holland this evening,' said Bartholomew, sounding formal even to his own ears, as he struggled to compose himself. Why did that maid have such an effect on him every time he caught a glimpse of her? He'd barely said two words to the woman since he'd met her, but something about her made his pulse race. And if he was not mistaken, she was also attracted to him.

'Well then, if my niece is not to join us for dinner, we may as well have another brandy. Hand me your glass, man, I'll top it up.'

The following morning, it was a bleary-eyed Bartholomew who made his way down to the breakfast room. Thankfully the room was empty when he arrived. Peters informed him that Holland would not rise until eleven, and Georgia usually had breakfast brought up to her in her room. Bartholomew sat down to a plate of cold meat and cheese, and worked his way through a whole jug of coffee. When it was finished, he felt a little more ready to face the day. He resolved to be more careful the next time he was in company with Holland and the brandy decanter.

He had not yet seen Agnes, the maid, that morning, but his night had been disturbed by vivid dreams of her. He tried to bring his thoughts back to Georgia – it was *she* he was here to court – but it was Agnes's face he saw in his mind's eye, Agnes's voice he heard, Agnes's hands he imagined caressing him.

He shook his head. He had to pull himself together. Agnes was a maid, too lowly for him to consider as a wife. He needed a woman with status, and definitely one with money. He had to focus on Georgia. The two women were superficially alike – both were blonde with green eyes, slight figures and clear complexions – but Agnes had sharper features and a more knowing, worldly manner, whereas Georgia's face was round and plump, and her attitude more like that of an overgrown child.

The sound of light footsteps on the stairs pulled him out of his reverie. He glanced out of the window; it was indeed a fine day. The breakfast room was at the front of the house, and there was a fine view across the promenade to the beach. High white clouds scudded across a brilliant blue sky, and the wind was whipping the sea into a frenzy of white water. He looked forward to a walk with Georgia. The fresh air would clear his head for certain.

He folded the newspaper he'd been reading, and went out to the hallway. The sun shining through the half-moon-shaped fanlight above the door made a dancing pattern on the tiles. Georgia was standing by the bottom of the stairs, one hand on the newel post, the other clutching a bonnet. She was wearing a pale-green silk dress, trimmed with brown lace, and with her golden hair shining in the sunlight she looked like spring embodied. Without a doubt she was a pretty young thing.

'Good morning!' he said, giving a small bow. 'I was sorry not to have the pleasure of your company last night, but your uncle made me most welcome. I trust you are fully recovered today?'

She smiled, her cheeks dimpling prettily. 'Yes, I am perfectly well, thank you. And ready for some exercise, if you would care to walk with me?'

'I can think of nothing I would like more. It is windy out – you will require a shawl, I think.'

'I shall ask Agnes to fetch me one,' she said, and she pulled the servants' bell-cord.

Bartholomew felt the now-familiar surge in his chest at the

thought of another glimpse of Agnes. But it was Peters who answered the bell, and was sent upstairs to fetch the shawl.

The wind was indeed strong, and Georgia slipped her small, gloved hand through his arm to steady herself as they walked eastwards along the promenade, with the wind at their backs. They nodded at other walkers. They must make a handsome couple, he supposed – Georgia with her blonde daintiness and tiny waist, he with his upright bearing, fine shoulders and bushy side-whiskers.

After a while, they approached the busy part of town, in front of the Regent's Pavilion and the bottom end of the Old Steine gardens. Georgia proposed that they went onto the beach to walk back. It was rough going over the pebbles, and the wind sent a fine spray from the sea into their faces, but it was invigorating.

'Marvellous place to live,' Bartholomew said. 'With this on your doorstep and the Assembly Rooms for entertainment, you have everything you could want.'

'I suppose so,' Georgia replied. 'Though I confess I preferred living in the country. I only moved to Brighton after my father died, when Uncle Charles took me in.'

'And how would you feel about living in London?' he asked. If he married her, that would be where they would live, for that was where most of his property and business interests were.

She shuddered. 'I should think it would be too big and brash for me. All those people, and so little space. At my father's house in Lincolnshire I would go for long walks across the fields, seeing no one except a few farm labourers. It was blissful.'

He smiled. 'I had you down as a party girl – I thought you enjoyed the excitement and glamour of the Assembly Rooms. You were there last night, were you not?'

'My uncle insists I go to every ball. I missed having a proper coming-out in London, as I was in mourning. But he is desperate to find me a husband. Oh!' She put her hand to her mouth. 'I should not be saying this to you. But I have always found you so easy to talk to.'

'I am happy to listen, my dear Miss Holland.'

'Oh, call me Georgia, do! You know, I quite think of you as another uncle – no, as a *favourite* uncle. Do you mind?'

He did mind; a favoured uncle was hardly the kind of man she would want to marry. But he laughed and shook his head. 'Not at all, Georgia.'

'Good!' She stopped walking and turned to face him. 'May I ask your advice about something, please? It is perhaps a little personal, but it is the kind of thing a girl would talk to her favourite uncle about…' She lifted her eyes to his.

He raised his eyebrows questioningly. Perhaps if he gained her confidences, he would then be able to gain her affections.

'It is about my marriage prospects,' she said, blushing. 'I – I think that I have some money held in trust, from the sale of my father's property, and that when I marry my husband would be in control of that money. But I confess I have no idea how much it is. Am I rich, Mr St Clair? Am I a good marriage prospect for some eligible young bachelor? Oh, forgive me if I embarrass you with such talk!'

'If I am to call you Georgia, you must call me Bartholomew. And no, you do not embarrass me. But I cannot answer you. I am afraid you must discuss this matter with your real uncle who is, I believe, a trustee of your estate as well as being your guardian. You are right: you *should* know what you are worth. Some men might court you only for your wealth, and not for yourself.' He coughed.

'But surely not Mr Perry,' she said, blushing and turning away.

Bartholomew straightened his shoulders. 'I'm sorry, I'm not acquainted with the gentleman of whom you speak.'

Georgia turned towards the sea and gazed at the horizon. 'I have met him several times at the Assembly Rooms. He has called on me a few times in the afternoons. I believe he may propose to me.'

'And will you accept?'

'Oh, Bartholomew, I do not know! Do you think I should?'

'Is he rich?'

'He works for his father who is a wine merchant. I believe he owns a small house in Kemptown. But doesn't love matter more than wealth?'

'Do you love him?'

'Yes, I think I do…'

Bartholomew thought hard. He needed to turn Georgia away from this Perry fellow, without also turning her away from him. He'd won her trust, and surely that went a long way as a foundation for a good marriage? Besides, he needed her inheritance. He needed to switch on his charm.

He stepped towards her and took her hands. 'Georgia, my dear, although it sounds harsh, I do not think you should marry for love. You need to think of your future comfort. Think of the children you will have, and the kind of life you would like them to lead. If you marry this man Perry, you might have a couple of happy years to begin with, but then the realities of lower-middle-class life would kick in. Could you really live in a small Kemptown house, having been used to your uncle's substantial property? You would only be able to afford a minimum of servants – a cook perhaps, and a maid-of-all-work. You are used to having your own lady's maid, and a very fine maid she is.' He cleared his throat. 'My advice, which you may not want to hear, is to be practical when it comes to marriage. Accept the best proposal you can get, from the richest man, who will be able to keep you in a manner which befits your class. Put thoughts of romantic love aside. As long as you respect and trust the man, and don't find him wholly repulsive, you will be able to love him in time. Love grows, my dear. The enduring type rarely arrives fully formed.'

Georgia had kept her gaze fixed on the horizon for the first part of this speech, but now she looked deep into his eyes. 'But where will I find such a man? No one else has made me a proposal, or indeed, shown any interest in me. And I know I am a burden to my uncle; the sooner I marry and move out of his house, the better, as far as he is concerned.' She brushed away a tear. 'Forgive me. If only my father were still alive, he would know what to do. I miss him so much.'

Bartholomew pulled out his silk handkerchief and gave it to her. 'It is barely a year since he died, isn't it? Of course you miss him still.'

He realised there was a chance for him here, if he played the game right. He watched as she dabbed at her tears with the handkerchief. 'I think I know what your father might have advised,' he said, gently.

She looked up at him in surprise. 'Please, tell me.'

'Marry a man you like and trust, and who can provide a secure future for you. Someone who is already established in life, perhaps a little older than yourself. Someone of whom your uncle approves. Someone…well, someone like me.'

He watched as her eyes widened, and a smile began to play at the corners of her mouth. 'Do you mean to say…'

'I do mean to say… I mean, Georgia, I would consider it an honour if you would agree to be my wife.' Well, the words were out, the deed was done. If she said yes, there was no going back.

Her smile widened, and she raised an eyebrow. 'Bartholomew, I did not suspect you cared for me in that way! I am flattered, honoured, and, well… I suppose you want an answer…' She turned away, gazing out to sea as though the answer would be brought to her on the crest of a wave.

'You do not need to answer immediately, my dear. Take time to think about it, if you need to.'

She nodded, then turned back to him with a flirtatious smile. 'You carried me once, along the promenade in the snow. That was fun. I cannot quite imagine Mr Perry doing such a thing.'

'And is that the kind of behaviour you would like in a husband?'

'I believe it is *required* behaviour in a husband.' She held out her hand. He took it and kissed her fingers.

'In that case,' he said, hoisting her up into his arms as she squealed and giggled, 'I shall demonstrate my suitability as a husband, and shall carry you down the beach.'

'Not into the sea!'

'What is your answer?' He took another few steps towards the waves.

She squealed again. 'You said I could take time to think about it!'

'You may think about it – in the sea!' The waves were now lapping at his boots.

'But my feet will get cold and wet!'

'That did not bother you at New Year. Do you say yes?'

He made as if to drop her. She clung tightly to his neck, and, laughing, gasped out a yes.

His debts would be paid, his future secure. How easy it had been to influence her! She would make him a perfect wife. He held her more firmly, and bent his head to seal their agreement with a kiss.

'Mr St Clair, Miss Georgia, is everything all right? Has something happened? Do you need any help?'

It was Agnes, clutching a shopping basket, her eyes wide with concern. Where had she appeared from? Had she followed them? How much had she overheard? Bartholomew stepped back from the water's edge, and placed Georgia carefully on the bank of pebbles above the water line. He coughed, embarrassed.

'Oh, Agnes, I am perfectly all right. You gave me quite a surprise, appearing like that. You mustn't mind our larking about. I am so excited – I am engaged to be married to Mr St Clair!' Bartholomew felt momentarily embarrassed by the way Georgia had blurted out their news, like an overexcited child.

'Congratulations, I am sure,' said Agnes. 'You have torn your gown.' She pointed to a seam at the bodice which had come away.

'Oh!' Georgia twisted to inspect the damage. 'Well, never mind, you can mend it for me later.'

48

Agnes nodded curtly, then turned on her heel and walked up the beach, her head held high.

Bartholomew watched her go, his heart racing, his palms sweating. She'd had that effect on him, yet again. And had there been a touch of hurt, disappointment perhaps, in her eyes?

'She fusses so,' said Georgia. 'She acts as though she's my mother, although she is only a few years older than me. She says I am missing a woman's influence in my life. My mother died when I was born, and Father never remarried. But never mind her – we are engaged, and you, sir, were about to kiss me, I do believe.'

'I was indeed,' he said, taking a step closer to claim the kiss. But Georgia picked up her skirts and ran off, along the beach, laughing like a child. Bartholomew grinned and shook his head. She was not much more than a child, he must remember that.

In the evening, having spoken to Charles Holland who'd readily agreed to the match, telling him it was about time, Bartholomew sat next to Georgia at dinner. All through the meal she flirted prettily with him, treating him to glittering smiles, laughing at his witticisms, and pressing her foot against his. Once she even put her hand beneath the table, on his knee. Bartholomew felt his desire for her increase – she may have acted like a young girl on the beach but now she seemed all woman. As the dinner drew to a close and the servants cleared away the dessert dishes, he longed to be alone with her; to get a chance to hold her and kiss her.

'We'll set your wedding date sooner rather than later, eh, St Clair? No sense making you wait longer than necessary to claim your bride.'

Bartholomew reddened. It was as though Holland had read his mind. He nodded, and smiled at Georgia. 'I'd certainly like to marry as soon as possible.'

'We'll need to wait at least until the banns are read,' she said.

'Banns, my foot,' said Holland. 'St Clair'll purchase a licence.

He can get that in a day. We could have you married by the weekend.'

Georgia's face fell. 'Oh, but Uncle, but that's too soon to arrange any celebrations, or buy any new clothes!'

'He's pulling your leg, my dear,' said Bartholomew. 'We'll marry soon, but not quite as quickly as that. You shall have a new gown if you want one, and a bonnet, and petticoats, and anything else you desire. And for now, you shall have this.' He pulled the box containing the hair ornament out of his pocket and handed it to her.

He watched as she opened the box and gasped at the comb. The jewels sparkled in the candlelight and reflected in her eyes.

'It's beautiful,' she said, in a whisper. 'Quite the most beautiful thing I've seen. I shall wear it for my portrait, so that when I gaze upon it in future years I will always remember this day. In fact, I want to wear it at once. Ring for Agnes – without a mirror I can't put it in by myself.'

Charles Holland smiled indulgently, and reached for the bell-pull. A moment later Agnes entered. Her eyes widened as she saw the comb.

'A pretty piece, Miss Georgia. You are a lucky woman.' She removed a plain tortoiseshell comb from Georgia's hair, and replaced it with the emerald one. Her eyes flickered towards Bartholomew, as she tucked away a stray strand of hair. What was in those eyes? Jealousy? Of her mistress's betrothal, of her comb, of her fiancé? Desire? For the comb, or for him? She was standing behind Georgia, so close to Bartholomew he could feel her warmth, smell her soap. His skin tingled, and he pressed his foot closer still to Georgia's.

'There, miss. Looks very nice.' Agnes curtsied and left the room.

Bartholomew let out the breath he hadn't realised he'd been holding, and smiled at Georgia. 'I am glad you like it, my dear. When we are married I shall take you to visit the man who made it, at the shop in Bond Street. He shall make you a brooch to match it.'

'Watch it, St Clair. Don't spend all your money on trinkets for her. Women are all the same, you know. They take your money, your youth and your vigour, and leave you an empty shell. Now then, Peters, where's the brandy? Georgia, time you left us now. St Clair will be all yours soon – but for now, I want to enjoy his company for myself. You'll join me for a brandy or two, I take it?'

'Indeed I will,' said Bartholomew, holding out his glass for Peters to fill. He turned to Georgia. 'I shall see you in the drawing room later, my dear.'

Georgia pushed back her chair and stood, trailing her fingers over his shoulder. 'Don't keep him too long, Uncle, please.' She patted her hair comb and left the room.

'I wasn't joking about marrying her at the weekend,' said Holland, as soon as the door closed behind her. 'Sooner the better. I've enjoyed your company, but having that young filly about the place doesn't suit my lifestyle. She had nowhere else to go, when my brother died. He'd appointed me guardian and trustee of her estate, but frankly, I want shot of the whole responsibility. First time I saw you I thought you'd be suitable for her. An older, more sensible kind of chap than the young pups just after her money. Someone of whom poor Francis would have approved. Glad she accepted you – could have been awkward otherwise, especially with that colt Perry sniffing around. You did well to move quickly. Here's to a quick wedding and happy marriage.'

He raised his glass, and gulped the brandy down in one swallow. Bartholomew did the same. 'She'll be off your hands within a month,' he promised. 'I'll start making the arrangements tomorrow.'

'Where will you live?'

'In my Mayfair house, I expect. Or if she wants to stay in Brighton, I'll take a lease on a house here.'

'Take her to London. Women like being in the capital.'

He really didn't know his niece well, thought Bartholomew,

51

remembering how Georgia had told him how much she preferred the country.

'Will you release Agnes Cutter? To come with Georgia, I mean?' He hadn't realised he was going to ask the question until it left his lips.

'Hmm? Who's Agnes Cutter?'

'Georgia's maid. I – I believe Georgia's rather fond of her. If you can spare the girl, I will of course take over her employment…'

'Oh, that one. Of course. Part of the package, you might say. Another brandy?'

It was several more brandies before Bartholomew could take his leave, and adjourn to the drawing room. Holland decided to retire, and after pouring himself a nightcap brandy he went upstairs to bed. Bartholomew went through to the drawing room where Georgia was sitting alone, sewing a sampler. She looked up and smiled when he walked in.

'At last! I was beginning to wonder if you would ever come.' She put down her sewing and stood to greet him.

'I am sorry. Your uncle kept me talking a while. And now he has retired for the evening.'

'No matter, I only wanted to see you.'

'And I, you,' he said, taking a step towards her. She held out her hands to him. He took them and drew her towards him. 'Georgia, my dear, you have made me so happy by agreeing to be my wife. Let's get married soon. Next month?'

'In the summer,' she said, smiling up at him. 'I'd like a summer wedding, I think.'

He pulled her closer still, wrapping an arm about her waist. 'I'm not sure I can wait so long, Georgia, darling. Why not a spring wedding?' His head was swimming after the brandy, and her closeness was intoxicating. He bent his head towards hers, hoping to claim the kiss he'd been denied on the beach, earlier in the day.

But she pushed him away, with a giggle. 'Bartholomew, I do believe you have had rather too much brandy. I think you had better go upstairs now.'

He considered pulling her back, forcing the kiss on her but a distant, more sober part of his mind told him not to. This was no casual affair, no street-corner hussy. This was the woman he'd chosen to be his wife and bear his children. The woman whose money would save him from a debtor's prison. He must wait.

He let go of her and bowed. 'I am sorry, and you are right. Good night. I shall look forward to seeing you in the morning.'

He left the room before he made even more of a fool of himself, and took the stairs two at a time. She was but a girl, he reminded himself. She'd had little experience of men. She was right to rebuff him, in the state he was in. Tomorrow he would not let Holland fill his brandy glass quite so frequently. Tomorrow, if he found himself alone with her, he'd claim his first kiss. If he acted more like a gentleman, she wouldn't refuse him. He would taste those sweet lips at last, smell her skin, feel that soft body pressed against his. And the wedding would be in spring, whether she liked it or not.

Upstairs he turned towards his bedchamber, which was at the end of a corridor, near the stairs which led on upwards to the servants' quarters at the top of the house. As he reached his room, a rustle of petticoats made him turn, thinking Georgia had perhaps followed him up. But it was Agnes. She was carrying the green gown Georgia had torn on the beach. She stopped beside him.

'Is everything all right, sir? Are you in need of anything, *anything* at all?' There was a glint in her eye.

'I am quite all right, thank you,' he replied, stumbling slightly as he reached for his doorknob. She caught hold of his elbow to steady him. A shudder jolted through him at her touch.

'I think not,' she said. 'Wait, I will fetch you something to clear your head.' She opened the door to the servants' stairs and began to ascend.

Without really knowing what he was doing, Bartholomew followed. She glanced back, with an expression of mild surprise on her face which was quickly replaced by a half-smile. There was, if he was not mistaken, an invitation in that smile. He followed her to her room in the attic. She threw the dress she'd been carrying onto the narrow wooden bed, and began searching through a chest of medicine bottles which stood under the small window.

She chattered as she rooted through the box. 'My mother is a herbalist. She taught me all the old remedies. And, sir, believe me, they do work.'

At last she found the potion she'd been looking for and turned back to him.

'Here. This will clear your mind a little, and stop your headache in the morning.' As he took the bottle his fingers brushed hers, sending a sudden shock up his arm.

She was looking directly at him, that half-smile at the corners of her mouth, her eyes wide and bright. She felt it too, he was sure. She'd felt that jolt – she wanted him as much as he wanted her.

He put the bottle down on the washstand, and stepped forward. She didn't move. He put a hand to her cheek, and brushed it gently with his thumb. She turned her face towards his hand, nuzzling against it, and took his thumb in her mouth. All the while her eyes were on his.

He could stand it no longer. He pulled her roughly towards him and covered her mouth with his, kissing her fast and furious. She kissed him back, and snaked her hands around his back, under his jacket. He could feel the thrilling warmth of them through his shirt. He kissed her face, her neck, her throat where the coarse wool of her dress met her soft, soap-scented skin. He was mad with desire for her and pushed her backwards, towards her bed. She lay down, crushing Georgia's gown, and drew him down on top of her. He tugged up her skirts as she reached for

54

his trouser fastenings, and a minute later he was inside her, grunting and panting, thinking of nothing but the moment they were in, and *her*.

My dear Barty, it is at this point in my narrative that you will no doubt have begun to despise me. How could I, on the very day of proposing marriage to one woman, take another to bed? My defence, for what it's worth, is merely that I was intoxicated by Agnes. When I was with her, with or without a gut full of brandy, I could not think clearly. I was at the mercy of my lustful feelings for her. She knew, I believe, that she had this hold over me. And she was as besotted by me at that time as I was by her, as she later confessed to me.

You might want, having read this far, to throw this manuscript down in disgust, and hear no more of your father's indiscretions. But, my dear son, bear with me please, for you must know the truth. Steel yourself, Barty, for there is worse, far worse, to come. And some of it, I must write as though Agnes herself is telling the story. She was loyal to me, in those days, and told me everything, or at least, almost everything, that passed in private between her and Georgia.

Chapter Six

Hampshire, April 2013

The day we moved into Kingsley House was one of those bright blue April days, when the air is rich with birdsong, the sun shines with golden promise, and the hedgerows explode with blossom. The newly unfurled leaves on the huge beech tree were an electric lime green, and the grass, in its first growth since the winter, rivalled them in intensity of colour. It almost made your eyes hurt to look out at the day.

The removal men whistled as they carried our furniture and cartons into the house. Lewis and Lauren were taking huge delight directing them – 'Lounge!', 'My bedroom at the top!', 'Kitchen!' – according to what was scrawled on the boxes in marker pen.

'Can you put my curtains up, Mum?' Lauren called down the stairs.

'Dad, when are you going to plug in the telly? *Deadly Sixty*'s on, and I don't want to miss it. They're doing tarantulas this week.' Lewis was apparently bored of directing removal men.

'Katie, any sign of the box with the kettle in? I could so do with a cuppa,' Simon said, as he staggered past me carrying two boxes at once.

'Mind your back! Why are you shifting boxes anyway, aren't we paying blokes to carry them in?' I said.

'These got put in the living room but they're books, should be in the study,' he said. 'They'll go on those big built-in shelves in there. Fabulous piece of carpentry, that. Wonder how old it is?'

I smiled. It was one of my favourite features in the house too. And if Simon was wondering about the age of it, it'd surely only be a matter of time before he started wondering about the people who used to live here…and then I'd be able to spend many happy hours filling him in. I still hadn't mentioned the fact my ancestors had lived here.

'I reckon it's mid-Victorian, possibly even earlier,' I said. 'I've found the kettle but we've no milk or teabags. Don't suppose you've come across my laptop and genealogy research notes?'

'Look in the fridge,' he grunted, as he passed me again with another box marked BOOKS. They were mostly mine.

'What?' I went out to the kitchen and opened the fridge. Bless the Delameres, they'd left us a pint of milk, a plastic bag with a dozen teabags in, a bottle of orange squash and a packet of chocolate digestives. I pulled the kettle out of a box and turned on the kitchen tap to fill it. The water ran brown.

'Hmph. Looks like we've inherited rusty iron piping,' said Simon, looking over my shoulder.

I guessed the house would need new plumbing, then. I shrugged. It's what you have to expect when buying an old house. I ran the tap for a minute until it cleared, filled the kettle, then searched for somewhere to plug it in. There was a single socket at worktop height, and a double beneath the table. When we refitted the kitchen we'd have to rewire and add plenty more sockets.

It wasn't long before the van was unloaded, the removal men

tipped and gone, and we were left amid a sea of cardboard boxes. Thank goodness this was such a large house: there was still space to move around the boxes and shift furniture. We made the kids' rooms habitable then headed into the village centre for an evening meal at the local pub, the White Hart. It was just a five-minute walk up the lane. The pavement was narrow and I was thankful Thomas no longer needed to sit in a pushchair.

'Great idea, this,' said Simon, as he sat down with his pint. 'I'd thought we'd get a takeaway but it's so nice to escape the chaos for a couple of hours.'

'Agreed. Well, here's to our new life in North Kingsley!' I raised my glass of Pinot Grigio and clinked it against his Guinness. Lauren and Lewis picked up their glasses of Coke and clinked too, while Thomas put his thumb in his mouth and cuddled up beside me. Although he was four, he was still very much our baby and tended to act it, especially when he was tired.

I gave him a hug. 'Aw, as soon as we've had dinner we'll go home and I'll read you a story and put you to bed, sweetie.'

'Our proper home?' He gazed up at me with wide, worried eyes.

'Our new home. You've got your own lovely bedroom now. No more sharing with Lewis.'

Wrong thing to say. He still looked worried and his lower lip began to tremble. 'I don't want to sleep on my own. That house is scary. There might be ghosts.'

'You can sleep in my room tonight,' said Lewis. 'Can't he, Mum? Just till we get used to the new house.'

I smiled at my lovely thoughtful eleven-year-old. 'Yes, of course he can. It'll be strange for all of us tonight. But we'll feel better in the morning when we're not so tired.'

We'd sold our Southampton house to a buy-to-let investor, who'd made us an offer during the twins' birthday party back in February; we'd negotiated the sale price while a horde of pre-teens ran riot having a balloon fight around us. There was no chain, so we'd been able to move on a day which suited us. The survey on Kingsley House had been worrying at first glance, but all it said when you boiled it down was that the house was old, and had the kind of problems you'd associate with old houses. Simon dismissed it as a waste of money, declaring he could have written it himself without ever having seen the house. Our removal company had packed for us earlier in the week, and had turned up at eight a.m. to load up the van. It had been a very long day. No wonder poor Thomas was so tired and tearful.

The food arrived, and we all tucked in to battered cod and chips, burgers for the kids, followed by steaming treacle pudding and custard. Perfect comfort food, and it hit the spot quickly. Soon the children were laughing together; Lauren was telling whispered stories about the grizzled old men who were sitting on bar stools clutching pints of real ale, making Thomas giggle uncontrollably. It was good to hear.

'Looks like a pretty old pub, this one,' said Simon, gazing around at the low beamed ceiling, dark wood panelling and stone window seats.

'I like it, it's got character.' I wondered whether Bartholomew or his father William had ever sat in this pub. Probably not, they'd been too high up the social scale to drink in the local hostelry. But Barty, at least in his later years, had certainly frequented this place. Vera Delamere had told me as much, recalling the village gossip about him.

Across the room, screwed to a wall beside the bar, was an old map. I got up to go and inspect it. It showed the village as it was in 1852. It was much smaller then: the railway had only just reached North Kingsley and none of the housing estates had been built. I picked out the high street, with the White Hart pub clearly marked. Following the road out of the village centre I found our house, surrounded then by outbuildings and stables, with far more land than I'd imagined.

'Come and look at this,' I called to Simon.

He came over, with the remains of his pint, and peered at the map. 'Wow, is that our house? Look at all the land it had then. Shame it's all been sold off. I wouldn't have minded a huge garden. Could have bought a ride-on mower.' He put on a wistful expression. 'Always wanted a ride-on mower, you know. Ah well, next house…'

I gave him a gentle thump on the arm. 'I'm not moving again, Simon. Well, not until it's time to downsize, like the Delameres. This is our forever home, as the estate agents put it.'

Simon gulped down the last of his beer. 'Nothing's forever, Katie, but right now I'm certainly not in a hurry to move again. Well, I think we'd better get young Thomas to bed before he implodes. Good of Lewis to let him share his room for tonight.'

'I suspect Lewis wants the company too,' I said.

We gathered up children, coats and Nintendos, and set off to walk the couple of hundred yards to our house. Simon hoiked Thomas onto his back, and the other two kids skipped ahead. I wondered how long it would take for them to get to sleep tonight – they were still buzzing with excitement about their new home.

'Hey, look,' said Simon, pointing to a small turning. 'Stables Close. That's where the stables which once belonged to our house must have stood.'

'Did we once have stables, Dad? Does that mean I can have a pony?' Lauren asked.

'Only if you go back in time, love,' Simon said.

Lewis grinned. 'That would be cool, going back to the olden days.'

We reached the front door. I pulled out my key, slotted it into the lock and turned it. It gave the satisfying click of a well-oiled mechanism, and the door swung open with a low creak. I flicked the hall light switch on, and sighed with happiness.

Simon grinned at me as he pushed past and climbed the stairs, Thomas still clinging to his back. 'Good to be home, eh, Katie?'

Oh yes. So very good to be home. To think this wonderful old house, with all its layers of history, some of it my family's history, was now ours. I offered up a silent promise to the ghosts of residents past that we'd respect their memory and the house as we brought it back to life.

The twins started their new school the next day, and Simon was back at work. I dropped Lewis and Lauren off at the local primary they would attend for just one term before moving on to the comprehensive, then drove home with Thomas and began the mammoth task of unpacking. Thomas was surprisingly helpful; so were the twins when they came home buzzing about their new school. We made good progress, not helped at all by Simon returning home late, tired and grumpy.

'Christ, Katie, there's boxes and paper everywhere! Could you not have flattened them as you went along, or put them out in the garage? I can barely move in this hallway.' He kicked an empty box to make his point. It knocked against a small table, sending the telephone tumbling to the floor.

'For goodness sake, Simon!' I bent to pick up the phone and put it back in its base unit. 'I've been busy all day unpacking. Kitchen's done, so are the bedrooms.'

'Well, that's something, I suppose. If we can just get these boxes out of the way so we can move around the house...'

'Feel free. I'm knackered, and am doing nothing more tonight.' I glared at him, daring him to suggest I do it now. 'And why are you so late home anyway? I was hoping you'd get back a bit earlier today, so you could help. It's gone eight, already.'

'I had a five o'clock meeting. And it's still an hour on the train, plus twenty minutes either side. What's for dinner?'

'*We* had lasagne and chips. There's some lasagne left, I could microwave it for you.'

'Reheated pasta – yuk. After my long day in the office.'

'Either that or a sandwich. Which you can make yourself.' I turned on my heel and went upstairs before he could see the tears in my eyes. I was just tired, I knew. But why had he agreed to work late on the first day in our new house?

61

'Why's Dad cross?' asked Lewis as I got to the top of the stairs.

'He's tired. So am I. And it's your bed time.'

'All right, sorry, Mum. I was just coming down to tell you Thomas is crying.'

I'd spent an hour reading him stories and cuddling him to sleep earlier, so this wasn't welcome news. I sighed and went in to him.

'What's up, sweetheart?' I said, crouching down on the floor beside his makeshift bed.

'Lewis is being too noisy. I can't sleep.'

I kissed his forehead. 'I'll tell him to be quiet. He's coming to bed now anyway.'

'And I can't find White Ted.'

I could sympathise with that. My laptop and folders were still unaccounted for. White Ted was probably in the still-sealed box of cuddly toys in a corner of Thomas's room, but I really didn't feel up to rummaging through it right now. But if I didn't, who would?

'I'll find him. You snuggle down now and I'll be back with him soon.' My knees groaned as I stood up and crossed the landing to Thomas's room. Ripping open the box I up-ended it in the middle of the floor. It could be sorted out tomorrow. Thankfully White Ted turned up among the assorted cuddlies, and I picked him up gratefully.

Simon appeared at the doorway. 'Sheesh, is that the way you unpack? No wonder the house is such a tip.' He grinned – it was clearly meant to be a joke, but I wasn't in the mood. I glared at him.

'Aw, love, let's not argue. Sorry I was narky when I came in,' he said, crossing the room to give me a hug. I leaned against him for a moment, enjoying the comfort but not quite wanting to forgive him yet, then went to give White Ted to Thomas.

On Saturday, after homework and an exploratory walk with me around the village, the children spent the afternoon reorganising and playing in their rooms while I did some housework. Simon had gone to visit his mother in the Southbourne nursing home where she now lived.

'How was your mum?' I asked Simon when he returned home in the early evening.

He sighed, and sat down heavily at the kitchen table. Recognising the signs of a tough day, I opened the fridge and pulled out a bottle of Pinot Grigio I'd put in there to chill, ready for this moment. I poured him a generous glass. The kids were happily snuggled up in the sitting room, watching a Disney DVD.

'Thanks, love.' He took a swig, then sat, glass held in both hands, staring at a spot on the table. I waited. It had been six months since I last saw Veronica, and if I was being honest, I'd say I wouldn't mind if I never saw her again. We hadn't taken the children to see her for nearly a year. It's not that we didn't love her – it's just that visiting her had become so stressful and upsetting for all involved.

'Mum was, I guess, worse than last time.' Simon took another gulp of his wine. I sat down beside him, ready to listen, if he wanted to talk about it. He didn't always.

'Did she know you?'

'Sort of. She thought I was Dad. Funnily enough, that's easier than when she thinks I'm a complete stranger. At least I can talk to her then, without her calling the nursing staff to get me ejected from her room.'

I rubbed his shoulder in sympathy, but he shrugged my hand away.

'She talked about her younger days. When she'd first met Dad, and they played at the same tennis club. How he'd asked to walk her home, and she'd said yes, then led him the long way round so as to spend more time in his company.' Simon smiled. 'Luckily I knew that story – it was one they always told – so I was able to chip in at the right moments. We had a bit of a laugh about it.'

'Well, that was nice, at least.' God, it must be so hard. Simon lost his father to cancer twelve years ago, and now he was losing his mother to dementia. All that was left of her was these occasional snippets of old memories, washed up like flotsam. We'd had to move her into a nursing home eighteen months earlier, when she'd stopped letting her carers into her home, thinking they'd come to rob her. A year ago she stopped recognising me and the children. Five months ago she didn't know who Simon was, and he'd come home that day and sobbed on my shoulder like a little boy.

He still visited her every fortnight, making the long drive down to the Dorset coast, spending ten minutes or three hours with her depending on whether his presence upset her or not. We'd explained her illness to the older children, who'd taken it in their stride, the way children do. Little Thomas didn't even remember her when we showed him a photo of himself as a baby, sitting on her lap. Simon had pressed his lips together and turned his face away. The idea that our youngest would grow up knowing only one set of grandparents pained him, I knew.

He refilled his wine glass, took a sip, then a deep breath, and looked at me. 'She also talked about how she'd never been able to have children, how she and Dad decided on adoption. And about the day they collected me from the children's home. She still thought I was Dad, and went through the whole story, saying do you remember, Peter? do you remember? And of course I *do* remember it, but from an entirely different point of view.'

'But you've heard her talk about that day before, love,' I said.

'Yes, but on those occasions she knew I was there. Today she thought I was Dad, and was talking as though I, Simon, her adopted son, wasn't present.'

I scanned Simon's face for clues as to what she'd said, how he'd taken it. He looked drawn, the way he always looks after visiting Veronica. But was he more upset by her stories this time? Had she said something distressing? Before she was ill she'd always talked about that day with warmth and affection. The chubby blond four-year-old running full pelt into the hallway of the children's home in pursuit of the resident cat, and stopping abruptly when he saw her and Peter standing there in their coats and hats. His formal greeting, parroting what he'd been taught: *Good afternoon, Mr and Mrs Smiff*. His shy smile when Veronica told him he could now call her Mummy, and Peter, Daddy. The wondrous moment when he first slid his warm, sticky hand into hers, as they led him outside to their car and his new life.

'What did she say that was different?' I asked, as gently as if he was still that shy little four-year-old.

'She spoke about her fears that it wouldn't work out, that I might change their relationship and not for the better, that despite all the visits they'd had with me before it became official she might find it all too much and have to send me back. I never heard her say anything like that before. I'd always grown up being told that I was special because they *chose* me. That their life wasn't complete until I joined the family.'

He took another gulp of his wine. His eyes sparkled. My big strong rugby-playing husband, close to tears. We might have had our ups and downs lately, but seeing him like this broke my heart.

'Katie, it hurt, you know? To hear that she'd thought they might have to send me back. Even now, after all these years.'

'She didn't know what she was saying.'

'She did. She just didn't know who she was saying it to.'

I rubbed his shoulder. I didn't know what I could say to comfort him. 'Perhaps you should stop visiting her. It wouldn't hurt her, she wouldn't even realise anything had changed.'

'It's my duty. She's got no one else.'

'But it just upsets you. I hate to see you like this. And it's not even as if she's your real m—'

Whoops. Wrong thing to say, or nearly say. Simon glared at me. 'She's my mum, Katie. She, and no one else.' He knocked back the rest of his wine and stood up decisively. 'Well. Enough of that. Where are our gorgeous children?'

'Sitting room, watching *Jungle Book*.'

'Great, I love that film! Mind if I join them while you're making dinner?' He didn't wait for an answer, but sashayed off across the hallway, singing something about the bare necessities of life. I heard Thomas squeal 'Daddy, Daddy!', ticklish giggles from Lauren, and the clap of a high-five, 'Yo, Dad!' from Lewis.

The next day, Sunday, was grey and rainy. There was no hope of going out anywhere, so we decided to get on with the unpacking. There were still piles of boxes in the corners of rooms, waiting to be sorted out. Some boxes contained things like photo albums, outgrown toys and old school books. Those would go in the loft above Lauren's room as soon as we'd installed a loft ladder. That was the only part of the house we'd not yet explored. The hatch was sealed shut and Simon didn't want to open it up yet. 'Time enough,' he'd said. 'Plenty to sort out down here before we venture up there. Right then, what shall we tackle today?'

'The study,' I said. 'Let's unpack the books and files, and fill up those shelves. I'll give them a dust and polish first while you get the kids settled doing something.' I hoped my family tree research folders would turn up somewhere among the books.

I made us a cup of tea, then went back to the study armed with a damp cloth, dusters and polish. The shelves and cupboards needed a thorough clean before we could put anything onto them. The wood was dark with age, with a deep patina from centuries of beeswax. Walnut, perhaps, I thought. I pulled open the fold-down desk where Vera had put the tea tray on my first visit, and reached deep inside with my damp cloth to get the dirt out of the corners.

'That's funny,' I said.

Simon looked up from the box he was opening. 'What?'

'The panel at the back inside the desk is loose. Oh!'

I'd pushed on one side, and the panel had opened up. I bent down and peered inside. There was a small drawer behind, made of the same walnut wood but looking less aged. It had a tiny metal ring as a handle. I gently pulled on it but it didn't move.

'It's stuck.'

'Let me look,' said Simon, and I moved out of the way. He gave a tug, and then joggled the drawer from side to side to free it up. Gradually he eased it out of its slot.

'There's something in it,' he said.

'Dead spiders?' I suppressed a shudder.

He reached in and pulled out a small bundle of dusty, beige cloth. 'This has been in there a long time, I'd say.'

I held my breath while he cradled the bundle in one hand and unwrapped it with the other. It was a black hair comb, with some sort of stones set along the edge. Simon rubbed at the stones with a finger. 'Green glass,' he announced.

'Let me look.'

He handed the comb to me. My fingers were instantly blackened where I touched it. 'I think this might be silver, badly tarnished,' I said. 'Let's see.'

I went out to the kitchen with it, followed by Simon. Under the kitchen sink I found a jar of silver dip. I dipped a corner of a duster into it, then rubbed at the comb. Yes, it was silver. Gradually the true colour of the metal revealed itself on the top edge. The stones too began to glow.

'Simon, I think these are emeralds, not glass. Some kind of precious stone, anyway.'

'Could be,' he said. 'I guess a jeweller's shop would be able to say for sure.'

I slotted the duster between the teeth of the comb and sawed back and forth. The books were forgotten as we both sat at the kitchen table, me cleaning, Simon watching, until the whole comb shone. It was a beautiful piece.

'Wow,' said Simon, as I held up the comb.

'Some lucky woman wore this in her hair,' I said. 'I wonder how old it is? Victorian, or maybe even earlier?'

Simon rolled his eyes. 'More likely it belonged to Mrs Delamere – you'll have to give her a ring and ask her.'

He was right. I'd have to check whether it was hers. I must admit, I hoped it wouldn't be. As I turned the comb over in my hands I felt a tingle – like the one I'd felt when I first entered the house. A kind of connection. Somehow I knew this had belonged to a woman in my family. Georgia St Clair, perhaps, or Bartholomew's mother Constance.

'Wonder why it was hidden away like that?'

'To keep it safe, I'd guess. No burglar would find that drawer. Come on – let's get on with unpacking the books.'

As I stacked the shelves, I found myself thinking about the comb. Who had worn it? Who had bought it for her? Why had it been hidden away in the back of the desk?

I phoned Vera Delamere that evening, and described the comb and where we'd found it. She was delighted to hear from us and wanted to know all the details of our move, how well we were settling in, which child had been allocated which room. She knew nothing about the comb, as I'd expected, but sounded as intrigued as I was, wondering who it might have belonged to. So the comb was mine to keep. I found a velvet padded jewellery box, tucked the comb inside it, and put the box in my bedside drawer.

The house had given up its first secret. Would there be more to follow?

Chapter Seven

Brighton, May 1838

She was certainly a pretty girl, thought Agnes, as she stood behind Miss Georgia at the dressing-table mirror, brushing her hair. She had a sweet face, unblemished by time or hardship. Though she'd lost her poor papa this last year, the grief hadn't marked her at all. Agnes felt a sudden rush of love for her young mistress.

'How shall I do your hair, miss?' she asked. 'Shall I pin it all up? Will that work with your new bonnet?'

'Oh, Agnes, don't pin it *all* up,' said Georgia. 'Leave some ringlets. The fashion is to have them tumbling down from beneath the bonnet, in front of one's ears. So that's what I shall have.'

Agnes frowned. 'We should have twisted your hair in rags last night, if you want ringlets. But I'll do what I can.' She began pinning up the back section of hair, leaving a few strands at either side. If she heated a poker a little in the fire, she'd be able to twist the hair around it to make the curls.

'It is my wedding day, remember, Aggie. A girl should have the hairstyle she wants when she's getting married.' Georgia pouted a little, then sighed. 'I'm sorry, dear Aggie. You are right

– I should have thought of the ringlets last night. Will you do your trick with the poker?'

'I will. And you will look lovely. A worthy bride.'

Georgia smiled, and caught hold of Agnes's hand over her shoulder. 'You are so good to me. Don't ever leave me; I could not manage without you. I shall be sure to ask my new husband to increase your wages.'

'Thank you, miss.' Agnes finished pinning the back of the hair into a neat chignon, and began carefully heating the poker in the fire.

'He is a fine man, is he not? Do you like him, Aggie?'

Agnes kept her back turned to her mistress, in case Miss Georgia caught sight of the flush which spread across her face and throat. If only Miss Georgia knew quite how much she liked him, and in precisely what way. She cleared her throat. 'He will make you a fine husband indeed, miss.'

'But do you like him, I asked?'

Agnes turned back to Georgia with the heated poker. ''Tis not for me to like or dislike him.' She picked up a lock of hair and carefully wound it around the end of the poker. ''Tis whether *you* like him or not, is all that matters. Now keep still lest I burn you with the poker.'

'Oh, I do like him. He is clever enough, handsome enough, and fun enough. And my uncle likes him.' Georgia fingered the ringlet Agnes had made. 'But I am not sure that I actually *love* him. Does that matter?'

Yes, Agnes wanted to shout. Yes, it matters! If you don't love him, leave him for one who does! But she bit her tongue. 'Love will grow, Miss Georgia. If you like him and respect him, those are the seeds and soil from which love grows.'

'You sound just like him! He said something like that on the very day he asked me to marry him. Oh, how I remember that day!'

And I, too, thought Agnes, remembering how he'd taken her

for the first time on her narrow bed, crushing Georgia's silk gown. She felt a pang of guilt. If only Mr St Clair wasn't her mistress's fiancé. She felt torn between love and loyalty to Miss Georgia and her overwhelming desire for Miss Georgia's intended. She unwound the last strand of hair from the poker. It sprang back into a perfect curl. She smiled. 'There, miss. Ringlets, as you wanted.'

Georgia admired her reflection in the mirror. 'Do I need a spot of rouge?'

'You are lovely as you are, miss. Naturally pretty.'

'Do you think Bartholomew loves me?'

'I am sure he does. Shall I help you put on your wedding gown now?'

Georgia leapt to her feet and clapped her hands, as excited as a child on her birthday. 'I've been longing to wear this gown! It's beautiful, isn't it? Oh, can you imagine Bartholomew's face when he turns and sees me walking up the aisle wearing this?'

Agnes could imagine it. His face would soften into a smile. He would hold out his hand to his bride, and his eyes would not leave hers. He would whisper something sweetly in her ear, making her eyes light up. But Agnes was not imagining Georgia standing beside Mr St Clair at the altar. It was herself she pictured there.

'And you too must have a new gown!' Georgia ran to her closet and pulled out the pale-green gown she'd worn on the day Bartholomew proposed. 'Take this one, Aggie dear.'

Agnes blushed. Why had she picked *that* one to give away, of all her gowns? 'Oh, miss, I couldn't take that one. It suits you so…'

'And it will suit you too. Your colouring is just like mine. Why, we could almost be sisters, don't you think? You the older and wiser one, me the silly younger one.' She giggled. 'You must wear this gown when we next go out and about together. People will wonder why Bartholomew chose the younger sister rather than the older one!' She pushed the dress into Agnes's arms.

Ah, but he had chosen *both* sisters, thought Agnes, with another surge of guilt at her betrayal. One for her status in society and one for her skills in the bedroom. She took the dress and draped it over the back of a chair. 'Thank you, miss. It's a beautiful gown.'

'Well, if it needs altering to fit you at all, I suppose you can do it today while we are at the church. I shan't be needing you again until later, after the party, so your time is your own. Now then, help me get into my wedding gown!'

Agnes bit her lip as she held out the gown for Georgia to step into. She'd expected to be asked to come to the church to witness the wedding as a guest. She and Georgia had always been so close – yes, almost like sisters! But Georgia could be so self-centred at times. She was thinking only of herself, her outfit, her hair. Her wedding.

Agnes felt a pain in her chest as she once again pictured Bartholomew standing at the altar. Painful though it would be, she resolved to be at the church and witness the wedding for herself. And she'd wear the green gown – the gown on which they had first made love. Maybe he'd see her and remember that day…

The day was grey and overcast, with rain threatening from the west. Bartholomew sighed as he drew open the curtains of his bedchamber and looked out across the barren beach and steely sea. Georgia had so hoped for a day of sunshine and warmth; she'd wanted to walk to and from the church via the promenade. But that was not looking likely now. He would send for cabs to collect them, and ask the drivers to wait outside during the ceremony. Georgia would not want to spoil her new ivory silk gown.

It was three weeks since he had proposed to her. Charles Holland had been keen for them to marry and move out as soon as possible, but Georgia had insisted on time to make preparations, get a new gown made, prepare a trousseau. And Bartholomew had needed to find a house to let, as Holland had made it clear they would not be welcome to stay in his house after the wedding. Tonight, their wedding night, was to be their last night in the Brunswick Terrace house. Tomorrow they would move to a smaller property at the eastern end of Brighton, in Sussex Square where they would stay for the summer at least, before moving to London for the winter season, if that is what Georgia wanted.

Bartholomew whistled as he finished dressing, tying a dove-grey cravat about his neck and buttoning his jacket. Rain or no rain, it was his wedding day, and he was happy.

He sauntered down the stairs for breakfast, which he ate alone. Georgia was to take breakfast in her room, and meet him at the church. Holland was not yet up; he never rose before eleven. There were no other house guests – Bartholomew had expected Holland to invite friends and relations for the wedding, but none had arrived. It seemed Charles Holland was Georgia's only living relative. Bartholomew also had no relatives coming. His mother Constance had been dead eight years, and he was estranged from his father, who had refused to bail him out of a financial crisis a few years back. He supposed he should make things up with his father. He resolved to write and tell him of his wedding. He had time this morning to do so; there was nothing else to do other than read the morning paper, then wait until the cab arrived to take him to the church.

A couple of hours later, Bartholomew was standing at the altar of St Nicholas's church, watching Georgia walk up the aisle on the arm of her uncle who was giving her away. A handful of their Brighton acquaintances were gathered in the pews behind him – they were the only people invited to the ceremony, and the wedding breakfast which was to be held afterwards, in Holland's dining room. Bartholomew nodded to his friend Henry Harding who stood smiling beside his wife Caroline. He caught the eye of Charles Holland's neighbour, portly Mrs Oliphant, who scowled at him and pursed her lips. No doubt she was disapproving of something as usual. Young Perry had of course not been invited.

Georgia looked beautiful: her new ivory gown was made of good silk and fitted perfectly. Her pale golden hair hung in ringlets cascading out from under her bonnet, which was adorned with white roses. She carried more white roses, tied with silk ribbon, and looked like an ethereal snow princess. Bartholomew smiled as he remembered the evening they'd met, and how she'd skipped along the snowy promenade oblivious to the cold.

There was a flash of green at the back of the church. Bartholomew peered towards the door – some latecomer, no doubt. He turned his attention back to his bride. Georgia smiled shyly as her uncle handed her to Bartholomew. He smiled back at her, imagining unbuttoning her gown, slipping it off her shoulders, peeling back her layers of petticoats... In a few minutes she would be his wife; in a few hours he could claim her soft, white flesh as his own. In a few days, her money would be in his account and his debts paid off.

Agnes slipped into the back of the church after Mr Holland and Miss Georgia had entered. She had not asked permission to attend the wedding, but, as Miss Georgia's maid, and the nearest thing she'd ever had to a mother, Agnes felt justified in being there. In fact, Miss Georgia ought really to have invited her properly. She'd put on the green gown, paired it with her Sunday best bonnet, and had tucked some lace into her bodice. Thankfully it had not rained this morning, although it had threatened to, or her gown would have been ruined. She'd had to hurry from the house to the church to get there in time. She sat in the shadows of the last pew to watch the ceremony unfold.

Dearly beloved, we are gathered here in the sight of God, and in the face of this congregation, to join together this man and this woman in holy matrimony...

Miss Georgia looked beautiful. Agnes felt a glow of pride at what she'd accomplished with the girl's hair and dress. The simple bouquet of white roses was perfect, adding to the girl's innocent, virginal look. Agnes smiled wryly – she'd not be virginal for very much longer. Her about-to-be husband was a lusty fellow, who would no doubt claim his bride roughly at the first opportunity that evening. She should know. Her inner thighs still felt raw from his visit the previous night. She sighed. It would, she supposed, be the last time. At least for a few months, while he enjoyed the pleasures of his fresh young wife. But he would return to Agnes's bed in time, she was sure. If, that is, she stayed in his employment.

Which, of course, she would. She knew – she had known since the first time Mr St Clair had come to her room – that she would never leave him. There was something about him which thrilled her. He had an animal passion – there was an intensity to his love-making which she craved. Since that first time, he'd come to her several times a week. And she had sat on her bed, almost unable to bear the wait, having to stop herself from going to find him in his bedchamber.

...if either of you know any impediment, why ye may not be lawfully joined together in matrimony, ye do now confess it...

Oh, confess, Mr St Clair! thought Agnes. Confess you are in love with another woman!

Last night he had told her their affair must end. For the sake of Georgia. He'd said Agnes should find herself a husband. But he'd said it without conviction, and Agnes had answered him with an equal lack of enthusiasm.

Wilt thou love her, comfort her, honour, and keep her in sickness and in health; and, forsaking all other, keep thee only unto her...

It's only words, Mr St Clair. They mean nothing. You don't need to keep yourself only for her. Come back to me!

But Bartholomew answered, gazing directly at Miss Georgia as he spoke clearly so that everyone in church could hear, 'I will.'

As Mr St Clair slipped a ring onto Miss Georgia's finger, Agnes straightened her back and raised her chin. She'd lost him, for the moment, but he'd come back to her sooner or later, of that she was certain. And she would be ready for him. If only Georgia was marrying someone else. Anyone else. Then she would be able to feel uncomplicated, unconditional joy on her mistress's wedding day, instead of this complex whirl of emotions.

The vicar announced a hymn, and asked people to turn to the relevant page in their hymn books, which had been distributed on every pew. Agnes picked hers up, and flicked through it, frowning at the squiggles and patterns which filled every page. Something else which differentiated her from the new Mrs St Clair, she supposed. She'd rarely attended the small school in her home village, preferring to stay at home and learn the skills of a herbalist from her mother.

She opened the book at a random page, and hummed along with the music, thankful there was no one in the pew beside her to notice that she could not read. When she had first begun working for Georgia, the fourteen-year-old had been first shocked and then amused at Agnes's illiteracy. She'd tried to teach her to read, but Agnes had felt it beneath her dignity to stare at children's picture books with a young girl as tutor. Now, she wondered if being able to read and write would have made any difference to her fortunes – would it have given her more of a chance with Mr St Clair?

When the service was over, Agnes stayed sitting behind a pillar at the back of the church until everyone else had left. It had finally started to rain, so the newlyweds, Mr Holland, and the guests quickly bundled into the waiting cabs to return to Brunswick Terrace. Agnes rose, stretched her back, and stood in the doorway of the church, watching the rain. If her circumstances had been different, and she'd been a rich heiress like Miss Georgia, it might have been *her* marrying Mr St Clair today. But she was only the daughter of a woodcutter. She knew her place. She might have already won Mr St Clair's heart, but she could never have won his hand. The best she could hope for would be to remain in his employ, and wait for him to resume their affair.

She waited in the church porch until the rain eased off, then hurried along the back streets to the back entrance of the Brunswick Terrace house. The kitchen was bustling with activity as the wedding breakfast was prepared. Mr Holland's regular cook had hired some temporary staff to cope with the party, and they were all running hither and thither, being scolded by the cook, as Agnes passed through. Not for the first time she felt thankful that she'd managed to rise above being a kitchen maid. Being a lady's maid was several steps up the ladder, and was a much easier and more pleasant job.

Becoming a kept mistress would be better still. In her own little house, with her lover visiting every few days bearing gifts… It was a dream, but could she make it a reality?

Upstairs, in Miss Georgia's room, Agnes set to work making the room ready for the night. She threw the nightgown Miss Georgia had been wearing into a laundry basket, and brought out a new lace-trimmed one in fine linen from Miss Georgia's trousseau. She tidied the perfume bottles and hair brushes which littered the dressing table, and put away jewellery. The silver and emerald hair comb was lying discarded on the dressing table. Agnes picked it up and turned it over. It was a fine piece of craftsmanship. She unpinned her cap, let down her own blonde locks, and caught them up again with the comb, turning her head this way and that to admire herself in the mirror. For a moment she considered replacing her cap, on top of the comb. She could say one of the temporary maids had taken it. Miss Georgia would never suspect Agnes, not after so many years of faithful service.

But no. Best not to do anything which might risk her position. Reluctantly she removed the comb and placed it into Miss Georgia's ebony jewellery box, then put the box away in a drawer, out of temptation of any thieving maids who might pass by.

She turned back the bedclothes, laid the new nightgown on the bed and, with a sigh, left the room. Her time was her own

77

now, until Miss Georgia needed help to get ready for bed, later this evening.

Finally the guests were gone. Henry Harding had been the last to leave, giving Bartholomew a hearty clap on the back and a wink as he left. Bartholomew knocked back the last of his brandy and put the glass down on a side table. He glanced across to his pretty young wife, who was twisting her wine glass back and forth by its stem.

'A nightcap, St Clair?' said Charles Holland, who was slumped in his usual armchair, brandy decanter to hand.

'Just a small one,' said Bartholomew, holding out his glass. He'd already drunk a fair bit, but it was his wedding day, and one more wouldn't hurt.

Georgia stretched, and yawned ostentatiously. 'I am so tired. It has been a long day. I think I shall retire, now. Uncle, would you ring the bell? I shall need Agnes.'

Bartholomew stood, and kissed her hand. 'I shall not be long, my sweet. Do not go to sleep.'

She blushed and bowed her head, then left the room.

Holland kept Bartholomew talking for a while, over another couple of brandies. The hall clock had chimed midnight when he finally put his glass down.

'Well, man, I shouldn't keep you. Not when you've a pretty new wife to deflower.' Holland chuckled, but the laugh turned into a spluttering cough.

Bartholomew rushed over and looked for a glass of water to administer, but there was none. He poured another brandy, and held it to Holland's lips. The older man was red in the face and spluttering, but he took a sip of the brandy. It seemed to ease the cough.

'Ah, that's better,' he said, wiping his mouth. 'Thank you. Now then, off upstairs with you. Leave me here on my own. Once you've moved out tomorrow, I'll need to get used to it again.' He coughed again.

The man drinks far too much, thought Bartholomew, as he finished his own brandy. So did he, he supposed, but then he could hold his drink well. It had never yet made him choke. And his nose and cheeks weren't a ruddy mess of broken veins like Holland's.

'If you're sure, I'll take my leave. Good night, sir. It's been a splendid day. Thank you once again for hosting our wedding.' He bowed, and left the room. Now then, off to his wife's bedchamber. A picture of Agnes, laid back on her narrow bed, hair splayed across her pillow, thighs exposed, flashed through his mind. He banished it immediately and tried to imagine Georgia instead: her soft white flesh and youthful curves. The sooner he'd had experience of her the better. He needed to forget about Agnes, and the only way to do that was to find his pleasures elsewhere, in the form of his pretty new wife.

He took the stairs two at a time, and turned along the corridor to Georgia's room. As he approached, the door opened and Agnes stepped out. She looked momentarily startled to see him but quickly regained composure. She looked beautiful, wearing a pale-green silk gown he thought he recognised from somewhere. Perhaps it had been Georgia's. It suited Agnes better.

'Mr St Clair, your wife is ready for you,' she said, with a half-smile. She dipped in curtsey, but her eyes remained locked with his. Embarrassed, he stepped past her, and put his hand on the doorknob of Georgia's room. He paused, and glanced back at Agnes. She was still standing there, the sides of her skirt still clutched in her hands from the curtsey.

He raised his eyebrow questioningly.

'Go on, then,' she said, nodding at the door. She smiled, then turned and walked along the corridor towards the servants' stairs, her head high and back straight, as always.

He watched her go, then shook his head. You've a wife now, he told himself. Forget about the maid servant. He twisted the doorknob and entered Georgia's room.

Agnes went up the stairs to the servants' floor and quietly entered her room. She took off her maid's cap, hung it on the back of a chair and let down her hair. She placed her hairpins carefully into a small saucer on the washstand. She sat down heavily on her bed, her head in her hands. A single tear ran unchecked down her cheek.

It would all change now. Nothing would ever be the same. She'd helped Georgia prepare for tonight: she'd held her hand, explained what it was that Bartholomew would want to do, told her how wonderful the act could be for two people who loved each other. She'd made Georgia look as alluring as possible, ready for her wedding night. She'd banked up the fire, lit candles and drawn the curtains, making the room as comfortable as possible for the newlyweds. And she'd practically pushed the man she loved into the arms of his new wife. There was nothing more she could do; nothing more she could be expected to do.

Why oh why hadn't she been born rich, a member of Bartholomew's own class? Why couldn't it have been *her* he met at the Assembly Rooms on that cold January night? Why couldn't it have been her he married today? She would have made him happy. They were so well suited, in bed at least, and she was sure that counted for a lot. Men were happy when their physical needs were satisfied. Men didn't stray if their wives provided what they needed and wanted.

She lay back on the bed, and imagined what was happening now in Miss Georgia's room. Would Georgia be able to satisfy him? In time, Agnes supposed, she would, assuming she enjoyed lying with him. What if she didn't? Agnes smiled, and dashed away her tears. Well then, Bartholomew would come back to *her*. And as long as she could continue to avoid a pregnancy, there was no reason their affair should not continue. The sponges soaked in vinegar had done the trick so far. She silently thanked her mother for passing on her wisdom.

Georgia was sitting on the edge of her bed, wearing a long

white nightgown. Her hair was loose and had been brushed over her shoulders. Her hands were tucked under her thighs, and her back was rounded, her shoulders drooped. She looked like a child, sent early to bed for some misdemeanour.

As Bartholomew entered she looked up and smiled shyly at him. 'Should I be in the bed already? Agnes said…'

'Come here to me,' he said, holding out his hands to her. She rose, and took a step towards him, but stopped short.

'Have you been drinking very much brandy?'

What was she, his mother? He bit back a retort. 'Only one or two more, after you left. To keep your uncle company. He will be lonely when we leave. Come, kiss me.'

'He wants nothing more than to live alone again,' she said. She held out a hand to him, but did not step any closer.

He caught her hand and pulled her roughly to him. Leaning over her, he covered her mouth with his, and brought his other hand up to her breast. It felt small and soft beneath the nightdress. Not like Agnes's firmer, more rounded breasts. Damn it, she was his wife, and he would make himself desire her, and she him!

She leaned back, and turned her head to the side to escape the kiss.

'I can taste the brandy on you.' She pushed him away. 'Oh, Bartholomew, oh, that taste, I am sorry, I think…' She ran to the washstand at the side of the room and leaned over the bowl. 'That taste, it makes me feel….' She retched into the bowl, then stood straight, and brought her hand up to cover her mouth.

'You are not well,' he said, flatly.

'I am sorry. What must you think of me, pushing you away on our wedding night? But, that taste… I don't think I can… Perhaps tomorrow, perhaps if you don't drink any brandy…'

He stared at her. So she was turning him away, on their wedding night! She was dictating how much he should drink, within hours of becoming his wife. He opened his mouth to say something, but thought better of it. She was so young. Give her time.

He turned on his heel and left the room, without another word. Walking fast along the corridor, he passed the door to his own bedchamber and went up the servants' stairs.

Up on the top floor was a woman who would not turn him away, brandy or no brandy.

Chapter Eight

Hampshire, May 2013

A week or so after moving in, Thomas began attending the reception class at the local primary school. He looked so adorable in his uniform – grey shorts, white polo shirt and bright blue sweatshirt emblazoned with the school logo of an oak tree under a rainbow.

With Thomas out of the house from nine till two, I had more time each day, both to get on with work on the house, and to explore the local area. On one meander through the village, I turned right up a lane just beside the White Hart. The lane soon petered out into a bridleway, sheltered by high hedgerows of hawthorn, bramble and the occasional oak tree. The hawthorn was in full bloom and its sweet scent mingled with birdsong filled the air as soon as I was out of the village.

A wooden sign marked the start of a footpath, which led over a stile then along the side of a field planted with rape, its uncompromising yellow flower making the day feel warmer and sunnier than it actually was. The ground rose gradually then, after another stile on the far side of the field, more steeply, up a small hill. The hilltop was covered with low gorse and bramble, a wide chalky path winding its way to a quartet of benches surrounding a triangulation point.

The view in every direction was stunning. To the south you could see North Kingsley and further away, Winchester, red-brick and sprawling. To the east, the M3 motorway, emerging from a cutting and heading purposefully London-wards. To the north, farmland and gently rolling hills as far as the eye could see. Same to the west, the view broken only by the railway line, fighting its way out of the Winchester housing estates and business parks into open countryside. North Kingsley's own little station, from which you could board a slow train north to London or south, via Winchester, to the coast, was tucked in a valley at the foot of the hill, a couple of miles away from the village centre.

The story goes, so Steve, the landlord of the White Hart had told me, that when the railway was being built, the Irish navvies camped up here. Since then the hill, previously unnamed, had been known to locals as Irish Hill. Not on the OS maps though, where it just appeared as an oval-shaped handful of close-packed brown contour lines.

I liked Irish Hill. It looked like a good place to come to think. I sat down on the west-facing bench watching a train speed southwards, not stopping at North Kingsley.

Simon always took the fast train from Winchester whenever he went to London. I wondered what time he would come home today. Usually he'd be home by seven. At least, that had been the usual before we moved here. These last couple of weeks he'd returned after nine, most nights. He'd phone me around six – 'keep my dinner warm, Katie', or 'don't bother cooking for me, I'll grab something on the way home'. I didn't know what was keeping him out so long. When I asked he muttered about working late, or going for a drink with a team-member who's leaving, or train delays. If I asked for details he was evasive.

A bird of prey was circling overhead, making use of the wind currents up the side of the hill. I wondered what type it was. Maybe a buzzard, or a red kite. Now that we lived in the country I felt I should know such things, so I could point them out to the children. Maybe I should buy a book on birds.

It crossed my mind to wonder whether Simon was having an affair. It's the clichéd, obvious conclusion to draw when one's husband is late home and cagey about where he's been. But Simon? Would he really? I shook the thought out of my head and watched the bird, yes I think it *was* a red kite, circle higher and higher on the thermals. Another one joined it briefly, then dived downwards and alighted in a tree near the bottom of the hill.

Who was she? Someone from his work, perhaps? I imagined going through his pockets, checking his phone for texts, inspecting his shirt collar for lipstick marks. That's what the cuckolded wife is supposed to do, isn't she? But Simon, my Simon – surely it wasn't something he'd ever do? We had a strong marriage, even if things hadn't been easy lately, and he'd been in an almost continual bad mood, what with the stress of the house move, and the worries about his mother's health. We'd always been totally honest with each other. Maybe I should just sit him down and ask him straight out?

I leaned forward, arms on knees, and hung my head. There were some tiny purple flowers among the grass and clover beneath the bench. I picked one and looked at it closely. So beautiful, so delicate. If I asked Simon straight out, that would be admitting I suspected him and didn't trust him. Which, if I was wrong, would undermine our relationship. I couldn't risk that. I'd have to find proof before confronting him.

I twirled the purple flower between finger and thumb until the stem crushed and the flower head dropped to the ground. It was time to go. Thomas needed to be collected by two, and Lewis and Lauren finished school an hour later.

I spent the afternoon cleaning the house while the kids bounced on the trampoline we'd erected in the garden, and climbed in the old beech tree. Simon rang to say he'd not be back until after nine again; he was held up at work with an urgent problem. Either he really was working too hard or he was hiding something. Thomas was in bed, the other two children were playing in their rooms already washed and pyjama'd, and my laptop had finally turned up in the last box we'd unpacked in the study. There was time to immerse myself in my family history. At least it would take my mind off worrying about what Simon was really doing.

I had stacks of notes on the St Clairs, and piles of birth, marriage and death certificates. It had cost a small fortune sending off for all those certs but I treasured them, and relished every new snippet of information I discovered. One day I would write the whole lot up as a book, and get it properly bound. It would be my gift to my children. Here's who you are, and where you came from. From your mum's side, anyway. Your dad doesn't know who his own parents were, and isn't even interested. The idea of not even knowing the names of your parents unsettled me. It would be like building a house with no foundations on quicksand – nothing beneath you to hold you up.

'It's not like that at all,' Simon had said, when I discussed this with him, years ago when he'd first told me he was adopted. 'Who you are has nothing to do with who your birth parents are. Sure, they might have passed on genes for ginger hair or chubby ankles but who you are – who you *really* are – is down to your upbringing and your life experiences. For which I have my wonderful adoptive parents to thank.'

Still, if it was me, I'd want to know names if nothing else. So I could go backwards into the past and find out where I came from.

I sorted the certificates into date order. Birth and death certificates are like the book-ends of a life. They define an ancestor's period. Born there, on that date. Died then, in this place. Before you've established those basic facts, ancestors are ghost-like beings. They must have existed, else you wouldn't be here, but you know nothing about them. Tracking down their births, marriages, deaths, entries on census forms gradually makes them take shape. It adds flesh to the bones, so to speak.

The earliest certificate was Bartholomew and Georgia's marriage certificate from 1838. It showed Bartholomew St Clair, occupation 'Gentleman', of Sussex Square, Brighton, marrying Georgia Holland, on 15th May, 1838. Georgia was just seventeen, and a ward of her uncle, Charles Holland of Brunswick Terrace, Brighton. The wedding was witnessed by Charles Holland and a Henry Harding.

I peered at the signatures of the couple. How wonderful to see my great-great-great-grandparents' own handwriting! Bartholomew's backward-leaning scrawl; the style of a man of business who was used to writing a lot. Georgia's elegant copperplate; a lady's handwriting, perfect for genteel correspondence with her friends, still showing signs of the schoolroom she had so recently left. Only seventeen when she married! Bartholomew was thirty-three.

I'd ordered the birth certificates of all of Bartholomew and Georgia's children. They'd had four children – Barty, the eccentric old man who'd inherited the house and lived here till the 1920s; William, my great-great-grandfather, and, between the boys, two daughters who'd died in childhood, Elizabeth and Isobella. I put all the certificates into date order.

Then there were the death certificates. Those for the little girls were so sad. Elizabeth had died aged just three of 'a fever, eight days duration', and Isobella died aged ten of consumption. I looked closely at the dates. William, my ancestor, had been born only two weeks after the death of Elizabeth. Had his birth been a comfort to Georgia, I wondered – had the arrival of a new baby somehow helped her get over her loss? I couldn't imagine losing a child. These days if a child dies it's a tragedy, something a parent never really gets over. But back then it was sadly all too common.

My research was interrupted by Lauren thundering down the stairs, a sniffling Thomas close on her heels.

'Mum, Lewis says there are ghosts in this house! He's made Thomas cry!'

I sighed, picked up Thomas and went up to sort them out.

'Lewis, what have you been saying to Thomas?'

Lewis was sitting on his bedroom floor surrounded by mounds of Lego. He looked up at me, all wide-eyed and innocent. 'I said nothing, Mum.'

'Well, why's he crying, then?'

'Dunno. Maybe he's tired. You should put him to bed.' Oh great. Now my own eleven-year-old is giving me parenting tips.

'I would, but how's he going to sleep if you've been filling his head with ghost stories?'

'He started it. He said he'd heard wailing in the night.'

'Thomas?'

He sniffed and buried his face against my neck. 'Ghosts were going woo-woo last night. I heard them.'

I hugged him close. 'Sweetie, it was probably the wind. Sometimes it gets in the chimneys and goes woo-woo. I heard it too.'

'I'm frightened of the wind going woo-woo in the chimley. Can you stop it getting in?'

'No, sweetie, I can't. But it's only air.'

'Ghosts are only air too,' said Lewis, unhelpfully.

I glared at him and shook my head. 'Lewis, pick up all this Lego. Why on earth did you tip it all out anyway?'

'I'm trying to find all the bits of my Star Wars MTT tank.'

'Your what?'

'The one I got two Christmases ago from Granny and Granddad.'

Oh yes. The one that cost about eighty quid. He made it once, threw out the box, then muddled the pieces in with all the rest of his Lego. The instructions got torn in a fight with Lauren.

'Well, good luck with that. I'll be hoovering in here tomorrow so make sure you've picked it all up by then. Come on, Thomas. Time for bed.'

I carried him out of Lewis's room and into his own. I pulled his jumper and T-shirt off over his head, tickled him, and tried to blow a raspberry on his tummy. He pushed me away.

'Will the wind go woo-woo in the chimley tonight, Mummy?'

'It might do, sweetie. The weather forecast said there'd be more strong winds tonight but then tomorrow it'll get better and we'll have some sunshine. That'll be nice won't it – just in time for the weekend. I want to take you all for a walk up a hill I've found. You can see for miles from the top.'

'I don't want the wind to go woo-woo tonight.' His bottom lip trembled.

'Once you're asleep you won't hear it. Come on, into these jim-jams, then let's go and scrub your teeth.'

'How do you know if the woo-woo is ghosts or the wind? If they're both made of air like Lewis said?' He held on to my shoulders while I tugged his pyjama trousers up.

'It's always the wind. There are no ghosts.'

'Lewis said there was. He said there's always ghosts in old houses. I don't want to live in an old house with ghosts and chimleys. We didn't have ghosts and chimleys in the other house.'

'No, and you didn't have your own room there either. And you like having your own room, don't you?' I led him by the hand into the bathroom.

'Not when there's ghosts in the chimley. Can I sleep in your bed tonight?'

'We'll see. Start off in your own bed. I'll come and check on you when I come up to bed. So will Daddy, when he gets home.' Whenever that might be. 'OK? Now, here's your toothbrush.' I handed him the brush with a dot of paste on the bristles and watched as he carefully scrubbed his teeth. He kept his serious little eyes fixed on mine. I smiled at him, in what I hoped was a reassuring way. Outside the wind was picking up, and rain lashed against the bathroom window. Simon had better get home soon. It was not a night to be out.

I read three story books to Thomas, hoping to push ghosts out of his mind with tales of baby bears going to the moon in a cardboard box and mother elephants trying to find five minutes' peace from their lively families. At last he looked sleepy, and I kissed the top of his head and tucked his duvet around him.

'I'll come in and see you again after Lewis and Lauren have gone to bed. And I'll leave your door open, OK?'

He nodded, and snuggled down beneath his duvet. For the time of year it was surprisingly cold.

I gave the older children their deadline to be ready for bed, and went downstairs to make a cup of tea. On the kitchen table was a letter for Simon which had come in the morning post. I picked it up. I'd been curious about it all day. The address was handwritten, in a writing I didn't recognise, on a plain white envelope. The postmark was London. It had been sent to our old house, and forwarded by the Post Office.

I replaced the letter and moved Simon's dinner, all plated up, into the microwave ready to reheat when he finally came home. I glanced at the clock. Eight-thirty. Presumably he was on the train by now. I picked up my phone and called him, but the phone went straight to voicemail. Where was he? Should I confront him or what? I didn't want to think about it. Instead I went back to the study and continued with my research. I'd received in the post a CD of details from a local family history group. It was a transcription of church records from several churches north of Winchester, including our local one, St Michael's. I was hoping to find where Bartholomew and Georgia were buried.

I stuck the CD in and keyed 'St Clair' into the search box. Minutes later, I'd found that both Bartholomew and Georgia were buried in St Michael's graveyard. I'd guessed they would be, but it was great to be sure. Not only that, the CD included a plan of the graveyard with each block labelled. My ancestors were apparently at the top end furthest from the church. On my next free day, I'd go and look for the grave. They'd been buried in the same plot, even though they'd died a year or so apart, in the 1870s.

A blast of cold air raced through the house, and the front door banged. 'Blimming heck, it's blowy out there! Brrr!'

Simon was back. I took a deep breath and went to meet him in the hallway.

'Hi, Katie. Had a good day?' He gave me a peck on the cheek, dumped his briefcase just inside the study and went through to the kitchen to pour himself a glass of wine. That was something else I'd noticed. He was drinking much more than usual, and was opening wine almost every night when he got home.

'Usual kind of day. Went for a walk. Cleaned the house. Sorted some paperwork. You?'

He sighed. 'Tiring. Long. *Very* long. Kids still awake?'

'They're ready for bed but still playing. I said they could stay up till nine.'

He looked at his watch. 'It's five to. I'll say hello then I'll chase them into bed.' He took a large gulp of his wine then put the glass down on the kitchen table.

I poured myself a glass of wine and regarded him. He didn't look like a man cheating on his wife. He looked like a man who'd had a tough day at the office and was simply glad to get home at last. I decided to keep quiet and say nothing. For now, at any rate.

'I'll reheat your dinner. There's a letter on the table for you. Oh, and can you reassure Thomas there's no such thing as ghosts – Lewis has been winding him up.'

'Thanks, love. Let me hang up my coat first, I'm dripping wet. This is a proper summer storm. Hope our chimneys will stand up to it!'

Great. Now I'd spend a sleepless night worrying about the chimneys, as well as Thomas. 'They'll be all right, won't they?'

'Course they will. They've all got iron bars tying them to the roof, in any case. Don't worry. Where's this letter?'

I handed it to him, and watched his face closely as he glanced at the writing, frowned slightly, then tossed it back on the kitchen table. 'It can wait. Now then, the kids.'

While he was upstairs I heated up his dinner. The letter lay on the table, glaring at me. I knew where Thomas got his overactive imagination from, at least.

Later that evening we curled up on the sofa in the sitting room with a glass of wine each, and listened to the rain lashing against the windows and the wind howling in the chimney. It did sound spooky – I could understand why Thomas had been frightened. He was sleeping soundly enough tonight. I'd been upstairs twice already to check on him. Lewis was the only one lying awake, complaining the noise was keeping him awake.

'Quite a storm, this one,' said Simon. 'I bet we'll lose some roof slates. I'll have to check in the morning.'

'My poor broad beans,' I said, thinking of the little plants I'd tied onto canes only a few days before. They stood no chance.

I wondered again about the letter. Simon had opened it as he ate his dinner, read it quickly and tucked it into his pocket without a word.

'Simon,' I said quietly, 'who was that letter from?'

'What letter? Oh, um, just an old friend.'

'Who?'

'No one you know.'

Hmm. I knew, or thought I knew, all his old friends. At least all the ones he'd kept in touch with.

'Ah ha,' I said, poking him gently in the ribs. 'It's from an ex-girlfriend, isn't it? That's why you're being cagey! Which one – that Sarah you went out with in college? Or the girl from your school days, what was she called, the one you said had the teeth of a racehorse and the eyes of a frog?'

He laughed. 'No, I described Jenny as having the *legs* of a

racehorse and the eyes of a *deer* – wide, brown and beautiful.'
He looked at me. 'Katie, you're jealous!'

'No I'm not!' I protested. 'I'm just curious as to who sent that letter. No one sends personal letters these days. It's all email.'

'Well, it's as I said, from an old friend. Kind of. Yes, a woman, if you must know. Hey, a new detective series is starting tonight. Shall we?'

He picked up the remote control and switched on the TV. Clearly he wasn't going to tell me anything more about the letter, at least not now. *Who Do You Think You Are?* was on as well, so I set that to record. I'd watch it on my own some other time. Simon, of course, had no interest in that programme.

The storm didn't let up all evening. We went to bed around eleven, with the wind still moaning in the chimneys and the rain pounding at the windows. I think it was around one am when we heard the enormous crash. The house shook, as though a ten-ton truck had smashed into it. I sat bolt upright, while Simon rolled instinctively out of bed and was on his feet before he was even awake. A small chunk of ceiling plaster fell down, scattering dust and debris over our duvet.

'What the...'

'What was that?'

'Something hit the house!'

'An explosion?'

'The kids!'

We both ran from the room – me to Thomas's room and Simon up to Lauren's, while he shouted for Lewis. We'd agreed years ago who would go to which child in the event of an emergency: the thought of leaving one child to burn in a house fire while we both rushed to save another is unthinkable, so our 'training' kicked in without either of us speaking.

Amazingly, Thomas was still sleeping, his duvet askew, and White Ted half under his head. I grabbed him anyway, folded him over my shoulder still sleeping, and ran downstairs with him.

Simon was just behind, with a terrified Lauren in his arms, Lewis holding onto his pyjama trousers saying, 'What's going on, Dad? I heard a bang…'

We were all in the hallway before we stopped to take stock. We were all safe. There was no sign of fire – no smoke detector had gone off, no smell of burning. Simon checked the living room – safe in there, so I lay Thomas on the sofa. Lauren snuggled down next to him, pulling a throw over them both. Lewis sat on the floor, leaning against the sofa.

'Stay there, kids, unless we shout for you to get out. Katie, stay in the hallway while I check the house.'

He checked the study, all clear, then went through to the kitchen. I heard him gasp, 'Shit!' then he came back to me. 'You'd better come and look at this, love.'

I followed him through. The kitchen window was broken, shards of glass covered the floor and the wind was inside, bouncing off the walls like a caged banshee. Simon threw me a pair of gardening shoes which were lying on the kitchen doormat, and I slipped them on, and flicked on the light switch.

A huge branch from the beech tree had come through the window, and was resting now on the remains of the casement, its leaves dipped in the sink, its twigs entwined with a shattered vase of flowers that had been on the windowsill.

'Oh my God!' I said. 'What a mess!'

'The whole tree is down,' Simon said, peering past the branch through the remains of the window. 'I'd better go and check.' He pulled a mac off its peg by the back door.

'No, leave it till the morning,' I said. 'There's nothing you can do now. Especially not while the storm's still raging.'

'I guess not,' he agreed. 'I'll get the sleeping bags and some blankets. Let's all sleep downstairs in the lounge for the rest of the night. Good thing it's Saturday tomorrow.'

I went back to the kids to tell them what had happened.

Thomas and Lauren were asleep, but Lewis listened wide-eyed while I whispered the news in his ear.

'Can we plant it again?' he asked. 'Cos I like to climb it.'

I smiled, shook my head and ruffled his hair. 'We'll have to plant a new tree, and watch it grow. You can help with that. When we've cleared away the beech.'

He nodded seriously, then snuggled into the sleeping bag Simon had brought, and settled down to sleep on the hearth rug. I did the same, and eventually drifted off to sleep reflecting on the loss of the tree. It must have been only a sapling when my ancestors lived here. Perhaps one of them had even planted it?

Chapter Nine

Hampshire, November 1876

Where were we, Barty my son, in this sorry narrative? I have not been well. I put it to one side for a week or so, while I lay abed and coughed and vomited as though my body was trying to rid itself of demons inside. There __are__ demons inside me – as you are beginning to realise. Demons which made me take another woman to bed on the day I proposed to my wife, and take her again on the day I married. Demons driving me to drink too much brandy and whiskey, until I, although aware of what I was doing, no longer cared, and no longer thought of the effects of my actions on others.

Poor sweet Georgia. She was not much more than a child when I married her. Frightened and inexperienced. Did anyone even tell her what to expect on her wedding night? Quite possibly not. She deserved better than me; brute that I was.

We did, of course, eventually consummate our marriage. It was about a month later. We had by that time moved out of Charles Holland's house, into a small but adequate apart-

ment in Sussex Square. It faced sideways into the square, so there was not the benefit of a direct sea view, but Georgia pronounced it charming, and the rent was reasonable. I wasted no time furnishing it with taste, using Georgia's inheritance, or what was left of it after I had paid off my creditors. Agnes, of course, moved with us, and took a rear-facing room on the top floor, one which was not overlooked at all. I was a frequent visitor to that room in the first month of my marriage, until Georgia finally overcame her scruples and allowed me into her bed.

And so it was that by the summer of 1838, Georgia was with child, and I confess I was excited at the prospect of producing an heir. Let us pick up the narrative again at this point, from Agnes's point of view. She told me much of what happened between herself and Georgia, either at the time or later. The rest, the parts she kept secret, I confess I have guessed at. Pour yourself a whiskey, dear Barty, and read on.

Brighton, July 1838

Agnes rubbed Georgia's back as she vomited for the third time that morning into a basin. Georgia was sitting on a chair in the corner of her bedchamber, while Agnes hovered around, trying to comfort her mistress.

'Let it come up, ma'am,' she said. 'You will feel better once it's out of you.'

Georgia groaned. 'I had no idea being with child could make you sick.' She retched again, and Agnes took a damp cloth and mopped her brow.

'I remember my ma had terrible sickness with all of hers. She were sick for months each time. But the babies were all born bonny and healthy. She said the sicker the mother, the bigger the baby.'

Georgia moaned again. 'I'm not sure I want too big a baby. How on earth do you get it out? Oh, there's more…' She vomited again.

Agnes stroked the younger woman's hair. 'There, there, miss. I'll make you a potion for your sickness, if you would like it. Something with ginger in, to take in the morning afore you get out of bed.'

'Oh, would you, please? Anything to stop this torture.'

Georgia straightened up, took the damp cloth from Agnes and wiped her mouth. She looked green and haggard. She was too delicate to bear a child, Agnes thought. Now if *she* was pregnant with Mr Bartholomew's child, she would be blooming with health at this stage. For a moment she allowed herself the fantasy – a baby in her arms and Mr Bartholomew looking on as a proud father. But it would not happen. She was careful, always, that she should not fall pregnant. For all the while there was no outward, visible sign of their affair, they could continue it. Mr Bartholomew still crept up to Agnes's room two or three times a week, sometimes coming straight from his wife's room to hers. But if she were to get caught… Agnes shook her head slightly to stop the thoughts. If that happened, she would lose the man she loved, and that, she thought, she could never bear.

'What is it? You look suddenly sad,' said Georgia, as she splashed her face with cold water from a basin.

Agnes shook her head, and pasted a smile onto her face. 'No, ma'am, I'm not sad. Are you feeling better? I'll help you dress and then I'll make that potion for your sickness. You should take a walk along the sea front. The fresh air will do you good.'

'You're so wise, Aggie.' Georgia rubbed her face with a towel and smiled. 'What would I do without you?'

I know what I'd do without you, thought Agnes. I'd claim your husband for my own. She said nothing, but busied herself clearing away the bowl of vomit and laying out Georgia's clothes. It was a fine day. Perhaps she'd be able to walk on the sea front herself later on, if the master and mistress went out for a while.

When Georgia was dressed and had gone downstairs to break-fast, still declaring she would not be able to eat a thing, Agnes went to the kitchen to collect some ginger and various herbs from Mrs Simmonds, the cook-cum-housekeeper, then took them up to her room, along with a flask of water. She laid the ingredients out on a small table, and opened up her herbalist's box, from which she removed a small bottle. Her hand hovered over a small box of powder, and she bit her lip as she remembered something her mother had taught her...

She returned to the table, and began chopping the herbs finely and mixing them with some crushed ginger in a little water. When she had made a watery paste she picked up the little bottle, ready to decant the mixture into it. She bit her lip once more, then looked back at her box. If the mistress were to have a baby, it would change things. All the while Georgia was pregnant, Mr St Clair would no doubt come to her, Agnes, for his comforts even more than usual. But afterwards, as a father, a family man, perhaps he would no longer want to keep her as a mistress. Perhaps he would then want to be faithful to his wife, the mother of his child, and would cast Agnes aside like a worn-out coat.

She could not allow that to happen. She took out the box of powder and considered it. Angelica root and dried pennyroyal leaves. Nothing very exotic but if her mother was right about their effects on a pregnant woman... Could she do that to her beloved young mistress? Hurt her, cause pain and grief, to keep her affair with Mr St Clair going? It was a hard decision to make. But she would do anything to keep him. Anything.

When she'd finished bottling the potion, she took it to Georgia's room. Once more she hesitated, putting the bottle back into her pocket, until, pressing her lips together firmly she took it out again and placed it on the washstand. It would certainly ease the girl's morning sickness and, after all, wasn't that what she'd been asked to do? In any case, Georgia was too young and delicate for child-bearing. She was doing this for the overall health of her mistress. Yes, it was all for the best.

Next morning, she mixed some of the potion with water and gave it to Georgia to drink before she got out of bed.

'It's mostly ginger, ma'am' she told the girl. 'With a few other things mixed in. 'Twill settle your stomach afore you rise, and will stop the sickness.'

Georgia drank it quickly and grimaced. 'Ugh, that's quite unpleasant. I can taste the ginger but there's something else in there as well, I do believe. Mint perhaps? Where did you learn this recipe?'

'From my mother, ma'am. She is a herbalist as I think I have told you before. In her village she is called on to make potions for all sorts of ailments. I have learned some of her skills.' Agnes turned away as she spoke.

'Well, I am most grateful to her for teaching you. Should I get out of bed now or stay here a while longer?'

'Give it a few minutes to take effect, while I get your clothes ready for the day.'

Later, when Georgia had risen, dressed and was downstairs eating a hearty breakfast, Agnes slumped down on her mistress's bed. The ginger had worked, and Georgia had not felt queasy, but what of the other ingredients? Would they work in the way her mother had taught her?

Two weeks later, the couple were hosting a dinner party. Agnes had let out Georgia's best, deep-red satin gown for the occasion. Although she did not yet have a baby bump, her waist had thickened and her breasts swollen. Thankfully the seams of the gown were generous enough to allow it to be let out, but it wouldn't fit her for long. Georgia's long, pale gold hair was piled high on her head in a complicated arrangement of curls. The silver and emerald hair comb held up the back of her hair, its jewels catching the light whenever she moved. Agnes was pleased with the effect.

'You look so beautiful, ma'am,' she told Georgia, who was sitting at her dressing table putting the finishing touches to her outfit. 'You will have a splendid evening.'

'Bartholomew is going to tell our friends this evening, that we are expecting a child,' Georgia said, smiling happily and admiring her reflection in the mirror. She fastened on a pair of emerald earrings. A distant clock struck the hour, and both women listened and counted. 'Eight o'clock – our guests will soon arrive. I must go down.' She stood and smoothed her skirts, patted her hair and left the room.

Agnes pottered about tidying up and, as so often, wondered what it would be like to be the lady of the house. How well *she* would look in that ruby-red gown. How witty and charming *she* would be, to Bartholomew's friends. She sighed. It could never be.

Bartholomew stood in the drawing room, welcoming his guests as they arrived for the dinner party. The maid-of-all-work, Polly, had put on her smartest uniform and a clean cap, and was answering the door and showing them in. Bartholomew was delighted with Georgia's appearance when she came downstairs. The deep-red dress looked stunning against her pale blonde hair. She was blooming – he liked her fuller figure. Pregnancy suited her. Well, as far as he was concerned, they could have a large family. Georgia had said how much she wanted children and as there was always Agnes to turn to while Georgia was indisposed, there seemed to be no reason not to have a string of children. One a year, perhaps. With Georgia's inheritance they easily had enough money.

The first guest to arrive was elderly Mrs Oliphant, a neighbour of Georgia's uncle. Bartholomew's heart sank; he'd been hoping Henry Harding and his wife would arrive first. Mrs Oliphant was a widow who spent her time nosing among the affairs of others. She was wearing an enormous black gown, with several strings of pearls draped around her fleshy neck.

'Welcome, my dear Mrs Oliphant. I trust you are well?' He gave a small bow and raised her offered hand to his lips.

'Tolerably so, Mr St Clair. But suffering in this August heat. How I long for the cool autumn days. Mrs St Clair, Georgia, my dear, you are looking remarkably well! You've put on a few pounds, I believe, and it suits you. I never did hold with young women being too thin.'

Georgia blushed. 'I am indeed very well, Mrs Oliphant. I find the summer warmth more to my liking than you, perhaps. I do so like to be able to stroll along the beach and watch the bathers.'

Mrs Oliphant shuddered. 'Another thing I don't hold with – sea-bathing. If God had meant us to swim, he'd have given us flippers like a seal. I do hope you don't bathe yourself? It's really not becoming for a young woman in your station in life.'

Georgia was spared from having to admit that she had indeed tried sea-bathing, by the arrival of Polly announcing more guests. It was Henry and Caroline Harding. Bartholomew greeted his old friend warmly, while Caroline, who wore a simple pale-blue gown trimmed with ivory lace, joined the women.

'What news, old man?' said Henry, clapping Bartholomew on the back. 'How's married life suiting you? Your wife is looking more radiant than ever. I'd say marriage is suiting *her*, all right. She'll be providing you with a son and heir before too long, I'd say.'

'We're both very happy,' said Bartholomew. 'And you may very well be right about that son and heir.' He gestured to Polly to pour them all a glass of sherry. Harding glanced towards Georgia and raised his eyebrows. She blushed and instinctively put a hand to her midriff.

'Ah, congratulations are in order, I see,' said Harding to Bartholomew, in a low voice. 'Or are you keeping it quiet for a while?'

'We may announce it later tonight. Charles Holland is coming, and he should hear it first. After all, Georgia's his only niece, and

102

if she has a son, Holland may very well want to make the child his heir, too.'

'Which is all good, what?' said Henry. 'I heard your doorbell just now. I suppose that might be Holland arriving.'

It was. Polly showed the old man in. He slumped immediately into a chair, puffing breathlessly.

'St Clair, a brandy, if you would, to revive me.'

'Of course. Polly, brandy for Mr Holland.'

'Are you quite well, Mr Holland?' asked Mrs Oliphant. 'Did you walk here, perhaps? It is too warm to be out walking. I don't hold with doing anything much in this heat. You would have been wise to take a cab, as I did. It is a long way here from Brunswick.'

'I did take a cab. It's those darned steep steps up to St Clair's front door which has me gasping. Ah, brandy, thank you.' He took the glass from Polly and gulped it down, causing him to cough uncontrollably. Georgia rushed to his side and helped him pull a handkerchief from his pocket to cough into.

'Uncle, are you sure the brandy helps? I fear it makes you cough so, it can't be good for you.'

'Nonsense, it's the exertion of climbing those steps which made me cough. I shall be quite all right in a moment.' He waved his glass at Polly. 'Keep it filled, there's a good girl.'

The dinner party progressed well. They dined on pheasant, quails' eggs and fresh plums. As he'd predicted, with a constant supply of brandy and no further physical exertion, Holland had no more coughing fits. Bartholomew thought, however, that he looked greyer and somehow diminished since the wedding. Mrs Oliphant kept up a constant stream of disapproving chatter about the things she didn't hold with. Bartholomew was tempted to ask her, just what *do* you approve of? but restrained himself, and engaged Henry Harding in a discussion about the new railways which were being built in the north of the country, and whether or not to invest in the various newly formed railway companies.

'They'll build some down here before too long,' said Henry. 'A London to Brighton line, perhaps. Imagine, you'd be able to get to town in just two or three hours.'

'That'd be marvellous for business,' agreed Bartholomew. 'But surely it'd be too expensive to build. It's not like in the northeast, where there's coal to be shifted from mines to ports. We've no need for a railway here in the south. I'll not invest in them, that's for sure.'

He was interrupted by Mrs Oliphant, who was sitting to his right. 'Mr St Clair, I think you should attend to your wife. She is looking unwell. With all your business talk with Mr Harding, you have failed to notice. I must say, I don't hold with business talk at the dinner table.'

Bartholomew glanced at Georgia who was at the opposite end of the table. She was indeed looking pale, and was leaning over the table, clutching at her stomach. Mrs Harding was holding her hand and murmuring sympathetically.

He jumped to his feet and went to her. 'My dear, are you all right? Did something we ate disagree with you, perhaps?'

She groaned. 'I don't know. It hurts – like someone is stabbing me… ohhhh!'

'There, there, do you feel sick?' asked Caroline Harding.

'No, just… ohhhh. Fetch Agnes, Bartholomew. She'll know what to do.'

He had already rung the bell. Polly answered, and rushed away at once to fetch Agnes.

By the time Agnes arrived, Georgia was doubled up on a small sofa, moaning. She would not let anyone near her. Agnes rushed to her side, and held a whispered conversation. She said something to Georgia which made her moan again, and thump a cushion in despair.

Agnes stood, and turned to Bartholomew. Her face was drawn and shocked.

'Sir, I fear your wife is losing the baby. We must get her upstairs to bed. Please send for a doctor, immediately.'

Bartholomew felt the words hit him like a punch to the gut. So many women lost the babies they were carrying, but this one was *his* baby, and he had not considered the possibility that it could be lost, so early on. He'd only just got used to the idea of becoming a father. And what if losing this child left Georgia unable to have any more? What would be the point of his marriage if not to produce children?

He felt a gentle shake of his shoulder. It was Henry Harding. 'St Clair? Come on, man, collect yourself.'

He shook the thoughts away, and called to Polly to run to fetch Dr Stockett, who lived but a few streets away.

Agnes and Caroline Harding helped Georgia to her feet, and with one woman on either side of her, managed to get her to walk, bent over, to the stairs. It was slow progress going up, as she stopped to groan every few steps.

Charles Holland announced he was no use at all in female crises, so if someone would call him a cab, he'd quietly drink brandy until it arrived to take him home. Mrs Oliphant tutted and said she didn't hold with drinking too much brandy, neither did she hold with young wives getting pregnant too early in their married lives, as it so often ended this way. She decided to share Holland's cab back to Brunswick.

Bartholomew retired to the drawing room with Henry Harding, where he paced up and down. He heard the front door open as Polly returned with Dr Stockett, and again as Holland and Mrs Oliphant left to take their cab. Harding kept topping up Bartholomew's brandy glass.

'Don't fret, man. Caroline lost a couple like this, before producing Henry Junior. Georgia'll be right as rain in a couple of weeks, mark my words. And she'll be pregnant again in no time, if you do your job right, of course.'

'I should go up, to see her…'

'No, leave this to the doctor and that lady's maid of hers. It's no place for a husband. There's nothing you can do, anyway.'

The door opened and Caroline Harding entered, looking drawn and worried. 'The doctor says there is no hope for the baby. I am so sorry, Bartholomew.'

'Is Georgia all right?'

'As well as can be expected. Her maid is doing a good job of calming and comforting her. I came downstairs because there's nothing more I can do.'

'Thank you. You have been very kind. I will ring for Polly to fetch you some refreshments.' Bartholomew crossed the room to the fireplace to pull on the bell-cord.

'No, don't trouble your servants.' Caroline glanced at her husband, who nodded.

'If you don't mind, old chap, I think Caroline and I will take our leave now. We are only getting in the way, here. But if there is anything we can do, please call on us.' Henry Harding patted Bartholomew on the shoulder as he headed towards the door. 'We can show ourselves out.'

Upstairs, Georgia was lying on her bed, covered by a light blanket, while Agnes sat at her side holding her hand. Dr Stockett was washing his hands.

'Well, as I said, keep to your bed for the next few days. When the bleeding stops you'll feel better. If it doesn't stop in a week, call me again. In a month you'll be ready to try to conceive again.'

He dried his hands on a towel and picked up his bag. 'Don't fret, Mrs St Clair. That won't do you any good. Plenty of women miscarry their first pregnancy and then go on to have half a dozen healthy children. I'll see myself out.'

Agnes tightened her lips. Well, he'd better see himself out, because she had no intention of letting go of Georgia's hand to see him out. The poor girl. She had taken it very hard, and was still in a lot of pain. Agnes felt a brief pang of guilt. She'd caused this, with her potion. She hadn't wanted to hurt Georgia. But she couldn't have allowed the pregnancy to continue. A baby would spoil things. It was better this way.

When the doctor had gone, Georgia sobbed. Agnes passed her a handkerchief, and pressed her hand.

'Ma'am, you heard what the doctor said. Try not to cry too much. Grieve a little for the lost baby but only a little, for it was only a very young soul that was lost. Not like a real child.' How would Georgia cope with losing a live child, one of two or three or ten years old? Agnes considered how her mother had lost four of her children before they reached their fifth birthdays. As the eldest, she could remember every one of those heart-breaking funerals for her tiny brothers and sisters. Each time her mother had cried quietly as the coffin was lowered into the earth, then she'd gone home, taken off her good Sunday clothes and got straight back to work.

'I so wanted to give Bartholomew a child,' sobbed Georgia. 'Now he'll think I have failed him as a wife. He might not want me any more.'

Agnes turned away, and busied herself folding the towel the doctor had used. 'Come now, ma'am. It's not your fault, and I don't believe your husband will think that it is.'

'Why has he not come up to see how I am? I believe he doesn't care!'

'A woman's sickbed is not the place for a husband. That's why he hasn't come up. He will no doubt call on you tomorrow, when the worst is over.'

Georgia sniffed, and wiped at her eyes with the handkerchief. 'Oh, Agnes. You are my true friend. Don't leave me tonight. Sleep with me, here in my room, please? I will feel so much better if you are by my side all night.'

'Well, ma'am, I…'

'Don't say no, Agnes! Please, stay with me. If I had a mother or a sister, perhaps I would manage, but I have only you. Say you'll stay!' She pushed herself up onto her elbow and clutched at Agnes's hands.

'Very well, ma'am. I will stay with you tonight. I shall call Polly to make up a down-bed upon the floor.'

Georgia clutched even more tightly at Agnes's hands, stopping her from reaching for the bell-cord. 'No, lie beside me in my bed. There is plenty of space, look, I shall move over. Then I need not let go of your hand all night. It will be such a comfort.'

Agnes suppressed a sigh. 'As you wish, ma'am. Let me go just for a moment, so I can prepare myself for sleep.'

'All right, but just for two minutes. Be quick as you can!'

Agnes left Georgia to fetch herself a nightdress from her own room. She was about to go up the stairs to the top floor when a quiet cough made her turn. It was Mr St Clair. He gestured to her to go on up, and followed her.

'Is my wife feeling better?' he asked, when they were out of earshot of Georgia's room.

'A little, sir. But it will take time for her to recover completely.'

'As I thought.' He took a step closer to her. 'Lie with me tonight. I feel the loss of the baby too. You will be a comfort to me.' He held her face and kissed her, deeply.

She kissed him back, and then pulled herself away. 'Sir, I cannot. Not tonight. Mrs St Clair has asked me to stay in her room tonight.'

'You are turning me down, for her?'

Every fibre of Agnes's being wanted him – her skin tingled at his touch and as always, his closeness made her feel more alive than she'd ever been. But she backed away from him, and put a hand against his chest to keep him away. She needed to make amends for what she'd done to Georgia.

'Her need for comfort, sir, is greater than yours this evening. I must do my duty to my mistress.' She picked up the items she needed from the room and turned on her heel, leaving him standing there alone.

***

Ten months had passed since Georgia's miscarriage. Agnes and Georgia were out, enjoying the spring air, and walking through the Old Steine gardens, heading towards the sea. It was a fresh, pleasant day and Agnes was enjoying the exercise. They had done a little shopping and she was carrying the purchases. Passing the bandstand, she noticed that a band was just setting up ready to play.

'Ma'am, would you like to stay and listen a while?' she asked, hoping that the answer would be yes. She wanted to stay out, mingling with the people, enjoying the mild sunshine and fresh air.

'No. I am becoming tired,' replied Georgia. 'I think we have had enough exercise for one day. Perhaps tomorrow, we could return, or maybe Bartholomew will bring me.'

Agnes pursed her lips. Maybe he would bring you, she thought. He'd never bring me. She forced a smile to her face. 'Very well, ma'am. It has been a tiring day. Let's go back before the crowds build up.'

'Yes, let's. But if there's a quiet bench, let's sit a while first. There is…something I would like to talk to you about.'

Agnes paled, imagining the worst. Did Georgia suspect something? But they were so discreet, always making sure Georgia was tucked up in bed, sleeping, before they crept to the same room. True, recently they'd been using Bartholomew's more comfortable room rather than going up to Agnes's, but even his room was at the other end of the corridor from his wife's, so surely she wouldn't hear anything?

'There's a seat over there, beneath that tree. Will that do?' Agnes led the way. Might as well get this over with. The bench sat in dappled shade beneath an ornamental cherry tree, laden with blossom. She brushed some fallen petals off the seat and helped Georgia sit down. She did look tired. And a little pale. Surely she wasn't still grieving for the miscarried baby, after so many months?

Georgia took Agnes's hand in hers, and regarded her for a moment. Agnes kept her expression bland and hoped she was not giving anything away in her eyes.

'You are such a good maid, no, more than a maid. A friend. You have worked for me – how long, now?'

'Must be four or five years now, ma'am. Since you were a young lady of fourteen.'

'But you worked in our house before then, didn't you?'

'Yes, since I was thirteen, and you were a child of five summers. I was a housemaid to start with. Then your father, God rest his soul, asked me to act as your lady's maid.'

'He made an excellent choice. You've been more like a companion than a maid.' Georgia sighed. 'I need to ask you, as my dearest friend, to keep a secret for me. Will you do that?'

Agnes nodded. 'Of course, ma'am.'

Georgia looked down at her hand holding Agnes's, and blushed slightly. 'The thing is, I…I'm with child, again. But I don't want to tell Bartholomew, yet. He was so upset last time, when I lost the baby. I couldn't bear for him to go through all that again…'

Agnes's eyes widened, then she smiled and squeezed Georgia's hand. 'But ma'am, this is good news! Many women lose their first baby. My ma said the body must practise first before it can grow a baby properly. Don't you fret about this one.'

'I have been feeling sick again. Would you make me that potion to prevent it, as before?'

'Of course I will, ma'am. I shall make some right away as soon as we are back home. I have my herbalist's box and I think Mrs Simmonds has some ginger in the kitchen.' Agnes glanced at Georgia. Did she want the *same* potion as before? Or the *proper* potion to stop sickness? And could she bring herself to give it to Georgia again, now that she'd seen the pain and grief it had caused?

Georgia reached over and hugged Agnes. 'Thank you. What would I do without you? But we must keep this secret from Bartholomew for as long as is possible.'

'He will notice, when your waist starts to expand.'

'I shall wear looser clothes. I shall tell him when he notices and not before. Promise me you won't give me away?'

110

'Of course I won't, ma'am.'

Georgia kissed her on the cheek. 'It is such a comfort to me to know I can always trust you, dear Aggie.'

Agnes looked away. She liked Georgia, despite the girl being childish and silly at times. If only she wasn't married to Mr St Clair. But, if she wasn't, then Agnes herself would not have met him either.

The potion worked more quickly this time. Agnes made a large batch, but it was only a week later that Georgia came knocking on her bedroom door at dawn one morning, sobbing and clutching a blood-stained nightgown. Agnes took the girl back to her own bedchamber and made her comfortable.

'Don't tell Bartholomew,' Georgia begged. 'Make up some story, that I have a fever or the like. Oh, please, don't tell him the truth, whatever you do.'

'I won't, ma'am. I shall say you have a headache and must not be disturbed. But the doctor must know the real reason, of course…'

'No! Don't call the doctor. I do not want to see a doctor. You can nurse me, can you not? I have been through this before – there is not much the doctor can do in any case.' Georgia clutched at the bed sheets and pulled them up to her chin, her brown eyes huge and scared. She looked like a frightened doe. Once again, Agnes felt a pang of grief for her mistress and the trauma she was going through. But it had to be done.

'Very well, ma'am. If you insist.' Agnes poured her a glass of water and set it on the bedside table. 'I will tell your husband that you are unwell when he comes down for breakfast. Sleep now. I will bring you some laudanum for the pain.'

My dear Barty, you are wondering, are you not, how I can tell the tale of Georgia and Agnes conniving to keep this second pregnancy and its loss a secret from me. Well, the truth is that Agnes's loyalties lay principally with me during this time, and not with her mistress. She told me, that same morning, what

111

had happened. I had not known until then that my wife was with child. But while I sat drinking coffee and eating kippers with toast, Agnes perched on a stool beside me and told me of the chat on the Old Steine gardens bench. She told me too of the anti-sickness potion she gave Georgia, though it is my own, much later supposition, that the potion contained more than just ginger, and may have been the cause of the two miscarriages.

Poor sweet Georgia. So trusting of Agnes, that scheming witch. Though back in 1838, as you know, I was still completely besotted with Agnes. It was to be a considerable time yet before I saw her true nature.

There was a third pregnancy, and a third miscarriage, less than a year later. This one ruined our Christmas celebrations, as Georgia kept once more to her room, recovering. It too was kept secret from me by Georgia, but told to me by Agnes. And this time, did I see a glint of triumph in her eye as she told me? Was there a satisfied air about her, knowing of her power over both master and mistress? Our lives were in her hands. She had destroyed three of our potential children.

Or perhaps I am now super-imposing those thoughts on my memories, given my knowledge of the terrible events that were to come later.

I must rest a while now, and resume writing this manuscript when I feel a little stronger. When I resume it, we will skip forward a little, to the autumn of 1840. We had stayed living primarily in Brighton throughout this period, while I took occasional short business trips to London. My finances were at last in order, thanks to Georgia's money. Charles Holland was in decline. I did not expect him to last another winter. But it was not his health, or Georgia's failed pregnancies, that were my chief concern in the final quarter of 1840. No, it was the news, whispered to me one night while I partook of the pleasures of Agnes's body, that our precautions had failed, and that Agnes was with child.

Chapter Ten

Hampshire, May 2013

On the morning after the storm the full extent of the damage was evident. The tree, thankfully, had fallen across the garden rather than directly onto the house. Just that one lower branch had gone through the kitchen window, and another had caught on the guttering and brought it down. The tree had flattened part of the fence on the left-hand side of our garden, and its uppermost branches were entangled in next-door's rotary washing line – one of the houses in Stables Close. Its roots, typically for a beech tree, had been wide and shallow. They had toppled the old garden wall: about ten metres of it behind the tree had fallen and lay crumbling across the lawn and driveway. The kids' trampoline was a write-off; the tree trunk had fallen directly across it and had crushed it flat.

We all stood in the dining room, surveying the scene with open mouths.

'Can I go out, Dad? And climb in the branches?' Lewis tugged at Simon's arm.

'Not yet, let me check if it is safe first. Katie, we'll have to find a tree surgeon to come and help us deal with this. And get on to the insurance company. We need to get that kitchen window boarded up today.' Simon was already making a list of stuff to do.

'All in good time,' I said. 'How about we have breakfast first? I've got some sausages to cook.'

Simon shook his head. 'The kitchen's unusable, until I cut off that branch and clear up all the glass and leaves. Look, you can't get anywhere near the grill.'

I grinned. I'd already thought of that. 'I'll get the camping stove out.'

Lewis high-fived me. 'Great idea, Mum!'

While I set up a camp kitchen in the dining room and fried the sausages, Simon donned a pair of wellies and went out to survey our wrecked garden. Lewis watched from the kitchen door, hopping excitedly until he was allowed to go out. Lauren had discovered that the best view of the fallen tree was from her bedroom window. She climbed up on the windowsill and tucked herself behind the curtain to watch. Thomas was grumpy from his broken night's sleep and after staring wide-eyed at the branch in the kitchen declared he wanted to do nothing but watch CBeebies for the morning. That suited everyone, so on went the TV.

'It's going to take some major chopping up,' Simon announced, when he came back in for his breakfast.

'Can I climb on it first?'

'Yes, Lewis. I reckon it's safe enough. When you've eaten, and helped Mum clear up.'

'Yes!' Lewis punched the air.

'Can I, too?' asked Lauren.

'Sure. Put old clothes on,' I said.

They had a great time among the branches all morning. I helped Simon saw through the branch which had come through the kitchen window, and soon we were able to tug that clear,

114

sweep up the broken glass, leaves and twigs, and get the kitchen back into use. The kids were making a den in the upper branches of the tree. Soon they were covered in scratches, their clothes filthy and wet but their faces glowing and happy. Even Thomas came out to join them after a while, and Lewis helped haul him up onto the tree trunk, and steadied him as he walked along it, ducking around the branches.

We got the window boarded up, and a promise from a glazier to fix it properly within the week. The tree surgeon couldn't come until Monday at the earliest – he was overwhelmed with work following the storm. Lewis didn't see why we had to have the tree cut up at all.

'Can't we just leave it? Like in the New Forest, they just leave trees where they fall, and let them rot. Much more environmentally friendly.'

I smiled at his latest buzzwords. 'Lewis, if we don't cut up the tree, we've got no garden. Nowhere to kick a football. Nowhere to sit in the sun or have a barbecue. It has to go. Make the most of playing in it this weekend.'

And they did. The sun stayed out for the rest of the weekend, and the kids stayed out with it. I almost began to think like Lewis – let's leave the tree where it is. But our neighbours, Stan and Eileen, came round, asking when we would get the tree removed, pointing out the damage to their beloved dahlias and roses, not to mention the fence and rotary clothes line. They'd looked cross when they first called, but when they saw the damage to our kitchen and the wreck of our back garden, they softened.

'Bless you, that's some clear-up task you've got ahead of you,' Eileen said, shaking her head at the flattened trampoline.

'Well, if you need access to our side, you've only got to ring the bell,' said Stan. 'We'll be in all week. Your tree surgeon can come down the side passage if he needs to.'

'Thanks. Who owns the fence on that side?'

'That one's ours,' said Stan. 'Soon as you've got the tree sorted we'll deal with the fence. The insurance'll cover it. Come on, Eileen, best leave these poor folk to their work.'

We spent a few more hours tidying and clearing up, doing what we could. By mid-afternoon there was no more we could do. Simon joined Thomas making a complicated layout of wooden Brio train track in the sitting room, while the older children retreated into their Nintendos. I had a few free hours before it was time to cook the dinner.

'I'm off for a walk around the village,' I told Simon. 'Just to see whether there's any more trees down, or anything.' I needed to clear my head. Despite the drama of last night I still could not put Simon's evasiveness about his late nights, or the mystery of that letter, out of my mind.

He looked up from the floor where he was coupling various engines and trucks together for Thomas to push around the track. 'Buy some milk while you're out, will you? We're short.'

'And some sweeties for me?' piped up Thomas.

'Sure.' I blew them both a kiss, and set off on my walk.

There were several branches strewn across the village roads, and a couple of trees down in other gardens. The pavements were littered with smashed roof tiles, and I spotted a few wheelie bins in odd places, rammed into hedges, wrapped around lamp posts and at least two in the pond on the village green. Everyone was out sweeping their bits of pavement, picking up the rubbish and hauling pieces of tree out of the roads. People I'd not yet spoken to nodded and smiled at me as I passed, and commented on the damage. The old British Blitz spirit: we only ever talk to strangers when we're pulling together in the face of adversity.

In the village Co-op, everyone was talking about the storm, and the chaos it had brought.

'There are no trains running,' said one man. 'A tree's down across the line just outside North Kingsley station. Just hope they sort that out before Monday morning.'

I hoped so too, or Simon would have to drive to work. He'd hate that.

A tweed-clad woman shook her head. 'Terrible. And the church roof took some damage. Lots of tiles down. The vicar'll be wanting to start a church roof fund, I reckon. I'll have to host a coffee morning.'

I smiled. What a cliché: raising money to pay for a new church roof. Still, this was a small community and the church was at the heart of it. I decided to go up and see how badly it had been hit. Maybe I could look for Bartholomew and Georgia's graves, too, while I was there.

The church was tucked in behind the high street. You could go round by the road or cut up through an alleyway next to the White Hart. I took the alleyway, which brought me out at the back of the churchyard. A path led through a lych gate and wound its way among the graves and round the side of the church.

There were indeed some roof tiles down, smashed on the paths and graves, but not as many as the tweedy woman had suggested. I glanced up at the roof. To my untrained eye it looked repairable. She wouldn't have to hold too many coffee mornings to put that right.

So, how do you find a grave, among so many? Bartholomew and Georgia had both died in the 1870s. Would their graves even be readable after so many years? I wished I'd printed off the plan of the churchyard from the CD. I vaguely recalled that the St Clair plot was at the top end of the churchyard, so I headed up that way first.

I began reading the inscriptions on the graves either side of the path, then more systematically worked my way up and down the churchyard, scanning the graves for the name 'St Clair'. Some stones were badly weathered, their inscriptions worn smooth and unreadable. Some looked as though they'd been carved yesterday, even though they were a hundred years old or more. I guessed it depended on the type of stone used.

One corner of the churchyard was in good condition – no weeds, the grass cut neatly, and the graves cleaned of lichen and moss. A notice pinned to a board, blown over by the storm, announced the work of the St Michael's Churchyard Restoration Society. They met every Wednesday afternoon, apparently: new volunteers most welcome, just turn up at two ready to work, refreshments provided. The cleaned graves were a little clinical looking for my taste; I rather preferred the unkempt look of the untended graves. But if I didn't find Bartholomew and Georgia today it might be worth coming to have a chat to the society.

There were no St Clair graves in the restored section. I moved back into the untended part, and pushed my way through the long grasses and thistles to check the inscriptions.

Finally, I found them. They lay side by side, Bartholomew on the left, his stone tilted slightly left, and Georgia's tilted right. It was almost as though in death they were trying to keep apart from each other. Bartholomew's stone read: *In loving memory of Bartholomew St Clair. Departed this life December 19th 1876. 'For all my wrongs I do repent.'* And in smaller letters, at the bottom: *This stone erected by his son, B. St Clair. May the Lord forgive you.* Georgia's was simpler: *Georgia St Clair. Died April 14th 1875. Forever mourned.*

Here they were, my great-great-great-grandparents. Bartholomew presumably had dictated the words on Georgia's gravestone. Forever mourned – now there was a love story in those two simple words. They'd been married for over thirty-five years and how he must have missed her when she died.

His own gravestone was more puzzling. I guessed he'd requested before his death for the words 'For all my wrongs I do repent' to be put on his grave. And then Barty had felt the need to implore God to forgive his father.

I traced the words with my fingers. What were those wrongs? What had Bartholomew done that was so bad he needed to plead for forgiveness on his gravestone? As on so many occasions before,

118

I wished I could go back in time and be a fly upon the wall, watching their lives unfold, and knowing for certain what happened and why.

It was Tuesday before the tree surgeons could come to make a start on removing the beech. Lewis and Lauren were at school, and I'd dropped Thomas off at his nursery class by the time they arrived. The day was chilly and overcast, but at least no rain was forecast.

'Ted the Tree' was a scrawny looking man of indeterminate age, with wiry muscles and a wispy beard. Dressed in shorts, torn T-shirt and a tool-belt, he wielded his enormous chainsaw as though it were a carving knife. I was glad the kids weren't around to get in his way. His sidekick Jamie was a young lad of nineteen or twenty, tall and skinny, whose job it was to drag away the cut-off branches, feed the smaller stuff into a shredder and pile the larger pieces ready for cutting up into firewood. They were a good team, working efficiently, and by lunchtime most of the branches were gone, leaving just the main trunk of the tree stretched across the garden, plus its enormous roots pointing skyward beside the remains of the garden wall.

I took cups of tea and a plate of biscuits out to the men, as they sat on the trunk to eat their lunchtime sandwiches.

'Cheers,' said Ted. 'Such a shame, this tree must have been a right beaut.'

'It was,' I agreed. 'The kids loved climbing it, too. My husband was considering building them a tree house in it.'

Ted grimaced. I got the impression he didn't approve of tree houses. 'You'll have a right big hole when we get those roots out.'

'Mmm. And a wall to rebuild.'

'Yeah. Reckon a bit more of it'll fall when we cut those roots. See how they're wedged up against it? We can't take the rubble away, missus. You'll need a skip for that.'

'That's OK. I think we'll keep the old bricks and see if they can be reused.'

119

Ted sniffed. 'I'd put a smart new fence in, meself.'

I gave him a non-committal smile and passed the biscuits. Not everyone appreciated old things the way I did. But those bricks – they'd been there two hundred years or more. Of course I wanted to keep them and rebuild the wall if we could!

The men spent the afternoon attacking the main trunk with their chainsaws. Gradually the tree grew smaller and smaller until there was just a ten-foot section of trunk and the fan of roots left. Jamie dragged the trashed trampoline down to the end of the garden, out of the way. They worked on the root ball then, cutting off what they could, and digging underneath on the side the tree had fallen, where the roots were still buried in the earth.

I left them to it while I went to fetch the children from school. The kids were excited to get home and find the huge pile of logs, ready to be turned into firewood, which filled half our driveway. I warned them not to climb on the precarious-looking pile, and went to check on Ted's progress.

I found him standing on the edge of the root-crater, while Jamie knelt at the bottom, scrabbling in the dirt with his hands.

'How's it going?' I asked.

Ted pointed in the hole. 'Found something. Down there. Jamie's just checking it out, now.'

'What is it?' I peered down.

'Bones,' said Jamie. 'Probably a dog or something. All mixed up in the roots of this tree.'

I shuddered. Someone's pet, buried at the foot of the tree.

'Collect them up,' I said. 'I'll rebury them somewhere further down the garden.'

Jamie pulled out a couple of pieces of bone and laid them on the side of the hole. He began pulling at another piece whose end was just visible in the tangle of roots. It came free suddenly, and we all stood staring in shock at what he was holding.

I'm no expert on bones, but it looked to me unmistakably like a human femur.

Ted gasped. 'Jesus! That's no dog. Pass it here, lad.'

Jamie dropped the bone as though it was burning him and scrambled out of the hole, wiping his filthy hands on the back of his jeans.

Ted picked it up and examined it. 'Well, that's a first, in all my working life. Never come across no human bones before.'

'Do you reckon there's more?' I asked.

'Can't imagine only a leg was buried, so yep, I'd say there's more.'

I felt sick. Human remains, in our garden, where our kids had been playing! 'Oh God. What do we do?'

'Best call the police, I'd say. Don't worry, they're not going to think you've done away with your husband or anything like that.' Ted laughed, pleased with his own joke.

'Mummy, why do we need to call the police?'

I hadn't noticed Lauren, who'd come out through the kitchen door and was standing behind me, her eyes wide and worried.

'Back inside, love. There's some chocolate cake left if you'd like a slice. Cut some for the boys too, would you?'

'What's that? Is it a bone?' Lewis had appeared beside his sister. Thomas, too.

'Inside, the lot of you,' I said, and shooed them back through the kitchen door. I sent them through to the living room, with instructions to put a DVD on.

There's always a danger with family tree research that you might unearth a skeleton in your family's closet. But a real skeleton, buried in the garden of a house owned for most of its history by your ancestors? I shuddered. Who was it, and how had he or she come to be buried there?

Chapter Eleven

Brighton, October 1840

Bartholomew paced up and down in the study of his Brighton house. Really, Agnes allowing herself to become pregnant was too much. She'd always assured him she knew how to prevent it, and that she wouldn't get caught. Bartholomew knew she pushed some sort of sponge soaked in vinegar up inside herself before they made love but had left it all up to her.

And now the woman was pregnant. He sat down at his writing desk and drummed his fingers. What was he to do? No, what was *Agnes* to do. One thing was for certain, he was not going to bring up the maid's child as his own. He'd provide for it if necessary, but it would not live in his house. Assuming it lived at all...

He stopped drumming his fingers and stared at the wall. There was a thought. Did the pregnancy need to continue? Agnes's mother was a midwife as well as a herbalist – surely Agnes had picked up a few tricks on how to be rid of an unwanted baby? Yes, that was the best answer for everyone. And maybe soon Georgia would be pregnant again and would manage to keep the child this time. It was such a shame that it was his wife and not his mistress who suffered recurrent miscarriages. In an ideal world his wife would bear a string of healthy children while his mistress remained barren.

There was a tap at the door. 'Come in,' he called.

Agnes entered the room, her head held high. Her cheeks were more rounded than usual, and her figure was beginning to swell. Whatever they were going to do about this baby they needed to do soon, before anyone, Georgia especially, noticed.

'Sir, you wanted to see me? I should warn you, your wife is in the drawing room and might hear us, if we make too much noise.' She stepped close to him and raised her face to kiss him.

He pushed her away. 'I have not summoned you to my study for…that. That is for the privacy of my bedchamber. Was last night not enough for you?'

She blushed and took a step away. 'Last night was, as always, magnificent. I do believe it is better than ever now that I am with child.'

He coughed. 'That is what I wish to speak to you about. You know, of course, that you cannot continue with this pregnancy while you live here. Soon it will start to show, and people will gossip. Georgia, especially, is likely to guess and I cannot allow that to happen.'

She blanched and sat down on a fireside chair. Without asking permission, he noted.

'Sir, do not send me away. I – I love you, I think you know that, and it would break my heart to be away from you.' She gazed up at him with eyes as green and wide as Georgia's.

'I am afraid I must send you away. You cannot stay here when you begin to swell. The only other option…'

'Yes?'

'Is if somehow you lost the baby. As my poor wife has lost all hers.' He held her gaze as he said this.

She gasped. 'Do you mean for me to lose the baby deliberately?'

123

'Perhaps your mother knows how this can be achieved. I think we could spare you to pay her a visit. You could stay with her for a fortnight. It must be many years since you last saw her.'

'Sir, I do not want to visit my mother. Besides I know all her methods…'

'In that case…'

'…but I must be clear about this.' She stood up and looked him directly in the eye. 'I do not wish to lose this baby. I wish to carry the baby to term and give birth to him. Whether or not you will acknowledge the child as your own.' She sat down heavily again and covered her face with her hands. 'Forgive me for speaking so bluntly.'

Bartholomew straightened his back and hardened his eyes. 'If you insist on having this baby, you must go away from here. Soon.'

'I will go to my ma's after all, then. And when the baby is born? Will I be welcome here? Will I still have a job?'

'Yes. You may return.'

'And my baby?'

'You will leave it with your mother, or with some other charitable soul. You will not bring the child back here.'

She stared at him. 'You're forcing me to choose between my child and you.'

He did not answer, but held her gaze, keeping his eyes steely. She was but his mistress, a plaything, albeit one he was besotted with. But that did not mean he had to acknowledge any brat of hers as his own.

She sniffed haughtily. 'And, pray, how will my ma afford to feed and clothe the child?'

'I will send five guineas a year. There is nothing more to discuss. I wish you to leave this house within the week.'

'A week!' Agnes clutched at his arm. 'But what will I say to my mistress? You know how she depends upon me for everything.'

He prised her fingers off his sleeve. 'We will say that your

124

mother is ill and has sent for you to nurse her. And that I have given you leave to stay with her until she is completely well again. While you are away, Polly can do your duties, and Mrs Simmonds can employ another housemaid.'

Agnes spoke quietly. 'If I do return, will we continue as before?'

Bartholomew turned away. 'We shall see.'

Agnes pursed her lips together. 'Very well. Excuse me, sir, for I have duties to attend to now.' She left the room, without waiting for his permission.

He sighed and sat down heavily in the chair in front of his desk. He would miss her; at least he would miss the comfort he found in her arms. But while she was away he knew he must wean himself off her. He was married, to a good woman who deserved better treatment. He must work hard at his marriage to try to make it a successful one. Keeping the affair with Agnes going would do his marriage no good at all. The forthcoming separation from her would be the perfect opportunity to focus more attention on his wife, and perhaps, finally learn to love her, as she deserved.

Agnes strode quickly up the two flights of stairs to her room at the top of the house. How dare he! How could he send her away like this, and refuse to accept his child? He'd more or less told her to abort it. He'd made it clear she could have either the child or her job, but not both. And *he* came with the job. At least he had, but even that seemed uncertain now.

She sat down on the bentwood chair in her little room and buried her face in her hands to think. What was she to do? She would not, *could* not abort this baby. It was part of her, and part of him. It was made from their union, which made it special, sacred. Finally she understood what she'd put Georgia through. The thought of losing her baby was unimaginable. So there was only one option for the short term, and that was to go to her ma's as arranged, and have the baby there.

Maybe, in her absence he would come to realise how much

he felt for her. Maybe he would bore of his wife in that time. And when she came back he would cast off his wife to be with her. She would then persuade him to reclaim their child... Yes. If she played her hand right, she could sort this situation out.

Three days later, Bartholomew came to her room at night. It was the first time she had been alone with him since he'd told her she was to leave. She smiled as he entered the room, but what she really wanted to do was shout and scream at him. Did he not love her? Did he not want her any more? How *could* he send her away?

They made love on her narrow wooden bed. She clung to him, relishing the feel of his weight on her, the warmth of his breath on her neck. He would change his mind. After doing this, how could he even think of parting with her? When it was over, she sighed with pleasure and nestled into his arms.

But he pushed her off, got up from the bed and rebuttoned his breeches. 'I cannot stay here any longer,' he said. 'I only came to tell you I have booked you a place on the coach to London for the morning. You can change there to catch one to Lincoln. I shall give you ample money to get you home to your mother's. Pack your things tonight.'

In the morning, her box packed, Agnes went to help Georgia dress for the last time. Georgia was sitting on her bed, her eyes red-ringed. As soon as Agnes came in, she leapt to her feet and clutched at Agnes's hands.

'Aggie, dear Aggie, Bartholomew tells me you are leaving us! How can this be?'

Agnes remembered the lie Bartholomew had instructed her to tell, and spoke it woodenly. 'It is my mother, ma'am. She has been taken poorly and is asking for me to go to help her.'

'So it will be just a few days, until she is recovered?'

'I fear it will be longer.'

'A week?'

'Perhaps, or a month, or...'

126

'No! I forbid it! You can stay a fortnight and no longer. Your mother can hire some nurse to look after her.'

'My mother cannot afford a nurse…'

'You have sisters? They can nurse her.'

'They have families of their own, ma'am.'

'And so do you! You have me. I cannot spare you.' Georgia turned her back on her maid like a petulant child.

Agnes swallowed a sigh and stepped forward to put a hand on her mistress's shoulder. 'I shall come back as soon as I can. My mother might recover quickly or might even die. I shall not stay longer than I have to, I promise.' That part was true at least. As soon as the baby was born and a wet-nurse found, she would return to Bartholomew and find a way to persuade him to accept her child.

Georgia spun around and slapped Agnes's hand from her shoulder. 'You don't understand! I need you here, *now*. I – I am with child again. How can I manage the pregnancy without your help? I shall soon start feeling sick again and will be in need of your potions. And if…if I should lose the baby again, I shall need you to nurse *me*.'

Agnes suppressed a gasp. This was bad timing indeed. 'You will be all right without me, ma'am. Perhaps this baby will hold. Mrs Simmonds can make you some ginger biscuits which will ease your sickness. I will instruct her before I go.'

'No, don't tell her. She will tell my husband. And I must keep it secret from him, as before, in case I lose the baby. Oh, how will I ever manage? Two weeks – you must and shall come back to me within two weeks. Promise me that, dear Aggie?'

'I shall do my best…'

'Do not abandon me!'

'Very well, I promise…'

Georgia flung her arms about Agnes's neck. 'Thank you, thank you. I know you will not let me down. You are my very best friend, dear Aggie, and so kind to rush to your mother's side in her hour of need. Rush back to me, in mine – that is all I ask!'

Three hours later, Agnes was on the stagecoach heading northwards. As the coach bumped and jolted along the rutted road, she felt the first, unmistakable movement of the baby in her womb. Instinctively she put a hand over it and smiled to herself. She would make a future for herself and this child, one way or another.

Bartholomew frowned as he watched Georgia pushing her food around her plate. It looked as though she had eaten nothing of this dinner. And she'd barely touched her breakfast this morning, having had only a bite of toast before hurriedly excusing herself and rushing from the room. She was missing Agnes, he knew, but surely that couldn't be making her ill? The maid had been gone three weeks now, but as far as he could see, Polly had been doing a perfectly adequate job. Really, he did not run the sort of household which required a dedicated lady's maid. Georgia would have to learn to do without.

Georgia laid down her knife and fork and pushed her plate away. 'I'm afraid I'm not very hungry.'

'Are you ill? You have barely eaten anything all day.' He looked at her with concern.

'I – I'm quite all right. I just have no appetite for the meat and vegetables. Perhaps I'll try a little pudding, later.'

'Some wine, my dear?'

Georgia blanched. 'No, thank you. I'm afraid wine seems to turn my stomach these days.'

He frowned again. 'There is something wrong. You are keeping something from me.'

She sighed, and looked down at her lap. He waited patiently, recognising that it was best not to push her too hard for an explanation.

'Very well. I will confess it – I am with child. But I fear that I might lose it as I did before. Agnes helped me so much then, and now she is not here I am frightened.'

She looked up at him, her eyes wide and glistening with tears.

128

He felt a surge of tenderness for her. 'Oh my love, that is such marvellous news!'

He pushed back his chair and went to kneel beside her, taking her hands in his. She was carrying his child, and this time maybe the pregnancy would – *must* – succeed.

'I have been so sick, Bartholomew. Every morning. It is horrible!'

'All women are sick in the early stages, as I understand it, my dear. You must be strong, and bear it.' He kissed her fingers.

'When it happened before, Agnes made me potions to stop it. Oh, when will she return? She has been gone three weeks now, but she promised me she would stay away no longer than a fortnight.'

'My love, her mother is gravely ill…'

'But she promised me! Oh Bartholomew, will you write to her and urge her to come back soon?'

He shook his head. 'It would do no good. She cannot read, remember?'

'She will ask her local reverend to read the letter. She said that is what people in her village always do when they receive letters.'

He patted her hand, and stood up, brushing the knees of his trousers. 'She will come back when her mother no longer needs her, I am sure. Until then, do you wish for me to employ another maid? Is Polly not adequate?'

Georgia sniffed. 'Polly does the job well enough but Agnes, well, she is more like a friend than a servant.'

Bartholomew pressed his lips together for a moment and returned to his seat. 'My dear, it does no good to become so attached to a servant. What if she decided not to return to us? What if she found herself a job elsewhere? Or found herself a husband? She's only a maid. A good one, I grant you, but only a servant.' And it would do you good to remember that yourself, he told himself.

The door opened and Polly came in with the pudding. It was

a jam sponge, with a jug of custard. She placed it on the sideboard and cleared away the dinner plates. Bartholomew and Georgia watched her in silence, Georgia sniffing slightly and dabbing at her eyes with a lace-edged handkerchief.

When Polly had served their pudding and left the room, Bartholomew smiled at his wife. 'Now then, this looks good, doesn't it? Please try to eat a little. You must keep your strength up, for the sake of the baby. And we'll have no more talk of Agnes. She might return or she might not, but I don't want you to fret about it. You have Polly to see to your needs and me as your friend.'

Georgia smiled weakly at him and picked up her spoon. He was pleased. With Agnes out of the way and a baby coming, perhaps their marriage would become stronger and maybe he'd begin to love her the way he felt a husband should.

It was a long cold winter. Georgia was sick for a couple of months and then, as her condition started to show, the sickness subsided. During the middle months of her pregnancy she glowed with health – her cheeks were plump and pink, her hair glossy. It suited her. Bartholomew found himself more and more attracted to her. He began spending many more nights in her room, and took pleasure in her swelling body. Georgia seemed to enjoy making love with him more than she had done before, and their increased intimacy made them both happy. They stopped going out or having visitors, and settled into a comfortable routine of sitting beside the fire in the evenings, reading to each other or playing cards, before going up to spend the night in Georgia's room.

It was late February when the black-edged envelope arrived, brought in by Mrs Simmonds while Bartholomew and Georgia were lingering over their coffee in the breakfast room.

Georgia put down her cup with a clatter. 'Oh, no, my uncle? Has he…?'

'I think not. Such news would have been hand-delivered. This has come by the mail-coach.' Bartholomew picked up a letter knife and slid it under the seal. He quickly read the letter.

It was his father. Though they had not been close for many years, Bartholomew still felt a pang of pain at the news of his passing. The letter had been written by his father's solicitor, Frederick Fitzwilliam. Mr St Clair had apparently been out riding when he'd had a seizure, and had fallen from his horse. He'd probably been dead by the time he hit the ground, so said the doctor who'd inspected the body after he'd been brought back to his house.

'Who, dear?' Georgia gazed at him with wide, worried eyes.

'My father.'

'Oh, love, I am so sorry!' She heaved herself to her feet and hurried around the table to stand behind him, her swollen belly pressed against the back of his head. Her hand was on his shoulder, and Bartholomew reached up to hold it.

'We were not close, as you must be aware. He chose not to attend our wedding.'

'I know, but still. He was your father.'

Bartholomew nodded. 'Yes, and I was his only son. And his heir.'

'Do you inherit?'

'His Hampshire estate. It is small, but pleasantly situated, on the edge of a village north of Winchester. It is where I grew up. I shall sell it, of course.'

'But why? Could we not live there?' asked Georgia. 'Maybe just for part of each year? You know I always preferred the country life. I grew up in the wide open spaces of the Lincolnshire fens. Hampshire has always sounded to me like such a pretty county. And I've always thought the country is the best place in which to bring up a child.' She took his hand and placed it on her belly, where Bartholomew felt the baby kick as though in agreement with its mother.

Bartholomew rubbed his chin. He'd never considered returning to Hampshire. But she was right: now that they were to become a family, a small country estate might be a more suitable home than a seaside apartment or London townhouse. The house would need work, of course, but he could afford it if he used some of Georgia's inheritance and gave up the lease on the Brighton apartment.

'Well, my dear, if it's what you want. I will need to go there this week for my father's funeral and to sort out his affairs. Perhaps after the baby is born we could…'

'Why not before? I could come with you to the funeral, to support you.'

'Surely you should not travel in your condition, my love?'

Georgia raised her chin in a determined little gesture that Bartholomew knew all too well. It usually meant that she'd made up her mind and would do all that she could in her own sweet way, to get what she wanted.

'I'm perfectly able to travel. Dr Stockett says the baby won't come for another three or four weeks. It's not too far to Hampshire, in any case. We could get there in a day.' She smiled at him, and draped an arm around his shoulders. 'Besides, I would very much like our baby to be born in the country. I do believe village midwives are better than town ones. And think of all that fresh, country air! It would do me so much good. Brighton is so busy these days, it is becoming quite polluted and will soon be as bad as London.'

'Well, if you're determined, love. I shall write to the housekeeper there immediately and let her know we are coming. We'll leave the day after tomorrow. But I shall go alone to the funeral – the stress would not be good for you.'

She bent down to kiss him, clearly pleased with this arrangement. He pulled her onto his lap, and wrapped his arms around her and the baby. He would become a country gentleman, spending his days riding and shooting. And soon he would become a father.

Chapter Twelve

Hampshire, May 2013

It was hard to explain to the police, when I phoned them. Bones in the garden. Buried beneath a tree that had fallen in the storm. The policewoman I spoke to asked why I was certain the bones were human. I told her about the femur. She was tapping away on a keyboard as I spoke, and told me a police car would be with me within an hour.

As I put the phone down, I realised Lewis was at the kitchen door. His eyes were wide.

'Wow, Mum, who do you reckon it is? Maybe a Roman legionary soldier? Or a Saxon king? Or maybe someone who used to live in this house before us?'

'We've no idea how old the bones are. Or even if they are human.'

'You said on the phone they were definitely human.'

'Well, that was to get the police to come and look. We don't really know. Maybe it's a deer?'

At that moment Ted tapped on the back door and put his head inside. 'Better come and look at this, Mrs Smith.'

I followed him outside, pushed Lewis back in and shut the door. Jamie was sitting on a garden chair staring in horror at the crater. Ted pointed into it.

'I went back down to scrabble around a bit more. Definitely human.'

It was a skull. Roots grew through the eye sockets and the back of it had broken away, but it was recognisably a skull. I felt sick and yet fascinated at the same time.

'The police are coming in an hour or so. I think we'd better not disturb it any more.' I nodded towards Jamie. 'We'd better take him inside. Looks like he needs a good strong cup of sweet tea.'

'Aye. Come on, lad. Tea's on offer.'

While they drank their tea, Ted told Lewis, who simply would *not* go and watch Disney while a real-life adventure was unfolding in his own back garden, all the gory details. I called Simon and filled him in on what had happened. He said he'd get home as soon as he could. No late meetings today, then. It clearly took a crisis to get him home at a reasonable hour.

The police, when they arrived, consisted of a middle-aged sergeant with a beer-gut, and a lanky youthful constable who looked as if he could be Jamie's twin. Both yawned as they walked through the house and I felt like apologising for keeping them up.

Their attitude changed as soon as they saw the skull.

'Bloody hell, missus,' said the older one. 'We thought it would be animal bones. That's definitely human. Gonna have to call in CID.'

'I did say on the phone they were human bones,' I protested.

He didn't answer that but went out to his police car to radio the detectives. Meanwhile, lanky constable pulled a reel of tape from a pocket and began cordoning off our garden.

I called Simon again. The phone went straight to voicemail. 'I hope you're on your way home,' I told him. 'Half our garden is now being treated as a crime scene.'

'Do you carry a gun?' Lewis asked the constable.

'Ha, no!'

'Not even sometimes? When there's a murder going on, and the murderer has got all the rest of the family trapped inside a house as hostages and won't let anyone come in or out? Don't you have to hide in the bushes in the garden and stake him out till he gets nervous and either comes out or shoots himself?'

'Kid, you've been watching too much TV.'

'Lewis, leave the policeman to do his job.' I ushered him back inside for the hundredth time that day. Lauren and Thomas had given up on the DVD and were standing in the hallway, wide-eyed and silent.

'Mum, what's happening?' asked Lauren, her eyes sparkling with tears.

I decided to come clean. Better they should know and understand there would be no harm come to them, than have them scare themselves with their overactive imaginations.

'Under the tree, the workmen found some bones. They're probably very old, but we think they might be human.'

'Or chimpanzee,' said Lewis. 'Their skeleton is just like ours.'

'Well, OK, or chimpanzee. In any case, because they might be human, we had to tell the police, so they can investigate.'

Lauren frowned. 'Someone got buried in our garden under the tree?'

'Looks that way.'

'How did they get buried *under* the tree?'

'Perhaps they were buried before the tree was planted. I said they were old.'

Thomas slipped his little hand into mine. 'Are skeletons the same as ghosts?'

'No, sweetie. There are no ghosts here. Just a few old bones.' I glared at Lewis as I answered Thomas, before he got any bright ideas about scaring his brother.

'Whoever it was,' said Lewis, 'they were murdered.'

'Well, no, we don't know that it was a murder…'

"Cos why else would the body be buried in the garden? Has to be a murder, doesn't it, Mum? Someone who lived here killed a visitor or a servant or something, and then hid the body so they wouldn't get caught and have to be hanged.' Lewis looked triumphant.

Lauren stared up at me. 'Is he right, Mum? Was it a murder? If you get murdered you become a ghost, so's you can avenge your death!'

'No ghost!' Thomas wailed. I scooped him up and he began sobbing on my shoulder.

'Right, kids, that's quite enough. There's no such thing as ghosts and even if there was, there are none here. So, I don't want to hear any more mention of them. All right?'

'Sorry, Mum. Sorry, Thomas.' Lauren stroked Thomas's arm. He kicked out at her, and carried on sobbing.

'Come on, how about you all go back to that DVD while I talk to the policemen. Off you go, now. Lewis, get everyone a chocolate biscuit.'

'Yay!' Lewis punched the air and scampered off to the kitchen for the biscuits. Sometimes children are so easy to please. I put Thomas down, and Lauren put her arm around him and led him back into the sitting room. She was clearly feeling guilty about scaring him so much.

I sat in the kitchen and considered what Lewis had said. If it was murder, perpetrated by someone who'd lived here, then it was quite possibly something to do with my ancestors. I shuddered. This wasn't quite the kind of family history you really want to find.

The detective arrived five minutes later, and introduced himself as DI Bradley. He was tall and wiry, with close-cropped red hair. He shook my hand with a firm grip and I instantly liked him.

'So, Mrs Smith, you've dug up a skeleton in your flower bed, I hear?'

'Something like that,' I laughed nervously. 'Come and see.'

The sergeant showed him the findings. A photographer had come along with DI Bradley. She took several photos of the tree, its root ball, the bones Ted and Jamie had pulled out and the ones still in the hole. When she was finished, DI Bradley pulled on a pair of latex gloves and knelt down beside the pile of bones on the edge of the hole.

'Human.'

The fat sergeant rolled his eyes.

'Yes, sir. Which is why we called you in.'

'Old.'

'I'd say so, yes.'

DI Bradley stood up. 'We'll get the bones carbon-dated by forensics. We can also look at dendrochronology, to determine the age of the tree, which will tell us the minimum age for the bones.' He smiled, and regarded the remains of the trunk. 'But I reckon we're looking at something at least a hundred years old. No danger of you being implicated in any way. Nonetheless, we have to check it out.'

'Of course. We only moved in about a month ago.'

'If you have contact details for the previous owners, I may need to talk to them.'

I nodded. 'But if the skeleton is a hundred years old it goes back before their time too.'

Back to Barty St Clair's time, I thought. Suddenly, I remembered what Vera had said about the eccentric Barty. Did he have something to do with it? Had he buried the body, and was that why he never let anyone into the house? Somehow, finding the skeleton was bringing the past into the present. Those people from my family tree research, who had only been names on census returns and birth, marriage or death certificates till now, were taking shape, and in a rather alarming way.

'Are you all right, Mrs Smith? You look a little pale.' DI Bradley put his hand on my arm. I realised I was shaking slightly.

'I'm fine. It's just a bit of a shock, that's all. Even though it's clearly very old.' I opened my mouth to say something more, something about my ancestors having lived here, then thought better of it. I still hadn't told Simon what I knew of the house's history.

He nodded. 'We'll have to do a bit more digging, I'm afraid, to retrieve all the bones. You won't be able to use your garden until we've finished.'

'That's all right. As you can see, we can't use it anyway until the tree's been disposed of.'

'That'll keep you in firewood for a couple of winters, I'd say.'

'Yes. At least one good thing has come of this tree falling.'

'Finding the bones is a good thing, too,' DI Bradley said, gently. 'Once we've finished dating them we can arrange for a proper reburial or cremation. Lay the poor soul to rest at last.'

I turned away and went back inside, before he noticed the tears welling up in my eyes.

As I entered the house I heard a car outside, then the sound of the front door opening. Simon was back. I rushed through to the hallway and hugged him tightly. He kissed my hair and patted my back. It had taken a macabre discovery to get him home early, and away from his mistress if there was one, but right now I needed the comfort of his embrace.

'Katie, it's OK, I'm here now. What's happened? Are the bones human?'

'Yes, definitely.' I took a deep breath and blinked a couple of times. 'We've got a detective here now. They're going to carbon-date the bones but they're probably over a hundred years old, judging by their position under the tree.'

'Wow, fascinating! What do the kids think?'

'Thomas is scared there might be ghosts again, the other two are as thrilled at the adventure as you seem to be. Come on, come and see for yourself.'

As we went through the kitchen we met DI Bradley who was

on his way out. I introduced them and the detective shook Simon's hand.

'I'm off for now. We'll send a crew to get the rest of the bones out tomorrow, then you'll be able to let your tree surgeons finish their job. Till then, the hole's out of bounds.' He winked at Lewis who'd come through to listen. 'Got that, young man?'

Lewis nodded solemnly.

'How long until the results of the carbon-dating are known?' I asked.

'About three weeks, I'd say. We'll let you know. If the bones are as old as I guess they are, we'll probably never know who it was. Ah well, can't solve them all.'

He strode across the hall and let himself out.

I took Simon outside to see the remains of the tree, the hole and the bones, now protected from the elements by a white tent.

He whistled and shook his head at the scene. 'Who'd have thought it? Must have been a terrible shock for you, Katie. You OK now?'

'I'm fine. A bit shaken. I can't help wondering who it was.'

He shrugged. 'Like the detective said, we'll probably never know. Whoever he or she was, and how they died – well, it's all long in the past, nothing to do with us.'

But it *was* to do with us. It was our garden, and, depending on the age of the bones, there was a good possibility it was something to do with my ancestors. I realised it was time I told Simon the truth about the house's history. I must have looked as though I was hiding something, because he suddenly caught hold of my arm and turned me to face him.

'What, Katie? What is it?'

'There's something I meant to tell you – about the house,' I began. 'I – well, I'd been here before.'

'What do you mean, before? Before what?'

'Before we moved in. I came here to see it…'

'Yes, we all did, with that smarmy young estate agent…'

139

'No, I mean before that. I'd already met the Delameres.'

'What do you mean?'

'Do you remember, I came to see a house back in November, the one...'

'November?' He frowned at me, trying to work out what I was talking about.

'The one where my ancestors used to live?' There. I'd said it.

'Ye-es, I remember... so are you saying...?'

'It was this house, Simon. I'm sorry, I didn't tell you before because, well, I thought...'

He rolled his eyes. 'Katie, how do I make it clear to you, I'm not interested in the past, or who lived here before, or where you've come from. I only care about who you are *now*, not who your great-great-whatever-grandfather was. Why should I care in the slightest who owned the house before us? What does hurt, though, is that you kept it secret. What did you think I'd do, refuse to buy it?'

'Well, yes. You might have – you might well have thought that I'd spend even more time researching, and that would have pissed you off. Don't deny it, Simon, you know you wouldn't have wanted to give me any reason to spend more time on genealogy than I already do. But anyway, the thing is, those bones, they might well have something to do with my ancestors.'

He laughed. 'Unlikely.'

'Simon, think about it: if the bones are dated to any time between about 1800 when my four-greats grandfather built the house and 1923 when Barty St Clair died, then it's almost certain that a St Clair knew something about the body. How could a body be buried in the garden and the owner of the house not know anything about it?'

He shrugged. 'Still, nothing to do with us. What's past is past. Anyway, I reckon the bones'll turn out to be far older. Medieval, perhaps. Come on. Don't know about you, but I reckon it's wine o'clock.'

He went inside to find a bottle. I stood for a moment longer, gazing at the remains of my garden. Great-great-great-uncle Barty, did you know about this? Did you know who was buried here? Once again I wished I could travel back in time and simply question him.

I followed Simon inside and gratefully sipped the wine he'd poured for me. I sat down in the living room for a few minutes, then made a decision.

'Simon, I'm going to give Vera Delamere a ring. To warn her that DI Bradley might get in touch with her. Also she might know something…'

'If Bradley's right about the age of the bones then they date from before her time, love,' said Simon. 'I'd leave it, if I were you.'

'…know something about the history of the house, I was going to say.' I fetched my address book and looked up the Delameres' new phone number.

Vera was, of course, horrified to hear of the discovery. 'To think we lived there all that time without knowing there was a body rotting there beneath the beech. The tree my boys climbed in when they were children. It doesn't bear thinking about, does it?'

As expected, she'd known nothing about it. The beech was already a mature tree when she and Harold had moved in. 'Maybe old Barty St Clair had something to do with it,' she said, echoing the thought I'd had. 'It might explain why he never let anyone in the house.' She sighed. 'I suppose we'll never know. But what an exciting discovery, although I can imagine it must have been rather traumatic for you. You are all right, aren't you, dear? And your husband and children?'

'We're fine, thank you. Yes, it certainly was a shock,' I said. 'Vera, who lived here before you and Harold?'

'It was a probate sale when we bought it. It had been empty for years. Since the war, I believe. Yes, that's right, it's coming back to me now. The Army requisitioned it during the war, and

RAF officers from the old airfield at South Kingsley lived in it. When we moved in there was still evidence of their occupation – cigarette butts, playing cards caught under the skirting, even an old gas mask in the under-stairs cupboard.'

'Wow, how fascinating to find all that stuff!'

'We just thought it was mess. Back then, in the 1950s, everyone was trying to forget the war and move on. Not like now, when we're all much more interested in the past and what's gone before.'

Except for Simon, I thought.

'I think it was a London family, quite well-to-do, who'd bought the house after Barty St Clair died,' Vera went on. 'They used it as a country retreat, up until the war. And after the war they never came back, and it was put up for sale when the last of them died. Perhaps the bones had something to do with them?'

'Perhaps. Well, hopefully DI Bradley might be able to tell us in a couple of weeks.'

'As long as that? Gosh, I don't think I can wait! Mysterious jewelled hair combs and skeletons in the garden – how many more secrets does Kingsley House hold, I wonder? You will ring again, as soon as you have any more news, won't you, Katie?'

I promised I would and, after ringing off, jotted down what she'd told me about the history of the house, before I forgot it all. Vera wasn't the only one wondering if we'd uncover any more secrets here.

After we'd had dinner, put Thomas to bed and sent the other kids upstairs to their rooms, Simon and I settled down in the sitting room with the remains of the bottle of wine.

He topped up his glass, then sat back in his armchair and regarded me.

'Katie, there's something I need to talk to you about. I know today's been a little traumatic, and I'm sorry to dump something else on you, but I really need to talk about this tonight.'

I raised my eyebrows in surprise. This didn't sound like Simon. He wasn't the kind of man who needed to talk through his problems. He usually kept quiet about them and told me only after he'd resolved them himself.

'Go ahead, love,' I said.

He sighed, and twiddled his wine glass by its stem. 'Not really sure how to tell you this.'

'Just say it, Simon, whatever it is. Today seems to be the day for coming clean. I've already told you my secret – about my ancestors having lived here.'

He snorted. 'What I have to say is a little more important than that.'

I felt a cold hand clutch at my guts. Oh Christ, he wasn't going to tell me he was leaving me for that other woman, was he? Surely not?

He gulped at his wine and took a deep breath before answering. 'OK. Well. I think I told you once about Sarah, the girlfriend I had at university? We broke up amicably when we left uni and got jobs in different towns. We wrote to each other for a while but then it fizzled out.'

'Yes, I remember.' I took a sip of my wine. Where was this going?

'I haven't heard from her for over twenty years.'

'Er, so?'

'Turns out she was pregnant when we broke up. She didn't tell me at the time. She never told me.' His voice sounded strained. He took another gulp of his wine, then looked straight at me. 'She kept the baby. It was a girl. She's twenty-one now. I didn't know about her until last week. She's my daughter.'

143

Chapter Thirteen

Hampshire, March 1841

It was a good thing, Bartholomew thought, that the railway had reached North Kingsley. It was only a year earlier, in 1840, that the line between Winchester and Basingstoke had been completed, and the little station of North Kingsley opened. Travelling here had been so much easier than he'd remembered. Perhaps he should have invested in the railways after all.

They were met at the station by Old George Fowles, in Bartholomew's father's phaeton. George was greyer and more bent over than Bartholomew remembered, but his toothy smile was as wide as ever.

'Good to see you again, sir,' said the old man. 'It be many a year since I had the pleasure. Sorry it be under such circumstances. Your father were a good man, God rest his soul. And I'm delighted to meet your lady wife, and all.' He bowed and raised his cap at Georgia, who smiled sweetly in return. 'You be coming to live down along of North Kingsley again, sir?'

Bartholomew helped Georgia into the phaeton, and climbed up beside her. Her enormous swollen belly had made the journey from Brighton difficult and uncomfortable for her, and he was sure she was very thankful it was now almost at an end. He nodded at Fowles. 'For a while at least. It's good to see you too, George. Is your good wife keeping well?'

'Ah, she's not too bad, thanking you for asking, sir. She's got a touch of the old rheumatics, but aside of that she's the same as ever. Lord, it must be nigh on ten year since you last lived down along of us.' Old George heaved the trunks onto the back of the phaeton and climbed up himself. He flicked the reins, and the two horses shook their heads and began to walk on.

'Easily ten years. I think I was last here for my poor mother's funeral,' replied Bartholomew, as the phaeton clattered over the cobbles outside the station.

'Aye, and now here for your poor father's. It be set for tomorrow afternoon, up yon St Michael's church at top of the village.'

'Yes, I'm aware of the arrangements from his solicitor, but thank you,' said Bartholomew.

Old George coughed. 'We was wondering were you ever going to come and live in the house, or was you going to sell it off? And what would become of Mrs Fowles and me in that case. We're not so young as we once was, and there'd be no finding another place at our age.'

Bartholomew leaned forward and patted the old man's shoulder. 'You've been faithful servants to my father. You'll always have a job with me for as long as you live. I'm not intending to sell the old house and I'll not cast you out.'

'Ah, thanking you, sir. That be very kind.' The old man grunted and lapsed into silence, as the horse trotted along the lane leading from the station towards the village, three miles to the east. It was a beautiful early spring day, cold but sunny, the sky a fresh, sparkling blue. The countryside curved and rolled away from them, fields either luminous green or still brown, trees in new leaf, with sweet-smelling hawthorn hedges either side of the lane.

Bartholomew smiled. He'd forgotten how pleasant the country-side could be.

Beside him sat Georgia, looking about her and pointing out red kites wheeling overhead, a pair of rabbits in a field, a lone deer startled by the rattling phaeton taking cover in a small wood.

'It's beautiful, Bartholomew. Doesn't it make your soul soar, just to be here? I'm sorry it's under such sad circumstances, but forgive me, I cannot help myself. We shall be so happy! And our child shall be born healthy and strong, fed by such wonderful fresh air.'

He laughed. 'A baby needs more than fresh air to grow strong, my love. But yes, it is beautiful and I am happy too, despite the events which brought us here. Remember, I had not spoken to my father for many years. His passing is not so very upsetting for me.' He put his arm around her shoulders and she nestled into him, resting her head against him as the phaeton made its way eastwards towards North Kingsley.

Soon, the phaeton pulled up outside a flat-fronted, Georgian house, set just outside the village. It looked much as Bartholomew remembered, although in need of some renovation and a new coat of whitewash.

'Well, here we are. Welcome to Kingsley House,' he said.

'It's perfect!' Georgia pushed back the top of the phaeton and grinned in delight. Bartholomew lent her his arm, and she heaved herself down from the carriage. She climbed the three steps to the front door, which opened as she approached. Mrs Fowles stood in the doorway, round and smiling, holding her hands out in welcome.

'Come in, Mrs St Clair, I'll put the kettle on and fetch you some refreshments. Oh, the journey be so long from Brighton, you must be fair famished, and in your condition too! So brave you are, Mrs St Clair, to travel such a way. And Mr St Clair, why, how good it is to see you again after all these years! So lovely to have young people in the house again. Your poor father, God rest his soul, he were so quiet in those last years. Never went anywhere, never had no visitors, did nothing except read his books and exercise his horses. Such a quiet life he did lead, and us along with him. Ah, what am I prattling on for, and keeping you on the doorstep! Come in, do, the parlour is made ready for you and my Old George will light the fire when he has done with the horses.'

'No need for a fire yet, it's a warm enough day,' said Georgia, as she crossed the wood-panelled hallway and entered the parlour. 'Tea, however, would be delightful.' She smiled at Bartholomew as Mrs Fowles bustled away to make the tea. 'What a lovely welcome. You'd never think she only had two days' notice to make the house ready for us. Look, there's even fresh flowers on the table!'

Bartholomew had to admit it, the room looked most inviting. Although the furniture was old and worn, it was clean and bright, and the housekeeper had done a good job of arranging it. If he spent a bit of money sprucing up the place and buying some new furniture, it could be an acceptable place to live. And certainly Georgia seemed to like it very much.

The funeral took place the following day, at St Michael's church in the village. Bartholomew insisted that Georgia remain at the house, telling her a funeral was no place for a woman in her condition. There were not many in attendance – Bartholomew's father had been something of a recluse in his later years. Besides, he'd outlived most of his closest friends. Bartholomew gazed around at the clutch of people who stood at the graveside as he cast the first handful of dirt onto his father's coffin. Old George Fowles and his wife, the parson, the landlady of the local inn, a half-dozen of his father's acquaintances from the local gentry, who exchanged a few desultory words with Bartholomew. He recognised no one besides the Fowleses. Despite having been estranged from his father for the previous ten years, he found himself grieving for him. He wished he'd allowed Georgia to accompany him – he would have welcomed her sympathy during the funeral service.

He shook his head slightly. Well, what was done was done. There was no chance now to make amends, and no point in looking backwards. Especially not with so much to look forward to.

The funeral over, he shook hands with everyone and walked back through the village to Kingsley House, with George and Mrs Fowles following him, two steps behind.

Bartholomew wasted no time getting the house organised and fit for his wife and child to live in. He asked the Fowleses to engage some new servants – Mrs Fowles took on a kitchen maid and Old George, a stable boy. Mrs Fowles would act as Cook. Polly joined them from Brighton the following week, and was collected from the station by Old George. She turned her nose up at the worn furnishings and muddy lanes. Bartholomew fleetingly wondered what Agnes would make of the house, but quickly banished the thought. Her baby was surely born by now, but she had not returned to the Brighton house. Well, they had no need of her. Perhaps she had made a new life for herself, back in her parents' village. Good for her. He did not wish her ill, but he did not want her back in his life. She was nothing but trouble.

He made several trips to nearby Winchester by phaeton and train, to order new furniture including a crib for the baby, and to engage workmen to repair the rotting windows and replace missing roof slates. A carpenter came to fit a range of shelves, drawers and cupboards in the small room at the front of the house, which Bartholomew had chosen to become his study. There were open shelves on the top half, and carved-fronted cupboards below, with a line of drawers at the mid-height, and a fold-down desk. The whole thing was made of a rich burr walnut. He was pleased with the work. There was a place for everything, just as it should be. As he arranged his books and papers he wondered why he had ever moved away from the country. He felt at home here. It was, of course, where he had grown up. And when Georgia's confinement was over, they would pay visits to all the good families of the neighbourhood, and become a true part of the county society.

Georgia kept to the house and garden at this time, and busied herself making plans to replant the flower beds and prune the neglected fruit trees. She was so huge Mrs Fowles was convinced she was having twins.

'Mrs St Clair, I do think you should let the doctor see you, afore you goes into labour. If it is twins, 'tis better to know this before they start to come, so we can be prepared for them. Polly will need to sew a second set of baby clothes if 'tis twins.'

Georgia reluctantly agreed. She had not seen anyone outside of the house since she'd arrived, but Mrs Fowles was right. Better to be prepared.

When Dr Moore arrived, he was not the genial old man Bartholomew remembered from his boyhood. It was the old doctor's son, plump, red-faced, short-sighted Jonathon Moore, whom Bartholomew had once played with, fishing in the nearby stream and setting traps for rabbits.

'My father died last year,' explained the young doctor. 'I've taken over the practice. Good to see someone living in this house again, Mr St Clair.'

Bartholomew shook his hand. 'Call me Bartholomew, Jonathon. Good to see you again. You always did want to follow in your father's footsteps, as I recall.'

'Indeed, and I have, though my eyesight's a bit of a problem.' Dr Moore pulled out a pair of the thickest glasses Bartholomew had ever seen, and perched them on his nose. 'Still, I can make my diagnoses well enough by listening to my patients. And in your wife's case, I shall need to go by feel to see whether she's carrying twins or not.' He coughed and shuffled his feet. 'May I also offer my condolences on the loss of your father. I'm afraid I never attended him before his accident – he would have no one in the house except for your housekeeper. I called once or twice but sadly I was turned away.'

'Thank you,' said Bartholomew. 'He always was rather stubborn. Now then, on to today's patient, if you wouldn't mind.'

Mrs Fowles showed the doctor up to Georgia's room at the back of the house, where she lay on the bed in her shift, ready for him. Bartholomew paced up and down on the landing outside the door. He hoped it would not be twins. Although two sons were undoubtedly better than one, he feared for the additional difficulties a multiple birth would give Georgia. Childbirth was dangerous enough in any case.

When Dr Moore emerged blinking from the room a while later, he confirmed it would not be twins. 'Without a doubt, there's only the one child in there,' he said. 'One head, one rear, one pair of elbows is all I can feel. Going to be a bonny big baby, though. I reckon he'll make his appearance within a week or two now. I'll call on old Mrs Miller, who lives in the village, next door to the bakery. She's the best midwife around these parts. Send for her the moment your wife feels anything start to happen.'

'I will. Thanks, Jonathon.'

'You're welcome. You've got yourself a fine wife there, Bartholomew. Take good care of her, now.' The doctor folded his glasses and tucked them into his waistcoat pocket. He groped for the banister at the top of the stairs, and carefully descended, nodding to Mrs Fowles on the way out.

It was only five days later when Georgia's pains began. She had just finished her breakfast when she doubled over and groaned. A moment later she vomited.

'My dear, are you ill?' Bartholomew cried, jumping to his feet to ring the bell for Polly.

'I think – I think it may have begun,' Georgia gasped. 'Oh – I think I should go upstairs…' She hauled herself to her feet, clutching at her swollen belly.

'I shall help you,' Bartholomew said, hooking her arm around his neck. He gestured for Polly to support her on the other side. Another pain hit Georgia halfway up the stairs and the trio stood on the half-landing while she groaned through it. Bartholomew called for Mrs Fowles to send for the midwife.

At last they reached Georgia's room, and laid her on her bed. Polly arranged a pile of pillows under her head, then turned, blushing, to Bartholomew.

'Sir, it's not my place and I know as she's your wife but my ma always said a birthing-room is no place for a man…'

'It's all right, I shall leave as soon as she is comfortable. Georgia my dear, the midwife has been sent for. Shall I send Mrs Fowles in or…?'

'Oh, please do send Mrs Fowles in,' cut in Polly. 'I ain't never been at a birthing, and what if the baby comes quickly afore the midwife gets here?'

Georgia was gasping her way through another contraction, and only managed to nod her head at Bartholomew's question.

'Very well, I shall send her in.' Bartholomew took his wife's hand and kissed it. 'Good luck, my sweet. Be strong.' He turned and left the room, letting out a sigh as he closed the door behind him. Another few hours and he would be a father, God willing.

Mrs Fowles bustled past him up the stairs, carrying a pile of linens. 'Mr St Clair, sir, it will be a busy household until the baby's here, for sure. I am sorry I can't bring you your coffee this morning. If you put your head into the kitchen, the girl Libby will fetch you some.'

'It's quite all right, I shall manage. Has the midwife been sent for?'

'Danny the stable boy is on his way now, sir. It's a wild day out there, but she'll not be long. I've known Jemima Miller all my life and no better midwife could you ever hope for. Your wife will be in safe hands.'

'That's a comfort. Now you attend to my wife, if you please.'

'Right away, sir. Though I don't know as I'll be much use to her afore the midwife comes. Old George and I only ever had the one youngster, and I've not been at no other women's birthings. I'll do my best though, sir, be sure of that.'

Bartholomew nodded, and went down to his study. Outside it was raining heavily and a strong wind was wrestling with the trees. He lit the fire and opened up his pull-down desk, which the carpenter had recently completed. Might as well get on with some correspondence, he thought, while he waited for things to progress upstairs. He slid some heavy cream paper out of a drawer and sat down to write.

It was hard to concentrate, knowing what was going on up in Georgia's room. Despite himself, he could not help but wonder about Agnes – how had she fared giving birth to her baby? His baby too, he supposed, not that he would ever bless it with his name. Well, she was gone now, and likely he would never set eyes on the child, or see her again. And that was for the best. It was a chapter of his life he was not proud of, and needed to put behind him.

A commotion in the hallway roused him from his thoughts, and he stepped out of the study. Libby the kitchen maid was standing, wringing her apron in her hands, while Danny the stable boy stood white-faced and dripping.

'Like I says, Libby, Mrs Miller ain't able to come. You got to tell the master… Oh! Sir, I di'n't see you there, sorry sir, I'll be on me way now, sir.' He tugged at his sodden cap and backed out of the hallway, but not fast enough. Libby caught him by the ear.

'Danny, you've to tell the master what you jest told me, now. He should hear it straight from you, not garbled through another set of ears and mouth.'

'What is it, boy? Come on, out with it,' said Bartholomew.

The boy was blushing now, and staring at the puddle of water around his feet. Bartholomew realised he'd probably never been inside the house before, at least, not beyond the kitchen and scullery.

152

'Tell me what's happened,' he said, more gently.

The boy took a deep breath, then all his words came out in a rush. 'It's Mrs Miller, see. The midwife. She ain't able to come. There be another baby coming today and that one be lying cross its ma's body which ain't an easy birth. Mrs Miller got to turn the child to make it come out right. Ain't no one else can do that round here. And cos of that she ain't able to come here to see to the mistress.'

'I see. And is there another midwife in the village?'

'Mrs Miller is the only one,' answered Libby.

'Danny, you must fetch Dr Moore from Winchester. Saddle up the bay and ride as fast as you can!'

'Right ho, Mr St Clair, sir.' Danny tugged at his cap again, turned and ran out via the kitchen door.

'Libby, go upstairs and call Mrs Fowles out. Tell her what Danny said, and that she and Polly must cope alone. Don't let my wife hear.'

'Yes, sir.' Libby began to run up the stairs.

'Oh, and Libby?'

She stopped and turned.

'Do you have any experience of birthing?'

'No, sir. I'm second youngest of my ma's. Only ever seen lambs being born. Ewes make it look easy, but I know it ain't really.'

'Well, you might have to help, if Mrs Fowles requires it.'

A howl of pain from upstairs sent Libby scurrying up. Bartholomew stood helplessly in the hallway. He prayed that Georgia and the baby would be all right. But it was her first child, and he knew that a woman's first experience of childbirth was usually the hardest. And this was a big baby, according to Jonathon Moore. He thought of Georgia's slim, almost boyish hips and shuddered.

Time passed agonisingly slowly, while Bartholomew paced the hallway, glancing occasionally at the stairs. Libby ran up and down a few times fetching and carrying, but each time she care-

153

fully avoided catching his eye. Well, there was nothing he could do, and any news, good or bad, would reach him eventually. He resolved to return to his study and deal with some correspondence.

As he reached for the study's doorknob the doorbell rang. He looked around for a servant to open the door, but of course they were all busy upstairs. It was still pouring with rain so whoever the visitor was would be drenched. He crossed the hall again and opened the door.

'Can't you afford servants now, Mr St Clair? Or are they all too lazy? Good job I'm back. I'll soon set them in order.' A very wet, black-cloaked woman pushed past him into the house, and stood, dripping, in the middle of the hall. She threw back the hood of her cloak.

'Agnes!'

'Glad to see you remember who I am. Didn't remember to tell me you'd moved though, did you? I had to call at old Mr Holland's house in Brighton. He told me where to find you. You said I'd be welcome back, and there'd always be a job for me. So, here I am.' She bobbed a mock curtsey. 'By train, farmer's cart and Shanks's pony, if you're interested.'

Bartholomew opened his mouth to speak but at that moment, an animal-like wail came from upstairs. Agnes stared at him, wide-eyed. 'Is that the mistress? She sounds like… Oh! Is she in labour?'

'She is, yes. And the midwife is engaged elsewhere.'

'How long has she been screaming like that?' asked Agnes, as she divested herself of her cloak and dumped it in a sodden pile on a chair. Her wet hair clung to her face, accentuating her fine cheekbones.

Bartholomew glanced at the hallway clock. 'I don't know – two or three hours, perhaps?'

'It's not going well, then. I'll go up. I've helped at many a birth including four of my ma's.' She headed towards the stairs, but stopped, her foot on the first step, and glanced back at him, her green eyes proud. 'It's a boy, by the way.'

'A boy? But…how do you know?'

'Not hers. My child. Your first-born son.' She ran up the stairs as another scream shook the house.

Bartholomew returned to his study and sat down heavily. She was back. His heart beat with excitement at having been in her presence. She was as irresistible as ever.

Agnes followed the moans until she found Georgia's room on the first floor. A mousy young maid came out carrying an empty bucket as she approached, and scurried past her, giving her only a brief backwards glance. She pushed open the door.

Georgia was lying on the bed, her face almost hidden by her huge swollen belly. An elderly woman with a kind, round face was dabbing at her face with a damp cloth, while Polly, whom Agnes recognised from the Brighton house, was holding her hand and murmuring words of comfort. Agnes tutted. There was no one attending to the business end. She stepped forward.

'Hello, Mrs St Clair.'

Georgia groaned, gasped and opened her eyes. 'Aggie? Is it you? Am I dreaming?'

'No, ma'am. It's me. I have returned as I said I would. And just in time, by the looks of things.'

'Who are you, young lady?' asked the older woman. 'Are you a midwife?'

'I have some experience of birthing,' Agnes replied, as she rolled up her sleeves. 'My name is Agnes Cutter.'

'I knows her, Mrs Fowles,' said Polly. 'She were the mistress's lady's maid afore she upped and left her last year.'

'Well, whoever she is, if she knows how to birth a baby, she's welcome here,' said Mrs Fowles.

Agnes gave her a tight smile. 'Just going to have a look below and see how you're getting on,' she said, pushing Georgia's night-dress up over her bent knees.

155

'Must you go looking down there?' asked Mrs Fowles. 'Can't the poor soul keep her dignity?'

'Down there's where the baby will come out,' said Agnes. 'If I don't look how will I know how close the baby is? Now, ma'am, this won't hurt.' She pushed her fingers inside Georgia. Only two inches dilated. The girl had a way to go yet. She swept her finger round inside, the way her mother had taught her. That should speed things up a little.

Georgia gasped, then groaned as another contraction hit.

'Ma'am, try not to cry so loud. Think about your breathing, steady in, just a little, puff it out. The harder you think on your breathing the easier the pain.'

'Is the baby nearly come yet?' asked Polly.

'It'll be a little longer,' replied Agnes. 'Fetch me some tea. I've had a long journey. And some bread and jam.'

Polly snorted. 'Back to boss us around I see. I takes my orders from the master, the mistress and Mrs Fowles only.'

Mrs Fowles looked up. 'Fetch the poor woman some tea like she asked, Polly. She's here in place of the midwife, and very grateful for that we all are, I'm sure.'

Polly turned on her heel and flounced out of the room without another word.

Georgia smiled weakly at Agnes, her contraction now subsided. 'She's been doing your job, while you were away. Oh Aggie, I am so glad you are back. What took you so long – you said it'd only be a fortnight, and you promised me!'

'My mother was ill for such a long time,' Agnes sighed. 'But, ma'am, let's not speak of it. It is past, and I am here now with you, and will stay with you. But for now, we have more important matters at hand.'

'Your mother, of course. Did she recover?'

'Yes, she is quite well now.' Agnes turned her head away for fear Georgia might guess there was a bigger reason why she had stayed away so long.

'Well, I will leave you to it,' said Mrs Fowles. 'I shall bring in your tea in a moment, then I shall wait outside the door if you need more assistance.' She rose stiffly and left the room.

Agnes sat in the chair vacated by the old woman, and took over the task of sponging Georgia's forehead and holding her hand.

'I am so *very* glad you are back,' said Georgia again.

A couple of hours later, Georgia was making progress. Agnes checked her a couple of times. 'Won't be long now, ma'am, before your body wants to push the baby out.'

'How will I know when that is?'

'You'll know it, ma'am. There is no mistaking that feeling.'

Georgia squeezed her hand. 'You are so wise, Aggie. You know so much about childbirth – it's almost as though you've been through it yourself.'

'I – I was with my ma through four of hers. She is midwife in her village, and I have helped her with many other women's babies.'

'I am glad to hear it. Though I shall not…oh, oh, I think…it is coming, it is coming, ohhh!'

'Squeeze my hand. Push, ma'am. Push.'

'I am…ohhh!'

'That's good. Keep pushing with the pain. And now let me look…yes – I can see the top of the baby's head…'

Minutes later, the baby was born. Agnes quickly cut the cord with a kitchen knife Mrs Fowles brought in, tied it with a piece of string, and expertly swaddled the baby in a linen towel. She handed it to Georgia. The baby mewled and turned its head towards its mother.

'You have a healthy son, ma'am,' said Agnes, as Georgia took the baby.

Agnes remembered so clearly her mother passing over her own baby, just a few short weeks earlier. How proud she had felt! How strong the bond of love between mother and son had felt, right from the start. At the sound of this new baby's cry, her breasts began prickling. She'd weaned her son off her and onto a wet-nurse before returning to the St Clairs', but she was still producing milk. She hoped the wads of cotton tucked into her chemise would soak it up so she wouldn't show wet patches on her dress. How she missed him already. But she must be strong. There would eventually be a future for her and her son, here with Mr St Clair, if only she played her cards right. Meanwhile, she needed to bide her time and await her chance.

'Aggie, call my husband in, do. He must meet his first-born son!'

'In a moment, ma'am. When the afterbirth has come and I have cleaned you up a little. You wouldn't want Mr St Clair seeing you quite like this, I shouldn't think.' Agnes went to the door and called in Mrs Fowles and Polly. Might as well have some help now.

'You're right, as always, Aggie. Here, take the baby from me, please. Put him down somewhere. I fear I am too tired to hold him now.'

Agnes took the newborn and placed him beside Georgia on the bed, where he could smell his mother and feel her warmth. Strange that Georgia did not want to hold him. She remembered when her own son was born, she had not wanted to put him down at all. She had wanted the soft warm feel of him, the milky smell, the perfection of his tiny fingers and toes to fill her senses at all times. Her ma had to prise him away from her to allow her to sleep.

Later, Agnes washed her hands in a basin of fresh water brought by Polly and went downstairs, leaving Georgia resting, her baby sleeping beside her. He was not as handsome as her own son, she thought. His head looked too flattened, no doubt from being squeezed out through Georgia's narrow hips. Still, he was a good weight and looked healthy.

She tapped on the door of the study, and without waiting for an answer, opened the door.

'Sir, you have a healthy son.'

'And my wife?'

'She is well. She would like you to go up, now.'

'Thank you.' He paused at the door, and turned back towards her, his eyes shining. 'Thank you, Agnes,' he said, again.

Agnes followed him up the stairs and into Georgia's room. She watched as he fell to his knees beside the bed and clutched at his wife's hand, kissing it, too overcome to say anything. She watched as he picked up the child, cradled it gently, stroked its head and gasped at the perfection of its tiny features. She imagined how it would feel to see him bestow the same attentions on her own son; how perfect life would then be, if he loved her son the way he loved this one.

Bartholomew looked at Georgia. 'What shall we call him?'

She smiled. 'After you, I had thought. Bartholomew junior.'

'Very well. Welcome to the world, little Bartholomew.' He bent his head and placed a kiss on the infant's forehead.

Agnes felt emotion rise up and threaten to choke her. Blackness clouded her sight and she found it difficult to breathe. She stumbled out of the room and pulled the door closed behind her, then leaned back on it, breathing heavily.

'Are you well?' Mrs Fowles was peering at her, a concerned expression on her face.

'Just a little tired. I shall go and sit downstairs in the morning room. Perhaps you can send your kitchen girl to me with a cup of tea.'

Mrs Fowles blinked. 'Libby's in the kitchen. You can ask her for whatever you need. Shall you be staying here tonight?'

'Yes.'

'Well I must get Polly to make a room ready for you. Where is your trunk?'

'At the railway station in Basingstoke. Perhaps Mr St Clair will send a man to fetch it.'

'Perhaps he will. I will leave that for you to arrange.' Mrs Fowles pushed past her and into Georgia's room. As she entered, Bartholomew came out. His eyes were bright.

'Agnes! A boy! My little Bartholomew!'

'Yes, sir. I am very pleased for you.'

'This calls for a celebration. I think I would like a brandy. Care to join me?'

'No, thank you.' She would not raise a glass to this baby's health.

'Oh. Very well, then.' He began to descend the stairs, then stopped, and turned back to her. 'I forgot – in all the excitement, I didn't inquire – what name did you give your son?'

'Bartholomew, sir. After his father.' She watched as the words hit him like a fist. He pulled himself upright as if to absorb the blow, nodded curtly and continued on his way down the stairs.

Barty, my son. I have told you now the story of your birth and your naming. Two mothers; two babies born in the same month and given the same name; and one man, caught in the middle, by his own doing. I wanted to ignore Agnes's son, but I knew at that moment, once she had told me the child's name, that I would not be able to ignore the child completely. He was as much mine as the tiny mite Georgia was cradling upstairs. I would need to provide for him, one way or another. And with Agnes back in my household, things would no doubt change. Would I be able to resist her and stay true to my wife as I had promised myself? Should I send her away again? How would Georgia react? And could I do such a thing, after she had been such a help during the birth, indeed, surely, sent to us by God himself in our moment of need.

It was too much for me to contemplate right then. I went into my study and drowned my problems in brandy.

Chapter Fourteen

Hampshire, May 2013

Simon had a grown-up daughter? One he didn't know about until last week? I gasped.

But something didn't make sense. 'Simon, if you haven't heard from Sarah for twenty years, how do you know this?'

'I haven't heard from Sarah. But I've heard from her daughter. *My* daughter, I suppose I should say. Her name's Amy. She tracked me down via my university's alumni society and LinkedIn.'

'So, what does she want?' Simon stared hard at me. I kicked myself. That hadn't come out quite as I intended. 'I mean, why contact you now?'

'She lost her mum. Sarah died in a road accident last year. She'd never told Amy anything about me other than that I'd been at the same university as her, and my name. But when Sarah died, Amy decided she wanted to find me.'

'Oh, how awful about Sarah. That must be hard on the girl. Have you met her?'

'Not yet. She's written to me – emails and a couple of letters. She wants to meet.'

Simon's daughter. Did that make her my stepdaughter? Suddenly I realised this girl, this Amy, was half-sister to Lewis, Lauren and Thomas. They would have to be told. I looked up at Simon. He looked haunted and drawn. I guessed the strain of finding out he had a grown-up daughter had been difficult to come to terms with. And probably he'd worried and fretted about how I'd take it. I wasn't sure myself, yet, how I was taking it. I expected I'd need a few walks alone on Irish Hill to think it all through.

'How do you feel about it?' I asked him.

He shook his head. 'To tell the truth, I'm not sure yet. It doesn't seem real.'

A horrible thought struck me. 'Simon, it may sound stupid, but are you sure it is real? I mean, how do you know she really is your daughter? You've only got her word for it, she could be some kind of...'

'She's telling the truth. The dates work out. And in any case, why would someone make up something like this? It's not like I'm rich, or a celebrity or anything. There's nothing to gain by being my daughter.'

'Nothing to gain? There's everything to gain. She'll gain a father, the knowledge of where she's come from, a family history. She'll gain *you*.'

He smiled. 'Trust you to see it that way, love. I suppose it'll feel more real to me when I meet her. I will have to meet her, I suppose.'

'Yes, I think you must. She has a right to know her father, I think.' Though why did her father have to be Simon? I could see already that this was going to change our family dynamic, and who knew whether that would end up being for the better or worse?

He nodded. 'Though as she's grown up now, I don't see that I can be much use to her.'

'I guess that's for her to decide,' I said gently. Everyone had a right to know who their parents were, I thought. And their grand-parents, and great-grandparents. Knowing where you come from helps give you roots. 'So, have you made any arrangements to meet her?'

'Not yet. We've agreed to email a few more times before we meet up. Get to know each other a bit first. Besides, she lives in Durham. It won't be that easy, logistically speaking.'

It wouldn't be easy *at all*, and I wasn't thinking about the logistics. 'Sad about her mother dying.'

'Yes, poor Sarah. I don't know the details. I do feel sorry for Amy, losing her mother so young.'

Something occurred to me. 'Simon, you've been late home a lot recently. Is this why – is it something to do with Amy making contact?'

'Late? Have I? Oh, no. That's been due to working late. Mostly. And, um, a couple of drinks parties after work which I couldn't get out of. So, anyway, I think we shouldn't mention anything about Amy to the kids. Not until after I've met her and we've worked out what's going to happen next.'

'I agree,' I said. So the late nights weren't down to Amy. That mystery was still not solved. And his stuttered answer and swift change of subject didn't fill me with confidence. I ran a hand across my forehead. There was too much going on in our lives at the moment. We were barely settled in our new house. Simon had discovered a grown-up daughter he hadn't known about. He might be having an affair. And there was a skeleton in our back garden.

'Simon, I've got a headache. It's been a hell of a long day. I'm going to bed.' I got up, and poured the rest of my wine into his glass. I needed a half-hour or so on my own before he came up, to mull things over and try to straighten out my thoughts. I suspected I wouldn't get to sleep for hours.

The next day was a busy one. Simon decided to take a day's

holiday and stay at home, to help deal with the endless succession of police, forensic archaeologists and other scientific experts who traipsed through the house to the garden, examining the burial site and the remains of the beech. By the time I got back from taking the kids to school, the garden was swarming with people. I had the kettle almost continually on the boil, making cups of tea for them. It was worse than having the builders in. And every time I looked at Simon I thought about this girl, Amy. I kept trying to picture her. Would she look like an older Lauren? Or completely different, more like her mother?

By lunchtime the word had got out that a skeleton had been discovered in a North Kingsley garden. When the doorbell rang for the twentieth time that day, I sighed, wondering what species of policeman or scientist or nosy neighbour would be on my doorstep this time. But it was a reporter and a photographer.

'Sorry to intrude, ma'am, but we're from the *Southern Daily Echo*. Is it true you've discovered a body in your back garden? Could you tell us the full story?'

I gaped at him, unsure whether I should talk to the press or not. DI Bradley passed by on his way out, and gave me a reassuring smile. So it was OK to talk to them if I wanted to. I showed the reporters through to the dining room where they could see what was happening in the garden without getting in the way of the police work, and told them the story of the storm, the tree surgeon and the bones. Simon followed me in and sat with me, chipping in with comments every now and again. I may have been talking about the skeleton, but it was the more momentous news of Simon's daughter that was really on my mind.

I decided against mentioning that my ancestors used to live here. If the bones were of someone who'd been murdered, and one of my ancestors had had something to do with that…well, I wasn't sure myself how I felt about that yet. And I certainly didn't want to discover how I felt by reading articles entitled 'local woman is descended from long line of killers' in the papers.

Twenty minutes later it was the *Winchester Star* at the door. And then the *Hampshire Chronicle*. By two o'clock half the village were standing in the lane to witness us bag the big one – the film crew from *South Today*. I ducked into the kitchen and let Simon deal with that one. No way did I want to be on the local TV news! Simon seemed to relish it all – after they'd gone he told me he'd enjoyed the experience of being interviewed, speculating on who the bones might have belonged to, reciting what he knew of the history of the house.

'Did you tell them my ancestors used to live here?' I asked.

Simon shook his head. 'No, I kept quiet about that. You hadn't mentioned it to any of the papers so I guessed you didn't want it shouted about. Anyway, I can't remember the detail.'

I rolled my eyes. Of course he never bothered to store any information relating to my research. But God help me if I couldn't recall who England's fly-half was. 'Thanks for not telling them. I want to wait and see what the police find out first. We don't even know if the bones date from my ancestors' time. They might be earlier, or later.'

'They seemed to be hoping the body was more recent,' he said. 'Apparently a woman went missing from this village about twenty years back, and her body was never found. I think they wanted it to be her.'

'What did you tell them?'

'Just what we know – that the bones were under a large old tree. Let them tell whatever story they want. Anyway, I must set up the TV to record *South Today* this evening. Don't want the kids to miss their dad being on telly!'

I wondered whether Amy would see it and, if she did, what she'd think of her father. Then I remembered she lived in Durham, well out of *South Today's* broadcast range.

Work continued all day. A slice of the tree trunk was taken for analysis by a dendrochronology lab. DI Bradley explained that if the body had been buried before the tree was planted, determining the age of the tree would give us the latest date on which the body was buried.

The bones were gathered up and individually bagged and labelled. Two forensic scientists spent the day in the root hole, scraping at the earth with tiny trowels, uncovering more pieces of bone and a few fragments of part-rotted cloth. For a while there was discussion about whether there might be more than one body buried. Again, that made me shudder. It's one thing to discover a skeleton in your garden. Quite another to think that you live on the site of a mass murder. Late in the afternoon, the scientists decided they'd found the remains of just one, complete human. I breathed a huge sigh of relief. Simon laughed. 'Just the one body, eh? Thank goodness for that!'

It was almost dark before the police scientists finally packed up for the day, taking the bones, their tent and tools with them. DI Bradley called round just as we were clearing up after dinner. Thomas was already in bed.

'Sorry to disturb you again, Mr and Mrs Smith,' he said, as we invited him in to sit in the living room. 'I just thought I'd let you know sooner rather than later – we won't need to dig any more in your garden. You can get on with the clear-up job now, as soon as you like.'

'Aw, and here was me hoping I could get the police to dig over my vegetable plot as well,' joked Simon. 'But thanks for letting us know. It'll be good to get the garden back in action. The kids get so fidgety when they're not allowed outside.'

'Also, I just wanted to confirm that you know you're not under any suspicion yourselves,' said DI Bradley.

'Well, I may look a little careworn but surely not old enough to have committed a hundred-year-old murder,' I said, with mock indignation.

'Precisely.' DI Bradley smiled. 'But it's my duty to make sure you're aware. Right then, I'll be off and leave you to your evening. When we get the results of the carbon-dating and dendrochro-

nology in about three weeks' time I'll come back to let you know.'
He stood up, and shook our hands. 'Oh, and the lads said thanks
for all the tea and biscuits. We'll leave you in peace now.'

When he'd gone I turned to Simon. 'Well, we can move on as
regards the garden clear-up now. That's good. Don't suppose you
heard anything more from Amy today?'

'Who's Amy?' Lauren came skipping into the room, carrying
a huge armful of teddy bears, mostly pink.

'Just someone your dad—' I began.

'—works with,' finished Simon. 'No one you know. Why have
you brought all those bears downstairs?'

'I've grown out of them,' Lauren announced, dumping them
in a pile on the sofa beside me. 'Thomas can have them if he
wants.'

'They're probably a bit girlie for him,' I said. 'Maybe we can
donate them to the school summer fair. I think it's next month.'

'OK,' said Lauren, skipping back out of the room.

'Hang on a minute, young lady.' Simon jumped to his feet and
caught her by the arm. 'You're not going to leave those bears
there, are you? Pack them up into carrier bags and put them in
the spare room for now. We don't want them all over the sofa,
do we?'

She scowled, and went off in search of bags. Simon glanced
at me. 'You know, I can't help wondering whether Amy had pink
bears when she was little, as well. Did she like the same kind of
things Lauren does? I wonder what she looks like?'

I couldn't admit I'd spent all day wondering the same sort of
things. 'I'll bet you anything you like that she had at least one
pink teddy bear. You can ask her when you meet her.'

He put his arms around me and kissed my forehead. 'I might
well do that. Thank you, Katie, for being so understanding about
this. I didn't know if it would upset you.'

'Why's Mum upset?' asked Lauren, returning with a handful
of plastic bags.

'She's not. And we were just talking about the mess in the garden.'

'Oh. Where shall I put these, then?' She stuffed the toys into bags and thrust them towards me. A one-eyed pink Care Bear was sticking out of the top of one. I remembered buying it for her on her second birthday.

'Upstairs, in the spare room, like Dad said,' I replied. She flounced off with them.

'She's growing up,' said Simon.

'Yes. Seeing those bears get thrown out is like the end of an era. She's not a little girl any more.' I sighed. All this change in our lives, so much to cope with. 'But she'll always be *your* little girl.' I put my arms around him and quietly voiced my greatest fear. 'Don't let this Amy supplant her, will you?' He responded by squeezing me tightly and sighing into my hair.

Mum and Dad came to visit on the following Saturday. Ted the Tree and Jamie had been back on Friday to finish cutting up the tree trunk. Now we had a huge pile of six-foot-long logs to chop up into firewood, a mangled trampoline waiting to be taken to the tip, a pile of old bricks which needed to be built back into a garden wall, and a huge hole requiring filling with earth. Not to mention a trashed lawn and trampled flower beds. Dad had promised to help take the trampoline away and fill the crater. He and Mum were also intrigued, of course, by the story of the skeleton and couldn't wait to hear 'all the gory details', as Dad put it. I'd told them on the phone about the house having belonged to our ancestors. Dad was desperate to hear all about this, too. Simon and I had agreed, of course, not to mention Amy, yet.

It was the first time Mum and Dad had seen the house since we'd moved in. I gave them a guided tour, with Lauren skipping excitedly alongside, desperate to show Granny her room. Mum wanted to know all about what colours we'd paint the rooms, when we'd buy new curtains and carpets, and whether we'd replace the 1930s bathroom suite or not. While we were in our bedroom I took the hair comb out and showed it to Mum.

'Pretty. Are you going to wear it?'

'Not really my style. But I am fascinated to think about who it might have belonged to.'

'It might be worth a bit. You could sell it.'

Sell something that could have belonged to an ancestor? Not likely!

At least Dad was interested in the history of the house. 'Which St Clairs lived here? Remind me?' he asked, as we climbed the stairs to the second floor.

'It was built in 1799 by William St Clair, your great-great-great-grandfather,' I told him.

'Hey, my father was also William St Clair!'

'Yes, I know. It seems to have been a bit of a family name. There were at least three of them. The William who built the house lived here till he died in 1841. Then his son Bartholomew inherited it and lived here with his wife Georgia, and their children. The elder son Barty then lived here until he died in 1923. But we're descended from the second son, another William. He was your great-grandfather, Dad.' I showed him into the room we'd designated as a playroom.

'I bet the kids love playing up here. What happened to the house after Barty died?'

I told him what Vera Delamere had told me when I rang to tell her of the discovery of the bones.

'Delamere – that's who you bought the house from? So it's only actually had four different families owning it, for over two hundred years? The original St Clairs, the between-wars family who used it as a country retreat, the Delameres and now you.'

I hadn't thought of it like that. 'Yes. It's quite impressive, really. I hope we get to stay here as long as the Delameres did.'

Dad went to peer out of the window. This room was at the back of the house, with a good view of what remained of the garden. 'What a mess. I can see why you want my help, love.'

I went to stand beside him, and took hold of his arm. 'You don't have to help if it's—'

'Too much for me?' He laughed. 'I'm perfectly capable of doing a bit of spadework, young lady. Don't be writing me off just yet. I've worn my old clothes specially.'

I hugged him. 'Thanks, Dad. Shall we go down? Cup of tea before you start?'

'Thought you'd never ask. Yes, please!'

We went down where Simon already had the kettle on. Mum was poking around in the kitchen cupboards.

'I'd put your pans in that one, if I were you. Nearer the stove. And your plates over there. Do you want me to sort it out for you?' Mum's eyes gleamed. She liked nothing better than to organise a kitchen.

'No, thanks, Mum. If we move things around now, I'll never find them. I've only just got used to where everything is now.' Mum's face fell. I hugged her. 'But you know what, if you want to make yourself useful, I could do with a hand to sort out the linen cupboard. Everything's just piled in there topsy-turvy at the moment and I haven't even managed to find a set of sheets for your bed tonight.'

Mum rubbed her hands in glee. 'I'd love to help. Right then, it's upstairs isn't it?'

'To the left of the bathroom. I'll bring your tea up.' I grinned as she skipped happily out of the kitchen and upstairs.

'Right then, that'll keep Christine out of mischief. Let's get this soil shifted, shall we?' said Dad to Simon. The two men went out to begin work, while I got started on making lunch.

By the end of the afternoon, the hole was filled, the trampoline had been removed, the bricks were stacked tidily, my linen cupboard was neatly organised, and my parents were sitting exhausted but happy on a pair of garden chairs in the sunshine, watching the kids kick a football around the reclaimed lawn.

'Can't help but wonder who those bones belonged to,' said Dad.

'Mmm, me too,' I said, as I handed them a cup of tea each and put a plate of flapjacks on the garden table.

'Must be some connection with people who lived here, I suppose. Can't imagine some stranger coming in off the street and burying a body in a random back garden.' Dad laughed at his own joke.

'There'll be no way of finding out who it was,' said Simon.

Dad frowned. 'Well, if or when your policeman finds out the age of the bones, we could try to research likely candidates. Maybe there's some old newspaper report of a missing person? Actually, Katie' – he leaned forward in his chair, wagging a finger; I recognised the signs of a plan brewing – 'let me know as soon as you have the age of the bones. I'd love to have a go at researching who it might have been.'

'Will do, Dad.' I grinned. I'd already thought I'd like to try to do that research as well. It'd be great to have someone to help, and discuss it all with – someone who was actually interested in it, unlike Simon.

'What will you plant in that gap?' asked Mum, changing the subject. She pointed to where the tree had been. 'A nice rhododendron or a camellia, perhaps? Something to add colour?'

'Yes, something like that, I expect.' If Dad and I did manage to find out who had been buried here, that would help me decide what to plant, as a kind of memorial. I didn't feel I could explain that to Mum.

'As long as it's not another tree,' said Simon. 'I dread to think what damage that beech did to the house's foundations. In some ways I'm glad it fell. Although I didn't much like what was hidden at its roots.'

'I wonder what other secrets the house is hiding?' said Dad, gazing up at the attic windows.

Mum shuddered. 'Stop it, John. One skeleton was enough. More than enough!'

171

'What's in the loft? Above the second-floor bedrooms? There is a hatch, isn't there?' asked Dad.

'There is, but it's sealed shut. Not been opened for years, by the looks of things. To tell the truth, we've not had time to investigate it yet.' Simon shook his head. 'That's a job for another day, I think.'

Chapter Fifteen

Hampshire, May 1841

Bartholomew strode into the house in his riding boots. It was a fine morning, sunny but windy, and he'd taken the opportunity to go for a gallop across the fields. He felt invigorated. He should join the local hunt, he supposed, and get to know the local gentry. He called for Polly to bring some tea to the morning room, where he flung open the French doors at the back of the house. There was an iron bench set against the wall. He sat down on it, and tugged off his boots. Out of the wind, the day was a warm one, and promised to become hotter later on.

Polly arrived with a tray of tea, and a salver holding the morning mail. She brought out a small table to put it on, beside him.

'Will the mistress be joining you?' she asked. 'I can bring a chair outside if needed.'

'I shouldn't think so,' he replied. 'Agnes will ring for you to take tea upstairs if my wife requires it. Thank you, that will be all.'

Polly curtsied and scurried back inside.

Bartholomew picked up his tea cup and sipped it thoughtfully. He was worried. It had been two months since the baby's birth and still Georgia had not left her bed. To his limited knowledge, the usual lying-in period after a birth was around two to four weeks. But Georgia would see no one except Agnes and himself. Mrs Fowles was banished from the room, as was Polly. A wet-nurse from the village had been employed. Mary Moulsford trotted up to the house several times a day, and sat in the nursery feeding Bartholomew Junior, brought to her by Agnes. After he'd been fed, Agnes took the baby to see his mother for a few minutes, if Georgia was feeling up to it.

He wondered if he should send for Dr Moore to check her over. But although the doctor had seen Georgia once, a day after the birth, she had refused to allow him into her room since then. Agnes could take good care of her, she'd said. But maybe Bartholomew should call the doctor anyway, and insist that she saw him? There was definitely something wrong.

He put down his tea cup and picked up the post. There were two letters. The first was addressed in his London agent's familiar handwriting. Probably the report on his properties and invest-ments as he'd asked. He shuffled it behind the other letter. This envelope was edged with black.

Bartholomew frowned as he broke the seal. Black borders meant bad news, but he couldn't imagine who it could be. Since his father died he had no other living relatives. He flicked open the single sheet of paper inside and read it quickly.

The letter was from a Brighton solicitor, concerning the estate of Charles Holland. Georgia's uncle had finally breathed his last, after clinging to life by his fingernails these last couple of years. Georgia was his heir, Bartholomew believed. So there'd be more money coming their way, plus the house in Brighton. He drank the last of his tea and stood up, tucking the letter into his waist-coat pocket. Time to go and break the news to Georgia.

Upstairs, Agnes was sitting sewing in an armchair, while Georgia

174

lay on her bed staring out of the window. A small flask of medicine was on the bedside table – something Agnes had concocted for her mistress, no doubt. Agnes got up as soon as he walked in.

'Sir, your son is with the wet-nurse in the nursery at present,' she said.

'That's all right. I've come to see my wife. Please, continue with your work.' She nodded and sat down again, bending her glossy blonde head over her work. He remembered how it felt to bury his face in that hair, and kiss that slender white neck.

'Bartholomew?' Georgia heaved herself into a sitting position. He plumped the pillows behind her and kissed her forehead.

'Yes, my love?'

'Will you read to me? Perhaps something from Longfellow's collection?' She gestured to a book which lay open, face down, on the bedside table.

It was the perfect way to put off telling her the bad news. He picked up the book and began. After a minute or two he glanced up. Georgia appeared to be barely listening. She was picking at a loose thread on her nightdress sleeve. Agnes looked up from her sewing and smiled sweetly. She, at least, seemed to be enjoying it. He wondered what it must be like to be illiterate like her. A life without books or letters was not one he would enjoy.

There was a tap on the door. Agnes put down her sewing and went out, returning a moment later with the baby in her arms, cooing and clucking over him, and dabbing dribbles of milk from his face with a muslin cloth.

'Ma'am, the wet-nurse has gone to her own family now. Will you hold your son for a while, perhaps?' asked Agnes.

'Oh Aggie, I am so tired, I fear I might drop him.' Georgia yawned, and pulled her covers up to her neck.

'Let me take him,' said Bartholomew. 'Hello, Barty, my handsome little chap. Do you have a smile for your papa, then? Or one for your mama?' He held the child near to Georgia so she could look upon his face.

She turned her back, and closed her eyes as if to sleep.

He looked questioningly at Agnes, who stepped forward to take the baby again, and place him in a cradle. 'She is always like this,' she whispered.

'It's not right,' he whispered back. Louder, he spoke to Georgia. 'My love, there is news. Rouse yourself please, you must see this.'

Georgia sighed and twisted her head to regard him with her sad, lifeless eyes. He pulled out the letter to show her, but she waved it away.

'I am too tired to read it. Please, just tell me what it says.'

'It is your uncle. I'm afraid to say…'

'Has he died?'

'Yes, love. Three days ago. I am so sorry.' He took her hand and kissed it.

She sighed once more and turned back onto her pillow. 'It's of no importance. He never cared for me.'

'I suppose you will inherit his fortune – you are his only living relative as I understand it?'

'I am, but no. He will not leave the money to me. He told me many times I would get nothing from him; only my father's money.'

'Then who?'

'Mrs Oliphant, I suppose. They were very close.'

Bartholomew suppressed a gasp. That disapproving old busy-body! Who would have thought it?

'The funeral is to be on Thursday,' he told her. 'Are you well enough to travel to Brighton?'

'I cannot leave my bed, Bartholomew. I shall not attend.' She took a sip of her medicine and closed her eyes again. 'I think I should like to sleep now.'

He patted her arm and stood to leave. Agnes had resumed her sewing. She glanced up at him as he left, and gave a half-smile. He felt the familiar old stirrings – she still had that effect on him. But he must be strong and resist her. For the sake of the mother of his beloved son. Though in her current state Georgia was not much of a wife.

He nodded curtly at Agnes and left the room.

Halfway down the stairs he realised he had left the letter in Georgia's room. He turned back to fetch it, and eased the door open as quietly as possible to avoid waking her.

Agnes was bending over the cradle, her back to him. She was holding a pillow. He watched, horrified but somehow powerless to move. Surely she wasn't going to… She took a step closer to the cradle, then dropped the pillow on the floor, shaking her head. He coughed; she turned and reddened when she saw him.

'Oh, sir, you startled me,' she whispered.

'What are you doing with that pillow?' He crossed the room to retrieve the letter from the bedside table.

'I – my back was aching. I was going to prop it behind me in my chair while I sew.' She picked up the pillow and squashed it against the back of her chair as if to demonstrate.

Bartholomew shook his head slightly. He'd had the fleeting impression that she was going to smother the baby, though he did not know why. Agnes was a loyal and faithful servant – hadn't she come back to them, leaving her own child to do so? She loved him, he knew it. And surely no mother could ever hurt another woman's baby.

'Of course. Do you want to work in your own room, perhaps? Polly could sit with my wife for a while.'

'I would prefer to stay here,' she replied. 'There are no comforts for me in my own room.' She held his gaze as she said this, making it all too clear what comforts she was missing. The message was clear. Later, after she had gone to bed, he would go to her. There was no point denying them both. Georgia would never know. And who knew how long it would be until Georgia was better?

Something was still niggling at him. 'What is the medicine you are giving Georgia?' he asked, abruptly.

'It is just a tonic – a mixture of several ingredients – for the pain, for her tiredness. It eases her mind and allows her to rest. Sleep and time are the only true remedy in these cases.'

He nodded, and left the room. His wife was in good hands.

The weeks inched slowly by for Agnes. Her days were spent sitting sewing in her mistress's room. Mrs St Clair was getting worse, not better. She would barely talk to either Agnes or her husband, and would not leave her bed, or allow the doctor in. She would not hold her baby; she would only glance at him briefly when Agnes brought him to her, perhaps smile wanly, and then turn away.

Agnes had heard her mother talk of women like this, who turned in on themselves after a birth. It could take months or years before they were well again. In the meantime others had to care for the baby and the mother alike.

At least Mr St Clair was coming to her room again. Agnes smiled to herself as she sewed a new nightdress for the baby, remembering their love-making the night before. One good thing from Georgia's illness was that her husband had to turn elsewhere for his comforts, and of course, Agnes had been ready and waiting. She had not yet broached the subject of bringing her son to live with them, judging the moment not quite right yet. She needed to get Mr St Clair into a position where he needed her, and no one else would do. Then he would do whatever she wanted.

As long as Polly didn't make trouble for them. She had hissed at Agnes only that morning: *I knows about you and the master*. Something would have to be done about her, before she went blabbing to Mrs Fowles.

Georgia stirred, and groaned. It was mid-afternoon and she was waking up from her midday nap. Agnes put down her sewing and watched her.

Georgia sat up and stretched. 'How long have I slept?'

'Perhaps three hours, ma'am.'

'Three hours? I still feel so tired.' She leaned back in the bed.

Agnes crossed the room to plump up the pillows. 'Would you like me to fetch little Barty, ma'am? He is with Mary.'

'Who?' Georgia frowned.

'Mary Moulsford, ma'am. The wet-nurse.' Agnes realised Georgia had never set eyes on the wet-nurse. It had always been Agnes who brought the baby to and from her. In fact, from the way Mary curtsied to Agnes and called her 'ma'am', it was as though she thought Agnes was the child's mother, and mistress of the house. That was not a misunderstanding Agnes was in any hurry to clear up.

Georgia sighed. 'Oh yes. I remember. No, leave him with her. He needs to feed as much as possible, doesn't he?'

Agnes chuckled. 'There's no danger of him not feeding enough. He's a right guzzler, that one. He'll grow up fit and strong, you can be sure of that.'

'Good. My husband will be pleased with a strong, healthy son.'

'And you, ma'am? Are you not pleased with him too?'

'Yes, I am pleased with him. Of course I am. I'm his mother, aren't I? Why wouldn't I be pleased with my son?' Georgia sighed. 'I just wish I didn't feel so tired and ill all the time. Oh, Aggie, when will I get better? It can't be right to feel like this for so long.'

'Perhaps you should let the doctor see you, ma'am.'

'No! I can't have anyone see me like this.' Georgia sighed again and closed her eyes. 'I can't see what a doctor could do for me. It's like – it's like my body is well but my mind is not. A doctor cannot fix a person's mind. He cannot give me energy, can he? He cannot make me want to get up. He cannot make me love my son!' She burst into tears and buried her face in her hands.

Agnes rushed to her side and sat on the edge of the bed, an arm about her mistress's shoulders. It was hard to see any woman, a fellow mother, in such a state. Even if that woman had the one thing Agnes wanted above all else.

'Ma'am, calm yourself, please. It does not do to be so upset.

179

Come, take a draught of your tonic.' She poured a measure into a small glass and handed it to Georgia, who drank greedily.

'Thank you. You are right. I must be calm. Your tonic helps so much.' Georgia lay back against her pillow.

Agnes smiled. Of course the tonic helped. It was mostly laudanum, with a little lemon and sugar added to disguise the bitter taste. It relaxed her, of course, but also made her sleepy and lethargic. Agnes had been gradually increasing the dose. The more Georgia slept, the more time she could spend with Mr St Clair.

She stayed by Georgia's side, stroking her hair until she had calmed down.

'Aggie, you are so good to me. I must repay you, somehow.'

'Oh, ma'am, it is my job, and besides, I don't like to see you upset.'

Georgia smiled faintly. 'Nevertheless I should like to show my appreciation for all you do for me. Open my wardrobe, would you?'

Agnes did as she was asked.

'That deep-red gown – I don't think it would fit me now that I have had a child.'

Agnes took out the dress in question. 'Would you like me to alter it for you, ma'am?'

'No, I would like you to have it. It would look well on you.' She sighed. 'And I am not in need of any gowns these days, beyond my nightgowns.'

'Ma'am, I can't take this!' Agnes fingered the fine satin gown. Georgia had given her cast-off gowns before but never one as beautiful or fashionable as this.

'You can, and you shall. Go and put it on, I should like to see you in it.'

Agnes raised her eyebrows. 'Very well, ma'am. I shall be back in a moment or two.' She took the dress and went up to her own room to change into it.

The gown fitted her perfectly, as though it was made for her. She unpinned her cap and brushed out her hair so that it fell in waves onto her shoulders. On a whim, she took out the only piece of jewellery she owned – a set of glass beads Georgia had given her – and fastened them around her neck to finish off the outfit. Then she went back down to Georgia's room, tapped lightly on the door and walked in.

Mr St Clair was perched on the edge of his wife's bed. He stood up and gasped as Agnes entered.

'Agnes! You look... Look at you!'

Georgia smiled at her. 'I knew it would suit you. And it's a perfect fit. I'm glad I've given it to you. She looks lovely, doesn't she, Bartholomew?'

'Yes, indeed,' he replied.

Agnes smiled and went to stand before the full-length mirror to see for herself. She was aware of Mr St Clair's eyes following her around the room. Georgia was right. The colour did suit her. Her hair was glossy and bright, and there was a spot of colour in each cheek. Probably because of the presence of Mr St Clair in the room, she mused.

Georgia yawned. 'I am sorry; I think I need to sleep again, now. Agnes, would you wake me when you bring my dinner up, please. Till then, you are free to do as you choose.'

'Of course, ma'am. Thank you, ma'am.'

'Sleep well, my sweet.' Bartholomew kissed his wife and left the room with Agnes. As soon as the door closed behind them he grabbed her around the waist and kissed her.

'Sir! Polly might...'

'Polly is downstairs setting a fire in the drawing-room grate. Mrs Fowles is in the kitchen preparing dinner, with Libby helping. Old George is tending to the horses, along with Danny. And Georgia will be snoring already.'

Agnes giggled, and snaked her hands around him, under his waistcoat. 'She doesn't snore, sir.'

He kissed her again. 'Perhaps not. But she'll be asleep. Come to my room. I want you.'

Half an hour later, Bartholomew emerged from his room, checked the corridor then nodded to Agnes to follow him out. She was giggling a little still, and trying to smooth the creases from her red gown. He felt pleasantly satiated. Georgia had never allowed him to take her in the middle of the day. Their couplings had always been at night, under the bedclothes, with Georgia's nightdress pulled up only as far as was necessary. Unlike Agnes who was much less inhibited and, indeed, seemed to enjoy sex at least as much as he did.

'Come and sit in the drawing room with me,' he said to her, as they went downstairs. 'You can bring some sewing in, if you like. Georgia doesn't need you, and I would like some company.'

This was the first time he'd ever asked her to sit with him in the drawing room. She looked surprised but pleased, and nodded. 'I am making some new nightgowns for the baby. I should be happy to sit with you and work on them. I'll fetch them.' She turned and went back upstairs.

It was a gloomy afternoon, with dark clouds blocking the sunlight. Bartholomew went into the drawing room, and rang the bell for Polly to light the fire and bring some tea.

Polly answered the bell, with baby Barty in her arms. 'Sir, I would make tea, but what shall I do with the baby? The wet-nurse has gone home, the mistress is asleep and I can't find Agnes.'

Agnes walked in at that moment. 'I'll take him, Polly, so you can do what Mr St Clair requires.' She put her sewing things on a chair and took the baby. Polly glared at her, sniffed and flounced off. Bartholomew smiled to himself. There was no love lost between those two, for sure.

They were barely settled in the room with Agnes sewing, the baby laid on a shawl on the hearthrug kicking and gurgling happily, when the doorbell rang and Polly announced the arrival of Dr Moore. Not wanting the doctor to question why he was sitting in the drawing room with a servant, Bartholomew jumped to his feet and went out to the hallway to greet him.

'Jonathon, my old friend. Come in, take some tea with me in my study,' said Bartholomew, shaking the doctor by the hand.

'No, I can't stop long,' the doctor replied. 'I was passing and wondered how your good lady wife is? It has been some time since I last saw her. And what of the baby? Is he thriving?' He blinked short-sightedly at Bartholomew.

'Little Bartholomew is doing very well, thank you. He seems larger every time I see him.'

'Ah yes, they do grow quickly in the early days. That's good to hear. And Mrs St Clair?'

Bartholomew shuffled his feet. How could he explain how Georgia was? Jonathon would insist on seeing her, but she'd made it clear she would not see a doctor. He didn't want to upset her.

'She's coping…' he began.

'Ah, and there's the lady herself!' exclaimed the doctor, striding towards the open drawing-room door.

'What?' Bartholomew was startled. Had Georgia come down-stairs? But Jonathon was standing just inside the drawing room, looking directly at Agnes.

'You're looking well, Mrs St Clair. And if I may say so, what a charming picture of domesticity – the young mother sitting with her sewing beside the fire, baby at her feet. Well, it's clear you've recovered very well, and I'm delighted to see it.'

Bartholomew opened his mouth to contradict the doctor, but then said nothing. Best not to embarrass his old friend. He shook his head slightly at Agnes, who had risen to her feet.

'Don't get up, Mrs St Clair. I can't stop – got a house call to make in the village. Well, good to see that all is well in this household at least. Don't hesitate to call on me if you need me, Bartholomew.' He gave a small bow towards Agnes, and backed out of the room.

'I'll see myself out, old chap. Now then, where's the door handle got to?' He groped around on the panelling until Bartholomew took pity, stepped forward and opened the door for him.

Returning to the drawing room, Bartholomew sat down in a chair opposite Agnes. She regarded him with wide, questioning eyes.

'He's as blind as a bat, poor Jonathon,' he said. 'But you do look rather like her, especially in that gown and with your hair unpinned.'

Agnes said nothing, but picked up her sewing and bent over it, a secret smile playing at the corners of her mouth. Bartholomew watched her for a moment, feeling aroused once more. She really was quite special. If only she were Georgia…

Chapter Sixteen

Hampshire, June 2013

It was three weeks since the discovery of the bones in our garden. We'd bought the children a new trampoline, and had replaced the broken windows and guttering. The lawn was recovering well. The storm and its aftermath just seemed like a bad dream now. There was only the garden wall waiting to be rebuilt. Simon was planning to do that himself, but needed to find some suitable old bricks first, as some of the originals were unusable. He'd spent the previous weekend scouring local reclamation yards, looking for bricks to match the one in his pocket from our wall.

As far as I could work out, all the reclamation yards in the area were within a ten-mile drive. But Simon had spent a whole day at them, and had refused to take Lewis with him, even though the boy had pleaded to be allowed to go. I hated being so suspicious, but couldn't help myself wondering what Simon was up to. I was still fretting that perhaps he was having an affair, even though the more rational parts of my brain knew that he couldn't, wouldn't do such a thing. But I had no alternative explanation for his continuing late nights and now, whole weekend days away from home, or for his evasiveness when I asked him about them.

I was busying myself with drawing up plans on my laptop for a new kitchen, using some nifty free-to-download software to arrange cupboards and appliances, and change the work surfaces and cupboard doors at will. It was great fun, though my gut churned at the predicted expense of it all.

I'd just clicked on a cream-coloured option with wooden work surfaces when the doorbell rang. It was DI Bradley.

'Mrs Smith, sorry to disturb you without warning, but I was in the area and thought I would drop in. Is now a good time to bring you up to date on the investigation?'

'Er, yes, of course.' I stood aside to let him in, and showed him through to the kitchen where I put the kettle on. I could still remember his tea preferences – milk and one small sugar. He gazed out through the kitchen window at the restored garden.

'You've worked hard. That looks so much better than the last time I saw it.' He grinned, and sat down at the table. 'Well, you'll be pleased to know we've had some results back from the lab. The bones have been carbon-dated to some time around the middle of the nineteenth century. Definitely not modern, and I'm afraid young Lewis will be disappointed to find it's not a Roman legionary either. We can't be very precise with this technique, but it points to a date range of around 1840 to 1860. However, dendrochronology can be much more accurate, and we've calculated that the tree began growing in 1842. So my guess would be that she was buried around that time, and a sapling planted on the spot.'

I took a moment to take all that in. 'She?'

'Yes, sorry, I should have started with that. The remains are those of a woman, probably quite a young one. The osteologist – that's the bone specialist – said he can't be sure of anything more, but it was definitely female.'

I poured him a cup of tea, and placed it on the table in front of him. 'Any ideas as to cause of death?'

'None at all. As you know the skeleton was too much disturbed by the tree roots to be able to get any further clues.'

I regarded him carefully. 'Do you think, was it—'

'Murder?' he asked, raising an eyebrow. 'Impossible to say. And professionally, I can't say. But, off the record, the fact she was buried in a back garden and a sapling planted above, which would stop the area being dug over – yes, personally speaking, I'd say she was most likely murdered. Or at least, unlawfully killed. Possibly suicide. Otherwise she'd have been buried in the churchyard, you'd assume.'

I sipped my tea. Who was she? She'd been buried in the garden during the time my ancestors owned the house. So she was presumably someone known to Bartholomew and Georgia. The chances of finding out who it actually was would be remote, but worth a try and I knew I'd enjoy the research. And Dad had said he'd like to get involved as well.

But something worried me. '1842, that's, um, 170 years ago. I'm amazed the bones lasted that long,' I said. 'I'd have thought they would rot completely, or be so broken up by the roots they'd be unrecognisable.'

DI Bradley nodded. 'I thought that too, but our tree experts told me beech tree roots tend to be shallow and wide, unlike say an oak which puts down a deep tap root. It's one reason why beech trees are particularly susceptible to blowing over in storms. So if the bones were deep enough under the tree, the tree's roots would not penetrate them as much as you'd think.'

'How come they didn't just rot away completely?'

'Your soil is quite alkaline. That helped preserve them. And under the tree the earth would be dry, as the roots would pull all moisture out of the soil before it had a chance to get down to where the bones were.'

I nodded. That made sense to me. I could hardly wait for DI Bradley to go, so that I could make a start on the research. But he seemed to want to linger over his tea, and was enjoying the pack of biscuits I'd opened. Finally he got to his feet.

'Once all the reports have been completed, we won't need the bones any more. Strictly speaking, as they were found on your property, they belong to you, but if you want us to dispose of them, we can do that. They're not old enough to be of interest to a museum, so it's probably best if we get them cremated. Do you want to have the ashes?'

'Well, yes, I suppose so. We could scatter them back in the garden or...' I hardly liked to say it. If I unearthed any clues as to who she was, perhaps I could scatter her ashes somewhere of importance to her – near her home, or her family's graves. 'Yes,' I said, more decisively. 'I'd definitely like to have them, if I may.'

He nodded. 'I'll bring them. Thanks for the tea, Mrs Smith. You always provide a fine choice of biscuits.' He shook my hand, and I showed him out.

As soon as he'd gone I picked up the phone and rang Dad. There were three hours to go before I needed to collect Thomas from his nursery class. Time to get started finding out who the poor woman was.

Dad was fascinated by DI Bradley's revelations and definitely wanted to help with the research.

I was feeling daunted. 'How do we even begin to find out who she was?'

'Well, why not start with the residents of the house in 1841?' he said. 'Try to trace them forward. If you find them in the next census or find a death certificate for them, you can rule them out.'

'What if she died before the 1841 census and the tree was planted later?'

'In that case we'd have no chance of finding out who she was. But if the sapling was planted in 1842 the body was probably buried only just before, and that does fit with the carbon-dating range of 1840–60. So let's hope we're right, and she was alive at the time of the census. When exactly was it taken?'

'April 1841,' I said.

'OK. The other thing we could try,' Dad said, getting excited now, 'is local newspapers. Perhaps someone went missing. Perhaps there was some local scandal... Why don't you start with the censuses and I'll trawl through the papers? Quite a few are online. Or I could go to the library in Winchester and look at microfiches. Your mother will be delighted to have me out of the house.'

'OK, Dad, if you're sure you don't mind?'

'I can't wait to get started! I'll ring if I find anything. Bye, love.'

I grabbed my laptop, saved the kitchen designs I'd started on, and navigated to my genealogical research file. I already had a copy of the 1841 census for the house saved, so I opened it up.

Bartholomew St Clair, head of household. Obviously not him. Georgia St Clair, his wife. Right gender and age, but it wasn't her. She was buried in St Michael's churchyard, and I had her death certificate from 1875. Barty St Clair. Not him, he was only a few weeks old in 1841.

That left two servants: Agnes Cutter and Polly Turner. I looked at their entries in more detail. Both were listed as young, unmarried women.

I looked at the 1851 census for Kingsley House. Bartholomew, Georgia, their children Barty, Isobella and William. Their other daughter Elizabeth had been born and died between the two censuses. Servants Annie Barton and Eliza Montford. No Agnes Cutter or Polly Turner. Had they married, changed jobs and moved away, or...?

My next job was to try to trace these two women after 1841. It was harder going forward than going back. Going backwards, you know that someone must have existed, and must have had a birth registration. Going forwards was harder, as you have no clues as to when they died, or married, or moved area.

It was a nightmare. Researching the St Clairs had been relatively easy, as it is such an unusual surname. But there were hundreds of Cutters and thousands of Turners. I spent a couple of hours browsing the 1851 census, and possible marriage or death registrations for them, and got nowhere. I realised I'd have to be more systematic.

With just half an hour left before I needed to leave to collect Thomas, I decided to take a look at the neighbours of Kingsley House in the 1841 census. The village was tiny back then, and the total census for it ran to just a dozen pages. Maybe there'd be someone with a more unusual name I'd be able to track forwards, so at least I could rule out one person.

The next census entry after Kingsley House was for Stables Cottage. This listed a George Fowles and his wife Maria. Both were in their sixties; George's occupation was given as Groom, and Maria's as Housekeeper. With a jolt I realised that they probably both worked for Bartholomew St Clair in Kingsley House. And Stables Cottage was almost certainly where Stables Close was now – on part of the land belonging to Bartholomew.

I began compiling a document on my laptop for each person – Agnes, Polly, the Fowles couple – and started adding notes and possible matches. The clock in the hallway chimed two. I was late to collect Thomas! I leapt up, grabbed my keys and ran through the village to the school. Other parents and their children were already on the way home. I hated being late to pick up the kids.

Running as fast as my FitFlops would allow, I reached the school gate, crossed the playground in record time, elbowing the groups of chatting mums and skipping girls out of the way, and burst in through the classroom door. As expected, Thomas was sitting alone, his Thomas the Tank Engine rucksack on his back ready, his lunchbox on the table in front of him. His teacher was stacking tiny chairs on top of tables ready for the cleaners. She smiled sympathetically at me as I stuttered an apology, and waved at Thomas. 'See you tomorrow, Thomas. Don't forget to bring your picture in when you've finished it.'

'Hello, sweetie,' I said. 'What picture have you been working on?'

He pouted at me, and marched out of the classroom without taking my hand. My punishment for being Last Mum. I walked behind him until we reached the school gate, then took his hand anyway. He gave me a half-smile. The sulk was over already. 'What picture was Miss Cotton talking about?' I asked again.

'The one I've been doing of the ghosts and skelingtons in our house.'

'Oh. You must show me when we get home.' I dreaded to think what he'd drawn. Miss Cotton knew about our discovery – so did the whole village of course, after the piece on *South Today* and in the local papers. We were quite the local celebrities.

The picture turned out to be a typical four-year old scrawl of characters with huge heads, stickman arms and legs and no bodies. All had enormous Os for mouths. They were the ghosts, Thomas told me. The ones that went woo-woo in the chimney. Among the ghost figures lay lots of sticks and circles – apparently these were the bones. Thomas settled down at the kitchen table with his crayons to complete the drawing, then carefully wrote his name in spidery letters at the top, and put it back in his bag to take to school the next day.

Later that evening, as we sat around the dining-room table after our evening meal, I told Simon and the kids about DI Bradley's visit, and about the findings. Simon, for once, was home on time to eat with the kids.

Lauren nodded sagely at the news the bones were female. 'I knew it'd be a girl. The ghost is a girl, and I've always thought they'd be her bones.'

I frowned at her, hoping she was not about to scare Thomas again. 'What ghost?'

She rolled her eyes. 'The one who visits Thomas's room, of course.'

'She goes woo-woo in the chimley,' Thomas said. 'That was to warn us that the tree was going to fall. She's a good ghost, Mummy. Not a bad one.'

Ah. I hadn't realised the ghosts were now considered goodies. That probably explained why Thomas had seemed more settled in the house since the storm, despite the macabre findings in the garden.

'Have you actually seen this ghost?' asked Simon.

'No, Dad. You don't *see* ghosts. You just *feel* them. She watches Thomas play and looks out of the window at the hill,' said Lauren.

Lewis laughed. 'Yeah, and once she built him a really good Brio train layout. But I'll kill her if she touches my Lego. Oh, I forgot. She's already dead.'

Lauren thumped his arm. 'Don't be stupid. She's real. Just cos *you* haven't felt her. Me and Thomas know she's there, don't we?'

Thomas nodded vigorously. Simon and I exchanged a glance. Maybe it was time to change the subject. I'd heard that children can be more sensitive to supernatural phenomena, but I wasn't sure that I actually believed in ghosts myself…

After the children were in bed Simon and I sat outside on the garden chairs watching the midsummer sun slowly set. It was good to spend some time with him. The air was scented with honeysuckle and Eileen and Stan's newly mown grass. I told Simon the rest of DI Bradley's report, and that Dad and I had decided to try to find out who the bones could be.

'Are the police not going to try to do that?'

'No. They're not interested. The bones are too old to be of importance to anyone living, so they've closed the case.'

'OK. Well, don't you waste too much time on it. At some point we'll also need to close the case and get on with our lives.' He ran his hands through his hair. 'Although I don't much feel we can get on with life at the moment. This Amy thing – it's really difficult to concentrate on anything else. I keep thinking about her, wondering what she's like, wondering how it'll be when I finally meet her.'

I shrugged. 'It'll be OK. Awkward, no doubt, but you'll be fine. You'll charm her, as you always charm everyone you meet.'

He didn't appear to have heard me. 'What does she want from me, I wonder?'

'A link to her roots, I'd say. A blood relative. The knowledge of where she's come from.' I knew Simon would find this concept hard to grasp.

He looked at me, worry clouding his eyes. 'Do you think she'll want to meet her grandmother? My mother? What would I do? Mum would have no idea who she is. She doesn't even know who I am any more. I'd never be able to explain Amy to her.'

I squeezed his hand again. 'You could tell her about your mother, but no, I don't think I would tell your mum about Amy. And, because you're adopted, your mum is no relation to Amy. So it'd be fair for you to say you don't want to upset your mother by taking Amy to visit her.'

'You're right. I don't think I will tell Mum.' He sighed. 'Speaking of Mum, I'll be going to see her this Saturday afternoon. I'll try and get some gardening done in the morning. We should extend this patio, to fit a larger table, so we can eat meals outside in the summer. We should also get on with planning the new kitchen. So much to do, so little time!'

I'd completely forgotten about the kitchen plans. DI Bradley's visit had put all that completely out of my head. I fetched my laptop, and showed Simon where I'd got to. The stars were out and dew was settling on the grass by the time we went back inside. I loved midsummer. Those lovely long evenings made so much more seem possible. I was looking forward to the school summer holidays, too. We'd planned to stay at home this year and explore our local area. We'd have trips to Marwell Wildlife Park, Winchester to see the cathedral and its various museums – Lewis was desperate to see King Arthur's Round Table – and walks in the Downs and the New Forest. Only three more weeks until school broke up. In August it would be Thomas's fifth birthday. In September Lewis and Lauren were due to move up to secondary school. They'd be taking a bus from the village into Winchester every morning, and I'd only have Thomas to take to the village primary school. All change. My babies were growing up.

Chapter Seventeen

Hampshire, December 1876

Barty, my son, you have read this far and perhaps you are now beginning to tire of this narrative. Many men are unfaithful to their wives, perhaps even father a child with their mistress, so maybe you are not terribly shocked by what I have confessed so far. What then, did I do to haunt me throughout my life? What happened that I regret so much?

I cannot divulge the answers to those questions just yet. I must allow the story to unfold, piece by piece, step by step. But this I promise you, dear Barty, you will know the answers before the end. For it is soon now that I will reach the climax of this sorry tale. I must steel myself with a whiskey or two before I write this next section. I have made the earlier parts longer than I intended; perhaps because I was putting off reaching this part, and the deeds of which I am most ashamed. Well, I can put it off no longer. Time is against me – my cancer is taking hold, eating away at me from within, like the secrets I have long held. I grow weaker with every passing day,

but I must and <u>shall</u> finish this narrative, so that I hold no
secrets from you, my best-loved son.

I shall pick up the story again in early December 1841.
The autumn had been long, dark and wet. Georgia was still
confined to her room, seeing no one except myself and Agnes.
The wet-nurse had been dismissed, as young Barty, at nine
months old, was now eating gruel mixed with milk and sugar.
I shall resume the narrative with a scene between Agnes and
myself, one which pains me even now to recall, even after so
many years. My words and actions here, were they in some
part to blame for what happened after?

Hampshire, December 1841

It was a dark, gloomy afternoon, and Bartholomew was sitting
beside the fireside in the drawing room, half-heartedly reading a
newspaper. If only the rain would stop, he would go out for a
ride to clear his head. Georgia's ongoing melancholy, together
with the depressing weather, was affecting the entire household
and he felt the need to get out as often as he could. He toyed
with the idea of going away – spending the winter season in
London perhaps, leaving Georgia and little Barty in the care of
Agnes and Mrs Fowles. He could employ a nursemaid to help
them, perhaps.

He sighed. He knew that he could never leave the house while
things continued as they were. Aside from not wanting to leave
his sick wife and dear son, he knew he would not last long without
his nightly visits to Agnes's room.

As if she'd been tuned into his thoughts, Agnes tapped on the
door and entered, as usual without waiting for permission. She
was wearing the red satin dress that had been Georgia's, and
carried baby Barty on her hip. He was pulling at her necklace,
trying to get the beads into his mouth.

'Sir, your wife is asleep, and Polly is busy with the dinner. I have brought Barty in to see if you could watch over him for a while, as I have several chores to do.' She put him down on the hearthrug, and handed him a rattle from her pocket, which he proceeded to bang on the floor. 'If you don't mind me saying, sir, now that the baby is older it's time he had a proper nursemaid. Nursing Mrs St Clair takes up most of my time.'

Bartholomew moved a fire-guard into place, between Barty and the roaring log fire. 'You are right, we should probably hire a nursemaid. I shall speak to my wife about it.'

Agnes rolled her eyes to the ceiling. 'She'll not have much to say about it. She doesn't seem to care what happens. I'm more of a mother to that child than she is.'

'I know it. I'm grateful for what you do for my son.' He took a step forward, and put his arms around her. Little Barty shuffled towards them and clutched at his trouser leg and Agnes's skirt.

'And for what I do for you?' she whispered.

'Of course.' He nuzzled her neck, breathing in her musky scent. He would employ a nursemaid, he decided. If one had been here now to mind Barty, he'd have been able to take Agnes upstairs to bed…

She kissed him, and then pushed him away. 'Sir, it is time I spoke to you of what is on my mind. My own son, my own little Bartholomew – is it not time we brought him here to live with us?'

Bartholomew sat down and shook his head. 'How could we do that? How could we explain the appearance of another child to people?'

'Explain to whom? No one comes here.'

'There's Mrs Fowles and Libby…' He reached down and picked up Barty, and dandled the child on his lap.

'They're servants! Why do you care what the servants think?'

He looked up at her sternly. 'You too are a servant, might I remind you.'

'Servant, pah!' Agnes paced the room angrily. 'I'm more of a wife to you than she is. I raise your child and sleep in your bed. And yet you won't grant me my basic rights – of having my own son live in the same house as me.'

'Agnes, please remain calm. Mrs Fowles is only across the hallway and might hear. Your position in this house is only possible if we maintain the utmost discretion.'

She stopped pacing and turned to face him. 'I've been discreet, sir, you know I have. But I don't know that I can continue, without my sweet son at my side.'

'You have Barty to love. Is he not enough?'

'I do love Barty, but he is not mine and it is not the same.' At the sound of his name, Barty looked up and raised his little arms towards her. She reached down for him, and held him tightly against her.

Bartholomew regarded them. If only he was looking now at his wife and her child. Why did things have to be so complicated? Two women, two sons. He only wanted one of each.

'Agnes, I am sorry. There is no possibility of bringing your son here. If you really want to see him, you will have to leave us and go to visit him. If I hire a nursemaid for Barty and a nurse for Georgia, we can spare you for a week or so. We can tell Georgia your mother is unwell again. I will pay your fares, of course.'

She stared at him over Barty's head. 'If I go, my ma will insist I bring my son away with me. I told her the next time I saw her it would be to collect him.' She brushed away a tear. 'Besides, I know if I saw him I'd never be able to leave him again.'

'Then it seems you have three choices,' he said, sadly. 'Visit your family for two weeks and return to us alone. Stay here and continue as we are. Or resign your position and leave us for good.'

'If I leave, who'd be a mother to this one? Not her upstairs, that's for sure. It'd break this little mite's heart if I were to go.' She kissed Barty's head. He giggled and wrapped his little arms tightly around her neck.

197

'So stay, Agnes, please.' Bartholomew got to his feet and put his arms around both her and the child. 'We'll carry on as we have been, until or unless something changes.'

He felt her stiffen and then relax in his arms. 'You give me no real choice, sir. I'm not sure I could ever leave you, in any case.' She raised her face to his for a kiss. 'If something did happen, to the mistress, perhaps then we could be together openly, and bring my son to us to be a brother to Barty?'

He frowned. What did she mean, if anything happened to the mistress? Georgia was depressed, that was all. It happened to some women, after giving birth. Hardly life threatening, was it? But Agnes was nuzzling into his neck, and little Barty was pushing his face between them in the hope of a kiss for himself, and the thought slipped quietly out of his mind as he held them both tightly.

Oh, dear Barty, that was a tender moment indeed between the three of us. But it was only a day later that things in our little household turned truly black, and reached a point from which there was no turning back. Let us see the next scene through Agnes's eyes. She told me later, word for word, what had passed between herself and Georgia that afternoon.

Agnes was sitting in her usual place in Georgia's room, sewing a new nightdress for her mistress. She was beginning to resent the number of hours she had to spend each day sitting by Georgia's side in her room. Why couldn't Mr St Clair employ a proper nurse for his wife? If only Georgia would allow someone else to tend to her. Agnes could barely remember the days in Brighton, when they would go out to parks and pleasure gardens, visit shops, receive visitors. Georgia's world, and hers with it, had shrunk to this house, this room. Since she'd arrived in North Kingsley, she'd not left the house except to stroll around the garden for a few minutes when she was desperate for some fresh air. And all because her mistress had succumbed to deep melancholy, after the birth of her baby. Well, Agnes supposed if she was honest, she'd made it worse by giving Georgia such large doses of laudanum, but she wouldn't have had to do that if Georgia had responded to her baby the way women usually did. She'd so wanted a baby – how upset she'd been by those miscarriages! And now that she had one, she didn't seem to care for the poor little thing at all. It was so unfair. They were the wrong way around – it was Georgia who should be separated from her son, she wouldn't even notice. And Agnes who should have her baby with her. Agnes who should be married to Bartholomew. Agnes who should be mistress of this house. She recalled the conversation with Bartholomew the previous day, and the impossible choices he'd given her. Unless something happened it was clear there was no hope of being permanently reunited with her son.

Georgia was stirring. Agnes put down her sewing. With luck, Georgia would just take another draught of her tonic and go quickly back to sleep. Agnes had been gradually increasing the amount of laudanum in the tonic. It was easier to keep Georgia asleep as much as possible. It was probably slowing Georgia's recovery but at least it gave Agnes more time off duty – more time to be with Bartholomew either in his room or downstairs in the drawing room.

'Aggie? What time of day is it?'

'About three o'clock, ma'am. I heard the hall clock striking a few minutes ago.'

'So dark!'

'Usual for the time of year, ma'am.'

'Yes, I suppose it is almost winter. I fear I shall not leave this room until the springtime. Not until the gorse blooms on that hill I can see through the window.'

'Fresh air would help you, I believe, ma'am.'

Georgia shuddered. 'It looks so cold outside. The hill is just a black outline against the sky today. It's cold in here, too. Bank up the fire, would you, please Aggie?'

Agnes added a couple of logs to the fire. It was a mild day, not really cold at all, and certainly not cold in that room. But Georgia liked the room to be warm and stuffy. Sometimes she refused to allow the curtains to be opened at all, and Agnes would have to sew by candlelight. Or just sit doing nothing. Lord knows she'd done enough sewing over these last few months. No baby had as many nightgowns and bonnets as little Barty. Though she hoped that one day soon he might have to share them with another child.

'Dress my hair, would you, please Aggie? If my husband should visit me today I feel I should try to look more presentable.' Georgia heaved herself into a half-sitting position in her bed, and Agnes plumped up the pillows behind her.

'Of course, ma'am.' She fetched a hairbrush, and gently brushed Georgia's hair. It was thin, brittle and dull, not at all like the glossy tresses she used to have. She twisted the hair into a loose pile and pinned it with the silver and emerald hair comb.

'There. You look as lovely as ever, ma'am.'

'Thank you, Aggie, but I am sure I don't.' Georgia groaned. 'Oh, I am so tired.'

Agnes considered whether this was the hundredth or thousandth time she'd heard those words. 'I know, ma'am. Maybe have another draught of tonic?'

'I have had so much today. Should I really take it so often? Though perhaps I will, for it does make me feel better for a while.' She reached out for the bottle, which Agnes had topped up earlier in the day. She was running short on supplies of laudanum. She'd need to dispatch Polly to purchase some more. At least Mr St Clair didn't seem to mind paying for it. Anything, he said, to make it easier for his wife. He paid fewer visits to Georgia's room now. He too seemed bored by her illness and resentful of the restrictions it placed on his household. The way he had held her and the baby yesterday – it was as though he wished *she* was his wife and the mother of Barty.

'Ma'am, you have only had one dose of it today so far,' lied Agnes. She'd had at least three.

'Well then, another won't hurt.' Georgia gratefully took a swallow of the tonic, leaned back against the pillows and sighed. 'Sometimes I feel as though I don't want to go on. I'm tired of living like this.'

'Ma'am...'

'I'm sorry. Morbid talk. I used to run and skip, on the beach in Brighton. I can't imagine doing that now. I look at that hill through the window and know that once I would have run up to the top of it. Not now. I'm not at all the girl I once was. Sometimes I just wish it was all over.'

'No, ma'am. You must fight it, not give in to it.'

'I've no fight left in me. Bartholomew would be better off without me.' Georgia stared at the ceiling. 'So would the baby. What kind of a mother am I? He doesn't even know me.'

'Shall I fetch him for you?'

'He'd only cry if I held him, like the last time. Who is looking after him now?'

'He is in here, asleep in his cradle.'

'Good. Leave him. I shall try to sleep again. Stay with me, Aggie. Knowing you are there in your corner is a comfort to me.'

'Very well, ma'am.' Agnes sat down in her usual chair and picked up the sewing again. Soon the light would fade and she would need to light a candle, or move closer to the fire to see. But for now the light from the window was just about good enough. She threaded a needle with white cotton and began stitching delicate tucks across the front of the nightgown. It would be nice to own something like this herself, rather than the coarse gowns she usually slept in. She imagined wearing it herself, lying herself in the large four-poster bed Georgia was now tucked up in. Seating herself at the dressing table, arranging her hair with the silver and emerald comb, ringing the bell for some other maid to help her. Oh, why couldn't she have been born rich? If she'd been of a better class, Bartholomew might have married her and not Georgia. He'd be happier too, she was sure of it.

Bartholomew ate his dinner alone and in silence, as he did every night. Polly waited on him, sullenly. Really the girl was too much. He had a good mind to send her back to her family in Brighton, and employ a new maid-of-all-work, locally, and maybe a nursemaid too, to ease the burden on Agnes. He considered the evening ahead. Once the dinner things were cleared, he'd dismiss Polly and Mrs Fowles for the night, then see if Agnes was free to come and sit with him in the drawing room. As long as Georgia and Barty were both asleep Agnes would be able to come downstairs. And Georgia did little except sleep these days.

He pushed away his plate and poured himself a glass of brandy from the decanter on the sideboard. If Agnes was unavailable there'd be little he could do other than read the paper and drink brandy. Tomorrow he'd go out for a ride, if it wasn't raining. There'd been a lot of rain lately and the ground was sodden.

He rang the bell for Polly, and turned down the offer of a pudding. Brandy was all the dessert he wanted. He drank another while Polly cleared the table, then left the dining room and climbed the stairs to Georgia's room. He tapped lightly on the door with a fingernail, and it was opened by Agnes.

'She's asleep, sir,' she whispered.

'Good. Come down to the drawing room in half an hour. Drink a brandy with me.'

'Very well, sir.' Agnes smiled, that slow, seductive smile he knew so well. He resolved to bank up the fire in the drawing room – keep it nice and warm, throw some cushions down onto the hearthrug and, who knew, the evening might turn out to be a good one yet. Agnes appeared to have forgiven him for his refusal to let her bring her son to live with them. He hoped she would not raise the subject again.

'Is she any better today?' he asked, still standing in the doorway, his hand on the doorknob. He could just see Georgia's white face on her pillow, in the gloomy shadows of the room.

'No. If anything she is worse. She has been saying she wishes

202

it were all over, and that she was no longer a burden to you.' Agnes's eyes glittered in the candlelight.

'She is becoming a burden, it's true.' He sighed. 'I too wish this was over. It is sad to see her so wasted, she who was once so vital, so lively. She is suffering so much.'

'Yes, she is suffering. It is a shame we cannot end her pain.'

'If only we could. The poor girl. I married her for her youth and vigour, but now she is but a shell of her former self.' He drew the back of his hand across his forehead. 'Forgive me, Agnes. I should not speak to you like this. But, you, dear thing, know me so well. You know what I like, and what I want.'

Agnes regarded him silently, her green eyes meeting and holding his. She seemed to read something there, for she nodded, and set her mouth into a firm line. Turning away from him she picked up a discarded pillow and walked towards the bed. An image of her, cushion in hand, leaning over little Barty's cradle leapt into Bartholomew's head. But she was not walking towards the cradle in the corner. She was moving towards Georgia, who lay sleeping on her back, her hair spread across the pillow and her arms flung above her head like a baby's.

Georgia had been so beautiful when he'd first met her. He remembered how she'd made him carry her in the snow, so there would be only a single set of footprints for others to follow.

Agnes held the pillow in front of her. She was standing now at the head of the bed. She glanced back towards him. He gave the slightest nod, almost imperceptible.

She lowered the pillow slowly, carefully, quietly.

Georgia, on the beach in Brighton, the wind whipping at her hair as he asked her to marry him.

Why had he nodded? What had he consented to, with that nod?

She pressed the pillow onto Georgia's face, pushing down firmly on each side.

Georgia, dancing in her black gown, on the evening they'd first met.

Agnes had always known what was best for Georgia. No doubt she was now doing the right thing, the best thing, once again.

Her legs kicked a little, feebly. Her arms raised as if to fight, but soon slumped back onto the bed. The laudanum was sedating her.

Georgia, exclaiming in delight over the silver and emerald comb he'd had made for her. She was wearing it now, he saw. Its jewels glinted in the firelight.

But what was Agnes doing? Ending her suffering? The poor girl, wishing only that this phase of her life was over.

The kicks gave way to twitches, and still Agnes pressed down on the pillow.

Georgia, collapsing in agony as she suffered her first miscarriage.

He should stop her. He should cry out, rush across the room, snatch the pillow away. Why was he still standing at the door, his hand on the doorknob as though he was not quite in the room? He was not really there, not a part of this terrible scene at all. As long as he held on to the door handle none of it was real.

And now there was no movement at all, but still Agnes held down the pillow, and still he held on to the doorknob.

Georgia. Georgia. Georgia. His wife. His beautiful, sweet, loving wife.

Agnes turned to look at him. Her face was expressionless. 'Sir, I believe her suffering is over now.'

Over. It was all over. But it had all only just begun.

Feeling dazed he entered the room fully and closed the door quietly behind him. He crossed to the fireplace and added a couple of large logs to the fire, then lit a candle from a taper and placed it on a side table. He went to the window and pulled the curtains closed. It had been dark for some hours, and outside, it was raining softly.

There was something in the room that required his attention. But for the moment he did not quite want to turn his mind in that direction. He picked up the nightgown Agnes had been working on, and held it up.

'A fine piece,' he said. 'Very fine.' He folded it carefully and put it back onto Agnes's chair.

Agnes was still holding the pillow, but now she had lifted it from Georgia's face. Her lips were blue, and her skin was a deathly white. Agnes gently lifted her arms and folded them onto her chest, then pulled up the covers to her chin.

'She looks at peace, sir.'

'She does, yes. She sleeps in peace, yes.'

He rushed forward quickly as the blood drained from Agnes's face and she slumped to the floor. He caught her, knelt and cradled her head on his lap.

'Oh, my love, my love, wake up, come back to me,' he moaned. 'Georgia, my darling, my beloved wife, I'm here, wake up, please wake up!'

Agnes groaned and opened her eyes. She looked wildly around the room as if wondering where she was, and he saw in her eyes the memories of the last quarter-hour come flooding back to her. She sat up, leaning into him still.

'Oh my Lord, what have we done?' she said, in a harsh whisper.

'Ssh,' he said, holding her, stroking her hair. 'Ssh, don't wake...'

'She'll not wake,' said Agnes, her eyes wide. 'She'll never wake again! We've done for her!'

'...the baby, I mean. Don't wake him.' He bent his head and kissed her gently, on the lips.

'What are we going to do?'

'Do?' He tried to kiss her again, but she pushed him away.

'With *her*.'

He let go of Agnes and stood up, regarding his still, dead wife properly for the first time. The horror of what had happened finally struck him and he buried his face in his hands. What had they done? Agnes had done the deed, but he'd stood and watched, and had made no move to stop her. Oh, why had she done it? Why hadn't he stopped her? He ran through the events in his mind since he'd tapped on the door of the room, working through

205

a different sequence, a different outcome. He'd darted forward and snatched the pillow from Agnes, slapping her, then gathered a gasping Georgia in his arms and kissed her, vowing never to leave her side. He'd given a small shake of his head, not a nod, and Agnes had dropped the pillow at the foot of the bed, then come down to the drawing room with him, where they'd made love beside the fire. He'd tapped on the door and it had been opened by Georgia, out of bed and dressed, feeling oh so much better, and ready to come downstairs with him for the evening.

Agnes, still on the floor, clutched at his leg. 'What are we to do?' she asked again, her voice shocked and rasping.

He took his hands away from his face. The stark truth of Georgia's corpse lay in front of him. A string of possibilities ran through his head, thoughts tumbling over each other. They would both leave the room, then Agnes would come back a little later, scream to find her mistress dead in her bed, passed away in her sleep. But why would a young woman like Georgia simply die like that? She'd been unwell but it was a sickness of the mind, not life threatening. They would say she must have taken too large a dose of the laudanum. But couldn't doctors tell these days? They cut bodies open, and could tell whether too much laudanum had been drunk. He would get a knife and cut Georgia's wrists, let her bleed over the bed, say she had taken her own life? And have the stigma of a wife's suicide hang over him for the rest of his life? In any case, would a dead body bleed enough to make that look feasible?

As each possibility presented itself, he dismissed it. More and more he wanted things to be back the way they were. All he wanted was to live happily and quietly with an adored wife, producing a child every couple of years. But had things *ever* been like that? There had always been Agnes, since the day he'd met Georgia. He'd never fully devoted himself to Georgia. He realised he was wanting to return to something that had never been.

He glanced again at Georgia. What was he to do?

Chapter Eighteen

Hampshire, July 2013

'Give it me, Thomas!'

'No, I found it!'

'I need to show it to Mum. Give it here!'

'It's mine. I'll show it.'

'Thomas, give it!'

I closed my secateurs and tucked them into a back pocket, then crossed the lawn to see what Lauren and Thomas were squabbling about.

'Mum, he won't give me the piece of cloth he found. But you'll want to see it cos it looks like it came off the skeleton,' said Lauren, indignantly.

'It's mine, I found it.' Thomas stood in the middle of the flower bed where he'd been digging a trench for some radish seeds, with his feet planted wide, his chin jutted out and his hands clasped firmly behind his back.

'It's OK, Thomas. May I see what you found? Lauren, don't snatch it from him.'

With a suspicious look at Lauren, Thomas held out his clenched

207

fist and slowly uncurled his fingers. He was grasping a shred of grubby fabric. I took it carefully and examined it. It was clearly very old and rotten, almost disintegrating in my fingers.

'Is it from the skeleton?' Thomas asked.

'Possibly,' I replied. Simon and my Dad had filled the beech root hole with soil delivered from a nearby plant nursery, but the area had been so much disturbed and dug over it was possible that earth from around the skeleton had made its way to the surface. The forensic archaeologists who'd dug out the bones had mentioned finding some traces of fabric, perhaps a shroud or sheet that the woman had been buried in.

I peered closely at the scrap. It had probably been white or cream originally. There were a few lines of stitching running across it, tiny tucks of fabric neatly stitched. This was no bed sheet. It looked more like part of a garment. Perhaps a petticoat or nightdress.

'This is a good find, Thomas,' I said. 'It might have belonged to your ghost. Do you want to keep it, or may I have it?'

'You can have it,' he said, generously. 'But Lauren can't have it.'

'I don't want it, it's disgusting. Anyway, your radishes will never grow there. They need to be in full sunlight. Dad said.' Lauren stuck her tongue out at Thomas and stalked off to join Lewis on the new trampoline.

'Your radishes will be fine here,' I said, noticing Thomas's lip quivering. 'In the morning the sun shines on this part of the garden. Come on, I'll help you plant them.' I tucked the scrap of fabric into my pocket. Maybe it had belonged to our mystery woman, maybe not.

Suddenly I remembered the silver and emerald hair comb I'd found in the study drawer just after we moved in. Could that have belonged to the mystery woman too? And what about the sealed-up loft – when was it sealed up? Could there be anything more up there belonging to her, or to any of my ancestors? Simon was away visiting his mother for the day. I resolved to ask him to work on opening up the loft when he got back.

A spot of rain landed on my nose, and then another, and another, and suddenly the heavens had opened.

'Quick, inside!' I yelled to the children, who were already running across the lawn. They charged for the kitchen door with me in hot pursuit, until I realised I had washing on the line. I did an about-turn, grabbed the laundry basket and yanked everything off the line. By the time I was inside I was soaked, and so was the washing. I might as well not have bothered. Well there would be no more digging or any other gardening today.

'Mum, can I make some biscuits?' Lauren asked. 'From my recipe book Granny gave me?'

'Sure. You go ahead and start weighing everything out while I get changed,' I told her. She was good in the kitchen. And hopefully Lewis would amuse Thomas for a while – I could already hear them debating whether to build a robot from Lego or K'Nex. I felt the urge to do a bit of research. I could have another go at looking for those servants after 1841.

Once I'd got some dry clothes on I took my laptop into the kitchen, and sat at one end of the table, giving Lauren strict instructions to keep her biscuit-making at the other end. Flour and laptops don't mix well. She'd made these biscuits plenty of times before so only needed supervision rather than hands-on help. I was able to open up my research folders and start a bit of digging of a different kind.

Which is how we all were when Simon arrived home from visiting his mother. I was deep into following up leads on an ancestry website; Lauren had just put her cookies in the oven and had gone to watch TV while they baked, and Lewis was building a remote control K'Nex robot while Thomas 'helped'. All happy, all productive in our own ways.

The peace was shattered the moment he walked through the door.

'Hellish drive home in that downpour. Make us a cup of tea, love?'

'Will do. Just a moment while I save this…'

'Save what?'

'Oh, some genealogy research I was doing…hold on, won't take a second…' I wanted to quickly type up the last few details on possible Agnes Cutter or Polly Turner matches I'd found, before I lost them.

'Katie, for goodness sake! I've had a long day – had to deal with my mum who barely knows who *she* is any more, let alone who I am. The roads were a nightmare, there were three accidents on the M3 alone, and you can't even be bothered to get up and make me a cup of tea. What is it – your dead ancestors are more important than me? Is that it? Well, thanks very much. I'll make my own. You just sit there and commune with the dead.'

He stomped over to the kettle and snatched it from its stand to fill it, knocking a mug off the work surface in the process. It smashed on the tiled floor. Simon kicked a piece of it and it skidded across the kitchen towards me.

'Simon, stop it! I've got bare feet – don't spread the shards all over the place!'

'I'll clear it up. What's for dinner? I had no lunch and I'm starving. Did you think to get anything ready, or have you just sat there all day doing pointless research?'

'Why didn't you have lunch?'

'Because I was stuck in traffic and late getting to Mum's, all right? Did you have any? Did you feed the kids or did they have to take a back seat to your research too?'

Good grief, he was really losing it now. This wasn't like him at all. I knew he must have had a really bad day to blow his top like this, but even so, those jibes about ignoring the kids stung.

I grabbed a pair of gardening clogs from the kitchen door mat and put them on. 'Simon, calm down. I've not been researching all day – just for the last hour after it started raining. And it's not pointless. I might be able to work out who our skeleton was.'

'Who needs to know? Who cares? The past is past, Katie. Dead and buried. Whether or not you find out who she was makes no difference – to you, me, the kids or anyone who's actually *living*.' He stuffed a teabag into a mug and poured boiling water onto it, then flung the used teabag into the sink. Great, I'd have to fish it out. Why couldn't he put it straight into the bin?

'It's just interesting,' I protested.

'So interesting it takes all your time, and you can't even make me a cuppa when I get back after a shite day?'

The kitchen timer began bleeping. Lauren's cookies were ready. She peered in through the kitchen door, as if wondering whether it would be safe to enter. I hated the kids hearing our rows. We didn't argue often, not like some couples, but when we did it could be loud and heated.

'It's all right, sweetie,' I told her. 'Come and take your cookies out. Oh, put some shoes on first.'

'Why?'

'Daddy smashed a mug on the floor.'

'Oh yeah, that's right. I hurled it down in a fit of rage. Make me out to be an ogre, why don't you, Katie?' Simon stormed out of the room, tea in hand, past an open-mouthed Lauren.

She tiptoed over to me in her stockinged feet and climbed onto my lap. Eleven years old but not too old for a cuddle. 'I don't like it when Dad shouts at you,' she said.

'I don't like it either,' I said, hugging her. 'I guess he's tired after visiting Nanna Smith. Come on, let's get the cookies out before they burn. You sit here while I fetch your shoes. I don't want a little girl with cut feet to deal with on top of everything else.' I kissed her head then shuffled out from under her.

With her trainers slipped on but untied, Lauren dealt with the cookies while I swept the floor and put my laptop away in the study. I made myself a cup of tea, and put a few warm cookies

211

on a plate for Lauren to take to Simon, who was in the living room. I followed her through. She made a little curtsey as she placed the plate in front of him. 'Will there be anything else, sir?'

He stared at her, and I saw him fight back a chuckle. Lauren's childish charm had worked. 'I'll ring if I need you, shall I?' He nodded at the old servants' bell-pull, hanging beside the fireplace. Lauren curtsied again, and ran out.

I sat down beside him. 'Sorry, love. You've had a bad day, and I was insensitive.'

He put his arm around me. 'Yep, I had a terrible day. Guess I just needed to let off steam. I'm sorry, too.'

'Do you want to talk about it?'

He shrugged. 'Not really. Mum didn't know who I was, again. Thought I was "from the council", come to put her into a home. She couldn't even grasp she was already in a home. Got quite irate at me.'

'Oh, love.'

'Just something I have to deal with, I suppose. It's hard, though.'

'If she doesn't know who you are, it'd be understandable if you just, well, stayed away…'

He shook his head. 'No, I can't do that. When she's gone I'd regret it, wouldn't I?'

'Probably.'

He was right. There was no solution that I could see. He might talk about focusing on the living but there were times when the dead were an easier proposition. It was a terrible thing to think, but Veronica would be far less of a burden on Simon once she'd passed away. I couldn't exactly wish for it, but I knew that when the time came, I would certainly feel a sense of relief. And so, I suspected, would Simon, underneath his grief. In many ways, he'd lost his mother already.

'Well,' I said, 'I should probably go and get the dinner ready.' I got up to go.

'Thanks. These cookies will keep me going a little while,

anyway.' He pulled me towards him for a kiss, and slipped his hands into the back pockets of my jeans. 'Ugh, what's this?'

It was the scrap of fabric. 'Thomas found it, in the garden. Probably from the skeleton.'

'Ah, I see what set you off again on that infernal research.' He grinned. 'Did you find anything out?'

'Not yet.' I had a sudden idea. 'Simon, do you fancy going up the road to the pub after dinner tonight? I can ask Eileen if she'll sit with the kids for a couple of hours. She always said she wouldn't mind.'

He grinned. 'Great idea! I do fancy a pint or two.'

A couple of hours later, we were strolling arm in arm up the lane to the pub. Thomas was in bed and the older two were playing Monopoly with our neighbour Eileen. The rain had stopped and everything smelled fresh and clean, the dust of summer rinsed away. The dark clouds had parted and moved on, and a low evening sun was making everything seem manageable again.

I leaned my head against Simon's arm as we walked. 'Feeling better now?'

'Almost. Nothing a decent pint of Guinness can't sort.'

'My round,' I said, as I pushed open the door to the White Hart.

'OK. I'll find us a table,' said Simon, and wandered off.

Steve, the landlord, served me. 'You found any more skeletons in your garden, Katie? Or should I say in your closet? Ha! That's a good one, innit?'

I grinned. 'Haven't gone looking for any more, Steve. One's enough, in any case.'

He set my wine glass in front of me. 'Seven-forty, please. Any idea who that skeleton could be?'

I handed over a tenner. 'No. It was a woman, youngish, and she was buried before 1842. That's all the police could tell me, and probably all we'll ever know.'

213

'Aw. I'd want to try to find out who she was. Maybe start by researching people who lived in your house around that time? You can do it all on the Internet these days, you know.' He nodded sagely as he handed me my change.

I smiled. 'Maybe I'll do that.'

He topped up the Guinness and I took the two drinks to the table Simon had found, tucked in a niche at the far end of the bar. Steve's comments about skeletons in the closet had made me think of the one from Simon's closet, who went by the name of Amy. I wondered if he'd heard from her again. But after the day Simon'd had, I didn't want to be the one to bring up that particular subject.

I didn't have to. As I placed Simon's pint in front of him he looked up at me, his face drawn, his eyes tired.

'Love, I know we're out for a quiet drink, but I think I do need to talk to you about Amy,' he said. 'She's emailed me a few times lately. She's coming down to London soon from Durham, and wants to meet up.'

I sat down, and took his hand. 'Of course she wants to meet up. And when we talked before, you wanted to meet her too.'

'Yes, but now it's all becoming real, and close.' He took a long pull of his pint, then wiped away the moustache of froth with the back of his hand.

'Does she want to come here?' I asked. I wasn't sure it would be a good idea bringing her to our home on the first meeting.

'Yes, but she thinks we should meet in London first. She'll be staying there with a friend and has asked me to go up. She's even picked out a meeting place.'

'Where?'

'A pub. The Argyll Arms, just off Oxford Street. I know it – it's an old place with lots of little snugs. If we can get one of those to ourselves it'll be quite private.'

'Sounds perfect.'

'Katie, I'll admit it, I'm nervous as hell about meeting her.

What will she think of me? I got her mother pregnant then left and had no further contact with her!'

'You didn't know Sarah was pregnant, did you?'

'No, but maybe I should have gone to see her after we split up, made sure she was OK…' He sighed.

'She'd have thought you were still after her. Stalking her or something. You said you wrote to Sarah a few times. Did she ever write back?'

He picked up his pint and nodded over its rim. 'Once or twice.'

'So she could have told you she was pregnant, but chose not to.' I leaned towards him across the table. 'Simon, it's not your fault you didn't know about Amy. You can't beat yourself up about it. And if she's anything like you, she'll understand. She's probably as nervous as you are about meeting up.'

'She sounds really together in her emails.'

'Sarah brought her up well, then.'

'Do you think I should ring her first? Speak on the phone before we meet?'

'Do you want to?'

'Um, not really. I don't like the phone. You don't get any clues from expression and body language. No, I think I'd rather speak to her first when we meet face to face.'

I nodded. I would do the same. 'I'd like to meet her too, but I think you should meet her on your own the first time.'

'Yes, I will. OK, I'll email her back and try to set a date. Got to get it over with, I suppose.'

I smiled at him. Who knew how this would work out. Getting to know each other could end up being wonderful for both of them. Or perhaps there would only be a few meetings and then Christmas cards every year. But he had to give his daughter a chance. His daughter! It still made me gasp every time I thought of Amy in that way. I was gradually getting used to the idea but there was a way to go yet. And I wondered too what the children would make of their grown-up sister. It was Lauren I worried

215

about. She'd been a Daddy's girl from the moment she was born, and had relished being the only girl in the family. How would she react to finding out she wasn't his only daughter?

Simon had finished his pint, and stood up to go to the bar. 'Same again?'

'Please.'

He was back in a minute. 'Steve was asking about our skeleton.'

I grinned. 'Yes, he mentioned it to me, too. We are quite the local celebrities.'

'Everyone seems desperate to know who it is. I suppose I'll have to let you go on with that research after all, to satisfy their curiosity.'

I punched his arm. '*Let* me? What are you, my lord and master?'

'If only. Anyway, from your research so far, who do you think it might be?'

I told him about the two servants I was trying to trace to rule them out.

'You think it might be one of them?'

I shrugged. 'It makes sense to start with the closest people – those who lived in the house at that time. If I can't find what happened to them after the 1841 census then they're a possibility.'

'So, if you find them after 1841 then you rule them out, and if you don't find one of them, it could be because she was buried in our garden?'

'That's about it.'

'You're looking for a missing record, then. It's impossible to find something that's missing. By definition!'

He had a point. I took a sip of my drink. 'Well, even so, those women were part of my ancestors' household so I'm interested in them anyway.'

Simon frowned. 'Hey, you don't think your ancestor, this Bartholomew chap, bumped her off, do you? Like, if he was shagging a servant, and she was giving him grief…'

'Well…'

216

'Or, if she was pregnant, and he needed to bury the evidence… Tiny foetus bones could easily have disintegrated completely in the earth…'

'Simon! What a horrible idea!'

'Well, think about it. It's possible, isn't it? Or maybe his wife found out he was having an affair and killed the servant in a fit of rage. I hate to say it, Katie, but one of your ancestors could have been a murderer.'

He didn't look as though he hated saying it. There was a spark of ill-disguised glee in his eyes. Yes, it was a possibility, and one that had crossed my mind too, that Bartholomew or even Georgia might have had something to do with the body in the garden. But I hadn't wanted to dwell on this. They were family, after all – their genes were in me. OK, pretty diluted as they were so many generations back, but still. No one wants to think they're descended from a murderer.

'It's possible, I suppose,' I said to Simon.

'Aw, love, don't look so heart-broken about it,' he said. 'Who your ancestors were and what they did during their lives has little to do with who *you* are. It's how you were brought up and what *your* life experiences have been, that defines who you really are. Not what genes you've got. They might determine your hair and eye colour, but not how you act and react. Not what makes you tick.'

It was the age-old argument and one I'd had with Simon a hundred times. Nature versus nurture. As an adoptee he preferred to think he was a product of his environment, not of the chance encounter between sperm and egg of two people he didn't even know. I'd always suspected he maintained this viewpoint as a kind of excuse – to explain why he had no interest or desire in tracking down his birth parents – and as a compliment to his adoptive parents.

And now the tables were turned on him, and his own daughter was tracking down the birth father she'd never known. I wondered if this would change the way he thought about the issue at all. If she was like him at all, in the way she thought or acted, it would be nothing to do with her upbringing and everything to do with her genes.

But now wasn't the time to say this. Time would tell – after he'd met Amy, he might think differently.

'You're probably right,' I said. 'Anyway, Bartholomew was just one of my thirty-two great-great-great-grandparents. There are a lot of other people's genes in me besides his. I'll go on with the research to see if I can work out who the bones were.' I took another sip of my wine. 'And who knows, maybe we'll find more clues somewhere in the house or garden. Talking of which, we really must open up that loft hatch some time soon.'

'Yeah, yeah,' said Simon, nodding. 'I'll add it to the never-ending list of stuff to do, shall I?'

Chapter Nineteen

Hampshire, December 1841

Bartholomew looked again from the corpse of his wife to the face of his lover. Agnes was still curled on the floor at his feet, clutching his leg and staring up at him with wide, frightened eyes.

'What are we to do?' she whispered, her voice shocked and fragile. 'Oh God, what have we done?'

What indeed had they done? No, what had *she* done? It was Agnes who'd pushed down on the pillow, Agnes who'd smothered the life out of her mistress. Bartholomew stared at her. All he'd done was…nothing. He'd stood frozen, as though she'd put him in some kind of trance. It was her fault. All her fault.

A gurgle from the crib reminded him of Barty's presence in the room. He glanced over at the cot. Barty was sitting up in his cot and staring wide-eyed at his mother, lying dead on the bed. Had he watched the whole thing? Was the image of his mother's last moments imprinted on the back of his eyes? Would he remember this moment, when he was older and able to understand what he'd seen? Bartholomew shook his head to clear the thoughts. Nothing to be achieved by thinking about that. What was done was done. But what to do, now? He forced himself to think clearly. There was no going back. At his feet, Agnes sobbed, her face pressed against his legs. She had done this, but only he would be able to find the way forward.

First, they must hide the body. But where? It had to be somewhere she would never be found. He shook his leg free from Agnes's grasp and walked over to the window. Agnes slumped to the floor, her shoulders heaving with hoarse sobs. Barty watched as he pulled back the curtain a little, and peered out into the dark night. It had stopped raining. He could just make out the hill, where the Irish navvies had camped while they built the railway, a deeper black than the surrounding sky. There was a half moon, its light diffused by the cloud cover. Enough light to see by but not too much. He gazed around the shadowed garden at the back of the house. Perhaps...later, when Mrs Fowles had left the house and gone to the cottage she shared with Old George, when Libby had left for the night...he struggled to remember which way Polly's room faced, on the top floor. The front. It was Agnes's room which overlooked the garden. If they were quiet, they'd not be seen. He made a decision. Yes, it could be done. But it would take both of them, all their strength.

'Agnes, get up. Listen to me.'

She moaned, softly.

'Get up. Come on, you will need to help me.'

She crawled away from Georgia's bed, and pulled herself to her feet using the chair near the fire. She was trembling, and her shoulders were slumped. Bartholomew took a step forward, ready to catch her if she should fall. He took hold of her hands.

'Look at me.'

She slowly raised her head, but kept her eyes averted from his.

'Look at me, I said.' His voice was harsh. 'Agnes, you must be strong. You will hang for this, if it is found out. Do you want to hang for it?'

She shook her head. Tears welled up against her lower lashes.

He pulled her towards him and wrapped his arms around her. 'No. And neither do I. But we will both hang if she is found, and murder is suspected. We must hide her.'

'Where?'

He nodded towards the window. 'Out there. But later – when the household is quiet. Now, I must go and check whether Mrs Fowles and Libby have left yet. You must stay here, take care of Barty.'

She pushed him away, and stared at him. 'No! Don't leave me alone with her!'

'She can't hurt you. Besides, you must watch over Barty.' His tiny son was watching them still from his crib. With a jolt, Bartholomew realised that the baby was all he had left of his wife. He felt a surge of love for his son. Whatever happened, the child must be well looked after and provided for.

He went to the door, and turned to look back at Agnes. She sat down heavily on her usual chair by the fire, her face in her hands. 'I'll be back soon,' he said. He picked up a lit candle, removed the key from the door, went out into the corridor and softly pulled the door closed behind him. He paused a moment, then locked it, and tucked the key into his waistcoat pocket.

Downstairs all was quiet and dark. Cupping the candle flame with one hand he checked the main rooms, but all were empty. He went along the corridor to the kitchen, and found Mrs Fowles humming to herself, preparing meat for the following day's meals.

'Oh, sir, you startled me!' She wiped her hands on her apron and gave a little curtsey.

'I am sorry, I did not mean to.' It was most unusual for him to come to the kitchen. Indeed he could not remember ever coming here before, since he moved in. He wondered whether there was guilt written on his face, and turned away from her.

'Is there something you need?' she asked.

'No, not especially.' He cleared his throat. 'I was coming to see

221

whether you had finished for the evening. But I see you are still busy. When that is done, you are dismissed until tomorrow.'

'Yes, sir, thank you, sir.' She frowned slightly at him, and continued cutting the meat.

'Has Libby gone home?'

'Yes, sir.'

'And Polly?'

'Gone to her room already, sir. I said she could, once she'd cleared the dining room.'

'Good. Right then, I'll leave you to it.' He nodded to her, and went to his study. There was no fire lit, as he was not in the habit of using this room in the evening. But the damp chill of the room and empty grate fitted his mood. He put his candle on a side table, poured himself a brandy and sat down to wait until the house was clear.

He could hear the ticking of the hall clock, and an occasional faint sound from the kitchen. How easy it had been to end a life! As easy as starting one – no, easier, he thought, as he recalled the miscarriages Georgia had suffered before having Barty. He ran through the events of the evening once more, wondering again why he had nodded at Agnes, as she stood holding the pillow. One tiny nod, and his wife's life ended, his own and Agnes's in jeopardy if it was ever discovered. Why that nod? What had he been thinking? He stared at his brandy glass. It was the brandy; he'd had several before going upstairs, it had clouded his brain and muddled his thinking, making him nod when he did not know what he was agreeing to. Disgusted with himself, he threw his glass at the empty grate, where it smashed, shattering across the hearth.

There was a tap at the door, and Mrs Fowles peeped in. 'Everything all right, sir? Only I heard a crash…'

Bartholomew glared at her. Could he not be left alone with his thoughts for five minutes? 'I dropped my glass.'

'Oh, sir, I'll fetch a brush.'

'No need. Leave it till the morning. Impossible to see all the splinters by candlelight. Please, leave me be.'

She dipped her head and backed out of the door. 'Sorry, sir. Good night, sir.'

Bartholomew shut the door firmly behind her, and sat down again. His hand reached automatically for the decanter and before he knew it, there was another glass in his hand, a sip of brandy in his mouth, and the welcoming, comforting glow of it easing its way down to his gut. It would give him strength for what he still had to do that night. He leaned back in his chair and forced his mind to think forwards to what had to be done, not backwards on what could not be changed.

Time seemed to slow down as he formulated his plan. Eventually the kitchen noises ceased, and a discreet click of the back-door latch told him Mrs Fowles had left for the night. The hall clock chimed eleven. Would Polly be asleep by now? Probably, as she had to get up at six to clean the grates and set the fires. But it'd be better to give her a bit longer, to be safe. He resolved to wait another hour.

Agnes heard the distant hall clock strike eleven. Still no sign of Mr Bartholomew returning. She glanced again at the body of her mistress, lying cold and still, so still! on the bed. The flickering firelight cast ever-moving shadows around the room, shifting like spirits, dancing and mocking her. They were coming for her. Georgia's ghost had summoned them, to avenge her death and punish her murderer. Murderer! Yes, that was what she was. She had taken a life. And the life of a poor, innocent young girl whose only crime was to be married to the man Agnes loved. But he was as much to blame as she was. He had nodded to her – he had wanted her to kill Georgia, hadn't he? She had only done what she was told. That was all. She was a servant, and had simply carried out his wishes. It was his fault. All his fault. He'd made her into a murderer. They'd been happy the way they were, but now she was in danger of being caught and hanged. She'd loved

Georgia, like a daughter or younger sister, and now she'd lost her. And little Barty had lost his mother. Barty! She'd almost forgotten about him. He was still sitting up, sucking on a corner of his blanket, watching her. As she caught his eye he began to grizzle and lifted his little arms towards her to be picked up. Instinctively, she went to him and gathered him up. She turned her back on the body in the bed, not wanting Barty to see his dead mother. Had he seen what had happened here? Would he remember? No, he was far too young. Even so, the thought that he had been in the room while she had smothered the life out of his mother was unbearable. He began to grizzle more insistently, hungry now. She offered him the knuckle of her little finger to suck on, and rocked him gently. 'Hush now, little Barty,' she whispered. 'Aggie's here. Aggie won't let anyone hurt you.' She owed it to him, she realised, to make it up to him for the loss of his mother. Not that Georgia had ever been much of a mother to him. She kissed his soft head and cheek. 'Hush, Barty, my sweet. Aggie – *Mama's* here. Mama loves you.'

Downstairs, the hall clock struck twelve. A minute later Agnes heaved a sigh of relief as she heard the key turn in the lock. Thank God he'd returned. If she was left much longer in the room with Georgia she felt as though she would lose her mind.

Bartholomew looked drawn and haggard. Had the spirits been tormenting him for the murder, too? It would not be fair if they were punishing only her. The need to get out of the room, away from Georgia's still, white body, was overwhelming.

'Barty's hungry,' she told him as he entered. 'I think I'll need to give him some milk to get him back off to sleep.'

'Very well,' said Bartholomew. 'Fetch what you need from the kitchen. Mrs Fowles has gone home.'

Agnes put the fretful baby down in the cradle and hurried off. Thank goodness he'd let her out. As she passed the back door on the way to the kitchen, she paused a moment. What if she ran away? Her cloak was hanging beside the door. She could slip it on and go out into the night. Get herself far away from here. Go back to her parents and her son. Leave Bartholomew to deal with his dead wife. But if she ran away, he might blame her for the killing. When she had only done what he wanted her to do, hadn't she? It was all his fault. The authorities would not think that, though. They would always take a gentleman's word over that of a servant. And wherever she went, one day she'd be found. In any case, she knew that leaving Bartholomew was the one thing she could not do. She loved him more now than ever. And Barty needed her too. She could not abandon the poor little mite. Somehow, together, they would have to find a way out of this.

She went on to the kitchen, and filled an earthenware baby's bottle with milk from the jug in the pantry. She hurried back up the stairs to Georgia's room, and noted the relief in Bartholomew's eyes as she entered the room. He must have wondered if she would run away, too.

Barty guzzled the milk hungrily, gazing up at her with wide blue eyes as he suckled. He wouldn't miss his mother, she thought. He was far more attached to her than he'd been to Georgia.

When the bottle was finished, Barty's eyes were half-closed. She expertly rocked him to sleep and laid him in his cradle, tucking a woollen shawl around him. He looked so peaceful, so innocent. Oh, to be a baby with not a care in the world!

Agnes looked up from the cradle, at Bartholomew. It was time to deal with Georgia. She steeled herself to be ready to do whatever he asked of her.

He walked over to the bed. 'Come on,' he said. 'We must change her nightdress.'

Agnes shuddered. 'Why?'

'Because we must send the usual items to the laundry. There must be nothing missing. Put that new nightdress on her. The one you've been working on.' He gestured towards Agnes's sewing things beside her chair.

'It's not finished...'

'She'll not mind,' said Bartholomew, with a wry smile. 'Come, help me with her.'

Bartholomew held Georgia in a sitting position while Agnes tugged the nightdress off her, and replaced it with the new one. She felt a momentary pang of regret that all her hard work had gone to waste, and only a corpse would ever wear it.

They wrapped the body in a blanket. 'Help me lift her,' said Bartholomew. Agnes grasped the foot end of the blanket and together they managed to get the body downstairs, along the kitchen corridor and out of the back door. For such a slight girl, she was surprisingly difficult to carry. Exhausted, Agnes dropped her load as soon as they were out of the house.

'Come on, not much further,' urged Bartholomew. Agnes stretched her aching back muscles, gritted her teeth and hauled again. How far did he want to take the body? With a shudder Agnes recalled how he'd stared out of the window at the far-off hill. Surely he didn't expect her to carry Georgia that far? Thankfully, instead of going out to the lane, he directed her into the garden at the back of the house, and to a spot beside the wall, where a couple of straggly rose bushes climbed, last summer's rose hips still hanging forlornly from them.

'Put her down here,' he commanded. Agnes did so with relief, and arched her aching back.

'Wait here,' he said, as he ran off in the direction of the stables.

Agnes shivered. It wasn't particularly cold for the time of year, but she was dressed only in her everyday gown of light brown wool. She folded her arms and tucked her hands under her armpits. It was all right for Georgia, lying down there wrapped in a blanket. Not that a corpse needed to be warm. She considered rolling the body out of the blanket so she could wrap it around herself, but at that moment Bartholomew returned.

He was carrying two shovels. He passed the smaller one to her, and began to dig. She watched for a moment, then as he looked up and nodded at her, she began to dig too.

The month had been wet and mild, and the ground was soft and easy to dig. What if it had been frozen – what would they have done then? Well, it wasn't, and they were lucky. She concentrated on digging, following his instructions to make it deeper, wider, straighter. The earth smelled rich and damp. She knew that the smell would always remind her of this terrible night. Now and again she glanced back at the house.

'What if someone sees us?' she asked.

'Who could see us?' he replied, breathless from the exertion.

He was right. There was only Polly and little Barty in the house. She hoped Barty was still asleep. Polly's room in the attic was at the front of the house – it was her own window at the top on this side, from which she imagined curious eyes watching them, judging them. She shook the thought out of her head and got on with the job at hand. It was hard work, and sweat prickled her back beneath her woollen dress.

Soon they had a trench, long enough for Georgia's body, and three feet deep. Agnes stopped digging and leaned on her spade.

'That's big enough, surely,' she said.

Bartholomew shook his head. 'Deeper. Another foot.'

She sighed, and set to work.

Finally he pronounced the trench suitable, and bade her help him haul Georgia's body alongside it. Together they rolled the corpse out of the blanket and into the hole, where it fell with a dull thud.

Bartholomew picked up his spade and threw a shovelful of earth on top of the body.

'Wait!' hissed Agnes, remembering that Georgia had been wearing her silver and emerald hair comb. She kneeled on the side of the trench and leaned in, raking through the dead woman's hair with her fingers, trying to find the comb. Where was it? She must find it. It was too good to bury – it should be hers, now.

Bartholomew caught her arm and pulled her up. 'What are you doing?'

227

'Her comb...'

'Leave it!' He began quickly shovelling the mound of earth into the trench. With a sigh she followed suit. It was easier work than the digging, but her shoulders were tired and aching now. It was all she could do to keep going.

Eventually the hole was filled. Bartholomew spread the spare earth around the surrounding flower beds. He tramped down the earth with his feet.

Agnes gathered armfuls of dead autumn leaves which had blown under the hedge at the end of the garden, and scattered them over the disturbed earth. Despite her efforts, even in the faint moonlight it was clear something had happened here. How could Bartholomew think for a moment that Old George would not notice? Or Mrs Fowles, on her way to the kitchen garden? But she was too tired to think about this. He must have a plan, she assumed, and she would simply have to trust him. With her life.

'We've done enough,' he announced. 'Bring the blanket up to your room. Hide it with your dirty clothes tonight.'

'How are we going to explain where Mrs St Clair has gone?' she asked.

'We're not,' he replied. 'I'll explain the plan tomorrow. For now, my love, you need to get some sleep. Bring Barty to the cradle in your room. You must rise tomorrow at your usual time, as though nothing has changed.'

Agnes was puzzled but too tired to think about it. Bartholomew took the shovels back to the stables while she went back into the house with the muddy blanket as instructed. Inside she removed her ruined shoes at the door, and padded upstairs to her room in her stockings. She shoved the muddy blanket under her bed, then went back downstairs, wiping away traces of mud as she went. Bartholomew was in his study, with a large brandy glass in his hand. As she entered he poured another for her.

'You'll need this,' he said, and she drank it gratefully, the sharp fruity taste warming her from the inside.

228

He kissed her. 'Go, sleep. Be strong.'

She fetched the sleeping Barty from Georgia's room, and took him to her room. Kissing his soft head, she laid him down on her narrow bed. 'Perhaps you can be a twin,' she whispered, thinking of her own little son, miles away in Lincolnshire.

When she eventually lay down too, still clothed in her muddy dress, she cuddled little Barty under her blanket and fell immediately into a dreamless sleep.

Bartholomew's sleep was not nearly as untroubled. His mind was working overtime, as he worked out the details of his plan. He felt unhindered now by the effects of the brandy, and the digging had energised him. It was not until after the hall clock had struck four that he finally dozed off, only to dream of white arms emerging from the earth, clutching at his legs as he walked past, dragging him down into a muddy grave. He woke with the dawn, sweating, feeling more tired than when he had gone to bed. The events of the night were still so vivid – Georgia's legs twitching as Agnes held the pillow on her face, Georgia's still, white face staring up at him from the trench, Agnes's frightened eyes, watching him, trusting him to make it all right for them.

He rose, dressed quickly and went downstairs. Polly was still setting a fire in the breakfast room.

'Oh, sir, you be up early,' she said. 'I ain't finished the fires and Mrs Fowles isn't come yet to prepare breakfast, but I'll fetch you some tea if you'd like it?'

'Don't worry about the fire – I'll light it. But I would like some tea. Thank you.'

She curtsied and scurried off towards the kitchen. Bartholomew lit the fire then sat in an armchair, considering the day ahead. There was no sign yet of Agnes this morning.

Polly was back in five minutes with the tea things. He watched her as she arranged them on the breakfast table, poured him a cup, and set it on a side table next to his chair. When this was done, she stood before him and pulled something out of her pocket.

'Sir, I found this just inside the kitchen door, on the floor. Can't think how it could've got there. Has the mistress been up and about?' She handed him Georgia's silver and emerald comb.

His stomach lurched as he took it, and turned it over in his hand. He fought to keep his voice steady as he answered her. 'No, Mrs St Clair has not been up. Thank you for returning this.' She could have kept it, he realised. But she'd chosen to be honest. That would make what he had to tell her all the more difficult.

She curtsied and headed towards the door.

He called her back. 'Polly, don't go. There is something I need to talk to you about.'

She turned to him, her eyes wide as though she was expecting a reprimand. 'Yes, sir?'

'You are, I believe, missing Brighton, and your friends and family there?'

'Well, I…'

'It's all right. Of course you are. I see it now – it was wrong of us to take you away from there. But while Agnes was away, there was no one else. You did her job admirably.'

She blushed, and gave a little curtsey in acknowledgement of the compliment. 'I did my best, sir.'

'You did very well. And I shall write as much in the reference I shall give you.'

She gasped. 'Are you dismissing me, sir?'

'With three months' pay, and the fare back to Brighton, and a good reference – yes. You will be happier among your friends. It is unfair of us to keep you here.'

'I don't mind, sir, really I don't! What've I done wrong? Is it because of the comb? I didn't take it, really I didn't! More likely it were Agnes…'

'No, it's nothing to do with the comb. You've done nothing wrong, nothing at all. Don't make a fuss, otherwise I'll not give you the three months' pay. Now go, pack your box. Old George will take you to the station in time for the midday train.' It was

230

harsh, but necessary. He watched as her eyes filled with tears. She gulped back a sob and ran from the room. He wondered whether three months' pay was generous enough. Perhaps he should have given her more. But too much might have made her suspicious.

He went through to his study, wrapped the comb in a handkerchief and tucked it away at the back of a hidden drawer. Maybe he'd give it to Agnes, some day. Or maybe he wouldn't. It would remind him too much of Georgia.

There was a tap at the door of the study. It was Agnes. She looked as though she had barely slept. Her hair was awry and there was mud on the hem of her gown. The silly woman, still wearing the same dress as yesterday. Did she not have something else to wear?

'Get back upstairs,' he hissed. 'Change your clothes. Don't let Polly or Mrs Fowles see you like that, or they might suspect something.'

'I-I just needed some tea,' she stuttered.

'There's some in the breakfast room. Help yourself, quickly now. And take it up to Georgia's room. Stay in there with Barty as you normally would, and let no one in.'

'But, I…'

'Just do what I say, woman.'

She turned and left without another word. Bartholomew buried his face in his hands and slumped forward in his chair. God, this was so hard. And he still had to dismiss Mrs Fowles and Old George. But that would have to wait until tomorrow. He needed Old George today.

A sound in the hallway alerted him to Mrs Fowles's arrival. He took a deep breath and went out to her.

'Mrs Fowles, good morning,' he said.

'Good morning to you, too, sir. Getting colder it is. Old George reckons as we'll have a frost tonight. About time too, this late in December.'

231

'Indeed. Now then, I'm about ready for some breakfast. I'm afraid you'll have less help today, as I've had to dismiss Polly.'

'Dismiss Polly! But why? She's a good girl, I always thought...'

'I thought so too. But nevertheless, I've dismissed her, and I don't need to explain my actions to you. Can you ask Old George to take her to the station for the twelve o'clock train?'

'She's leaving today?'

'That's what I said. Now, about that breakfast?'

'Of course, sir. Right away, sir. Libby'll be here soon to help me I hope, since I don't have my Polly no more.' Mrs Fowles bustled away towards the kitchen, muttering to herself.

It was a difficult day. Old George took Polly to the station as planned. Bartholomew told Mrs Fowles that Georgia was sleeping, and that Agnes was nursing both her and the baby as usual. Mrs Fowles spent the day plodding up and down the stairs, leaving trays of food and bottles of milk outside Georgia's room, and eyeing Bartholomew with suspicion every time their paths crossed. In the late afternoon he called her into his study.

'Mrs Fowles, how long have you and Old George been working for my family?'

'Ooh sir, I would think nigh on thirty year now, for you, and your father before you. I remember you as a bonny young lad.'

'As long as that? Well, you've served us well.' He drummed his fingers on the desk, trying to work out the best way of saying this.

'Mrs Fowles, do you know what a pension is?'

'Well, I, er...'

'It's where an employer continues to pay someone after that person stops working for them, due to old age. It's to thank them for long and loyal service.'

'Yes sir, I did know...'

'And the time has come, Mrs Fowles, for me to pay you and Old George a pension. You will lose the cottage of course, but you have a son, I believe – in Kent, isn't he? Your pension will be dependent on you moving to Kent to live with or near your son. You will both continue to get half your current salary from now until the ends of your lives.' He looked up at her gaping mouth. 'I think that is fair, don't you? More than fair. Pack today, and leave on the morning train. I shall pay your travel expenses. Anything too large to carry can be sent on afterwards – leave me your son's address.'

'But, Mr St Clair, excuse me for speaking out of turn, but what're you doing? First Polly, then me and my George. What about Libby, and Agnes? Are they also to be sent away?'

'Yes, they too. Could you tell Libby for me – ask her to come to me here for a month's wages and a reference. I'll talk to Agnes later.'

'Are you and the mistress leaving here, then?'

'It's really none of your business, but if you must know, yes. I am taking Georgia away, for her health. It is clear that she has not thrived here at North Kingsley. I am shutting up the house. We'll be leaving by the end of the week and I don't expect to come back. So there'll be nothing for you to do here. Half-pay as a pension should be perfectly adequate.'

He stood up, to indicate the interview was over. She nodded her head and turned to leave.

'Mrs Fowles?'

'Yes, sir?'

'Thank you. This wasn't easy for me.'

'No, sir. Nor for me. Look after your wife and your little boy. I wish you well.' She sniffed, raised her chin and left the room with her head held high.

Chapter Twenty

Hampshire, July 2013

The summer was shaping up to be a good one. There were only another two weeks until the children broke up from school, and I was trying to make the most of my free time. We'd decided not to start any major work on the house until the kids went back to school in September, so we could enjoy our first summer here in North Kingsley. I had a long list of stuff to do before they broke up – planning the kitchen, deciding on its floor, units and colour scheme, lining up plumbers and electricians so we could hit the ground running in September, gardening and, of course, researching who the bones might have belonged to.

Despite all these items on my to-do list, it was a beautiful Friday and Irish Hill beckoned. I decided to take a walk up there in the morning, after dropping off Thomas at school. There'd be time enough to progress the chores or, more likely, the research, in the afternoon. It hadn't rained for weeks so the usually muddy track across the fields was dry and rutted. There were a few sheep grazing on the parched grass, who regarded me forlornly as I walked by. Up on the hill, the gorse and hawthorn had finished flowering so there was less colour than in the spring, but the view was as magnificent as ever. A heat haze made the horizon shimmer, and fields of wheat were beginning to ripen. In another month there'd be patches of sunshine gold all across the countryside, cheering the souls of all who looked upon it.

I needed my soul cheering. Simon, again, late home night after night. Refusing to talk to me if I tried to probe into why. It wasn't Amy. He'd arranged to meet her in London in a week's time, and although he was nervous about the prospect, we'd talked it over many times, and he was confident he was doing the right thing, in the right way. No, there was something else going on.

I climbed to the top of the hill and sat on the east-facing bench, to feel the morning sun on my face. A red kite wheeled above me, its splayed wing feathers silhouetted against the pale blue sky. I still occasionally wondered whether Simon was having an affair. His late evenings and evasive answers pointed to something like that, but his overall demeanour didn't. He acted like someone with a secret, but not a *guilty* secret. Just something he didn't yet feel as though he could tell me.

A thought struck me, as I watched the kite swoop down and disappear into a copse. Maybe Simon was tracking down his birth parents? Maybe Amy contacting him had made him want to trace his own roots? But if so, why on earth didn't he talk to me about it? I'd support him, he knew I would. I'd do it for him, if he asked. And then I'd trace his ancestry further back. I'd relish having another genealogy project!

The sun was too warm on my face and I felt as though I might be burning, so I stood and stretched, and moved to the west-facing bench, my back to the sun. I supposed you'd need to be careful tracing your birth parents, and be prepared for some shocks. It was a bit like genealogical research, although of course, much closer to home. You never knew quite what you might find. What if your birth mother was a prostitute, or your father a criminal? How would that make you feel?

I decided to go home. If I sat on Irish Hill all day, pleasant as it might be, I'd never get any closer to finding out who'd been buried in our garden and why. Time to try to track down those servants. Or not. I felt the familiar little buzz of excitement at the prospect of a couple of hours' uninterrupted research, and hurried down the hill.

Simon, thankfully, was home early that evening. We decided to have a barbecue in the back garden, and he set to work lighting the charcoal while I prepared some salads and sliced open burger buns. We had sausages, burgers and chicken wings, and I wrapped some strawberries in tin foil along with a drizzle of orange juice, to tuck into the embers afterwards for dessert. The kids loved barbecued food, and happily organised themselves into a mini-Olympics involving much bouncing on the new trampoline and scoring of goals in the football net, while we cooked the food and sipped a bottle of chilled Pinot Grigio. Sometimes, everything just slotted into place and life was perfect. Except for my niggling worries about whatever Simon was hiding from me.

'Mu-um,' said Lauren, in one of those wheedling tones where you just know you're going to be talked into something against your better judgement, 'you know how it's Friday, and there's no school tomorrow, and it doesn't get dark till ten, and it's a lovely warm evening?'

'Ye-es?'

'So can we all stay up late tonight? Playing out here? Until the stars come out? Even Thomas?'

Little Thomas stood beside his sister, with pleading puppy-dog eyes.

I looked at Simon and raised my eyebrows. 'Well, I don't see why not,' he said.

'OK, Thomas goes in when the first star comes out, and you and Lewis go in as soon as it's properly dark.'

'Yes!' The children ran off again to the end of the garden to continue their games.

'Nice to see them playing well together,' commented Simon. 'And including Thomas.'

'Yes. Though we might pay for the late night with grumpiness tomorrow.'

Simon topped up our glasses. 'Cheers, love. We're doing a great job with our kids, even though I say it myself.'

I clinked my glass against his and smiled. He was right about the kids.

'They're lucky,' he went on. 'Having each other, I mean. And you had Jo.'

'Jo and I didn't always get on, as you know!' My sister and I didn't get on too well even now. We were too alike in some ways and complete opposites in others.

Simon looked wistful. 'Maybe it would be different now, if I'd had a sibling. If Mum and Dad had adopted another child as well as me.'

'What do you mean?'

'I think it would be easier. I mean, dealing with Mum's dementia. There would be someone else who really understood, who remembered her the way I do, from childhood. And maybe if she had a larger family to gather round her, she'd remember more.'

'Maybe. But there would be no guaranteeing it.'

'At least there'd be someone to share the visiting with. It's hard, being the only one.'

I frowned. Simon only visited Veronica once a fortnight. 'Love, if you find it that hard to visit her, maybe just go once a month?'

He looked at me, and bit his lower lip. Then he sighed, put his elbows on his knees and stared into his glass of wine, cupped in both hands. 'I haven't told you, Katie. I didn't know what you'd think.'

'Haven't told me what?'

He swirled the wine around in his glass. 'I've been going to Mum's much more often lately. I found that on about half the occasions I visited, she was more with it – knew who I was and all that. So I figured that if I went more often, then overall there'd be more times when we could have a proper conversation. I thought it might help her keep her memories for longer.'

'When have you been going?'

'Two or three times a week. After work. I've been staying on the train down from London, and getting off at Bournemouth. Then I take a cab to her home. Spend ten minutes or an hour with her depending on how she is, then get the train back here.'

'That's why you've been late back so many times.'

He nodded. For a moment he looked just like Thomas, when caught with his hand in the biscuit tin. I could barely believe it. All those terrible thoughts I'd had, that he was cheating on me, when the only 'other woman' he was seeing was his mother. The darling man! I felt both relieved and mortified. How could I ever have suspected him?

I reached out to touch his hand. 'But why didn't you tell me?'

'I thought you might advise me against it. You always say I'm so tense and stressed when I come home from seeing her. You've told me I need to look after myself first, or I'll be no good to her. And you've often said I should go less often.'

'I wouldn't have stopped you from going, if you'd told me why you wanted to.' Did he really think I would? Was I that much of an ogre?

'I know, but you might have put me off. Put doubts in my head, even if you didn't mean to. But I knew I wanted to give it a go. It's kind of an experiment.'

'And is it working? Do you get more quality time with her?'

'A bit. Maybe once a week she's on good form. But I can't spend long, and I'm so tired – that all works against it.'

He looked as though he was going to cry. The stress he'd been under – all that extra travelling, dealing with his mother's illness, keeping it all quiet from me. All on top of the house move, the bones, not to mention the contact from Amy. No wonder he'd been grumpy at times lately. And I hadn't helped at all.

'Oh, love,' I said, taking his hand. 'You should have told me. It was a good idea, and would have been easier for you if I'd known what you were doing. I could have supported you more.'

'You've been fab. God knows what you thought I was doing for all those late nights.'

'Well, you said you were working late so I...'

'Believed me? Bless you.' He leaned over and kissed my forehead. I felt myself blush with embarrassment. God knows what he would think of me if he knew the wild ideas I'd actually had about why he'd been late back so many times.

'So what are you going to do now? It's too much for you to keep going there after work.'

He shook his head. 'I don't know. It's wearing me out, all this travelling.'

'Why don't we move her to Winchester? There are plenty of nursing homes near here. If she was just ten or fifteen minutes' drive away, you could see her as often as you like. Every day, even.'

Simon stared at me. I wondered whether I should say any more. Would he think I was interfering? She was his mother – he needed to be the one who decided what was best for her. But I'd started now. Might as well say it all. 'I know you always thought moving her would upset her too much. But in the long run it might be worth it – if she settled and you were able to see her without ruining your own health.'

'She barely knows where she is now, half the time.'

'Well then – it would make no difference to her. Does she have friends in the home?'

He grimaced. 'They're not really friends. Some days she'll chat to anyone who'll listen; on others she won't say a word. Depends on her mood. I think she'd be just the same with a different set of people around her.'

'So, what do you think?'

He sat in silence for a minute, staring at an overgrown Clematis which grew along the remains of the old garden wall. It needed a severe pruning. I made a mental note to do it after it had finished flowering.

'Maybe if she was nearby I could even take the children to see her. If it turned out to be one of her better days we'd stay, if not, we would leave early.' Simon looked carefully at me.

'I think that would be a great idea. The twins are old enough to understand that she might not always know who they are. And Thomas is young enough to accept anything.'

'I'll start looking at local homes then. As soon as possible.'

I raised my glass to him and we clinked them. 'Sounds like a good plan. But listen, Simon, keep me involved, all right?'

'Will do.'

He still looked thoughtful. I guessed it would take a while for him to work through the implications of having his mother closer. I poured him another glass of wine, and we sat watching the kids play, and discussing his mother and Amy. It felt good to be talking openly with him, knowing he was not hiding anything more.

There was more than one star out by the time I retrieved Thomas from the den the kids were making at the bottom of the garden, and carried him yawning into the house and straight up to bed.

Chapter Twenty-One

Hampshire, April 1842

It was four months since the death of Georgia. Four long months. Agnes couldn't remember how many inns they'd stayed in; how many trains they'd caught or stagecoaches they'd travelled in. It was all a blur. She wondered how on earth gypsies coped with this lifestyle – always on the move, never staying anywhere more than a few days. At each stage Bartholomew had a story ready for anyone who asked – they were travelling north to attend a relative's funeral; they were travelling south on business; they were on their way to visit friends. And all the while he'd introduced her as his wife, Georgia, and their baby, Barty. She was beginning to understand what the plan was, and how it might work.

He'd bought her new gowns – not maids' uniforms but ladies' outfits. She had a trunk full of them now – beautiful dresses in silk and satin, dainty slippers to match, exquisite Indian shawls and beaded reticules. He'd bought her a necklace of silver and pearl, a delicate golden filigreed brooch, an opal and diamond ring.

He'd taught her to mind her ts and hs, to lose her country burr, to hold out her hand and incline her head when being introduced to someone new. He'd reminded her to hold her head high, her back straight, and walk as though she was gliding on casters beneath her skirts. He'd taught her how to be a lady.

And now, finally, the time had come to return to North Kingsley. They'd taken a train from London to North Kingsley station, then Bartholomew had hired a cab to take them and their trunks to Kingsley House. Agnes gazed out of the cab at the fields as they passed, their spring growth just beginning to emerge from the brown earth. The hedgerows were bursting into bloom, celebrating the end of a long, cold winter. It felt as though they were putting on a display to welcome her back. It was a little over a year since she'd first come here, on that stormy day when Georgia had given birth to little Barty. Just over a year ago, but so much had changed. Barty had changed too; he was already beginning to walk, and was a big eater.

Her own son must also have had his first birthday, she realised with a jolt. As the months had passed, she'd thought about him less and less often. Her time was taken up with caring for little Barty, who now felt like her own child. His face lit up whenever he looked at her. When he cried, she was the only one who could comfort him. And she knew that when he began to speak, she was the one he would call 'mama'.

As the cab lurched its way along the rutted road, she realised sadly there was no place for her own son in this new life Bartholomew had forged for them. Although the people of the village had never met Georgia, they'd known of the birth of her baby. There would be no possibility of explaining a second baby of the same age. Agnes knew her dream of bringing her own son to live with them would never be realised now. He would have to stay with her parents. Besides, he wouldn't know her. Last year, her arms had ached to hold him whenever she thought of him. Now, with Barty to hold and cuddle, that ache had gone.

She put her hand on her tummy. If she was right, there'd be another baby before the end of the year. A brother or sister for Barty, and a cementing of her relationship with Bartholomew.

The cab was now nearing the village. Agnes caught her lower lip between her teeth. Would their plan work? Would people accept her as Mrs St Clair? After Polly and the Fowleses had been sent away, only a couple of people from the area – Libby, and Dr Moore – had ever seen both her and Georgia. The short-sighted doctor had once mistaken Agnes for Georgia, as she sat in her red gown beside the fire, with Barty on the hearthrug at her feet. That, Bartholomew had told her, was what had given him the idea.

Still, as the cab entered the village, Agnes pulled her veil over her face.

Bartholomew looked at her. 'Nervous?'

'A little,' she admitted.

He patted her hand where it lay on the seat beside her. 'It'll be all right. Trust me.' He gave her a tight smile, and leaned forward to instruct the driver where to go.

The house, when they arrived, felt cold and unwelcoming. Agnes carried a sleeping Barty upstairs to find a cot. She shivered as she passed Georgia's old room, and went on up to the room she'd used in the attic. She put Barty down gently, went to the window and gazed out across the garden. To think she was now to be mistress of this house! It was what she had always wanted, and yet…things were not quite as she would have them. Bartholomew had been colder to her than he used to be. He made love to her, and treated her as his wife, but – something was missing. Something she could not quite put her finger on. It was as though he'd buried a part of himself along with Georgia.

Bartholomew entered the room. 'Ah, there you are. What are you doing up here? This is not your room now. We will need this room for one of the new servants.'

He came to stand behind her. 'I must plant a tree in that spot.'

He nodded at the place beside the garden wall where Georgia was buried.

Agnes glanced down at that spot. It no longer looked newly dug. Last autumn's leaves still covered it, and a few bluebells had seeded themselves and were nodding their violet heads in the spring breeze. Why did he want to plant a tree? Some kind of memorial to Georgia?

'To stop anyone digging there,' he said, as if he'd read her mind.

The following day, after a makeshift breakfast of bread and cold ham bought the previous day, Bartholomew looked across the table at Agnes.

'Today we must start setting up our household. We need servants, and you, as the mistress of the house, must go out and employ them.'

Agnes gasped. She had not thought she would need to go into the village as Mrs St Clair quite so soon. But she realised the sense of it – sooner or later she would have to go out. They needed a cook, a kitchen maid, a house maid and maybe also a nursery maid. They also needed to stock up the kitchen, and Bartholomew would need horses and a man to look after them.

They would probably need a gardener as well, but not until after that tree was planted.

She went upstairs to the room she now shared with Bartholomew – his old room; thankfully he had not chosen to use Georgia's room. She chose a bonnet with deep sides, a veil and a shawl, and got herself ready to go out. One thing was certain, she thought wryly: she would never employ a lady's maid.

It was a five-minute walk to the village centre. Although she'd lived here for six months the previous year, she'd never been in the village apart from the day she'd arrived. And Georgia too had never been. She'd been too heavily pregnant when she arrived, and then too sick, confined to her room after Barty's birth.

Agnes held her head high as she walked up the lane. No one

would recognise her, so if she played her part right she would easily be accepted as Mrs St Clair, recovered at last from the birth of her baby.

As she walked through the village a portly woman passed her, with three small children tagging along behind. She nodded at Agnes. 'How'd ye do, Mrs St Clair.'

It was Mary Moulsford, who had been Barty's wet-nurse. Agnes nodded in response, feeling herself blush under her veil.

'May I be so bold as to ask, how is the little one?' said Mary.

'Barty? He's doing well, thank you. Fit and well, and growing quickly.'

'Glad to hear it, Mrs St Clair. And may I say, 'tis good to see you're back at the big house,' said Mary. She nodded, and went on her way.

Agnes smiled. So at least one person in the village knew her as Mrs St Clair. She walked on, more confident now.

How to find servants? Bartholomew had been unsure, but had suggested she should simply ask around, at the inn, the shops and the market. She decided to start at the inn – the White Hart.

The woman who stood behind the bar was large, with a red face and straggly grey hair which poked out from a grubby white lace cap. Her eyes widened as she took in Agnes's expensive, blue silk gown and Indian shawl.

'Yes, ma'am?'

'I'm looking for servants,' Agnes replied. 'I am, um, Mrs St Clair. My husband and I are recently returned to Kingsley House and we need some staff.'

'Ah, Mrs St Clair, how'd ye do?' The woman bobbed a small curtsey. 'You've come to the right place. My Annie be looking for work. She's very hard-working.'

'Does she have references?'

'Oh, no, ma'am. She's only fifteen and not yet had herself a job. I can vouch for her, though.'

'Very well, send her up to the house at two o'clock this afternoon,' said Agnes. Maybe the girl would do as a kitchen maid.

'Shame our Libby isn't here,' said the woman. 'She worked for you last year, and was very happy, at least until she were dismissed, if you don't mind me saying.'

Agnes blanched. She remembered the kitchen maid who helped Mrs Fowles. Libby had seen both her and Georgia, and would surely recognise her. She cleared her throat. 'Where's Libby now?'

'Oh, she have got herself a job in a big house up at Winchester. That be all thanks to the reference Mr St Clair wrote for her. It were such a good one – she had no trouble finding another job. Though it were a shock when you let her go so sudden like, and just before Christmas and all.'

'I am sorry for that,' Agnes said. 'My husband insisted on taking me away for my health, and once he'd had the idea, he wanted us to go immediately. And as you can see' – she smiled – 'it has worked and I am quite well now.'

'Well, I shall tell Libby you are back and in fine fettle next time she comes home on a day off,' said the woman. 'Mebbe if you're still looking for staff, she might want to come back?'

'Oh, no, if she has a good job in Winchester let her continue there,' said Agnes hastily. 'I am sure I'll find other servants. I'll look forward to meeting your Annie later on today. Good day to you, and thank you.'

She turned to leave, but the woman called her back. 'You be wanting a man for the stables as well? There's John Morris up at Hill Cottage as needs a job. And his missus might want to be your cook, now their sons have all left home. I did hear how you'd let the Fowleses go, and sent them off afar.'

Agnes nodded. 'Thank you, you've been very helpful. Would you send a message to them to come at two if they want the jobs?'

'I'll do that, thank you, ma'am.'

Agnes heaved a sigh of relief as she left the inn. The woman had accepted her as Mrs St Clair with no questions. And she'd made a good start in finding servants. She grinned as she walked back through the village to the house. This plan looked like it was going to work. As long as Libby never came near them.

***

A couple of weeks later, Bartholomew sat at the desk in his study, an opened letter spread before him. He drummed his fingers on the desk. How to reply to this letter? It was from his old friend in Brighton, Henry Harding. He was asking if he and his wife Caroline could pay a visit to Bartholomew and Georgia, and the 'dear wee baby boy'. June would be a good month – they were due to visit other friends in Bath, and could divert to Hampshire on the way. It'd be good to see where dear Bartholomew had grown up, and to be reacquainted with his 'sweet young wife'. Harding trusted Bartholomew would reply 'at his earliest convenience' as it had been far too long since he'd seen his 'oldest, dearest friend'.

Bartholomew picked up his pen, dipped it in the ink-well and began a reply.

My dear Henry,

How wonderful it was to receive your letter. I am glad to hear you and Caroline are both well and happy. As are Georgia and I, and dear little Barty is a wonderful addition to our family...

No, that wouldn't do at all. It read as though he was encouraging them to visit. He screwed up the paper and tossed it into the fireplace. Start again.

Dear Henry

Whilst I would love to have you and Caroline visit us, it is rather too soon after the birth of our baby and Georgia is not yet fully recovered...

But it was almost a year – how many women took a year to recover from childbirth? That letter too was crumpled up for kindling.

247

What if he simply didn't reply at all? But then Harding might decide to call anyway, especially if he was passing nearby on his way to Bath.

Or he could write and suggest meeting instead in Brighton, just himself, pleading that Georgia needed to stay with the child, but that he had business in Brighton so could combine that with a visit? That might work, but Harding would no doubt want to come to visit another time. It would just put the problem off, rather than solve it. No, he would have to think of something which would put Harding off for good.

He sighed, realising that he would never again be able to see any of his old friends or acquaintances. He'd have to drop them all – anyone who'd ever met Georgia. They'd been lucky while they travelled, that they'd not run into anyone he knew, though he had carefully steered well clear of Brighton.

He picked up his pen once more.

Dear Henry

I am afraid we will not be able to receive you and Caroline here at Kingsley House. Georgia has never recovered from the illness she sank into after giving birth, and is unable to tolerate any visitors. Her doctor advises absolute quiet and solitude. It is her mind, you see – she was never strong and is now more fragile than ever. Any disruption to her routine causes her great distress. As you know, it is almost a year since our son was born, and it is only now that Georgia is beginning to function at all. The doctor does not think we can expect much further progress. I dare not do anything that could set her back again...

The ink was barely dry on the letter when the doorbell rang, and a moment later the housemaid Annie tapped on the study door.

'Sorry to disturb, sir, there be a woman at the door,' she said.

'Well, show her in!' What was the girl thinking, keeping visitors waiting on the doorstep?

'I would, sir, only she looks a bit rough,' said Annie. 'Don't know why she didn't go to the back door. She be asking for someone called Agnes. I told them there were no one here by that name but she said this is certainly where she last were at, said she were working for Mrs St Clair. Should I fetch Mrs St Clair, sir? She be upstairs with the baby, I believe.'

'It's all right, Annie, I will go and speak to the woman. Show her into the drawing room.'

The maid curtsied and left. Bartholomew stood, straightened his waistcoat and went to see who this woman was.

Annie was right. She was certainly rough-looking. Standing in the middle of his drawing room, wearing dirty, torn clothes and smelling as though she'd never seen the inside of a bath tub, was a middle-aged woman. Her wiry grey hair stuck out at all angles from her battered straw bonnet. In her arms she held a small child – a baby really – about the same size as Barty.

'Mr St Clair?' She spoke with a coarse country accent.

'Yes?'

'I'm looking for my daughter. Her name's Agnes Cutter. She was maid for your wife, but your girl there says she's never heard of her.'

'Agnes, yes, I remember her,' said Bartholomew. He sent up a silent prayer that Agnes would not come downstairs to see who'd come to the door, and that Annie wouldn't take it upon herself to go and fetch her mistress.

'So where is she, hmm, sir?'

'Um, she left us. Yes, about, ooh, a year and a half ago...'

'When she were pregnant with this little one,' said the woman, holding up the child. The boy grinned at her and made a grab for her bonnet ribbons. She batted his hand away. 'Stop it, Tolly. Then she came back to you. At least she said she were coming back to you. You was in Brighton. I've been there looking for you, and they sent me here. Traipsed all round the country I have.'

'Well, she, um, never came back to us. She must have changed her mind, I suppose. We've not seen her in all that time. I'm sorry I can't help you, Mrs Cutter.'

The woman snorted. 'So she's missing, hmm? But you must know where she went.'

'I'm sorry.'

'She could be dead in a ditch somewhere. Being eaten by maggots. My own dear daughter!' The woman wailed, while the child watched her wide-eyed.

'Please, Mrs Cutter, sit down, don't upset yourself. Agnes was always capable of looking after herself, as I recall. She's probably found herself another position somewhere. I'm sure she's all right.'

Mrs Cutter sat down on a chintz-covered sofa, and sat the child on her lap. He had the same fair hair as Agnes, and something about his eyes reminded Bartholomew of his own son, Barty. With a start he remembered this boy too, was his son.

'Maybe you can still help,' she said. 'Agnes left her bairn with me and my husband. She said she'd come back for him, when she'd got the bairn's father to agree to take him. But she never did.' She looked at Bartholomew slyly. 'I don't suppose as you knows who the father is, hmm?'

Bartholomew willed his face to stay pale and impassive. 'I've really no idea, Mrs Cutter. My servants' private lives are up to them and nothing to do with me. Though it was most inconvenient for Agnes to fall pregnant and leave us when she did, especially when my wife was pregnant herself.'

'I'll not go till I've heard where she's gone,' said Mrs Cutter. 'A cup of tea would be welcome, hmm, after the distance I've come to get here. Get some milk for the child, too.'

'Very well. I'll send Annie in with some refreshments. Excuse me.'

Bartholomew left the room. He instructed Annie to fetch some tea and milk, then hurried up the stairs to find Agnes. She was resting on their bed, while Barty napped in his cot.

He stood beside her and placed a hand on her shoulder to

250

wake her gently. She rolled over and frowned. 'What is it? I was sleeping.'

'Your mother is here.'

'What? Here? Where?'

'Downstairs. In the drawing room. And she has brought your child.'

Agnes sat up with a gasp. 'My child? Our child?'

'Tolly, she calls him.'

Agnes covered her mouth with her hand. 'Oh, my word.'

'She is looking for you. I said you never came back to us, after you had the baby.' Bartholomew sank suddenly to his knees in front of her. He realised the possibility of their crime being discovered now was more real than ever. 'Agnes, you must stay out of sight. If she finds out you are here, then we are lost. You must not go down to her.'

'But, my son!'

'I will give her some money. Enough to keep her happy. And I'll send money each year, on condition she promises to stay away and keep the child away.' He nodded. Yes, that would work. Mrs Cutter would assume, if she hadn't already guessed, that he was the father and was paying her to stay away to avoid scandal. If she only knew how great the scandal he was trying to avoid really was!

'My own son...' Agnes stared at him, wide-eyed. 'My own darling baby!'

Bartholomew took her hands. 'Think, Agnes. If we're found out, it's the gallows for us both.'

'If I could just see him...'

A gurgle came from the cot in the corner of the room. Agnes rose instinctively to see to Barty. She picked him up and looked at him as though she was seeing him for the first time.

Bartholomew got to his feet, and crossed the room to embrace her and Barty. '*This* is your son, Georgia.'

She looked at him, with tears streaming down her face.

'Yes. *This* is our baby. And soon, we will have another. Send the woman away, Bartholomew. Tell her I do not know where Agnes has gone.'

He nodded, smiled, and kissed her forehead, then went back downstairs to get rid of Mrs Cutter.

A few minutes later, Agnes stood at the window holding Barty, watching as the ragged woman left the house and walked up the lane towards the village. She held the child on her hip, his head turned to face back towards the house. He seemed to be staring straight up at the window where Agnes was standing.

She nuzzled her face into Barty's neck, making him giggle. 'Mama loves you, Barty,' she whispered. 'Mama loves you very much indeed.'

Bartholomew had a reply to his letter to Henry Harding within a week. This one was curt and to the point. Harding, it seemed, had heard from friends that a Mr St Clair and his beautiful blonde wife had been seen at the Assembly Rooms in Bath, and someone else had made their acquaintance in Margate, and a third had heard it from someone else that the St Clairs and their baby son had been seen boarding a train at Euston station. All that travelling and socialising was not in keeping with what Bartholomew had told him about the fragile health of his wife, Georgia.

It was clear, Harding wrote, that for whatever reason, Bartholomew had decided to drop him as a friend. So be it. Harding would not write again. He wished them well.

Bartholomew sighed on reading the letter. It was the end of a chapter of his life. The old friends had been cut away, and now they had to look to the future, and make new friends. He rang the bell for Annie.

'Tell the cook to start planning a dinner party,' he said. 'We shall be inviting a dozen people, and I want to serve them the very best of everything.'

It was time to properly integrate themselves into the local society. He'd invite all the local gentry – the Gaskells from the big house over near Micheldever, Colonel Booth and his wife from the other end of the village, Frank Bonnington from Winchester who he remembered from his youth, and of course Dr Moore and his wife. It would be Agnes's launch into society as Georgia. And then they would be able to sleep easily, once Agnes was known to all as Georgia.

And, dear Barty, that is what we did. Dr Moore welcomed her as an old friend, peering at her through his thick spectacles and declaring her fully recovered since he'd last seen her. Agnes charmed all the guests, and made a close friend of the colonel's wife, Mrs Booth, who became a frequent visitor to the house. Soon we had return invitations, and thus built ourselves a social life, though we were careful to keep to those few, local people and not tempt fate by going to balls or gatherings in the larger towns. After a year or so, news came that Libby Barton had married and moved to Ireland with her husband. That brought us some peace of mind. On occasion I could even forget that there had ever been another woman. Only the beech sapling which flourished in its sunny spot beside the garden wall served to remind me of my dark past.

Chapter Twenty-Two

Hampshire, July 2013

When I got back from dropping off the kids at their various holiday activities, Simon was still not dressed. I went upstairs and found him in our room, a mound of shirts and jumpers strewn across the bed.

'Come on, love, or you'll miss the train. Have you had breakfast?'

He picked up a denim shirt, held it against a pair of jeans and shook his head. 'Too much like a cowboy. What? Breakfast? No. Can't face eating anything.'

'I'll make you some tea and toast. You must have something.'

He pulled a pair of beige cargo pants out of the wardrobe, and unfolded a Motörhead T-shirt, then threw me a questioning look.

'Too casual,' I said. 'And, Motörhead? For goodness sake, that T-shirt must be a thousand years old.'

He pouted. 'What'll I wear, then?'

Good grief, he was like a teenager on his first date. I did have sympathy though. It couldn't be easy, going off to meet his grown-up daughter for the first time. Simon had the day off work, and was to take the train to London to meet her. They were to meet in the Argyll Arms at eleven a.m. If all went well, he would take her somewhere for lunch.

I picked up a pale-blue polo shirt and a pair of jeans. 'Here. Safe, and comfortable. It's warm out, you won't need a jacket.'

He smiled gratefully and pulled on the clothes. I straightened his collar and tucked the label inside. 'Come on then, time for a slice of toast, then I'll drop you at the station.'

'Thanks, love. I can't believe how nervous I feel. Are my hands sweaty?' He held out his palms for me to feel.

'A little. She'll be nervous too, it's only natural. Try to take it easy, though, OK?'

He nodded, and followed me downstairs to the kitchen. I felt like his mother, not his wife, as I made him tea and toast and stood over him while he ate it.

'Have you got your phone, and your rail ticket? And your wallet?'

He checked his pockets, and nodded.

'Sunglasses?'

He raised a finger and went to fetch them from the hall table.

'Amy's present?' After agonising for hours, he'd bought her a dainty silver necklace. Nothing too showy or obviously expensive – just a little token gift that he hoped would say to her that he cared.

'No, Christ, what have I done with it?' He ran his hands through his hair and looked wildly around him.

'On the hall table. Next to where you found your sunglasses.'

He smiled sheepishly. 'Ah.'

'Newspaper, or book?'

'What for?'

'To read on the train.' For a man who commuted every day he was doing a great impression of someone who'd never travelled by rail before.

255

'Oh. Um, I'll buy a paper at the station.'

'OK. Right then, we'd better go, or you'll miss the train. Ready?'

He nodded, biting his lip like a five-year-old on his first day at big school. I ruffled his hair and ushered him out to the car.

An hour later I was back in the house with the washing machine, tumble dryer and dishwasher all on, chuntering away, doing the housework for me. I made a pot of coffee, and sat down with my laptop to do some research.

A little later I'd made some progress. I'd found George and Maria Fowles on the 1851 census: living in a village in Kent with their son. They were elderly, both over seventy. Maybe they'd retired from working for Bartholomew and had moved to Kent to end their days with their son. Well then, the bones in the garden did not belong to Maria. In any case, she was probably too old.

That only left Agnes Cutter and Polly Turner. There were so many Turners I'd found it impossible to be certain whether any of them were the Polly I was looking for, so I'd been unable to definitely rule her out. And as for Agnes Cutter, I'd drawn a complete blank. It was an unusual enough name that I felt I ought to be able to find her, either in the 1851 census, in a marriage registration or in a death registration. She was definitely in Kingsley House in early 1841 when the census was taken, but I couldn't find what had happened to her after that.

Unless it was she who'd ended up buried in our back garden?

It was an odd kind of research to do – normally you're hoping to find someone but on this occasion I didn't want to find her in any document after 1841. I didn't want to be able to rule her out.

Mid-morning, Dad phoned, and we swapped research news. 'There were twenty-three possible women in the village on the 1841 census,' he told me. 'Those in Kingsley House I left for you to do. And of the others, nineteen appear on the 1851 census and I have found death registrations for the other four.'

'Twenty-three! You must have spent ages researching,' I said.

He laughed. 'Yes, and your mother's going spare. I've loved doing it, though. So, either your skeleton is one of your missing servants, or she's not local.'

'What do you think?'

'We will never be able to be sure. I found nothing in the newspapers – no reports of missing women or anything of the kind. I'll have a look for these servants as well, in case you missed something. Oh, and guess what else I found?' He sounded excited. 'The National Portrait Gallery website has a search facility. Have you ever tried looking for any ancestors there?'

'No. Are there some St Clairs on it, then?'

'Sadly not our St Clairs. Then I thought of looking for the Hollands, and guess what – there's a portrait of Georgia!'

'Wow! Hang on, Dad, just opening up that website now. What did you put in the search box – Holland or Georgia Holland?'

'Georgia Holland. Have you found her?'

I had. There she was. I gasped to see her – my great-great-great-grandmother smiling demurely at me through my laptop screen. She was pictured standing beside a small table on which stood a vase. She was holding a bunch of garden flowers, and more flowers were strewn across the table, as though she was in the act of arranging them. I peered closely at her face. Blonde hair, caught up at the back and falling in ringlets either side of her face. Green eyes, creamy skin, round face. Her expression was sweet, naive – here was a girl who had yet to see the dark side of life.

'Wasn't she pretty! She must have been very young when this was painted.' I checked through my notes. 'Looks like it was painted around the time she got married. She'd have been about seventeen.'

'That's when she lived in Brighton as a ward of her uncle's, didn't she?' asked Dad.

'That's right. Hold on, just saving a copy of that portrait.' I right-clicked and saved it to my laptop. 'Isn't it brilliant seeing the face of an ancestor?'

'Certainly is. I've found myself wondering if I can see my nose or your forehead in her.'

I peered again at the picture. Perhaps there was something in the shape of her face? But she was only one of my thirty-two great-great-great-grandparents. It would be difficult to spot any kind of family resemblance. Then I saw it, in her hair, a row of jewels holding up her blonde tresses... I zoomed in, enlarging the picture until I could see every brush stroke.

'Dad, did you see what's in her hair? It's the comb, I'm sure of it. That silver and emerald comb we found in the bureau drawer. It is, look, the row of green stones in her hair – they're in the same pattern as the comb.'

'So the comb was definitely Georgia's?'

'Yes! Oh, wow. I'd wondered if it could have been hers.' That old buzz of excitement again, to think I not only had a picture but also owned something that had belonged to my great-great-great-grandmother!

'Which also means it didn't belong to that poor girl who ended up buried beneath your beech tree,' said Dad. 'Shame, in a way. I liked to think it might have been hers.'

I spent the rest of the morning going through my research and listing who had lived in Kingsley House at each census date. After Bartholomew and Georgia's deaths in the 1870s there was just Barty junior living here, with a couple of servants. But then on the 1881 census I noticed something I hadn't spotted before. The transcript of the census on the ancestry website listed a visitor staying with Barty at the time of the census – a man named Tommy Colter. But when I looked closely at the original hand-written census return on the website, I realised it had been transcribed wrongly. Not Tommy Colter, but Tolly Cutter.

Cutter. Agnes's surname was Cutter. Could there be any link between these two? Agnes Cutter was certainly the right age to be Tolly Cutter's mother. His age was given as forty on the 1881 census, so he must have been born in early 1841 or late 1840. He was a farm labourer, and his birth place was noted as Woodhall, Lincolnshire. Tolly was an odd name. I googled the words 'Tolly' and 'name' and found a names website. I gasped – Tolly was listed as a contraction of the name Bartholomew.

So: Agnes worked for Bartholomew and Georgia, and in late 1840 or early 1841 she may have had a baby out of wedlock, whom she named Bartholomew. The baby was born in Lincolnshire. But at the time of the 1841 census, she was living in Kingsley House with no baby. If it was hers, who was looking after him then?

I quickly began researching Tolly Cutter or Bartholomew Cutter, and found him as a baby in 1841 living with his grand-parents Mary Cutter, a midwife, and John Cutter, a woodman, in Woodhall. I followed him through the censuses – finding him in the same village and working as an agricultural labourer, marrying, producing three children, and then there was the visit to Barty St Clair around the time of the 1881 census. Why would Barty and Tolly have been in touch? Tolly was the child of a servant once employed by Barty's father. Why would he then come to stay with Barty, with whom he had no connection? Unless…unless both Bartholomews shared the same father… I could think of no other possible explanation.

It could be worth spending a few quid and ordering his birth certificate to try to find out more. I pulled out my pile of certif-icates to remind myself what was shown on them. Did birth certs always list the father as well as the mother? Flicking through them, something I'd not noticed before jumped out at me. Little Elizabeth's death certificate stated Georgia was present at her death. But there was something odd – instead of Georgia's copper-plate signature as witness, like the one on her marriage certificate, there was only an X, and a note written by the clerk: *The mark of Georgia St Clair*. I picked up Isobella's death certificate. Georgia was present at this daughter's passing as well. But once again, she had not signed it, and there was only an X.

It was puzzling. Had she been too distraught to sign her name, perhaps? It was the only explanation I could think of. But surely she'd have been able to write her name, even if her signature had come out as a tearful scrawl.

I tracked down Tolly's birth registration details and sent off an application for a copy of his birth certificate. It would take a week or two to arrive, but it would confirm whether Agnes was indeed Tolly's mother and with any luck, state who his father was. As for the mystery about Georgia's signatures, that was something to ponder on.

I'd just about finished when the doorbell rang. It was DI Bradley. He was carrying a small brown cardboard box, which he held out apologetically.

'We don't provide pretty urns, I'm afraid, but you'd said you'd like to have this.'

I put a hand to my mouth. 'Is it…is it her?'

'Yes, all that's left. It arrived on my desk a couple of days ago so I thought I'd pop round when I was next in the area.' He smiled and held out the box again.

'Thank you. Won't you come in for a cup of tea?' I took the box from him and stood aside, but he shook his head.

'Sorry, can't stop this time. I'm on a call.'

'More ancient bones?'

He laughed. 'Nothing so exciting. A break-in at a school. Probably just bored kids. When do they go back to school?'

'Not till September. Ages yet. I managed to get shot of them all today and have the house to myself but it's not always easy to keep them amused.'

'I bet. Well, do what you will with the ashes. The poor girl, whoever she was.' He nodded, and walked back to his car.

All too quickly the clock ticked around to three o'clock and it was time to fetch Thomas from his friend's house, then start preparing dinner for the kids. The twins were due back from their holiday club at five. I hadn't heard from Simon so did not know whether he'd be back for dinner or not. I wondered how his meeting with Amy was going.

In the end it was after nine p.m. before I heard his key in the door. I rushed out to the hallway to greet him, searching his face for clues as to how the day had been.

He was flushed and grinning from ear to ear. I looked around quickly to check the whereabouts of the kids – I'd already put Thomas to bed and the other two were ensconced in their respective bedrooms.

'Come into the kitchen,' I said. 'I'll make us a cup of tea and you can tell me all about it.'

He followed me through and sat down, still grinning. I filled the kettle and stopped myself from telling him to get on with it, let me know what happened. He'd need to tell me the story of the day in his own way, in his own time.

As I poured the tea he leaned back in his chair, put his hands behind his head and said, 'She's a cracker. Beautiful, lively, lovely girl. I'm so proud to be her dad.'

I smiled, and handed him the tea. 'It went well, then?'

'Brilliant. We got on so well. I think we've got quite a lot in common. She even played rugby for her college team.'

'Well, she's your daughter, you're bound to have a lot in common.' I felt an inexplicable pang of jealousy. He'd never talked in this way about Lauren. Or the boys.

'Yes, but it was more than that. We just clicked. She was nervous at the start, like I was, but after about five minutes we were chatting like we'd known each other for years. Except of course we knew nothing about each other, and so there was a lot to fill in.'

'Did she like the necklace?'

He nodded. 'At least, she said she did but I think it's probably not quite her style.'

I'd suggested it. Clearly got it wrong, then. 'It was the thought that counted.'

'Katie, she wants to come and visit us here. Meet you, and get to know her brothers and sister.'

'We'll have to tell them, then.'

'Yes. She wants to come in a couple of weeks' time, if that suits us. On a Saturday, for lunch, perhaps. I'll help cook.'

Yeah right, I thought. Cooking wasn't Simon's strong point.

'So we'd better tell the children soon, to give them time to get used to the idea of having a big sister before they meet her.'

'Yep.' He reached across the table and took my hand. 'I'll need your help with that, love. I've no idea how best to tell them.'

'Of course I'll help. It has to be both of us to tell them.' I felt tears welling up in my eyes.

'Thanks, love. You've been so great about all this.'

I shrugged. How else could I be over it?

262

Chapter Twenty-Three

Hampshire, December 1876

My dear Barty

This sorry narrative is almost at an end now. It remains only for me to bring you up to date, from those shameful events of 1841 to the present day. I shall do so briefly, for the main part of the story is now told, and there are thankfully no more shocks in store for you.

Agnes, as I have related, was readily accepted by the North Kingsley folk as Mrs St Clair. We were lucky in that no one of note in Winchester had known Georgia, so we were able to cautiously widen our social circles to that city. Agnes played her part well. She refined her speech and bearing, dressed herself immaculately – though never employed a lady's maid to help her – and learned to converse on any topic with anybody.

The only thing expected of a lady which she did not do was learn to read or write. I offered to teach her on several occasions but she did not want to learn, saying she would not be like a child, studying at my knee. She kept her ignorance well hidden. I would read out the morning paper to her, to keep her abreast of current affairs so that she could hold her own at dinner parties. Did you guess, Barty, that she could not read? Did you wonder why you never found her with a slim volume of poetry, or the latest novel, in her hand like other ladies?

It was about six months after the visit of her mother, on a cold night in December of 1842 almost exactly a year since we'd buried Georgia, that our daughter Elizabeth was born. Do you remember her, Barty? A delicate, fair child, so like her mother, yet so loving towards her father. You were only four years old when she died. She succumbed, like so many small children, to a fever. I remember how she lay, sweating and moaning, on that last day. Agnes stayed at her side throughout, eating her meals in the sick room, and leaving it only when poor Lizzie had breathed her last.

She was a good mother. She was good to you too, even though, as you have learned, you were not her flesh and blood. No woman could have been a better mother.

Your other sister, Isobella, you do remember, I know, because you have spoken of her. Her looks, of course, were more like mine, dark and heavy. Her personality was her mother's – she knew how to use her charm to get whatever it was she wanted. That charm worked on you too, Barty, didn't it? She could twist you any way she wanted. You adored her, doted on her, and would do anything she asked of you. You were blamed, I believe, for many of the pranks and escapades she initiated. And you took that blame squarely on the chin, preferring to be punished yourself than see your cherished little sister in trouble.

Poor Isobella suffered so much with the consumption. You spent hours by her bedside, praying for her recovery, but it was not to be.

And lastly there was William. He was born within a fort-night of Lizzie's death. He'll be good for your wife, said the doctor – he'll keep her busy, be a replacement for the child she's lost.

How wrong he was. Agnes, I think, never really recovered from losing Lizzie. She found it hard to care for little William, and I was reminded so much of your mother, Barty, and how she had suffered in the months after giving birth. I think Agnes too was reminded of that. Certainly she did all that she could to pull herself together, and get herself up and about again. Did she think perhaps that I would take up with some other servant, and do away with her, and bury her in the garden alongside Georgia?

No, of course not. I was never unfaithful to Agnes. Even after she became bitter and uncaring towards me, and our sham marriage became barren and cold, I did not stray. I had learned the dangers of infidelity. I would not do anything that might risk Agnes's anger, for who knows what she might have done, if provoked? She might have risked the gallows herself, and led a constable to Georgia's earthy grave, to spite me.

Yes, we were cold and bitter towards each other, beginning from the month of Lizzie's death and William's birth. And yet we had many more years together, shackled to each other by our shared crime. There was no escaping it. We dared not move, and I dared not go away for too long, for fear of a gardener taking it upon himself to turn over the soil around the beech sapling I'd planted beside the wall. I could get up to London and back in a day by rail, for business purposes. I never stayed away overnight. After our initial travels, we never left Kingsley House again.

William grew up healthy and strong, an independent little boy, who had little need for love, affection or company. Did he grow up like this because he received so little attention, or was that his natural constitution? Would we perhaps have loved him more if he'd demanded our love? We shall never know. I am proud of him – a successful London solicitor –

certainly he has brains and ambition and will do well in life. I hope in time he will marry, have children of his own, and thus continue the St Clair name.

Or perhaps you will, Barty? Though you are already past the usual age for marrying, it is not too late, and maybe you will find some sweet young girl who is prepared to accept what you can offer her.

But if that happens, Barty, you must promise me, you must bring her to live here. You must not sell this house. You, and only you know what is buried in the garden. It is your own mother there, beneath the beech, beside the wall. You must stay here as her guardian. You are her only living relative. You must remain here and look after her.

Agnes, of course, is buried in St Michael's churchyard, under a headstone engraved with Georgia's name. Soon, very soon, I fear, I shall join her. Entombed for all eternity with my partner in crime, while my true wife rots alone under the beech.

You will, I am sure, if you hadn't already done so when you reached that part of my confession, go to stand beside the beech tree. You might reach out a hand to touch it, wondering if it has taken some of its sustenance from the flesh and bones of your mother, disturbed and muddled now, no doubt, at its roots. Perhaps you will crouch and bury your fingers in the earth, in an attempt to touch some part of the woman who gave you life. Maybe you will go there often. Or maybe you will stay away, averting your eyes from the scene of such an atrocious crime, committed by your own father and the woman you called mother.

Whatever you do, don't, for heaven's sake, draw attention to that spot. Don't let anyone wonder what it is that draws you to it, or repels you from it. Just keep an eye on it, don't allow the tree to be cut down, replace it yourself should it fail.

Should Tolly Cutter ever call and make any claims on you,

please treat him with compassion, and make sure he is provided for. He is, of course, your half-brother, and as much your brother as William is. I have sent money monthly since Mrs Cutter's visit, but whether it reaches him or not I do not know.

I hope, dear Barty, that you live a long and happy life. You are named executor of my will, and apart from a legacy to William you inherit everything. You will be comfortably off, and will never need to work for a living, as long as you manage your investments well.

You no doubt hate me now, having read the entirety of this confession. Perhaps in time you will learn to live with what I did, and although I would never expect forgiveness, you might begin to understand my actions.

I can only apologise for my part in your true mother's death, and my subsequent deception allowing you to believe all your life that you were Agnes's natural son. I cannot imagine how you must feel now, knowing that the woman you called 'mother' was in fact your mother's murderer. It pains me to think of it, as it has done for so many years now. Finally, in writing this confession to you, I feel a small amount of relief of the burden of secrecy. But I have simply passed the burden on to you. I am sorry. So very, very sorry, believe me.

I am tired now, and my end draws ever nearer. I have but one final request to put to you – burn this manuscript. It must not be seen by anyone other than yourself. Do not be tempted to hide it away anywhere, even in the darkest recesses of the house, for surely someone might one day find it. Our secret must be buried for all time, just like your poor dear mother.

Goodbye, dearest Barty, my only legitimate child.

Chapter Twenty-Four

Hampshire, August 2013

'Mum, I'm confused.' Lewis spoke through a mouthful of toast.

'What, love?'

'So today, right, we're visiting Nanna Smith in her new home, but she might not know who we are. And if she doesn't, we're to pretend we're just random children off the street.'

'Er, yes, that's right.' Not quite how I'd have put it but he's got the gist of the plan. We'd been lucky – a nearby nursing home had a place for Veronica and we'd been able to move her into it within a week.

'Then tomorrow, we're meeting some random woman who's our older sister who we didn't even know we had, and Dad didn't even know about either. But we don't have to pretend with her, 'cos she knows who we are and everything.' He took another slice of toast from the rack and began slathering it with our homemade blackberry jam, made just the day before.

'Yes, Amy's coming for lunch tomorrow. And Granny and Granddad will come for tea.'

'And in case you weren't sure, poo-face, Granny and Granddad know who we are, and we know who they are. Ow!' Lauren got her ear flicked from her brother for her less-than-helpful comment. 'Anyway I can't wait to meet Amy. I always wanted a sister and now I've got one. It's going to be soooo cool.' I'd been delighted and relieved by Lauren's reaction when we told her she had a sister. She'd punched the air and declared the family numbers evened up at last. Lewis had simply shrugged.

'How come Dad didn't even know about her?' said Lewis. 'Like, he must have been there when he and Amy's mum...'

'Yes, well, obviously,' I cut him off, noticing Thomas's wide-eyed stare. Lauren sniggered. 'He split up with Amy's mum, and she never told him she was pregnant.'

'Wasn't she like, fat or something?'

'She must have been still in the early stages when they split up, so she wouldn't have been fat, yet.'

Lauren made a face at him. 'Derr.'

Simon entered the kitchen, running his hands through his hair. I recognised the signs of stress. Today was to be an experiment, to see if we could somehow restart some kind of relationship between Veronica and the kids. And with Amy coming tomorrow, we were extending our family in all directions. Who knew how the two meetings would work out?

'Ready to go in ten minutes?' I said.

Simon poured himself a coffee and nodded. 'I'll be ready. Kids, you ready?'

Thomas nodded solemnly. Lewis mumbled something through his toast and Lauren left the table and bounded upstairs.

Veronica's new home was a modern building on the outskirts of Winchester. It was set in leafy grounds, with wheelchair-friendly paths winding their way beside flowerbeds crammed with flowering shrubs. There were inviting-looking benches under rose-clad trellises and a pond with a small fountain and a couple of koi carp. Inside, a pleasant reception area led to the residents' lounge, which had patio doors opening to the grounds. Simon had loved the place as soon as he'd seen it. I smiled as I watched the kids hurtle through to the gardens to investigate the pond.

'Mrs Smith is in her room,' said a friendly nurse. 'She's getting on well but is not always confident to come out and socialise with the other residents. It'll take time for her to get used to her new surroundings.'

Simon called the kids and led the way along a ground-floor corridor to his mother's room. At the door, Thomas pestered to be picked up, and the twins hid behind me. It was a shame – they'd loved Veronica when they were little and she was well.

'Mum? How are you getting on? Do you like your new room?' Simon approached her cautiously, looking for signs as to how 'with it' she was today. She was sitting in her chair beside the bed, her hands folded in her lap and a piece of knitting discarded at her side.

'They've closed the window again,' she said. 'Open it for me, Peter, love.'

Simon bent to kiss her cheek, and opened the window. The scent of lavender filled the air – there was a bush just beneath her window.

'Why did she call Daddy Peter?' whispered Lauren.

'Sometimes she thinks Daddy is *his* daddy,' I told her. 'Go and say hello.' I gave her a little nudge forward.

'My name's Lauren,' she said, giving a little curtsey.

Veronica's face lit up with an enormous smile. 'What a pretty curtsey! You must be a ballet dancer.'

'I used to do ballet. When I was little. You came to one of my shows, when I was a Sunbeam. Do you remember?'

'No, dear, I've never been to any ballet shows. Except when Peter took me to see *Swan Lake* at the Southampton Gaumont. I loved it, you know. He fell asleep, didn't you, Peter? It was so embarrassing. I never let him take me again.'

'I've never liked ballet,' Simon agreed.

'I'm Lewis. I don't like ballet either.'

270

'I suppose you like football better, young man?'

'Yes, course I do! So does Thomas. But he's only four.'

'I'm five tomorrow.'

'No you're not. It's next week, isn't it, Mum?'

'So many children,' sighed Veronica. She looked at me. 'Are they all yours?'

'Yes, all mine.' Simon opened his mouth as if to say, his too, but thought better of it.

'Peter and I only had the one son. That was enough for us. A little blond boy. I don't know where he is, now. I think he must be in the playroom. Would your children like to run along and find him? He's about your age,' she nodded at Thomas.

I watched as Lauren bit her lip, and fiddled with the end of her belt. Then she went to sit on the bed beside Veronica. 'I'd much rather stay here and talk to you about ballet, Nan— I mean, Mrs Smith. I've never seen a proper ballet. Was it really lovely?'

'Oh yes, dear. Those lovely dresses – tutus, they call them. And the dying swan scene. So beautiful. Of course it wasn't Margot Fonteyn. I forget the name of the prima ballerina. I seem to be so forgetful these days.'

Lauren, bless the darling girl, took Veronica's hand and patted it. 'Don't worry, Mrs Smith. Everyone forgets things sometimes. I forgot where I put my Nintendo. Then it turned up in Lewis's room.'

'Nintendo?'

'It's a kind of game.'

'Like Cluedo?'

'Mum, what's Cluedo?'

'A kind of game.'

'Is Lewis your brother?'

'Yes. I've got two brothers. Lewis is my twin and Thomas is the baby.'

'I had two brothers as well. Frederick and Geoffrey. Geoffrey went to live in Australia. Such a long way away. I wonder why Frederick hasn't been to visit me. Is it tea-time yet, Peter?'

'I'll go and find out,' said Simon. He'd been fighting back emotions all the while Lauren had been chatting with Veronica. I guessed he'd appreciate a moment to collect himself outside of the room.

There was more disconnected chat of ballet and football and long-dead brothers who clearly still lived on in Veronica's mind. Simon returned with news that we could take a tray of tea things outside to the garden. The kids leapt up and down, delighted at the idea of freedom. But Veronica shook her head.

'Oh no, not in the middle of winter. It's far too cold out there, and there's nowhere to sit.'

'Yes there is, Mrs Smith. Come on.' Lauren took her hand and pulled her gently.

'And there are goldfish in the pond,' said Lewis, taking her other hand.

Veronica smiled and allowed herself to be pulled to her feet and out of the room. 'I don't know who these children are,' she said to me as she passed, 'but they are certainly very nice ones. Do you think they'll come again? Did Peter bring them?'

'Yes, I think they'll come again,' I replied, and Lauren nodded her agreement. Even Thomas nodded, his thumb in his mouth and his eyes fixed on this strange old lady.

The rest of the visit was a success. Veronica enjoyed the children's company and they kept up a steady stream of chatter. After a while Thomas forgot his shyness and went to climb up on Veronica's lap, to her delight and surprise.

'Peter, look, isn't he just like our Simon? Do you remember when we fetched Simon, from the children's home? He was just like this little boy. Blond and shy. And then he put his little hand in mine, and it felt so perfect. His hand fitted mine and I knew I was *meant* to be his mother.' She looked around the garden. 'Where is Simon now? I expect he's in the playroom. Why don't you children run along and find him? He's about your age, you know, little blondie.' She tickled Thomas who giggled in that infectious way young children have, and we all laughed along with him, though I noticed Simon's eyes were sparkling with unshed tears.

When the time came to leave, with promises to come back in a week, Simon was grinning from ear to ear. As we walked out to the car park, he put an arm around my shoulders. 'Well, I'd say that was a resounding success.'

'Absolutely.' I leaned into him. 'So what if she doesn't know who we all are, or how we're all related. She enjoyed the visit, so did we, and that's all that matters. She lives in the present, now, with snippets of past memories floating up every now and again.'

'Don't we all? Isn't that the only way we *can* live?' Simon stopped me mid-car park and kissed me. 'Great idea to move her closer. Thanks, love.'

The kids had been brilliant with Veronica. We took them to Paulton's Park for the afternoon as a reward. I only hoped they'd get on with Amy as well as they had with Nanna Smith. My stomach lurched as I wondered how *I'd* get on with her. My grown-up stepdaughter. I'd find out, tomorrow.

Chapter Twenty-Five

Hampshire, August 2013

'Lewis, have you tidied away your Lego from the living room? Lauren, help me empty the dishwasher, there's a love. Simon, have you got enough charcoal for the barbecue? We were a bit low last time, do you think you should nip to the garage and get some more? Oh, bugger it.' I swore as two plates clashed together as I pulled them from the dishwasher, and one chipped.

'Mum, that's a bad word!' said Lauren reprovingly.

'Yes, so don't you repeat it,' I said.

'Mummy, what's bugger?' said Thomas, as he whizzed into the kitchen on his scooter.

'Nothing, darling, now take that scooter outside to play please, we've got a lot to do in here before Amy comes.'

Simon passed through the kitchen on his way to the patio, ushering Thomas outside with him. 'I bought charcoal on my way home from work yesterday, there's loads. Oh Christ, she's not a vegetarian is she?'

I stopped unloading the dishwasher and stared at Simon. 'Is

she? You might have said so – that'll mean we need to rethink the meal completely!'

He scratched his head. 'Trying to think – what did she have to eat? I was so caught up in the moment, I didn't notice.'

Lauren put some cups into a cupboard and sighed. 'She had steak and chips, Dad. That's what you told us. You said she had the same as you and that's how you knew she was definitely your daughter.'

'Steak and chips, yes, that's right! And then treacle pudding and custard for afters. Got a healthy appetite, that's for sure.' Simon tried to ruffle Lauren's hair but she ducked away, rolling her eyes.

'Well remembered, love,' I said. 'So the barbecue is saved. It's the right weather for it, anyway.' It had been hot and sultry for a few days now.

A clatter at the front door announced the arrival of Saturday's post. 'I'll fetch it,' said Lauren, as she ran out to the hallway. She was making herself extremely useful. I wondered if she was trying to prove she was the perfect daughter, in case Simon preferred Amy. In my eyes, of course, she already was perfect.

'Just one for you, Mum,' she said, passing me a brown envelope. I was going to put it to one side when I noticed it had come from the General Register Office. Tolly's birth certificate, it had to be! Despite the chaos in the house and all that had to be done before Amy was due to arrive at midday, I just had to open it, there and then.

Mother: confirmed as Agnes Cutter, as I'd suspected. Place of birth: Woodhall, Lincolnshire, the same village he'd grown up in, cared for by his grandparents. Father's name was left blank. I felt a pang of disappointment. That confirmed he was illegitimate. I suppose it would have been too much to hope that Agnes had named the father of her child.

'What's that, Katie?' Simon had come back into the kitchen to fetch implements for the barbecue.

'Just a birth certificate I'd ordered. You know, my obsession with the past.' I stuffed it back into its envelope, to have a better look at later, in private.

'Whose? Anything to do with our mystery burial?' Simon was rummaging in a drawer for tongs and a fish slice. I pushed him away, opened the right drawer and handed him the tools.

'Possibly. One of the servants who lived here in 1841 who I've been trying to trace, had a baby. It's his birth certificate.'

'Let me see? No, on second thoughts, don't. We've got far too much to do right now. You're gradually hooking me into this family tree research, you know. I never thought I'd be interested, but what with the skeleton, and then the stuff that Amy said…'

'What did Amy say?'

'Oh, you know. About how important it felt for her to know where she'd come from. That's why she tracked me down, you see. She wanted to find her roots.'

Well, I could understand that, completely. I nodded, and was about to say something more, when Simon spoke again.

'She's got a point, I suppose. I'm beginning to get it now – this thing about wanting to know where you came from.' He gently flicked my bottom with the fish slice. 'Still think it's more important to look to the future though. That's more important than the past.'

'Oi, that hurt!' I flicked him back with a tea towel. 'The present's the most important, I reckon. Think about your mum. She just enjoys what's happening now, without worrying about what came before and what'll happen next, bless her. And *our* present, right now, is too busy to talk about ancient history any longer. Come on, you've got a barbecue to get ready, and I need to make a salad.'

Amy arrived right on time, armed with an enormous smile, presents for the children and flowers for me. While Simon hugged her, I took the flowers straight to the kitchen to find a vase, and to hide the emotions which welled up as I watched Lauren's eyes

276

widen in awe at the sight of her new big sister, and Lewis's feigned indifference hiding his obvious curiosity.

The afternoon was a complete success. By the time we were eating our barbecued bananas with grated chocolate (Lauren and Lewis's favourite dessert, and Amy declared it was her new favourite as well), it felt as though I'd known Amy for years. Afterwards she played football against Lewis and Thomas, blaming her long blonde hair for getting in her eyes and causing her to miss the goal. The boys won five–one. She'd bought Lauren a nail-art kit, and painted her nails a delicate lilac, with a diamante flower on each tip. Simon sat watching her, his expression a mixture of pride and wonder.

Mum and Dad arrived at their appointed time of four o'clock. Mum had even brought a gift for Amy – a box of Butlers chocolates, which Amy declared were her favourite brand. She kissed them both, and I had the impression she would not only happily adopt me and the kids, but also my parents and sister. She was a young woman in need of a family. I felt a glow of pride that we'd be able to provide that for her.

When the kids went inside to watch the *Clone Wars* DVD Amy had bought for Lewis, Simon handed us a beer each and we turned our garden chairs to face the sun. Between us, Simon and I told Amy the story of how we bought the house and what we'd discovered in the garden, and how we'd tried to find out who it could be and guess what might have happened. Mum rolled her eyes to hear it again, but Dad chipped in enthusiastically about his part in the research.

Amy was astounded. 'Bloody hell, talk about finding skeletons in the closet when you research your family tree – you found an actual skeleton! And you think it could have been one of those servants?'

'That's our best guess. But it'll be impossible to ever know for sure.'

'You said one of them had a son? So perhaps if there's any

DNA in those bones, it could be tested against DNA from her descendants?' said Amy.

Dad nodded. 'That's what they did with Richard the Third, after they found his bones under that Leicester car park.'

Simon laughed. 'Bit late for that. The police had the bones cremated.'

'Aw. What happened to the ashes?'

I nodded back at the house. 'They're sitting in a cardboard box on the kitchen windowsill right now.'

Amy looked shocked. 'You can't just leave them there. What will you do with them?'

I shrugged. 'That's the problem, I don't know. It doesn't seem right to scatter them in the garden, if she was murdered here. I thought of taking them up to the churchyard where Bartholomew and Georgia are buried but…'

'Not if there's any chance Bartholomew was the murderer!' said Mum. 'She'd hate to be scattered on top of her killer, poor girl.' I looked at her in surprise. It was the first time she'd shown any interest in who the bones had belonged to. But it was just like her to think first about the wishes of the dead woman.

'Take her somewhere neutral. Perhaps a local beauty spot or something?' said Amy. 'You could have a little ceremony, to finally lay her to rest.' She took a sip of her beer and sighed. 'It's amazing how much you've found out about your ancestors. And here's me, having only just met my dad.'

Simon opened his mouth as if to speak, but then just smiled and looked down at his beer bottle.

Mum tactfully gathered up empty beer bottles and took them back to the house, throwing Dad a stern look. He gave a half-smile and dutifully followed her inside.

'It must be very hard,' I said, gently.

'It was,' she replied, 'but now I've met him, and you and the kids, it's wonderful. I wish I'd known you all earlier. It means so much to me. Your parents are lovely, too.'

I wondered what Simon was thinking. He'd never wanted to track down his own biological parents. Maybe he'd feel differently now.

'I know what you mean, I think,' said Simon. 'Now that I've met you I get it – this urge to know where you came from. I never used to understand Katie's obsession with genealogy.' He looked at me, and then at Amy. 'But I still don't think I'd ever want to trace my own birth parents. Mum and Dad brought me up. I feel grounded enough in the past I had – I don't need to know anything about the alternative one I might have had if I hadn't been given up for adoption.'

Amy smiled at him. 'That's OK. I won't push you to find out who my grandparents were. But I'd like to meet your adoptive mum. Will you take me to visit her? I know she won't be able to understand who I am, but maybe you can say I'm a friend or something.' She bit her lip. 'I do understand if you don't think it would be a good idea.'

'I think we can sort something out,' he said. 'She's lovely, on a good day, and I think she'd like you.'

At that moment, Lewis came out of the house. 'Thomas is crying. He's going on about ghosts again.'

Thomas was right behind him, and came running into my arms.

'What's happened, sweetie?'

'I was up in Lauren's room and there are ghosts in the roof crashing around,' he sobbed.

'In the roof?' asked Simon.

'Banging on the ceiling and flapping.' He climbed onto my lap, snuggled into me and put his thumb in his mouth, a sign that he was tired.

'Maybe a pigeon has got into the loft,' Simon said.

I looked at him. 'You're going to have to get that hatch opened up then, at last.' I turned to Amy. 'I've been asking him for weeks to open it up. We've lived here four months now and have still not been up there.'

'Wow, unexplored territory!' said Amy. 'Why not open it up now? I'll help.'

'So will I,' said Lewis, hopping from foot to foot with excitement.

'Looks like we're going to have to,' said Simon. 'Come on then, troops.'

They marched inside, and I followed, carrying Thomas. I took him to the living room, persuaded Lauren to make room for him on the sofa, and switched the TV to CBeebies. With the bribe of a chocolate biscuit, she agreed to look after him while we investigated the 'ghosts'. I felt a twinge of excitement myself – finally the loft would reveal its secrets, if it had any. Remembering Georgia's silver and emerald comb I'd found hidden in the desk, it was not impossible that there could be something else, tucked away in a corner of the attic.

I went upstairs, followed by my intrigued parents, to find Simon and Amy manoeuvring a step-ladder under the loft hatch. Lewis was standing by, with a crowbar in his hand.

Simon climbed the ladder, and inspected the hatch. 'It's nailed shut. Getting it open will probably wreck it. I'll have to make a new hatch, after.'

I could hear the pigeon, if that's what it was, flapping about up there. 'It's got to be done. Come on, we'll hold the ladder steady.' Dad stepped forward, recognising his job in the proceedings, and took a firm grip on the ladder.

Simon rammed the crowbar between the hatch and its frame, and levered it back and forth. The wood splintered and a shower of dust fell down on us.

'Careful, love,' I said, following the unwritten rule that a wife and mother must advise caution at every possible opportunity. Lewis rolled his eyes and Amy grinned. Mum put her hand over her mouth. I knew she'd been thinking of saying the same thing.

'My mum used to be forever saying that, too,' Amy said, and Lewis giggled.

280

Simon gave one last heave on the hatch, and it gave way, swinging downwards on rusty hinges. He caught it before it knocked him off the ladder.

'Right, now we need to bring the long ladder in. It's too high to climb up from the step-ladder.' He backed down the steps, brushed the wood splinters off his shoulders and he and Dad went to fetch the other ladder in from the shed.

Lewis and I folded the step-ladder and propped it in a corner of the landing. A frantic fluttering ensued and we realised the pigeon had come down through the hatch. We managed to usher it into Lauren's room, and opened the window. After a few sickening crashes against the glass it found its way out, and headed over to Stan and Eileen's garden where it disappeared into their flowering cherry tree.

'Poor thing,' said Mum, already picking up feathers from the carpet.

'Did it hurt itself?' asked Lewis, handing her a bunch of feathers from his windowsill.

'Maybe a little, but it was able to fly, so I reckon it'll be all right,' said Amy.

I winced as a crash from the stairs signalled the return of Simon and Dad with the ladder. 'Sorry about that,' Simon said, nodding at a fist-sized chunk of plaster they'd knocked off while negotiating the turn in the stairs.

'Needs replastering anyway, when we can afford it.' I shrugged. 'Pigeon's out.'

'Oh, good. Well, we've come this far, might as well go up and have a look around. Lewis, can you fetch the inspection lamp from the under-stairs cupboard, and an extension lead? Plug it into the socket just inside Lauren's room.'

Lewis nodded and ran off to fetch the items while Simon pushed the ladder up through the hatch. Dad resumed his ladder-holding job.

A minute later, with the lamp in his hand, Simon climbed up, and disappeared into the darkness above.

'Well?'

'I can see where the pigeon got in. There are a couple of missing slates. We'll have to get them fixed before the winter.'

'Can I come up?'

'Yes, there's a bit of boarding down, and it seems firm enough.'

I climbed up slowly, and emerged into the stale, dusty attic air. Simon had hung the inspection torch from a nail in a rafter, and the light it gave was good enough to see the whole area. Only the area around the hatch was boarded over; an assortment of planks laid haphazardly across the joists. Simon pointed out a gap which I stepped over carefully.

'Can I come up? And Amy?' Lewis didn't wait for an answer, but scrambled up the ladder, quickly followed by Amy.

'I'll just stay and hold the ladder,' said Dad.

'Careful,' said Mum, sending Lewis and Amy into fits of giggles again.

'Is there anything up there?' called Dad.

'No, it's empty,' said Simon. 'Just cobwebs and a few dead leaves from the old beech. Must have blown in through the hole in the roof.'

'Wow, this is amazing!' said Amy. 'All this space – you could turn it into a games room or something. Put a Velux window in, and some proper flooring. It'd be a great place to play for the kids.'

'Yeah, cool! Can we, Dad?'

'You don't need any more space to play. We've got two spare bedrooms, for goodness sake! What we'll be putting up here is insulation. And I guess we could store stuff, like the Christmas decorations and camping gear up here, once I've put a proper loft ladder in.'

'Hold on, what's that?' I'd spotted something. Simon unhooked the inspection lamp and angled it towards where I was pointing at a corner of the loft. There was a small wooden box, pushed right up under the rafters. I got down on my hands and knees and crawled over. It was about the size of a shoebox, and filthy dirty. I pushed it back across the boards towards the others.

'Cool, a box of treasure!' said Lewis, crouching down to open it. 'Aw, poo, it's locked.'

'Pass it down to Granddad,' said Simon. 'We can probably prise it open, but let's do it in the daylight. The dust up here is making me sneeze.'

I almost fell down the ladder in my haste to find out what was inside the box, prompting Mum to shake her head and tut. Once we were all down, Dad carried the box out to the garden. Mum fetched a duster to get the worst of the filth off, and Simon fetched a variety of screwdrivers and chisels to try to get it open. In the end, the lock broke away with very little effort. There was a clash of heads as Amy, Dad, Lewis and I all leaned over it, each trying to be the first to see what was inside.

'Well, I'll go and make some tea while you all knock yourselves out over that musty old box,' muttered Mum, clearly feeling left out. No one answered her, as she slunk off to the kitchen.

I lifted the contents out carefully, and spread them out on the garden table. A mildewed hardback exercise book. A scrap of paper with something written on it, in faded brown ink. And a photograph, in a broken gilded frame.

Dad picked up the picture and studied it. 'This looks like a really early photograph. Ooh, Katie, is this who I think it is?' I looked over his shoulder. The grainy, sepia picture showed a seated elderly woman in a dark gown, a bearded man standing behind her, and two younger men standing stiffly at her side. At the bottom of the picture the name of the photographic studio was printed: *Brown & Sons, Winchester, 1872.*

My stomach flipped with excitement. It was the St Clairs, it had to be! 'Yes, I think it is! Georgia, Bartholomew, and their sons Barty and William.'

'She looks completely different to her portrait, doesn't she?' said Dad.

'Well, she's much older here. 1872 – that makes her…'

'Only about fifty. Hardly *old*, my girl,' said Dad, with mock indignation.

'She looks older than that,' said Amy.

'Yes, and even allowing for age, to me she looks nothing like the portrait we found online. Her face shape's completely different.' Dad frowned as he peered at the picture.

'I guess the portrait painter wasn't very accurate, then,' I said. 'But isn't it great to see an actual photo of your ancestors? Look at Bartholomew's whiskers, they're quite something!'

'This book's all just numbers. Maybe it's grid references to where the treasure is buried,' said Lewis. He'd been leafing through the notebook while we studied the photo.

'Let me see,' I said, and he passed it over. I opened it and flicked through a few pages. It was an accounts book. I looked closely at the list of outgoing payments. All were for the same day every month starting from May 1842 and continuing up to December 1876. Different amounts, but all documented as *Payment from B. St Clair to B. Cutter.* I picked up the scrap of paper. It was an address: *B. Cutter, c/o Revd. Richards, The Rectory, Church Lane, Woodhall, Lincs.*

'Dad, look at this.' I passed the book and paper to him. 'B. Cutter is Bartholomew Cutter, the servant Agnes Cutter's son, known as Tolly. His birth certificate arrived in the post this morning. He was brought up in Woodhall by his grandparents.'

Dad stared hard at me. 'If Bartholomew St Clair was sending money to Bartholomew Cutter, the son of his servant, that surely means…'

'…that Bartholomew St Clair was the father,' Simon finished triumphantly. 'Perhaps Agnes was making trouble for St Clair, so he killed her to keep her quiet, and buried her here in the garden. Which means our mystery woman must be Agnes, Bartholomew's mistress, fallen out of favour.' He slapped his thigh. 'Knew it would be something to do with sex, in the end. It always is!'

I frowned. Something didn't quite add up. 'Barty and Tolly were half-brothers, then. But Barty must have known about Tolly, because he had him here to visit in 1881. He was visiting here when the census was taken.'

'Which would mean Bartholomew didn't murder Agnes to keep his illegitimate son secret, as he must have told his legitimate son Barty about him at least. What a mystery!' Dad shook his head.

'And if the bones *were* Agnes, Tolly's mother, it'd be very strange to invite her son to stay, knowing his mother was buried in the garden.' I shivered at the thought.

'Maybe Barty didn't invite Tolly. He could have just turned up. Look, the payments stop in 1876,' said Dad, pointing at the last page of the accounts book.

'That's when Bartholomew senior died. Perhaps Barty didn't continue the payments, or didn't know about Tolly, until Tolly turned up five years later wondering what had happened to his money.'

Simon nodded. 'Yep, I bet that's what happened. Bartholomew senior was sending money, not just because Tolly was his illegitimate son, but because he felt guilty over murdering Tolly's mother.'

'Tea's up,' said Mum, returning across the lawn with a tray.

'Biscuits!' said Lewis. He grabbed a handful and ran off to jump on the trampoline.

Amy grinned at me. 'This is better than *Who Do You Think You Are?*' She stuffed a biscuit into her mouth and went to join Lewis on the trampoline.

'Well,' said Dad, as he took the cup of tea Mum offered him. 'I think that's as near to the truth as we're ever likely to get.'

***

The weather changed at the start of the next week. It was cooler, with a definite feel of autumn in the air. Amy had left late on

Saturday evening, hours after Mum and Dad, with promises to come back for a full weekend the next time. She was moving to London permanently so it would be easy to meet up. Simon had put a temporary catch on the loft hatch, to keep it closed until he'd made a new one.

We had a riotous birthday party for Thomas, who wore his 'I Am 5!' badge for a whole week. The kids went back to school, so once I was back from delivering Thomas to his new class – my baby, in Year One in big school! – my time was my own. I whizzed around the house cleaning and tidying, and had everything straight by midday. Time to go for a walk.

I collected the little box of ashes from the kitchen windowsill, put on my walking shoes and a fleece, and set off, up the lane past the pub and up to the churchyard. The grass around Bartholomew and Georgia's graves was in need of a trim again. I made a note to myself to come back here and tidy it all up, one day soon.

I sat on a nearby bench and regarded Bartholomew's grave. *For all my wrongs I do repent.* What wrongs, Bartholomew? Did you kill her, your servant Agnes? Could you really have done such a thing? And you, Georgia, did you know what he did? Did you know about his love-child – the other baby Bartholomew? I took out the box of ashes and gazed at it. These two sets of remains, just feet apart now, who had once lived under the same roof, and, if I was right, had shared the same bed on at least one occasion.

If I was right, I was descended from a murderer. But one who had covered his crime. It seemed no matter how hard you try, if an ancestor really wanted to hide something, then you wouldn't be able to find the truth. Once past, the truth could be buried, and often was. Future generations could never know everything about what had happened before their time – not if their ancestors had really wanted to hide something. You could research all you liked but you would never find out everything that happened to them, or why they made the choices they did.

It was time to lay Agnes to rest at last. I left the churchyard, walked up the lane and across the fields to Irish Hill. There was a light wind blowing at the top, and the clouds were beginning to lift and thin. The day might turn out sunny yet.

At the top I sat on one of the benches, and took out the box of ashes once again. Should I say some words? Amy had suggested holding a little ceremony, but that felt awkward and forced. After all, I hadn't known this woman. I wasn't descended from her. I gazed across the landscape in the direction of our house, which I could pick out quite easily now. Had this woman stood in Thomas's or Lauren's bedroom at the back of the house, and looked across to this hill, I wondered? She may never have walked up here, but she would surely have raised her eyes from her work and noticed it. It was as good a place as any for the end of her story.

I opened the pot, tipped it and walked slowly around the quartet of benches, allowing the fine-grained ash to gradually trickle out onto the ground. Some was blown away by the breeze. I liked that. Agnes Cutter, or whoever she was, scattered on the winds. Her remains were no longer buried, even if the truth about her was, and would remain so, for ever.

Dear Reader,

We hope you enjoyed reading this book. If you did, we'd be so appreciative if you left a review. It really helps us and the author to bring more books like this to you.

Here at HQ Digital we are dedicated to publishing fiction that will keep you turning the pages into the early hours. Don't want to miss a thing? To find out more about our books, promotions, discover exclusive content and enter competitions you can keep in touch in the following ways:

JOIN OUR COMMUNITY:

Sign up to our new email newsletter:
hyperurl.co/hqnewsletter

Read our new blog www.hqstories.co.uk

🐦 *: https://twitter.com/HQDigitalUK*

📘 *: www.facebook.com/HQStories*

BUDDING WRITER?

We're also looking for authors to join the HQ Digital family!
Find out more here:

https://www.hqstories.co.uk/want-to-write-for-us/

Thanks for reading, from the HQ Digital team

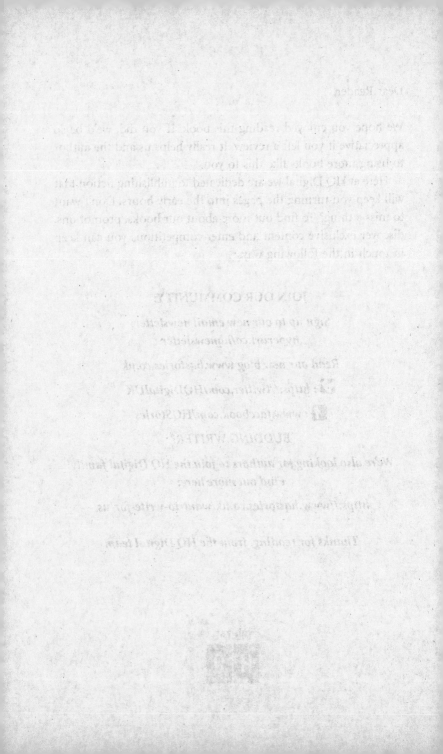

If you enjoyed *The Emerald Comb*, then why not try another gripping historical novel from HQ Digital?